THE
GIRLS
IN THE
WATER

Published by Bookouture
An imprint of StoryFire Ltd.
Carmelite House
50 Victoria Embankment
London EC4Y 0DZ
www.bookouture.com

ISBN: 978-0-34913-252-5
eBook ISBN: 978-1-78681-198-1

Printed and bound in Great Britain by Clays Ltd, Elcograf S.p.A.

Papers used are from well-managed forests
and other responsible sources.

MIX
Paper from
responsible sources
FSC
www.fsc.org
FSC® C104740

PROLOGUE

The slap came from nowhere, sudden and sharp. Her nail caught the boy's skin, slicing his cheek. He put a hand up, tracing the wet trail of dotted blood that bubbled to the surface of the wound. The boy looked at the magazine held outstretched in her other hand. Its opened pages, vivid in their accusations, showed an array of images: naked flesh, skin on skin; so many things he had heard about, but had never really seen this close up and in detail.

The child still in him wanted to laugh at the sight of bare bodies.

The child still in him remained scared of the ferocity of his mother's tongue, fearing her verbal assaults almost as much as the physical force of her anger.

'This is sick,' his mother spat. 'Why would you look at it? What's the matter with you?' She was shouting now. Her anger was visible in the red flare of her cheeks, in the fists that had formed at her sides and had turned her bony knuckles white. It was tangible in the venom with which her words were spoken.

The boy didn't want to feel this kind of anger, but in that moment – in so many moments before and after it – he hated his mother. Even at such a young age he recognised her hypocrisy, and he hated it. He hated this life and everything she had made him.

'Nothing to say, have you?' she snapped, his silence heightening her anger.

She grabbed the boy by the hair and dragged him to the kitchen. The sink was filled with dirty water left from the last lot of dishes that had been washed. Lifeless bubbles lay flat on the surface of the water, the occasional few giving their last sad pops before disappearing.

'Maybe we can clean your eyes out,' she suggested.

He didn't try to fight her, and later he would wonder why. He hadn't struggled as she had tightened her grip on his hair, or fought when she had shoved his face into the murky water. He never had. His mind went momentarily blank, as he had worked so long to train it to do. When his mind was blank, he could be anywhere. He could be anyone.

Sometimes the boy was a pilot. He had always liked the idea of what being a pilot might be like: of being able to go anywhere, his own hands navigating his destiny. That freedom. He would imagine the roar of the engine, the surge of the wheels on the runway; the tsunami in his stomach that would rise and subside as the plane left the ground and took its first steep tilt skywards.

Other times he was an actor. He would imagine himself on a stage, dressed as someone else, speaking someone else's words. He was someone else. His audience stretched in front of him, but he could never see them; they were shrouded in the darkness, the only lights focused upon him. He wanted to be someone else, anywhere else.

He held his breath under the water for as long as he could, snatching gulps of air when he was pulled back up. After what seemed for ever but was little longer than thirty seconds, his mother let go. He stood hunched over the sink, coughing and choking, his dark hair dripping water down his face.

*

That night, he lay in his single bed and imagined the most horrific images his young mind could conjure. When his mind was no longer blank it was filled with the purest kind of hate: a rage so intense that it sometimes scared him.

The boy hated his mother.

One day he would make her pay.

CHAPTER ONE

'You're in a good mood today.'

Detective Inspector Alex King glanced at her colleague, who was sitting in the passenger seat chewing on the corner of a thumbnail and watching her with a look that suggested good moods were something other people didn't generally expect of her. She didn't blame them. There hadn't been much to smile about these past few months.

'What's wrong with that?'

'Nothing,' DC Chloe Lane said, raising an eyebrow. She gave a slight smile whilst turning her blonde head to the window, presumably under the assumption that Alex would miss the look.

She didn't.

'You were singing,' Chloe said, her attention drawn to a young man struggling outside an off-licence with a dog that was almost as big as he was.

'I wasn't.'

'You were.'

'When?'

'Just then! Was that One Direction?'

Alex snorted. 'No, it definitely wasn't.'

It might have been, she thought. She hadn't been able to get that bloody song out of her head all morning, not since she'd heard it drifting from the kitchen when Rob had gone downstairs to make a cup of tea. He had put on the radio. She hadn't been sure how she'd felt about that: the tea making or the act of turning on the radio. It was all too familiar. They were supposed to be beyond all that now.

They'd been divorced for nearly three years, yet here they were again.

The adult part of Alex's brain knew she should have been sceptical about what was going on. Sex with an ex-husband, in the majority of cases, was destined to be problematic, yet, for whatever reason, Alex felt unwilling to expel him from her life for a second time. Didn't she deserve a break, just this once? Didn't she deserve a bit of fun?

You're forty-four not nineteen, she reprimanded herself. And where an ex-husband was concerned, there was never likely to be a no-strings scenario.

She shook herself from the thought. 'I think it might have been.'

She smiled. She turned up the car heaters. Chloe's face was disappearing into the folds of her jacket in an attempt to get warm. She was so slim that Alex found it unsurprising she was so susceptible to the cold. It was a bitterly chilly morning, but Alex didn't appear to feel the dip in temperature as keenly as her younger colleague clearly did. She'd often thought Chloe looked as though she could do with a couple of decent meals and some looking after, although her size didn't seem to impact upon her apparently boundless energy.

The sky stretching across the town that lay spread before them was grey and heavy, the threat of rain increasingly present as they neared Pontypridd. As they approached the exit that would take them to the town centre, Alex found herself struggling to remember the last sunny day this part of South Wales had seen, no matter how cold. The festive season had been characterised by grey afternoons and a steady stream of relentless rainfall, yet in its own way this had seemed fitting.

'Thanks for the lift, by the way,' Chloe said, breaking Alex's chain of thought.

'No worries. Heard anything from the garage?'

Chloe pulled a face. She somehow managed to look pretty even when she was grimacing. 'Yeah, got an email last night. Be cheaper for me to buy a new car. Third time it's happened. I don't really see the point in paying again.'

Alex cut across the roundabout that took them towards Trallwn. 'Is this your way of hinting at another lift tomorrow?'

Chloe shot her a smile. 'Would you mind?'

'Suppose not. I mean, I'm going this way anyway.'

Chloe's smile disappeared back into the folds of her jacket, and she turned her head to the window, watching the traffic slow to a crawl at the next approaching roundabout.

'Busy day ahead?' she asked, the words muffled.

Alex rolled her eyes. 'When's it not? Have you seen my office recently? There's a backlog of paperwork a foot high on my desk. You know, before I got promoted I used to think South Wales was pretty quiet. Be careful what you wish for, right?'

Her promotion to detective inspector had happened a few years earlier and life was now moving so quickly, in such a relentless rush of activity, that Alex often found herself worrying about the things she feared she might be missing. Her divorce had helped push this fear into a full-blown panic, but rather than stop to let life catch up with her she had pushed ahead, intent on holding on to her workload as the last passenger on a sinking ship clings to the only lifeboat.

'I think you'd get bored if things were too quiet,' Chloe said. 'But if you get a break and you fancy a drink, give me a shout. I'm usually designated driver, but I don't have a car. We'll have to bus it.'

Alex smiled. It was a nice thought. They'd managed a night out just after Christmas: one so wild she'd been back home by ten thirty. Chloe was sensible for her age, which suited Alex just fine. She didn't need to be made to feel any older than she already did.

'A break,' Alex said. 'Just imagine that.'

The station loomed ahead of them, as grey as the sky that formed the backdrop behind it. It stood on a corner in the middle of Pontypridd town centre as though keeping an eye on the local residents, and Alex had often wondered why they couldn't do something to make the place look a little less hostile, although she imagined colour might have defeated the intended purpose of its existence. It appeared they weren't there to be cheerful.

The thought of the day that stretched ahead of them pushed her reluctantly from the car. In truth, Chloe had got her right. Not having something to do or somewhere to be gave Alex too much time and space to think about the things that haunted the silent hours of the night when she would lie in her room and find them gathered at the bedside, ready to make sure she hadn't forgotten them. Perhaps the thought of a pile of paperwork and an afternoon locked in the office wasn't too unappealing, just for today. She presumed she should make the most of being confined to the realms of the station while she was given the rare opportunity.

CHAPTER TWO

It was late January; the kind of January that holds everything still in its grip, its fingers embedded in the hard ground and its breath staining the air with shivers. She knew all about the cold, despite being indoors. She had been there for days – exactly how long, she couldn't be too sure – and with every hour, and with every next humiliation inflicted on her, she grew colder in her bones, hoping for death to relieve her.

It occurred to her that no one might have realised she was missing. Moving from friend to friend, from sofa to sofa, had always seemed such a good idea; in fact, it had been her sole method of survival for the previous eighteen months. She couldn't stay still, which now, bound to this chair, seemed sadly ironic. She could go weeks without speaking to what family she had left, and those 'friends' she had stayed with she now realised were nothing of the sort. She didn't even know them, not really. She had used them; they had used her. She had got what she deserved in the end, she supposed.

Would anyone now notice she was gone?

The only person she had really spoken to about how she was feeling – the only person she had allowed herself to get remotely close to during the past few months – was here, and now there was no getting away from him.

The room was dark, the only window boarded up with thick wooden slats. There were drapes hanging from the walls, black and heavy, but she didn't know why they were there or what they were hiding. Sometimes, she couldn't see anything. Her eyelids felt weighed down and when he wasn't there she would allow herself to close them, though she never slept. She didn't think she'd slept for days. How long would it take before it sent her into madness?

She had cried at the start. When she'd woken to find herself in that unfamiliar place, tied to a chair by a man whose face she couldn't see, she had cried, screamed; begged. She had offered him things that repulsed her, but he didn't seem interested in any of it. He didn't seem interested in her.

What did he want from her?

It was so difficult to try to piece together the events that had led up to her being here. There were things she remembered, but so many more that she didn't. She had been to work, that much she remembered. She sometimes shared a taxi home with one of the girls she worked with, but she couldn't remember anything about the journey home. She couldn't remember that there'd been a journey.

She was tied to a chair, at her wrists and by her ankles. Her arms were pulled awkwardly behind her, cutting off her circulation. She had tried to squeeze her hands through the tight loops of the ties holding her in place, wear them down against the wooden slats of the seat, but her results had only left her with raw skin and broken hope.

She wasn't getting out of here alive.

On the first day, the man had cut her nails. She had been left alone for what felt like for ever, her vision blurred by tears and her mind clogged with dark thoughts of the ways that this man might end her life. She tried to kick out, thrusting her hips forward to send the chair tipping to one side, but when she toppled with it she realised she had only made things worse, and she stayed there like that, tied to the chair with her right arm deadening beneath her until her captor made his silent return.

When he came back, he tilted the chair upright, moving it as though she was weightless. She spoke to him, but he refused to reply. When he released her hands from the knotted cable ties, a surge of adrenalin rushed her and she swung an arm at the man, clawing at the dark mask he wore over his face. It was then she felt her life had ended, because it was then she saw him for the first time. Might things have been different had she never seen his face? She would never know.

The realisation of who he was had made her sick. She threw up down the front of her top, chunks of the slop he had fed her some time during the previous evening spattering the cotton and lacing the air with an acidic, rancid tang.

Then the evening came back to her. She remembered seeing him. She remembered how pleased she had been to see him.

Later, as her memory returned in fragments, she remembered accepting a lift from him.

'Why are you doing this?' she asked him through tears. 'I've never done anything to you.'

Her body tensed as he reached into his pocket and produced what looked like a small black box. He unzipped it and drew out a small pair of nail scissors, which he used to slowly cut away her sick-stained top. She didn't bother fighting him this time. Instead, she sat in the dark, shivering in her bra. He had scissors in his gloved hands, and her ankles were still bound to the chair: she couldn't go anywhere. Fighting him would only anger him further, and then where would that leave her?

'Please,' she said, as he pulled the last strip of cut fabric from her body. 'Please say something.'

The man pulled a chair that matched hers in front of her and sat before her, taking her left hand in his. When his eyes met hers, briefly, she wondered why she hadn't seen it before. Of course it was him.

'I don't understand,' she said.

Her nails were long and painted. He cut them methodically, filing each right down to the skin. At the third finger, he realised the nails were false. The realisation enraged him and he ripped at each furiously, bending them back and tearing the glue from the nail beneath. She cried out in pain. The noise only encouraged him.

He left the room.

The girl looked around her, desperately searching for something she could use to try to hit him with.

He returned. He sat back down in front of her. There was a pair of pliers in his hand.

'No,' she pleaded, hot tears stinging her eyes once more. 'Don't. Please.'

She struggled with him, but her efforts were futile. He hit her across the face, once, with an open hand, a blow hard enough to send her body reeling and the chair toppling back to the floor. He straddled her fallen body, reaching again for her hand. One by one, he ripped the real fingernails from each of her fingers.

At some stage, she passed out. She couldn't remember everything that had happened between then and now, only that she had woken to find all her nails missing and her hands caked in dried blood. Her wrists were bound to the chair again; this time, at her sides where she could see them. She had screamed at the sight of her bloodied hands, at the memory of the pain and at the pain she still endured in the aftermath of what had been inflicted upon her, but her screams had gone ignored and she had finally fallen silent, still thinking about how she might escape this place.

Still knowing that she couldn't.

When she had calmed slightly, she managed to shuffle the chair across the room, dragging it over the exposed wooden floorboards. She made it to the door, but when she got closer she could see it was locked. It had taken all her energy just to cross the room and a wave of frustrated tears swept over her, engulfing all hope and drowning her future.

She waited for death, praying for it, but it didn't come.

Upon his last return, he finally spoke to her. He dragged her in the chair back to the side of the room where he had originally placed her and stood behind her, his hands resting on her shoulders, weighing her down. She heard him remove something from his pocket before she felt him take her long ponytail in his hand. The next thing she heard was the sound of scissors slicing through her hair, cutting the ponytail loose from her head.

'I thought you might be different,' he said, 'but you're just like all the rest.'

Her breathing had quickened upon his return to the room. Now, with him standing behind her and with her own hair tossed, severed, into her lap, she felt her heart slow until she was sure it would stop.

His hands tightened on her shoulders.

'I'm sorry,' she said quickly through her tears. 'Tell me what you want from me… tell me what I've done wrong. I'll do anything, I promise.'

She didn't mind begging now. Not when death seemed this close.

He was disappointed in her words. She was going to say anything she thought it might take to appease him. Her desperation – her pathetic snivelled words – only made him hate her more.

She waited for him to say something. She thought that if he spoke to her again, she might be able to get him to stop what he was doing. If she could get him to talk, and properly, she thought maybe she could talk him down. She thought maybe all hope wasn't lost.

Then he cut her throat, and all her thoughts left her.

CHAPTER THREE

Alex crouched alongside what was left of the body at the water's edge. The river was high that morning and faster than usual, gushing south with an urgency that implied danger, as though the water wished to rid itself of something; which it had earlier that morning, spitting the corpse on to the riverbank where it was later discovered by an unsuspecting jogger who had ventured between the trees seeking privacy to relieve himself.

Alex turned her head and tried to find a clean pocket of air to inhale through the mask she wore. She felt sick to her stomach, yet the scene of crime officers milling around the tent and on the path along the park beyond seemed unaffected, as though young women washing up on riverbanks was an everyday occurrence in the city. She knew that after seventeen years in the force she should have become more inured to the realities of death, but it was yet to happen. She would shake it off, put on the face she wore to work each morning and move the images of what she'd seen to the back of her mind, from where they would later resurface to haunt her.

The north end of Bute Park had been shut off; the rubberneckers who had gathered to gawp at the drama unfolding had been moved along by officers. In the summer months, this area of the park would be packed with families and students, the stretch of widening river just a couple of hundred metres or so along becoming a swimming pool where, on better days, sun worshippers could cool off. Teenagers would jump from the bridge, competing with one another, showing off to friends.

At this time of year though, not even the most foolhardy would brave the water.

A tent had been erected to protect the body from the elements – though it had already been subjected to a prolonged assault in the water – and uniformed officers were now performing zone searches of the surrounding areas of parkland and riverbanks. Photographs had been taken, documenting the decomposition of the corpse and the abuse that had been inflicted on the young woman's body both before and after death.

Alex had never seen a victim such as this. Her body was blistered and swollen, the water having ravaged and bloated her. Her ankles were tethered with cable ties; her wrists, the same. From them, tattered scraps of plastic carrier bags lay like litter on the ground, torn by rocks and the weight of water.

Something had gnawed at her skin, chewing through the girl's flesh until angry red welts scarred her body. She was covered in bruising. On both hands, every nail was missing. The river might have ravaged her, but unthinkable horrors had been inflicted long before the water had its way with her.

What sort of person could do this to another?

Alex stood for a moment to ease the pressure on her calves, but found herself unable to turn away. Turning her face from the victim seemed disrespectful, as though doing so would mean leaving the girl alone in this state of degradation, abandoning her when she most needed someone to stay. She might have a weak stomach, but Alex refused to walk away from someone in need, and quite often the dead needed her help more than the living.

'Who did this to you?' She spoke softly, as though the dead young woman – this girl –might somehow find a way to respond.

Did she know her killer? Most did, and random attacks tended to be frenzied. This seemed premeditated, methodical. Why were her nails torn from her hands? Was she alive at the time? Why was she brought here?

There was a gust of breeze as the pathologist re-entered the tent.

'Don't take it the wrong way, but I was hoping not to see you again so soon,' Helen said.

Alex's path had crossed with Helen Collier's during two other recent cases, and Alex shared her sentiments. She had been hoping for a quiet new year, but was beginning to think 'quiet' was destined to be something unknown to her and the rest of the team.

'Barbaric, isn't it?'

Alex said nothing. A pair of lifeless eyes stared up from the hollows of a water-eaten face.

'The fingernails,' Helen said, crouching beside the body and tentatively taking the left hand in her own. 'I'd say this was done while she was still alive.'

Alex winced. 'The markings to her wrists, you mean?'

The flesh at the young woman's wrists was cut in angry stripes suggesting a struggle to free herself from wherever she had been held. Alex scanned the length of the young woman's body – her top half in just a muddied bra, her bottom half wearing a pair of leather-look leggings that had been torn in the river – and felt sadness sweep over her. How frightened must she have been when facing her own death? How brave she had been to continue to struggle, even when she must have realised she was fighting a battle she couldn't possibly win. There was no question of whether she was already dead when her body had been put in the river. The deep cut of her throat clearly marked her final moments.

'Looks as though she put up a good fight. As much as she was able to, anyway.'

Helen Collier crouched at the body. 'Here,' she said, gesturing to the young woman's head. 'Her hair's been cut.'

She worked her fingertips gently beneath the head, moving it slightly to one side so that Alex was able to see the tangled hair that lay stuck to the girl's scalp, matted with dirt from the riverbed. 'I'm no hairdresser, but I'd say that's been cut off at a ponytail.' She lifted her gloved hands to the back of her own head and motioned a snipping action, as though Alex had been otherwise unable to imagine what she'd meant. 'I'd say your killer kept himself a souvenir.'

'How long do you think she's been in the water?'

Helen lowered the dead girl's head, letting it rest back on the ground. 'Not as long as someone was hoping. The stage of decomposition suggests no more than two weeks. These,' she said, moving a gloved hand to the scraps of plastic tethered to the victim's wrist, 'were probably intended to keep her down longer. Presumably long enough for the body to decompose altogether.'

They discussed the remnants of the carrier bags attached to the victim's wrists. It seemed likely they had been loaded with weights – rocks, perhaps – in order to pull the body beneath the water and conceal all evidence of the crime. That would explain the choice of point of entry where the girl's body was placed into the river. This was one of the deepest parts, and in most cases where bodies were submerged in water they resurfaced at or near the place where they had entered.

If the woman had been put into the water here, how had someone managed to get her to this point? The park was inaccessible to public vehicles. It would have been impossible for someone to carry a corpse this far into the park without being seen, even at this quieter time of year. The gates were locked at ten o'clock, meaning no one was able to gain access at night.

Helen seemed adamant that the body would have entered the water close to the place where the young woman had been found, but how had that been possible?

Alex looked back at the dead girl lying on the riverbank. Her heart swelled with a sickness she knew would stay with her until they caught whoever had been responsible for the brutalities inflicted upon her.

Until they did, this face would remain with Alex, the horrors of the girl's final minutes haunting her.

CHAPTER FOUR

There were six people at the support group that evening: two volunteer leaders and four group members. Everyone was sitting in their coats because the hall was so cold; the three-bar electric heater that had been pulled as far as its lead would allow was offering little but the smell of burning dust, and the row of windows that lined the far wall was intent on letting in the cold, despite the ancient velvet curtains pulled to shut them out.

Sean Pugh gave a spurt of chesty coughs, as if to demonstrate how cold the place was.

'Rachel,' Tim said, giving the shy girl at the far curve of their circle a smile. 'Hope you're feeling better this week.'

Rachel's pale face coloured pink at the acknowledgment, and Tim turned his attention to the rest of the group.

'Would anyone like to get us started?' he prompted. 'What sort of a week have we all had?'

'Shit.'

Tim turned to Carl. Six feet two on a short day, Carl Anderson's legs seemed to fill the space in the centre of the circle.

'Why's it been shit?'

Carl shrugged. 'Groundhog Day, innit? Same shit, different day.'

'How's the new job going?'

Carl gave another shrug. 'All right.'

His words may have been few, but Carl's anger radiated in an aura around him. The other members of the group seemed indifferent to his festering rage; all except Rachel, who was careful to keep her distance and always made a point of sitting to the side of him, and never opposite where she would be forced to look directly at him for prolonged periods of time.

Before Christmas, Carl had told the group he would be starting a new part-time job as a bouncer at a club in Pontypridd. Now just a few weeks in, Carl already seemed disaffected by his new employment. He wasn't the type of person Tim Cole and Connor Price had had in mind when they'd started the support group. The group had been started with the aim of helping young people in the local area overcome anxiety and depression, yet Carl didn't seem to suffer with either. Nor was he that young. He was just angry, and his anger was starting to make everyone else's anxiety tangible.

'Anyone do anything different this week?' Connor asked, keen to take the focus away from Carl. 'Last week we talked about meditation.' Christ, he thought. Meditation. Another of Tim's hippy-dippy theories. Come spring, he'd have them all out in the street hugging the nearest available tree. Still, if it kept the focus off Carl and away from Tim for at least five minutes, it was bound to be worth it. 'Anyone try it?'

Carl gave a snort which went ignored by the rest of the group. Rachel shifted awkwardly in her seat, and Connor considered the idea that perhaps it was time this man left for good. He was making people uncomfortable and if they were unable to be comfortable here then the whole purpose of this group was lost. He might agree with Carl's scepticism about Tim's proposed remedies, but at least he was attempting the politer thing by hiding his derision.

Connor was adept at hiding his true feelings. It was becoming quite a skill.

'I tried it,' Sarah said. She flicked a long length of blonde hair away from her face. 'It was good. Really good.' She dragged the vowels in her words, stretching their meaning into ambiguity.

'What did you try?' Tim asked, reaching for his beanie hat from the floor. He put it back on, protecting his bald scalp from the snapping cold of the village hall. Beside him, Connor shifted. Sean shot him a look that went unnoticed by Connor but, for Sarah, demonstrated the intended effect of her words.

'You know… just breathing. In and out… slowly.'

Her eyes stayed fixed on Connor, challenging a response.

'I found meditation really useful when I first came out of prison,' Tim said, oblivious to the looks that were being passed between certain other members of the group. The volunteer leaders encouraged group members to be honest about themselves and their pasts, always starting with themselves and their own experiences in order to develop an atmosphere of trust. There was nothing Tim had held back: he had shared stories of his drug addiction, his brief period of homelessness; his even longer period of residence as a detainee at Her Majesty's pleasure. Connor wondered if he shared too much. Being honest was good; being too honest could be fatal.

'The funny thing is,' Tim continued, 'people assume that being in prison is the difficult bit, but if you keep your head down and don't make yourself any enemies, it's not. Actually, it's being released that's the hard part. You come back out into the world, you think you've got nowhere to go and nothing to live for. It's tough. Sometimes just being able to step away from things makes life a lot clearer. You need that time for yourself. Did you find that, Sean?'

Sean Pugh had sat quietly taking it all in, or appearing to. Tall, skinny, and with a sleeve of tattoos that depicted the array of things he believed were to blame for his life's early downward spiral (he had given the group a guided tour of his arm at his second meeting, proudly declaring that what he carried with him and could keep an eye on could never defeat him), he had spent three years in prison for car theft and armed robbery and was now, still only twenty-two, unemployed and living back at his mother's house.

'Uh? Sorry, what did you say?'

'When you left prison. Did you try meditation to help yourself readjust?'

Sean looked at Tim as though he'd just spoken to him in a foreign language. 'Uh… no. I listened to a lot of music though. You know, to chill out.'

Connor Price let the conversation pass over him. He kept an eye on Sarah, his mouth fixed in a grimace. Rachel's attention was distracted from Tim's next question about what sort of music Sean had listened to; instead, she found herself engrossed in the silent exchange taking place between Connor and Sarah: in the twitching of jaws and the narrowing of eyes that seemed to form their own muted conversation. Carl pulled his phone from his pocket and checked the time.

'Are we going to the pub tonight?' Connor asked, interrupting the debate.

Invariably, the group sessions often began in the hall and ended in the pub. The cold was usually a good enough excuse, although they never seemed to need one. Carl never went. Connor presumed he didn't want to be seen out in public with them in case Carl saw someone he knew. Explaining he was out with his support group likely wouldn't help the hardman image he seemed so keen to project.

'I'm up for it,' Tim offered.

There were a few nods and mutterings from the remaining members of the group. Connor got up from his chair and turned the heater off, unplugging it and moving it back to the far side of the room. The others returned their chairs to the corner, stacking them noisily.

'Anyone heard from Lola?'

Connor turned to look at Tim. He shook his head.

'She said she'd be coming back after Christmas,' Sarah said.

'But no one's seen her?'

Sarah shrugged. 'She's never been that regular, has she?'

Connor turned back to the wall, busying himself with rolling up the cable of the electric heater. It didn't need doing – he just didn't want people looking at him. He didn't really feel like going for a drink. He didn't want to go home either. The problem was, Connor didn't really know what he wanted. Except the one thing. The need for *that* never seemed to leave him.

CHAPTER FIVE

Alex sat on the edge of a desk in the main investigation room of the station and looked at the image of the murder victim pinned to the board in front of her. The team had assembled, discussed, and dispersed, and on any other day Alex might have been due to head home. Now she wasn't going anywhere. Murder victims couldn't be made to wait for office hours, she thought. While there was something she could be doing, she would make sure she was doing it.

'What you thinking?'

Alex became aware of the superintendent's eyes on her. He was still sitting at one of the computers, so quiet that she had forgotten he was there. She had never liked having to address the team in front of him, always feeling reduced to her teenage self, keen to impress a favourite teacher. It was ridiculous, especially after all these years of working together. She and Harry Blake had known each other for years, and he had always treated people fairly. During her ongoing fertility treatment, the superintendent had been an unlikely ally. He had fought her corner when the nonsensical rules regarding time off work for treatment had stated Alex should use her days off as unpaid leave. According to the police service's rules, IVF treatment was a 'lifestyle choice'. Like having a boob job, Alex remembered thinking at the time.

'Oh, you know me,' she answered flippantly. 'Nothing much.'

Harry raised his eyebrows, knowing the opposite was always true. Alex never switched off. There was always something going on behind those dark eyes, even when she stoically refused to share it with anyone.

'How was the body transported through the park to the river?' Alex said, thinking aloud. 'The victim was small, but no matter how easy she might have been to carry, how the hell would anyone get across that kind of distance without being seen?'

Harry ran a hand over his short greying hair, looking past her as he pondered the question. 'How late does the park stay open?'

'According to the council's website, pretty late even through the winter.' Alex gestured to another of the computers. The website was still up on the screen, left from where she had studied its details before addressing the team. 'Someone must have had vehicle access to the park. It's the only thing that makes sense.'

She gestured for Harry to join her at the computer.

'The pathologist seems certain the young woman's body was placed in the water at or very near the place where it resurfaced. The only plausible theory is that someone transported the woman to the river in some sort of vehicle. Yet according to this there's no public access to the paths.'

'What type of vehicles have access to the park?' Harry asked, his attention still fixed on the website.

Alex slid from the desk and into a chair beside him, moving a fingertip across the keypad of the opened laptop. She typed the words 'Cardiff Bute Park vehicle access' into the search engine and a huge list of results was thrown up. It took little time for her to find a council file that was open to public viewing which documented a brief history of the park and assessed the suitability of its current access points.

'Read this.'

The park had been open to the public since 1947, having previously been the private gardens of Cardiff Castle. Since being opened for public use, the park had gained only two additional access points.

According to the council's document, a need for additional vehicular access was justified by the volume of vehicles that required entry to the park for services such as supplying the nursery, setting up and dismantling equipment and staging for events, maintaining and managing the water flow in the Dock Feeder, maintaining the riverbanks, and for general upkeep of the gardens.

Cooper's Field was the area of the park most often used for events. Alex had been there on several occasions. Back during her days in uniform she had worked at events such as Party in the Park: long, sticky hours when she would be grateful for the sighting of a drunken scuffle just for something to break up the monotony of the day. As a civilian she had stood in the field with an army of fellow numbered women, waiting to start Cancer Research's now-famous Race for Life event that was held there every summer. Trying not to linger for too long on the tributes and photographs pinned to the backs of the pink T-shirts swarming the spaces in front of her, because running was difficult enough without a thick lump of sadness stuck in the throat.

Alex hated to run, but she hated bloody cancer with a far greater intensity.

She glanced at Superintendent Blake, who had recently made his return to work. She had missed his presence at the station. God, he could be cantankerous at times, but he was honest and he was fair, which were admirable traits in a world that often lacked these two seemingly uninspiring qualities. Eighteen months earlier he had been diagnosed with prostate cancer. It had hit his family hard; in particular, his two children who were aged eleven and twelve at the time. Treatment had followed. His doctors reported an encouraging response to the radiotherapy, but had advised him to take it easy and allow his body time to recover.

With typical Harry Blake pig-headedness, he had decided to ignore them.

Alex smiled at the thought of Chloe's first encounter with the superintendent after he'd returned to work. It hadn't been obvious at the time whether it had been more embarrassing for Harry or for Chloe, but it had provided Alex with amusement for the rest of the day. Chloe had transferred to the department during his time off, and upon his return Harry had mistaken her for an A-level student there on work experience – and Harry didn't have much time for work experience.

The reception Chloe had received was less than welcoming, but amusing for everyone else. Harry, feeling it necessary to acknowledge the girl's presence, had asked if she had any relatives at the station. Chloe, having realised the error of judgement he'd made, deadpanned that her dad was locked up in cell number four. It was the only time Alex had ever seen Harry's face redden, but Chloe's had matched it when she'd found out who she'd been speaking with.

It was true that Chloe looked younger than her twenty-six years, but once Harry had got to know her, he quickly learned there was a lot more to the young woman than met the eye.

Alex had always thought there was more to be discovered, but Chloe kept her personal life just that. And Alex could understand that.

'The North Gate entrance is right in the city centre,' Harry said, snapping Alex from her thoughts. 'That would mean someone drove along the main road and turned into the park whilst carrying a corpse in their vehicle.'

Alex felt sick at the thought. She had seen this poor girl only shortly after her body had been dragged up from the river. It was going to be a long time before she stopped seeing her.

She forced her thoughts back to the park. There were no events held in Cooper's Field during the winter, so that eliminated one group of vehicles. The words 'maintaining and managing water flow' meant nothing to Alex, but she would need to find out exactly what was involved. As for the nursery and the gardens, were gardeners even employed during the winter months? It had always seemed to Alex to be a seasonal sort of job. She had planted daffodil bulbs in her front garden one year and had been rewarded the following spring with seven tiny flowers that had managed the course of a week before wilting and giving up. It really didn't qualify her as an authority on the subject.

'Let me find the street.' Alex leaned across the desk and reached again for the keyboard. She searched for Boulevard de Nantes in Google Street View and located the place where a vehicle that might have transported the woman would have made its turn into the park. The access point was near a set of traffic lights, parallel with the pedestrianised top end of Queen Street, a popular shopping street in the middle of the city centre.

'You'd think those traffic lights would have cameras,' she said, 'but possibly not. I'll get on to it first thing in the morning, find out if they exist and whether the bloody things were actually turned on.'

And then what? she thought. The body had been in the water for anything up to two weeks, according to Helen Collier. Someone was going to have to sit through up to two weeks' worth of CCTV footage in order to identify every vehicle that had entered the park during that time.

Whose week was she going to make by handing them that entertaining task?

'In the meantime,' Harry said, 'you should probably go home.'

'Probably.' She caught his look and raised both hands in mock surrender. 'Two minutes,' she lied. 'Then I'm out of here, I promise.'

Alex minimised the Internet page and waited to watch the superintendent leave the room. She then searched for the bank of profiles she had earlier retrieved from the missing persons database. If this young woman had been in the river for anything up to two weeks, someone must surely have missed her during that time.

Thinking she might be kept occupied by the surprisingly long list of missing people the database had thrown up, Alex went into the quiet corridor and down to the small staffroom to make a cup of coffee. The vending machine in the corridor produced what could only be described as water that smelled vaguely of coffee, deemed worth keeping for emergency caffeine needs should the kettle ever decide to spontaneously combust, which it had decided to the previous week.

There was something irrepressibly tragic about the image of a missing person. Even the photographs that had captured joyful moments – wedding days, graduations, sun-bleached beach holidays – were made eerie by the subject's updated status as 'missing'. Smiles became saddened, eyes dulled; gestures became fake somehow, as though the soon-to-become-missing person wished to emphasise that moment in an effort to erase a fate they were subconsciously aware of. As though somehow they had known back when the photograph was taken – had known all along, really – that at some point they would be leaving the world that existed on the other side of the camera.

Alex sipped her coffee as each face greeted her in turn. Missing sons, missing brothers, missing wives. Everyone meant something to someone, even those who might not have believed they did. Where did the missing go? What happened to those people who left their homes one day, heading for work as they did every other morning, and simply disappeared from their lives? It seemed to Alex that it should no longer be possible for a person to just go missing, yet every year thousands did.

Her finger hovered over the keypad, lingering over an image. A young woman – a girl – was sitting on a low wall in a back garden, a small square of overgrown lawn behind her. She wore a summer dress, pale blue with spaghetti straps, and a pair of sunglasses was pushed up on to her head. Her long hair was swept to one side, over one shoulder, and the ghost of a smile sat upon her lips, as though giving in to it might cause her fragile frame to shatter.

The young woman seemed to call to Alex in silence through the screen, and though she had looked so different when the image had been taken, Alex had no doubt that this was the girl whose body had been pulled from the river.

CHAPTER SIX

The group had gone to the pub and ordered drinks; all except Carl, who had made his excuses and left. If no one else noticed that Connor and Sarah had simultaneously disappeared after the drinks had been taken to a table in a far corner – the kind of spot that most of the group was happy to opt for in order to be lost to the rest of the room – then Rachel Jones at least had spotted them, and she sat with her back turned slightly to the others, her dark eyes watching the empty corridor down which Connor and Sarah had slipped away.

*

Connor followed her to the toilets, reached for her elbow and pulled her into the cold night air of the small enclosed smokers' area.

'What are you playing at?'

'What?'

Connor exhaled loudly and pressed a hand to the brick wall of the pub, his body blocking hers and stopping her from leaving, though they both knew she wouldn't have left even had it been an option.

'You know what. All those innuendos in the meeting. You've got to stop this, Sarah, please. If anyone finds out—'

'If anyone finds out what?'

He should never have stayed out with her that first night all those months ago, he thought. They hadn't been to the pub that night; they had stayed at the hall and he could still remember that night so clearly, all the truths and the admissions that had been spilled by not just them but by other members of the group. He had felt the connection instantly, like some sort of invisible length of thread that passed across the room and pulled him towards her, and she to him. He had felt she understood him, and at the time that had been exactly what he'd needed.

And now it was everything he didn't.

He might have been initially attracted to her because he had thought she understood him, but the only attraction that had kept him going back was the one he kept feeling in his trousers every time she stood too close to him. The one he was feeling now, even though his brain was telling him how stupid he was and how much trouble this woman could cause him.

'What you did earlier, the way you spoke like that at the meeting. It wasn't you.'

'You don't know me.'

Perhaps that was true, and why wouldn't it be? They all professed to honesty, but the real truth was that they all kept their darkest secrets hidden, buried in their own heads. If they didn't, they wouldn't need the support group.

'This has to stop, Sarah.'

She shifted her weight from one foot to another, her body tilted at an angle and her arms folded across her chest. She hated it when he said her name like that. He was older than her, but not by much, so how did it always manage to sound like some sort of reprimand, like a teacher berating a student or a parent scolding a wayward child?

He thought she was going to argue with him, but instead her folded arms relaxed and she breathed a gulp of night air before saying, 'I know.'

He exhaled. 'I'm sorry. It's my fault, all of it. I should never have let it happen. And I don't want you to stop coming to the meetings, but if you feel you have to then I'm sorry for that too.'

What was he saying? He didn't care if she stopped coming. It would make his life a lot easier if he never saw her again. But if he told her that, she might decide she had nothing to lose. She would tell the rest of the group what they'd been up to, and then everything would really go to shit.

Sarah closed her eyes. 'I don't want to stop coming.'

'Then what happened earlier. It can't happen again.'

'I know,' she said, looking at him. 'I'm sorry.' She didn't want to make a scene, but going quietly still felt like giving in to Connor. Things had always been on his terms. They met up when it suited him; he answered her calls when it suited him. He picked her up and put her down and expected her to be available whenever it was convenient for him.

How was that fair?

It had started as fun. She knew it was wrong, but didn't she deserve a bit of happiness after everything that had happened to her? He had made her feel wanted. She hadn't meant to have feelings for him. They'd just happened by themselves. Now she couldn't make them go away. She had tried, but they just kept coming back.

'I don't want us to stop seeing each other.' She hated the desperation in her voice. She had heard it before, in another life that seemed so long ago now, and she thought she'd left that old Sarah behind.

Apparently not.

Connor sighed and lowered his head, focusing on the ground between his feet. 'It can never be what you want it to be. You know that, don't you?'

'It doesn't matter,' Sarah said too quickly. 'What's wrong with this, with the way things are now? I won't make a fuss, I promise. I won't say anything. We can just keep things as they are. No one will know.'

She might have hated the fact, but she didn't want to be without him. She had tried being on her own. She couldn't do it. Eventually, he would come to realise that he didn't want to be without her either. She just had to be patient.

Connor was shaking his head. 'I can't do this any more. I'm sorry. It's too risky.'

He didn't even meet her eye to say the words, and when he went back into the pub, Sarah waited outside, allowing the cold air to dry the start of tears that had caught at the corner of her eyes. He would change his mind, she thought. One way or another, she would make him see sense.

Connor used the toilet before heading back into the pub. No one seemed to notice he had gone; no one except Rachel Jones, whose quick eyes fixed upon him as he re-entered the bar. Connor took his seat without making eye contact.

One thing had made itself obvious that evening. Rachel knew what was going on between him and Sarah.

CHAPTER SEVEN

Chloe Lane sat in the bedroom of her flat and stared at the screen of her laptop. She rarely watched television. When she needed company, she sought it online, sneaking a peek into other people's lives via Facebook. Most of the people she was friends with online she never saw in the real world. They were people she had known at university, first in Cardiff and then in London – 'known' meaning she had once lived on the same floor as them, or had sat in the same lecture hall. There were people she had met during her first few years with the police, although she wasn't bothered if she never saw any of them again.

Chloe never added anything much to her own timeline, happy to keep her private life just that. Not that there was much to write about, she thought. But if other people wanted to tell her what they were doing, it seemed rude not to pay them some attention. These things that had become normal and everyday – boasts of workout sessions, photographs of impressive (and often less than impressive) cake attempts, daily updates on the progress of babies who did nothing but eat, sleep and shit (and what else could they be expected to do, really?) – were a welcome distraction from things like corpses on riverbanks.

They were a distraction from the ghosts that stood in the shadows of Chloe's day-to-day life.

She rubbed the heel of her hand against her eye, pressing back the need for sleep. She was tired, it had been a long day, so why she now thought to check her emails this late she wasn't sure, as though some sixth sense had driven her to turn on the laptop and had then led her away from Facebook and towards something that would stop everything else dead in its tracks.

She should have tidied up a bit. The rest of the flat was neat and orderly – she didn't own enough for things to become cluttered – but her bedroom was a different matter. The wardrobe unit that framed the head of her bed was filled to bursting, with more clothes crammed into the set of drawers beneath the window. Her make-up bag spilled its contents across the top of the unit, used face wipes smeared with concealer and mascara waiting to be thrown away. These were the things that allowed her to be someone else. Every morning when she dressed and applied her make-up, Chloe felt as though she was donning a disguise.

She sat in bed, shivery in her pyjamas and reluctant to put the heating on when she would soon be asleep anyway. She glanced across at her phone. That afternoon, she had sent a text message to Scott – a man she had met a few months earlier, who, in those months, she had let down more than probably merited forgiveness – but he hadn't replied. She couldn't blame him. She wondered whether one day she might ever be able to get beyond all the things that stopped her from ever getting too close to somebody, but for now she very much doubted it.

Looking again at the screen of the laptop, Chloe felt a shiver pass through her. This time she knew it wasn't just the temperature that had prompted such a physical response. The first message received weeks earlier, just before Christmas, could have been put down to error, or perhaps some sick prank from somebody who knew too much about her. But this, the second: this was no coincidence. She stared at the words on the screen.

Found him yet?

She checked the day the email had been sent. She hadn't logged in for a few days, but it had been received that day. She checked the time it was sent: four thirty that morning. Chloe ran a fingertip across the mousepad and clicked the search bar at the top left corner of her email page. In it, she typed the words 'the serpent'. The screen buffered as her useless Internet connection decided on whether or not it was going to work. Then there it was. The first message, sent almost a month earlier.

Reaching to her bedside table, Chloe took a pen from the top drawer and searched for an opened envelope or the back of a receipt on which to write. She found a tattered old notebook hidden among the debris of the drawer. She knew she wouldn't forget it, but she wrote it down anyway, scrawling the email address hurriedly on the first clean page she came to.

theserpent@hotmail.com

She ran a hand over her face in another attempt to push away the tiredness that had previously beckoned her to her bed. She had drunk a coffee not long before, with sugar she didn't usually take, and now she wished the blast of caffeine would actually do what it was expected to and make her feel a little more alert. Her heart pounded in her chest. She had been waiting years for something, anything, and now this, as though someone else knew who she was looking for. There was only one 'him' she had ever sought. It couldn't possibly refer to anyone else.

Pushing the laptop from her, Chloe went to the wardrobe in the corner of her small bedroom and reached for the suitcase that lay on top. It was heavy, weighed down with papers and documents, and she strained as its weight eased on top of her. She wasn't sure how she'd ever been able to get it up there in the first place. Over the years, this suitcase had travelled with her between every move. Perhaps she had grown accustomed to carrying the weight of its contents with her.

Without it, what did she have, really?

She took it to the bed, unzipped it and flipped the lid open.

It had been a while since she had opened the suitcase, yet everything inside it was as familiar to her as her own reflection. She reached past files of papers to the photo album that lay beneath and sat on the side of the bed before opening it. It was an old album, with a green satin cover. Its edges were battered and its front cover tea-stained, but Chloe considered these imperfections evidence of love. Here was the proof that she had returned to this album, returned to its pages, time after time: sometimes with smiles; often with tears.

Here was the evidence that she had never forgotten him.

From the pages, their faces looked back, young and laughing. Ice cream smiles and limbs swinging from park monkey bars; staring back at her were all those early days: the days before they'd learned about the things that made them different. These were the days before everything had gone wrong and all the bad things became irreversible.

His life – his death – had been blighted by a question mark, and Chloe was the only person prepared to search for the answer. Those happier photos were the minority. In the others, she saw both their faces as she now remembered them, as she believed in her heart she would always remember them: distant, lost; always thinking of something else.

Always thinking of somewhere else.

And it shamed her now that it had been so long since she had held his face in her hands, as though that absence over time had meant she had forgotten him. She never had. For the past eight years he had followed her, ever present, continuous, like some unfinished sentence that had never come close to a full stop.

The sense of an ending frightened her, but the thought of never finding one was even more unbearable.

She slipped a finger beneath the page and turned to the next, offering sad smiles to the faces looking back at her. Everything she had done had been with the intention of this. It was time she got back to what she was meant to be doing.

It was time to tell DI King the truth.

CHAPTER EIGHT

The following day, the next of kin of the young woman Alex feared she'd identified on the missing persons database attended the station after an early morning visit from uniformed officers. Alex sat in one of the station's interview rooms opposite a woman she suspected might not be as old as she looked. The woman was frail, using a stick to balance herself when she walked, and when she'd taken the seat opposite Alex it seemed to have taken all her effort, visibly exhausting her. Alex went to fetch her a cup of tea, subtly using the offer as an excuse to leave the room and give the woman a few minutes alone to get her breath back.

When Alex returned, April Evans told her that she hadn't seen or heard from her granddaughter, Lola, in over two weeks. She had reported her missing just a week earlier, and Alex questioned the woman's delay.

'She's a bit of a free spirit,' April explained, wheezing the words from her chest. 'Always has been. She pops in, she pops out again – I can't keep tabs on her.'

'Can you describe Lola for me, please, Mrs Evans?'

The woman rummaged in her handbag and retrieved a mobile phone. She tapped the screen a few times, evidently not adept at how the thing worked. Once she'd found what she was looking for, she leaned over to show Alex the screen. It was a different photograph to the one that Alex had seen on the database the previous evening, but at the sight of Lola's face, her heart sank once again.

'Where was the last time you saw Lola?'

'At the house. Friday before last. She popped in for some of her things, she said. Stayed long enough to manage a quick cup of tea with me. Look, I know not seeing her for a week seems a long time, but it's nothing unusual for her. She's twenty years old, she's got her own life. She doesn't want to be seen living with her nan. She stays with friends, with her boyfriend. I used to try to get her to check in every now and then, but she wasn't having any of it. I tried her mobile during the past week when I started to get a bit concerned and every time it went straight to answerphone. That's not like her. That phone is always on. That's what made me contact the police.'

Alex listened to the woman's words, unable to escape the underlying detachment that came with them. April Evans had reported Lola missing, but it had taken a whole week before she did so. She spoke of her granddaughter in the way a casual acquaintance might. What had their relationship been like in recent months? She was about to have to tell the woman that they'd found a body in the river – that now she'd seen another photograph of Lola she believed there was more than a possibility the dead girl was her granddaughter – and ask if she would make a formal identification.

'A body was found yesterday morning,' Alex told her, 'in the River Taff at Bute Park. There were no belongings on the body, so we've not yet been able to make a formal identification.'

The woman glanced down at the darkened screen of the mobile phone she still held. Her granddaughter's photograph had now disappeared, blanked away by the fading of the screen. She was silent before looking back up at Alex.

'Have you seen her? Does it look like her?'

'I'm going to have to ask if you'd come with me to identify your granddaughter. I know this is very difficult for you—'

'It's fine,' she said quickly. 'Can we go now?'

Alex was stalled by the woman's reaction, her eagerness to view a corpse that might prove to have once been her granddaughter. There was no panic, there were no tears; she seemed calm somehow, as though she had expected the worst.

'I'll take you. I have to warn you though that the body was in the water for a while.'

April Evans nodded, acknowledging Alex's words as a warning. 'It's fine,' she said again. 'Where shall I wait?'

*

April Evans stood at the side of the table, looking over the body of her granddaughter as though observing the remains of a stranger. Alex still found it unsettling to look at Lola Evans, yet the young woman's grandmother had shown little emotion, reacting to everything with silence and nods. She stared absently at the bloated grey flesh of the girl, quietly absorbing the realities of Lola's final moments.

Looking away, April moved a hand to her mouth; the first signs of a reaction.

'Is this Lola, Mrs Evans?'

April nodded. She moved her hand from her mouth. 'Yes, it's Lola.'

She turned away from Alex and looked at the closed door that kept them shut inside the claustrophobic room. 'Her mother died when she was three. Cancer. When she was twelve, my son was killed. Knocked off his motorbike by a drunk driver. She's seen more suffering in her life than most twice her age.'

Alex wondered whether the family's tragic background went some way to explaining the woman's strange, perhaps delayed, reactions to the sight of her granddaughter's tortured and decomposed body laid out on the table in the pathologist's identification room. It was almost as though April Evans expected darkness to lurk at her door.

'Who did this to her?' April asked, turning back to Alex. There were tears in her eyes, stubbornly fought back with pride and defiance.

'I don't know,' she told her. 'But I promise we'll do everything we can to find out.'

CHAPTER NINE

Alex and Chloe were joined by the rest of the team and the super-intendent in the station's investigation room. A photograph of Lola Evans provided by her grandmother was pinned to the board at the far end of the room, highlighting the empty white space that surrounded it. They had very little to go on. Lola Evans was twenty years old and lived with her grandmother despite rarely being there. According to her grandmother she was often out until the early hours and she spent a lot of nights staying at friends' houses. She worked as a self-employed mobile beautician although April Evans hadn't seemed convinced this was the only way she'd made her money. When questioned further about what she meant by the comment, she gave an equally vague answer, merely stating that the lifestyle Lola seemed to have become accustomed to – the constant going out and the never-ending clothes she seemed to buy – was unlikely to have been funded through facials and pedicures.

'The post-mortem report on Lola Evans came back this morning,' Alex said, addressing the team.

'As we already know, there were several injuries inflicted on the victim, particularly to the hands and nails, and the assault was likely sustained over a period of time. We need to find out her last known whereabouts.'

Alex paused and turned to the image of Lola: a photograph of her taken on Christmas day, sitting at her grandmother's table beside what looked like a meagre celebratory meal. Thinking back on what April Evans had told Alex of the family's history, she guessed there was little worth celebrating at any time of year, but least of all during December.

Lola looked hung-over in the photograph, with heavy bags circling her bleary eyes and what looked like the previous evening's make-up darkening her skin. It also seemed glaringly obvious that she was unlikely to eat much of what was on her plate. The post-mortem report showed the ravages of anorexia on Lola's body over the years.

Looking at the sad eyes of the girl in the photograph – at the knife and fork that would no doubt have been pushed half-heartedly around the plate once the photo had been taken – made her life's brutal ending somehow all the more tragic.

'Lola Evans suffered from anorexia. She was hospitalised three years ago at the age of seventeen with a weight of just five and a half stone. Her grandmother said she made improvements with the help of various medical and psychiatric professionals but it was short-lived. Her family history is tragic, as you've already been informed. Now, initial indications would suggest that Lola wasn't taken at random.'

'The post-mortem shows no evidence of sexual assault.'

Alex turned to Superintendent Blake. 'No, so that rules out what might have been our obvious assumption. So what else? Lola was young, attractive, but obviously highly vulnerable. Who might have wanted to make her suffer in this way, and did that person know her? Lola's mobile phone is missing. The service provider has drawn a blank. She owned a laptop, but it wasn't in her room at her grandmother's house when officers carried out a search there. Dan,' she continued, nodding to a uniformed officer sitting close by, 'you went to the house, didn't you? If you could give feedback.'

Daniel Mason was a detective constable recently transferred from another unit. A few years older than Alex, he was one of the few men she'd encountered on the force who didn't seem to mind taking instruction from a woman younger than him. Ribald station banter often revealed more truth than anyone liked to admit. Dan had shown her nothing but respect and had fitted into the team as if they'd already known him for years.

'Not much to report back, I'm afraid,' Dan said, turning in his seat so that he was able to face the rest of their colleagues. 'Laptop missing, as DI King said. No signs that Lola had been planning on going anywhere – no great amount of clothes missing and her passport was in the bedside drawer. There's a suggestion from her grandmother that she might have had a boyfriend, although she doesn't seem too sure about it. The bag of equipment Lola used for her beautician's job was in her room, so she hadn't been working for around two and a half weeks.'

'Not at that job, anyway,' Chloe chipped in. 'Didn't her nan suggest she might have been making money in other ways?'

The superintendent cut in before Alex could respond. 'I don't want us to spend too much time speculating on what other source of income she might have had, at least not until we've got some facts. I don't want anything to skew our perception of this young woman, OK?'

Alex nodded in agreement. 'The fact of the matter is, she was brutalised and whoever was capable of inflicting this kind of suffering on another human being needs catching.'

'He could do with a bit more than that,' Chloe muttered.

'Before he does it again?' Dan asked.

Alex sighed. 'Let's hope not. And let's not rule out the fact that "he" could be "she".'

She gestured to the other images on the board; in particular, to the close-up shots of Lola's hands and the bloodied fingertips from which her nails had been pulled out. 'This kind of torture is inflicted deliberately, with intent. Why the nails? Any link to her work as a beautician?'

'What?' piped up one of the younger male officers at the back of the room. 'She gave someone a dodgy manicure and they decided to get their own back?'

Alex wasn't in the mood for attempts at humour, particularly when they were in such bad taste. Her lip curled, as it often did when she was unimpressed. The look was enough to cast an uncomfortable silence over the room, especially when it was reinforced by the superintendent. If nothing else, the comment allowed her to allocate the task of watching the two weeks' worth of CCTV footage requested from Cardiff City Council.

'Her hair was cut off,' Alex continued, drawing the focus away from the young constable. 'Why?'

'Souvenir?' Chloe suggested, repeating the assumption that had been made by the pathologist at the scene.

'Perhaps. That might suggest she wasn't chosen at random. It would also suggest her murder was premeditated. We need to find out as much about Lola Evans as we can,' Alex said, bringing the meeting to a close. 'It appears she has a boyfriend, or someone her grandmother thinks she might have been involved with. He plays in a band that seems to be quite well known around Cardiff. Let's find him, see what he knows. If there are any developments, I want to be made aware straight away, please.'

The team began to disperse. Chloe Lane lingered at one of the desks, waiting to grab Alex's attention. 'I was wondering if I could have a word?'

'About this?'

She shook her head.

'Now?'

'No, no rush. Lunchtime?'

'I'll be in my office.'

Chloe smiled. 'Thanks.'

She didn't really know what she was thanking her for. Not yet.

CHAPTER TEN

Chloe stuck her head around the door of Alex's office and eyed the sandwich sitting unopened on her desk.

'That your lunch?'

Alex glanced at the cardboard packaging that housed the equally cardboard-looking sandwich. 'It's an attempt.'

Chloe gave a slight smile. 'It doesn't look that great.'

Alex placed her hands on the desk in front of her and turned in her swivel chair so that she was facing Chloe. 'What did you want to see me about?'

Chloe hesitated between the truth and a lie. She glanced at the clock on Alex's wall. 'Any chance I can tell you over a better lunch?'

*

Twenty minutes later, the two women sat at a table in the corner of a quiet café in the town centre, waiting for their food to arrive. Chloe didn't want to tell Alex the truth at the station, not with prying eyes and over-keen ears lurking in every corridor. For months she had longed to tell Alex the secret she'd been keeping, and for months there had always been something that had stood in her way. Now there was a pressing sense of urgency. The emails she'd received seemed to read as a warning.

'This can't be long,' Alex told her, shooting a look at the woman who had taken their order. 'I'm going to speak with some of the staff at the council this afternoon – find out exactly who had access to the park. Authorised access, that is. Obviously, whoever put Lola

Evans in the river could quite plausibly have been there without any authority. I'm not sure many people would look twice at a van driving through the grounds there – it's not that uncommon a sight.'

Alex was thinking out loud now, but she noticed Chloe seemed to be barely listening. 'What's the matter?'

'I need your help,' Chloe confessed.

Alex was the only officer – the only person – she trusted with the words she was about to speak. Life had taught her that even those closest couldn't be relied upon – that everyone had a second face and some chose to keep it well hidden – but Alex had proven to be exactly the type of person Chloe needed: someone honest, someone with integrity; someone with a sense of loyalty that dictated that once something had been started, she would see it through to its completion.

Alex studied Chloe questioningly, wearing that expression she seemed completely oblivious to: the expression that seemed to look right through someone and see things they'd not yet seen for themselves.

'What's the matter?' Alex repeated.

Chloe realised, much to her embarrassment, that tears had spiked at the corners of her eyes. She swallowed and took a sip of her tea. 'Does the name Emily Phillips mean anything to you?'

Alex put her coffee cup on the table and sat back in her seat. She recognised the name, but she couldn't picture the face and couldn't remember why it should mean something to her.

'Eight years ago,' Chloe said. 'She was found hanging from her mother's banisters.'

Alex's face fell. Of course she remembered Emily Phillips. Alex had attended the scene of what had initially been reported to police as a suicide. A teenage girl, just sixteen at the time, had been found hanging from the staircase of her mother's home, or so it had been claimed.

'I remember her. Did you know her?'

'It wasn't a suicide, was it?'

Alex's eyes narrowed. Where was all this leading, and why was Chloe so interested in this girl? Alex couldn't remember all the details, but she carried the main bones of the case with her – as she did with every case in which she'd had involvement – as though a part of her own skeleton.

'No,' she said tentatively. 'Why do you ask?'

'Please tell me what you know.'

Alex sat forward in her seat and leaned on the table, closing the distance between them. 'I know the same as everyone else does – it was public knowledge. Emily hadn't killed herself – she'd been strangled and the death had been staged to look as though she'd taken her own life. Pretty badly, by all accounts.'

There was other evidence that it hadn't been staged at all, but until she knew where Chloe's sudden interest stemmed from she wasn't going to volunteer any further details on the matter. What would Chloe have been at the time? Eighteen… nineteen? She hadn't been in the police then; she had no reason to be interested in this case.

As she spoke, Alex watched Chloe's pretty face grow pale. Her eyes became glazed yet her focus more intense, not faltering from Alex's.

'You met him, didn't you?'

'Met who?'

'The boy everyone thought had killed her.'

'Her boyfriend? Yes, I met him.'

General opinion was that the boyfriend had killed her after a drunken argument, yet there was something about it that Alex had never quite believed. She had been one of only two people who had seen him on that staircase and she remembered him now as she had found him then, clutching his girlfriend's body and sobbing into her hair; little boy sobs that had failed to subside even when Alex had managed, after what had felt considerable time, to coax his body from the dead girl's arms.

The case had been closed shortly after, when the boy had killed himself less than a week later.

'Chloe, what's all this about? Why are you asking me about this now?'

'Her boyfriend, Luke,' she told Alex, the words falling free before she had time to think twice about letting them escape her. 'He was my brother.' Chloe pushed a hand to her face as though willing back a further onslaught of tears. What use were they to him now? He needed her to be strong, to do what she should have done years ago.

'He didn't kill Emily,' she told Alex. 'And he didn't kill himself.'

CHAPTER ELEVEN

Sometimes Connor's head felt too full of the things of which he knew he would never truly be free. He had tried to fight them off, tried to shut them down, but they kept surging, like recurring nightmares, to break him, always managing to somehow take him by surprise though he spent every day expectantly awaiting their arrival.

He watched his son clicking away at the computer in the corner of the living room.

'Liam.'

Connor continued to watch the back of his son's head, knowing the boy had heard him. The click-clicking of the computer keyboard was grating on his last nerve.

'Liam!'

The boy turned slowly on his swivel chair, meeting his father's eye with indifference. 'What?'

'Fancy a game of football after dinner?'

Connor didn't know why he was wasting his time. He was more likely to get a game of football from the baby than he was from Liam; if nothing else, the baby would have been a more willing opponent. His son wasn't interested in spending time with him. He didn't really seem interested in anything beyond the bloody computer.

Liam pulled a face and made a noise that sounded too much like a teenager for Connor's liking before turning back to the screen. Connor knew he wasn't supposed to feel it, but he didn't really like his own son. He wasn't sure whether he liked the baby either.

The problem was, Connor didn't much like anyone, least of all himself.

Liam had been conceived when Connor had been home on leave from Afghanistan. His family was under the impression that his 'issues' – as they ambiguously liked to name them – had started upon his later return, but they had begun much earlier. Under duress, he had attended counselling. Under even greater duress, he had agreed to complete a short course that would allow him to run his own support group. He'd never had any intention of actually doing so, but once he'd met Tim Cole there he was railroaded into it, going along with the other man's plans in the hope that it would get him out of the house. The truth was, he hated listening to people drone on about their problems. I'm lonely, I'm exhausted, I'm fat... God, they got on his nerves. Still, he needed the group as a much-needed excuse for a night off once a week; the only time he didn't feel crippled by the weight of parental responsibility and supposed marital bliss.

The news of Jen's second pregnancy had been met with plenty of enthusiasm and excitement, but unfortunately for her little of that had been generated from Connor. Afghanistan changed everything. He didn't want this domesticated life he was living. In the kitchen, Jen was grappling a heavy load of wet washing. The baby was sitting in its highchair, red-faced and wailing.

All he heard was noise, but Connor realised these sounds went way past his family and ran far beyond the four walls of this house he was supposed to acknowledge as home. They consumed him, filling the space around him like the air he breathed. The memory of war tormented him yet, with a perverseness that left him questioning his own sanity; a part of him longed to be back there. There he had served some sort of purpose. Here he wasn't doing anything. What was the sense in any of this?

There was a clatter from the corner as Liam dropped something on to the floor. He cursed, the word he muttered audible enough to be heard by his mother in the kitchen, who appeared in the doorway of the living room with a face as red as the baby's and a wet bedsheet tangled around her arm.

'Liam! Naughty!'

Connor took his mobile from the pocket of his jeans and pretended to read an imaginary email he'd received just as his wife entered the room.

'You can turn that off now,' she scolded. 'Your dinner's almost ready.'

For a moment, Connor thought she was speaking to him.

He tried to remind himself the boy was only eight, but sometimes Connor felt his son was testing them both, and that his wife would pass this initiation with straight A*s while he was destined to be leaving at the end of the term.

Running away had certainly seemed an appealing option, on more than one occasion.

'Do you want anything?'

It took a moment for Connor to realise that this time she was in fact talking to him. 'What? Uh… no.'

She said nothing and returned to the kitchen. Connor watched his son traipse out into the kitchen, the boy ignoring his father's presence as he passed.

He reached for the television remote and switched channels, watching aimlessly as a panel of famous sports stars answered trivia questions in order to win money for charity. On the table beside the sofa, his mobile phone vibrated with a text message. He leaned over and swiped a finger across the screen before typing in his four digit passcode. A number he didn't recognise came up.

Tell your wife or I will.

Connor read the message twice. He glanced to the opened kitchen door, spying like an outsider on his family's dinnertime. He looked back at the phone, locked it, and went into the kitchen to feign happy domesticity.

CHAPTER TWELVE

Ethan Thompson had proven easy to find. He was working in a bar called The Lizard in Cardiff city centre and was bottling up the beer fridges when Alex arrived. A flyer for his band had been found during a search of Lola's bedroom at her grandmother's house, and April recalled Lola having said something about knowing the lead singer. 'Knowing' him turned out to mean she had been having regular sex with him, although Ethan was quick to point out that he hadn't been in a relationship with Lola.

Alex had acknowledged what April Evans had told her – that her granddaughter was very much a free spirit who didn't take too well to having to explain her whereabouts to anyone – but the fact that so many of those who were allegedly closest to her had little knowledge she'd even been missing let alone anything worse was something Alex was struggling to get to grips with. Had it just been that everyone had assumed she was with somebody else?

She had encountered a few missing children cases in which similar scenarios had unfolded, with both parents thinking the child was safely with the other. Alex realised mistakes could easily be made, but whenever there was a child involved she found it difficult to be sympathetic with a parent whose attention had been distracted. Her own childlessness made it easy to judge the inadequacies of others and believe she would do better. She would never allow a child to leave her sight. No harm would come to anyone in her care.

She followed Ethan Thompson to a table in the corner of the bar. This was completely different, she thought. Lola Evans was a young woman, not a child. Perhaps it hadn't been anyone else's business where she was or who she was with.

Or had it?

Ethan Thompson sat and Alex took a seat opposite him. He looked like a model from the pages of some alternative fashion magazine, she thought: that skinny, anaemic look young people seemed to prefer these days. His ears had huge holes in them filled with thick black coins of plastic that stretched his lobes like a spaniel's. Alex was pretty sure he was wearing eyeliner.

His dark eyes fixed themselves on her, and it was only then that Alex noticed how enlarged his pupils were.

'I don't get it,' he said. 'I saw the news, but they just said a woman's body had been found in the river. They didn't give a name, did they?'

'You play in a band?' Alex asked. She wanted to gain a picture of Ethan's social life; hopefully, find a link with Lola's. Lola had been found the morning before, on Tuesday, but the pathologist believed she had died anything up to two weeks earlier. Her grandmother claimed to have seen her eleven days prior to her body being found. Trying to pinpoint an exact timeframe was going to prove near impossible.

'Yeah.' Ethan faltered, as though it was a trick question and Alex was somehow trying to trip him up. He ran a hand through his hair – too long in Alex's opinion, but how most young men were wearing it – and twisted his lips in an expression of confusion.

The pupils seemed to grow bigger by the second. Alex wondered whether he knew which day of the week it was, never mind being able to recall the name of the band he played in.

What had Lola Evans seen in Ethan Thompson? He looked as though he needed a good bath and a decent meal, as well as perhaps a couple of weeks in rehab.

'Is this where you first met Lola?'

The young man shook his head. 'I met her in the club opposite. I was playing there with my band – she was with some friends. We got chatting at the bar. She came back to mine. You know how it is.' He pulled a face that suggested Alex didn't know how it was.

'When was that?'

Ethan fiddled with his stretched left earlobe. 'Couple of months ago. Maybe a bit more.' He put his hand on the table between them, his unusually long fingers splayed. 'Shit. I can't believe she's dead. She was a nice girl. Quiet, you know. Bit vulnerable. I like that.'

If he realised how odd his last statement sounded, Ethan Thompson didn't show any awareness.

'Vulnerable, in what way?'

Ethan pulled a face. 'I don't know. Like she needed looking after. I liked that, at first.'

'At first?'

He shrugged. 'Gets a bit wearing, you know what I mean.'

How wearing had it become? Enough to drive him to murder?

'When did you last see Lola?' she asked.

His eyes rolled up to the ceiling as though trying to fix the memory. 'Weekend before last. Saturday night. We grabbed some food together before she went to work.'

Alex narrowed her eyes. What beautician worked on a Saturday night?

'Work where?'

Ethan shrugged. 'She was a waitress or something. Evening job to earn an extra bit of cash. She mentioned somewhere, but I can't remember.'

'You didn't know where your own girlfriend worked?'

'Look,' Ethan said, raising his hands from the table, 'she wasn't my girlfriend. We were just having a bit of fun, you know.'

Alex's thoughts skipped momentarily to Rob and she felt a flush of shame at what she knew she'd been doing the past few months.

She didn't know what Rob believed was happening between them, but she was beginning to suspect whatever thoughts he'd had on the subject didn't match hers.

Had Lola seen her relationship with Ethan as more than just a bit of fun?

What did Rob think was going to happen as a result of all the nights they'd spent together recently?

'Where did you go?' Alex asked, snapping herself away from distracting thoughts.

'When?'

'You said you went for food before she went to work. Where did you eat?'

'Oh. Nando's. The one in the shopping centre in Cardiff.'

Alex made a note of the place along with the date. 'OK. If there's anything else we'll be in touch. Soon.'

Ethan gave her a nervous glance as he rose from his chair. 'I am upset about it, you know,' he said, as though trying to convince himself rather than Alex. 'I just, I didn't know her very long, you know? It's really sad.'

It was the most insincere expression of sadness Alex had ever heard. They still had only a limited picture of Lola's life, but had her confidence been at such a low ebb that she had seen nothing better for herself than gravitating towards young men such as Ethan Thompson? Alex knew very little of eating disorders or the psychological implications of such diseases, but the knowledge she had was enough to understand that Lola's condition might have resulted in extremes, and this might also have impacted upon her trust in other people. She could have distanced herself from people, but the fact that she went home with Ethan on the evening she met him – coupled with a lifestyle that seemed to suggest she moved from place to place quite freely – implied the opposite was true, and that Lola might have trusted other people too easily.

Statistically it was likely Lola Evans had known her killer. She looked at the young man opposite. Could those long, skinny fingers – could that young man who was little more than a boy – have inflicted the multiple injuries that had scarred Lola's body? Watching Ethan Thompson head back to the bar, Alex knew nothing was to be considered impossible.

CHAPTER THIRTEEN

Alex poured herself a glass of wine. Chloe didn't drink and Alex had often wondered whether there was a reason for it. It didn't seem appropriate to ask and it was none of her business. She made her a coffee and took a seat opposite her at the kitchen table. Chloe had brought an array of files with her, stacked at her side and labelled with an administrative prowess Alex could merely dream of. She seemed fraught and her hair was dishevelled, so far from the usually immaculate young woman in whose presence Alex found herself feeling inescapably old and dowdy.

'Have you had a chance to check the case history?' Chloe asked.

'Not yet. I had a corpse wash up on a riverbank, remember?'

The younger woman's face flushed. Alex had noticed she only ever blushed in front of women. With men, Chloe was defiant. She never backed down in the face of male banter at the station and her attitude towards Harry during their first meeting showed a tendency to be flippant if she felt threatened or undermined.

Alex wondered where her defences against men had risen from.

'Sorry,' Chloe said. 'I know the timing isn't great.' She reached for the top of her files and drew out a photograph. 'Emily Phillips.'

The smiling teenage face in the photograph was far different to the face Alex recalled. She hadn't wanted to remember, but the young girl with the belt tightened around her throat was an image that would be etched permanently on Alex's brain. Worse still had been the tear-streaked face of the teenage boy who had clutched on to the body, refusing to let her go.

'The coroner didn't think it was a suicide, did he?' Alex asked.

She didn't want to sound unfeeling, but she realised how difficult talking about this case would be for Chloe. If the young woman wanted her help, she had to accept Alex as things stood now. She would look at it from the eyes of a detective and nothing closer. Allowing herself to become emotionally embroiled in the details of the story's background wasn't going to be productive for anyone – least of all for Chloe – and the last thing she wanted was to encourage any false hope.

In truth, Alex remembered exactly why the death hadn't been believed to have been a suicide. The coroner reported that it would have been impossible for the girl to have positioned herself in such a way that her boyfriend claimed to have found her, and that was also an initial source of doubt: no one but the boyfriend had seen her 'hanging' at all. A post-mortem examination revealed that although she had been strangled by the belt, the markings to her throat suggested the belt had been tightened horizontally, and not from the angles that would have been evident had she been hanged from the staircase as claimed.

The boyfriend had claimed to have loosened the belt and lowered Emily's body upon finding her. It was obvious why he had so quickly become prime suspect in her murder.

'I know how it all looks,' Chloe said, having talked Alex back through the initial events, 'but I also know my brother. He'd never hurt anyone. He's not a killer.'

Alex sipped her wine and tried not to linger on the look of desperation evident in Chloe's expression. She noticed how she never spoke about her brother using the past tense. How had she been able to keep this to herself for so long?

'Your brother's name was Luke?'

'Luke Griffiths.'

'Your surname?'

'I changed it about a year after Luke...' Chloe drifted away from the end of the sentence. 'My parents... we fell out. I wanted a clean start. It's a long story.'

If Chloe wanted her help, Alex felt that at some point that long story was going to have to be told. She just wasn't sure it was the right time. Glancing at the files in front of them, it seemed evident they already had enough to keep them going. And none of this could be looked into properly until they had completed their current commitments and found the man responsible for Lola Evans's murder.

'I know Luke,' Chloe said, putting her drink on the table between them. 'And I know you were there – you were with him.'

Alex had been a sergeant at the time and had responded when the initial call had come in. She and a colleague had been first on the scene.

'Everyone was against him,' Chloe continued. 'Everyone thought he'd killed her. Only, everything was circumstantial. Where was the proof?'

Alex sat back in her chair and exhaled. 'I'd have to refer back to the case file,' she said, knowing that was a lot easier said than done. 'I can't guarantee that'll be easy. Look, I've never been asked to do anything like this before. Cases aren't usually reopened without some sort of new evidence having come to light, you know that. And you also know how much shit you could end up in if you go about taking matters into your own hands.' The original case had been led by a senior investigating officer who'd retired a couple of years later. Returning to it now would mean seeking the permission of Superintendent Blake. Alex glanced at the files on the desk. 'Please tell me this lot's not from the station.'

Alex couldn't remember much of the case that had followed. She hadn't been directly involved – had been working on another case at the time – but she had known how it had ended. She was worried that this was all too personal to Chloe. Her attachments to the people involved were inevitably clouding her judgement.

She shook her head and Alex sighed with relief. Chloe tapped the pile of files in front of her, as though her own belief in her brother's innocence was proof enough. 'This is what I collected. Evidence.' She eyed the look of scepticism etched on Alex's face. 'Look, I'll show you.'

For the next hour, and over Alex's second glass of wine, Chloe worked her way through the paperwork. She had documented everything she had gathered – newspaper clippings, photographs, handwritten transcripts of conversations between her and her brother – with a precision that bordered on obsession, but rather than convince Alex that the case was worth reopening, Chloe managed to dissuade her there was anything substantial that could be considered by a case review team.

'This all relates to Emily,' Alex pointed out. 'What about Luke?'

Luke's suicide had closed the case into Emily's murder. In the days that had followed her death, police had closed in on Luke, looking for concrete evidence that would be sufficient grounds for an arrest. But that, as far as Chloe was concerned, was the pivotal flaw in the logic of the officers who had dealt with the case: they had never found any. They had read Luke's death as an admission of guilt. Case closed.

'Luke didn't kill Emily,' Chloe repeated.

Alex wondered if she was really convinced of this as fact, or whether her insistence just showed a desperation to keep the possibility a reality.

'And he didn't kill himself,' she continued, reading the doubt in Alex's expression. 'I saw him that afternoon. He told me he was going to find out what had happened to Emily – that it was the last good thing he could do for her. I told the police what he'd said, but nobody would listen to me. I was little more than a kid myself – why would anyone take me seriously? And I didn't do much to help myself. I was in my first year of uni, I was drinking too much.'

Chloe's unspoken words left Alex with questions she didn't feel comfortable asking. Was this an explanation as to why Chloe didn't drink now? What had she done?

'Luke was scared, but he was determined,' Chloe said, shifting focus from herself. 'The following morning, they found the car. Does that sound right to you?'

Alex held back her response. Over these past few months working closely alongside DC Lane she had found herself developing a respect for this hard-working and resilient young woman. That hadn't changed, yet this seemed to alter everything. Alex couldn't help but feel in some way manipulated, as though Chloe's trying so keenly and so obviously to impress her had all been leading up to this: this moment when she would ask for her help.

A wash of disappointment swept over her and she shook it off hurriedly, annoyed at herself for her misplaced pride. 'I'll have to speak with the superintendent.'

Chloe looked panicked. 'I'm not sure that's a good idea. What if he says no? They don't know I've got any connection to either case. How's that going to look?'

Alex wasn't sure, but she knew that investigating a case without following the appropriate procedures would land them both in front of a disciplinary board, justifiably or not. The case into Lola Evans's death was already proving a difficult one; Harry certainly wouldn't appreciate one of his own making things even more complicated.

'Why now?' Alex asked. 'How long ago was this? Eight years?'

Chloe took her mobile from her handbag and showed Alex the email she'd received that week:

Found him yet?

Then she searched for the other, the one received weeks earlier:

How's the search going?

'I ignored the first one – I thought it'd just been sent to the wrong email address by mistake or something. I got the second one the other day, again from the same email address.'

'This could refer to anything.'

Chloe looked at Alex as though she had physically harmed her.

'Someone knows something. If I can find out who murdered Emily, I can find who was responsible for my brother's death. Someone killed him, I know it. Either that or he was being blackmailed, something, but I know he wouldn't have killed himself. I have to find out what happened, but I don't think I can do this alone. I know I'm asking a lot, but there's no one else.'

Alex put a hand to her forehead and dragged her fingers through her hair. How was she supposed to tell Chloe that neither of them could go through with this – that if they couldn't get permission to reinvestigate the case then going ahead and doing so anyway might potentially mark the end of both their careers?

It turned out she didn't need to say anything. Chloe had read the response stamped on her face.

'I'm sorry. I'm asking too much.'

'I understand why you want to do this. Well,' she hastened, knowing she could never truly understand what Chloe must have felt, 'not understand, obviously, but I can appreciate how difficult this all must be. I just want you to think very carefully before you make any next step.'

Chloe gave a wan smile, sat back and drained the last of the coffee from her cup. 'I will.'

She didn't need to say any more. They both knew she was going to go ahead, with or without the help of Alex.

CHAPTER FOURTEEN

Connor knew Sarah's shift pattern because he regularly met her once she had finished work. They would meet a few streets away where he would abandon his own car to get into hers. That day, he waited for her to finish her shift and approached her in the car park, taking her by the arm and trying to lead her around the side of the building. His fingers dug into her skin and she yanked herself away from him, voicing angry protestations.

'What the hell do you think you're playing at?'

'What are you trying to do?' Connor hissed.

'Well, I was trying to get in my car and go home.' She shoved her handbag back up on to her shoulder and pushed her long hair from her face.

'I thought we talked about this at the pub the other night? I thought we were going to leave it there.'

'If by "it" you mean "us" then we were,' Sarah said. 'And I have.'

She flicked a length of blonde hair from her face and Connor tried to ignore the reaction that stirred inside him. He didn't need any psychologist to tell him that he'd found a counteraction to his anger through sex – he'd worked that much out for himself, much earlier. The only time he didn't feel angry – the only time he found himself able to block out all the things that had gone before this and the life he'd left behind on the dirty ground of a foreign country – was when he was having sex.

His therapist had told him he should talk about how he was feeling with his family, that they would understand the complications he was facing. What the hell would he know about it, sitting there in his nice office never having done a proper day's work in his life? All he seemed to do was repeat back what Connor said to him, occasionally altering his words with a slight change in phrasing.

Would his wife understand his need to have sex with other women? He wasn't prepared to take a bet on it.

'So what was that text yesterday all about then?' he asked Sarah angrily.

'What text?'

Connor felt anger crawl up into his chest. He could usually control it – he'd been controlling it for so long now – but more frequently, it caught him with a need to suppress it, and an even greater desire to let it do as it pleased.

The only way he could release it would tear his life apart, if his family were ever to find out the truth. Even now, whilst so angry at Sarah – whilst hating her – he wanted to push her into her car and take her clothes off.

'You know what bloody text,' he said, shoving the car door closed as Sarah once again tried to open it. The shove was stronger than either of them expected and the door slammed shut, narrowly missing Sarah's fingers. She shot him a glare.

'I'm sorry,' he snapped, not sounding sorry at all. 'It's just…'

He glanced to the far side of the car park, where a woman was standing at the corner of the building. She was holding a black bin bag in each hand and wore a net on her head to keep her hair in place. Once the woman realised she'd been caught watching them, she turned away from Connor and Sarah, busying herself at the industrial-sized wheelie bins that were separated from the car park by wooden fencing.

'Here,' Connor said, showing her the message he'd received.

Sarah looked at him defiantly. 'Well, I didn't send it.'

Why should she care? She wasn't the one who was married and had kids. He had ended it – whatever happened next was his problem.

'Have you tried texting back?' she asked sarcastically.

'I tried calling. It keeps going through to answerphone.'

'Well, it wasn't me,' Sarah said quietly between gritted teeth. She pulled her arm away from Connor, opened the car door and threw her bag inside. 'You said it was over. It is.'

She got into the car and slammed the door shut. Connor stood in the car park, fists clenched by his sides, and watched as she drove away.

*

When she got back home, Sarah planned on going straight to her bedroom in a bid to avoid Grace, her flatmate. The plan failed: Grace was coming out of the bathroom as Sarah reached the top of the stairs and, as always, Sarah was unable to hide her feelings from her face.

'What's happened?' Grace asked. She flicked the bathroom light switch and stepped out on to the landing. 'You OK?'

Sarah shrugged. 'I'm fine. I just want to get showered and out of these clothes.'

Grace folded her arms across her chest. Sarah was a terrible liar; she always had been. Grace had known her long enough to know when she was trying to hide the truth.

'It's him again, isn't it?'

Sarah rolled her eyes, unable to hold back the reaction. 'Not everything has to be about him, you know.'

'But I'm right, aren't I?'

Sarah sidestepped her friend into the living room and threw her bag on to the sofa. 'Everything's always on his terms.'

Grace stood in the doorway, watching as Sarah sat down to take off her shoes. How many more times were they going to have this same conversation?

'Of course it is. That's how affairs work.'

Sarah looked up sharply. 'You don't have to be quite so mean about it.'

'I'm not being mean. I'm being honest. Married men don't leave their wives, Sarah, that's not how it works. I just don't want to see you hurt again.' She sat down beside her, aware Sarah was still sulking. She always did in the first few moments after being told the truth. It usually didn't take too long for her to snap out of it, although there had been a couple of occasions when Sarah's relationship with this married man had caused days of non-communication between them.

She wondered what it was about her friend. A few years earlier, when Sarah was just twenty, she'd been in an abusive relationship that had ended when she had been hospitalised. The ex-boyfriend was sent to prison for the assault and Sarah – after many tears and much therapy – seemed to be moving on with her life. Right until she found another Mr Wrong, that is.

'How about that night out you promised me?' Grace suggested.

'I don't know. I don't think I'm in the mood.'

'That's exactly why you need it,' Grace said, getting back up from the sofa. 'Come on. I'm not taking no for an answer.'

CHAPTER FIFTEEN

After Chloe left, the thought of spending yet another evening alone in her empty house was almost enough to make Alex want to call her and ask her to come back. Instead, she did what she recently tended to do when this feeling caught her off guard: she called Rob. It rang through to answerphone.

She stood at the kitchen sink and washed her wine glass, resolving not to drink any more. As her thoughts festered in the silence of the house, they naturally strayed towards her work. Her job was the only thing able to provide a distraction from the realities of her home life, and from a future Alex feared to linger on too long. Empty years – childless, loveless – seemed to stretch into the spaces ahead, leaving Alex filled with a dread that often kept her awake at night in the darkness of her now-lonely house.

There were things she couldn't make better – circumstances she was unable to change.

A young woman was dead, and nothing she or anyone else could do would be able to reverse that. But she could try stopping whoever was responsible before that person decided to end someone else's life.

She looked out on to the dark stretch of garden that lay beyond the kitchen window. It occurred to her that she should think herself lucky: she lived in a nice area at the top of the town just off the mountain road, in a large semi-detached house that had a generous stretch of garden behind it. Years before, these had been the things she had aspired to and worked for. Now none of it seemed to mean anything.

Alex was dragged from her thoughts by the sound of her phone ringing. She glanced at the screen. Rob.

*

Half an hour later, her ex-husband rang the doorbell. Until a couple of months ago, he'd still had a key to the house. He refused to use it, even now when they were sleeping with each other again. Alex had taken it back from him, careful to conceal the relief she'd felt at the gesture when he'd offered its return. They might be having sex, but Rob letting himself into the house using his own key would take things a step further than Alex was comfortable with.

'Everything OK?'

She leaned in and kissed him. They went upstairs to what had once been their bedroom and had wordless sex, the type that had formed a pattern during the previous months. It had started as exciting – there had been something dangerous in the unexpectedness of it all – but what had been thrilling in its spontaneity was increasingly becoming a routine, albeit one that, at that time, Alex felt her life needed.

Not for the first time, Alex realised that it wasn't Rob she had missed. She just missed someone being there. The house had become too big for her; too silent. The memories of it had become too noisy.

She wasn't even sure she had missed the sex. It was just good to feel his skin against hers, to have some element of physical closeness back, to be able, for those moments, to switch off from the rest of the world. She had always been physically attracted to Rob, even when she had become turned off by elements of his personality.

She didn't want to be with him. She hadn't wanted to be with him in a long time.

She realised she was using him.

She knew she should feel guilty at the thought, but she didn't. For reasons that she couldn't fathom, she couldn't bring herself to feel it.

'What's happening here, Alex?'

'I'm going to make a cup of tea. Do you want one?'

Rob put out an arm and reached for hers to stop her leaving the bed. 'You know that's not what I mean.'

Her back turned to him, Alex closed her eyes. She didn't want to have this conversation, not now. Not ever. They had stopped living in the moment years ago. Hadn't that been what had eventually driven them apart? Why had they always needed to know what would be happening in the future: tomorrow, the next week; the next year? The need to plan for the perfect family home: a building that had become filled with material things yet empty of anything with purpose or meaning. The need to know why nature, science, something was preventing them from becoming a family. The need to know whether they would ever be parents; the need to plan for the what ifs and the maybes, the maybe nots.

'I don't know what you want me to tell you.'

'Just tell me the truth.'

Alex found this ironic. Telling the truth had been their downfall, the reason for their divorce; telling the truth had caused such irreversible damage that Alex had begun to reconsider the mantra that honesty was always the best policy. Sometimes it wasn't. Telling her husband the truth – that a childless future was a future that scared her, and that, no, she was sorry, but she didn't believe they alone were enough – had been the final nail driven into the coffin in which their marriage had been buried.

But he wasn't her husband any more.

'It just is what it is,' she said, aware that if someone else had said the same to her she would have been tempted to throw the nearest available object at them.

Rob moved from the bed. She heard him reach for his clothes and put them back on.

'Is that all I get? That's what I'm worth?'

'No, of course not, it's just—'

'It's not really normal, is it,' he cut her off, moving to her side of the room and facing her so that she could no longer avoid looking at him. 'This.'

What was normal any more? Alex wasn't sure.

'I still don't know what you want me to say.'

Rob looked exasperated. There was something more. He looked hurt. The look made Alex feel even guiltier than she already did.

'Neither of us wants to go backwards, Rob, not really. That's never been what this was about.'

His jaw tensed. His mouth moved as though about to say something, but changing his mind he reached for his jacket from where it was slung over the end of the bed and headed to the door.

'I don't understand you,' he said, turning back to face her.

She said nothing. The truth of it was, she didn't understand herself either.

CHAPTER SIXTEEN

When she woke, she found herself in darkness. She couldn't move. She tried to free her arms from behind her back, but they were tied to the chair on which she was sitting. Something was shoved into her mouth, something like clothing, the cotton absorbing all the moisture so that her tongue, squashed against the roof of her mouth, felt dry. She panicked, tried to free herself, but her arms were tied back and her legs were fixed fast to the legs of the chair. She tried to scream, but only a muffled gurgle escaped her.

She tried to remember what had happened, but those past few hours were a tangle of blurred recollections. They had been talking, catching up, and then… she didn't know what had happened next. The room was cold and dark. Her head ached so badly. It was like every hangover she'd ever had all rolled into one, fierce and unforgiving. She was supposed to be going out with Grace, she thought. Was she late? What time was it?

Grace would be wondering where she was.

They'd had a drink together, she remembered. She had popped to the supermarket; she was only going to be twenty minutes. He had seen her there and they had gone to the pub just around the corner. Grace always took ages getting ready, so Sarah figured she wouldn't miss her for an extra half an hour. He'd offered her a lift home with the bags she had been carrying. As always, she had only gone in for a couple of things – a bottle of wine that she and Grace could share before they headed out – but she had got carried away and ended up with more than she could comfortably manage. She was appreciative of the offer – she'd decided not to take the car, having planned on not buying much and figuring she needed the exercise.

Now she wished more than anything that she'd taken it.

Tears coursed her cheeks, hot and fast. This couldn't be him, she thought. It couldn't be.

Why would he do this to her?

She tried to remember what they had talked about, but so much of the time after leaving the supermarket had become little more than a blur, and her head felt heavy, dragged down with the weight of something unknown. Had she had that much to drink? She was certain she wouldn't have, not when she had planned to go out later on with Grace.

There was a creaking somewhere in the darkness, on the other side of the wall to her left. Her eyes had adjusted slightly to the dark – enough to make out the heavy drapes and the wooden furniture – but whatever he had given her was making a double of everything, like an old photograph taken out of focus. At the sound of his footsteps in the next room, she felt her body freeze. She didn't know whether she hoped it was him or not. If it was him then everything she had thought she had known had been wrong. She had trusted this man. She'd had no reason not to.

Perhaps she could talk to him, find out why he was doing this to her. Maybe, somehow, if she could get him to free her mouth, free her words, he might allow her the time to change his mind.

She had never done anything to him.

If it wasn't him… she couldn't bring herself to think that far ahead. If the man who had brought her here, wherever here was, was a stranger, she had no idea what had happened during the past few hours. Did she hope it was him? She really wasn't sure which outcome would be worse.

Her heart faltered at the sound of the door handle, the heavy door creaking on its hinges as it was pushed open. A thin shard of light stretched across the dirty carpet, highlighting the dust-filled air of the room.

She tried to speak, but the words were muffled by the material filling her mouth. A low groan broke free from her, animal-like and desperate. He filled the path of what little light had existed, blocking it and sending her once again into a half-darkness where all her worst fears became imagined and played out in front of her. She was going to die here, she thought.

She was going to die and she had no idea why.

CHAPTER SEVENTEEN

Chloe sat in Alex's office discussing Emily Phillips's death in even greater detail. Alex didn't want to be found away from her duties in the middle of a murder investigation, but at the same time she didn't want Chloe to land herself in trouble. Unless she could keep her talking about it, Chloe might take matters into her own hands by trying to access the closed case files. Chloe Lane was bright and astute, but Alex was worried that where her brother was concerned the young woman was unable to see the bigger picture. She seemed blinded by loyalty, as Alex supposed any good sister might be.

Alex hadn't said she believed there was a chance Luke hadn't been involved in his girlfriend's death, yet Chloe had assumed that she was with her in her doubt. She acknowledged the grey areas surrounding the closing of the case, but that didn't mean she thought Luke innocent. Alex hadn't been directly involved in the case, despite having been the first officer to arrive at the scene following Luke's call. She had been assigned to another case, so her knowledge of what had followed was for the moment limited to what the newspapers had told her at the time, station gossip, and what Chloe had told her the night before. Everything she knew was therefore clouded in media sensationalism, hearsay or bias.

If she was going to help, she was going to have to access the case files, but when was she going to have the time to do that?

And how was she going to do it without getting them both into serious trouble? It couldn't be done, not without major repercussions. It wouldn't be worth it. If the evidence to clear Luke's name hadn't existed at the time, it wouldn't be discovered now. She was going to have to deter Chloe in her efforts, but how she was going to go about it Alex wasn't sure. The young woman's determination seemed unshakeable.

'Matthew Mitchell,' Chloe said, reaching into one of the documents she seemed to now carry with her at all times. She put a photograph in front of Alex, who looked at her incredulously.

'You've got photos?'

'Of course. This is Emily's half-brother,' she said, tapping the image of a sullen-faced young man, aged early twenties at the time the photograph was taken. 'Same father, different mothers. He had an argument with Luke the afternoon of the day Emily died. Emily had been upset about something – Matthew thought Luke was responsible.'

'And was he?'

Chloe shook her head. 'According to Luke, they'd been getting on fine. There'd been no argument. He didn't know what had upset her.'

'So you're assuming if Luke hadn't upset her, someone else must have?'

Chloe shrugged.

She must realise that all this is just 'he said, she said', Alex thought; nothing more than teenage drama that didn't amount to anything substantial when it came to looking at the facts.

'Matthew might have argued with Luke, but why would that have made him want to hurt his own sister?'

Chloe's face tightened. She pulled her long blonde hair back from her face and knotted it up in a messy bun. 'I don't know,' she admitted quietly. She reached for the file again and removed another photograph. 'Emily's ex-boyfriend,' she said, putting his photograph beside Matthew's. 'Callum Ware. My God, did this boy love himself.'

The picture showed a teenage boy in a beanie hat, flicking his fingers in a V-sign and smirking smugly for the camera.

'In what way?' Alex asked.

'Take your pick.'

'Why have you got him down as a suspect?'

Chloe sat back in her seat, taking her eyes from the photograph of Callum.

'Emily had finished with him not long before she started seeing Luke. I don't think Callum was used to girls dumping him; he did the dumping. It didn't go down too well, I don't think.'

Alex found herself wishing that this conversation had followed the pattern of the previous discussion she and Chloe had had about Luke and Emily, and that wine had formed an element of proceedings. It might be earlier than most people's breakfast time, but normal hours no longer applied to Alex. Last time, the wine had been enough to just about blur the edges of Chloe's irrational thought processes, but now, in the stark sobriety of the morning, Alex was unable to avoid the desperation in the young woman's face. Alex realised this was no longer just about seeking justice for Luke. For Chloe, proving her brother's innocence had become an obsession.

But she didn't want to be the one to shatter Chloe's dream of finding an impossible truth. It was nice to believe that all mysteries would finally be resolved one way or another, but Alex was experienced enough and old enough to have accepted the sad truth that sometimes, no matter how much will and good intention were involved, some secrets were never exposed.

And sometimes it wasn't necessarily a sad thing. Sometimes the truth was painful. Destructive. Sometimes it was better to remain ignorant of the thing you had always felt you needed to know.

'Chloe, none of this is evidence, you know that, don't you?'

'Patrick Sibley,' Chloe said, ignoring Alex and reaching into the file for a third photograph. 'He had a thing for Emily; everyone knew about it. He sent her flowers a couple of weeks before she died.'

'Where have you got all these photographs from?' Alex asked, glancing at the picture. Chloe's documentation of other people's details was beginning to look like borderline stalking.

'The Internet. People put them up because they want them to be looked at. There'd be no reason otherwise.'

The defensive tone with which Chloe's words were spoken cut a chill through Alex's office.

'You don't believe me, do you?'

She must have realised how irrational this all seemed, or else Alex's questions wouldn't have prompted such a reaction.

'I believe that you think Luke is innocent,' Alex said, trying to pacify her. 'I believe that you want the truth, but I also think you know deep down how difficult that truth might be to find. There was an investigation, Chloe.'

Chloe gave a bitter laugh. 'It lasted less than a fortnight. It was full of holes. Look at it. Please. I know I'm asking a lot, but if you won't help me no one will.'

Alex sighed and sat back in her seat. 'Have you already looked at it? Or are you too scared of what it might reveal?'

As soon as the words left her mouth, Alex regretted them. She heard them in the way Chloe had heard them, laced with a severity Alex had never intended. The reaction on Chloe's face was enough to reveal their impact. She reached for the photographs, gathering them quickly and shoving them back into their file.

'Chloe, I—'

'Forget it, please,' Chloe stopped her. 'I'm sorry, it's my fault. I should never have mentioned it. Please forget I ever told you.'

Without making further eye contact, Chloe left the office. Alex cursed herself, wondering how many more people she was going to drive away before the week was out. She pitied Chloe, but resurrecting this case now was inviting trouble. They had a murder investigation on their hands, a current case that needed their full focus.

*

Outside the office, Chloe stopped at the end of the corridor, her heart pounding against her ribcage. No one was going to believe her. Without evidence, people would just think she was crazy. Alex had probably already started. She had seen the DI's face as she'd talked her through each of the men she thought might have had an involvement in Emily's death; she had seen the scepticism and the doubt in the other woman's eyes.

Until someone believed her, Chloe knew she was on her own.

CHAPTER EIGHTEEN

On the computer screen beside Detective Constable Daniel Mason there was a still of Lola Evans and Ethan Thompson entering Nando's at just gone quarter to seven on the Saturday night: the last known sighting they had of her.

'Can't really miss them, can you?' Dan said.

Alex knew what he meant. The young couple were easily identifiable: Ethan with his unconventional dress sense and Lola, rake thin and lost-looking.

'How long were they at the restaurant?' Alex asked.

'Just over an hour.'

Alex nodded. This matched the information Ethan Thompson had given her.

'What sort of waitressing job had Lola been working that started so late?' Dan wondered aloud.

Alex shrugged. 'I suppose plenty of restaurants in the city wouldn't start to get busy until late.'

'Just goes to show how out of touch I am,' Dan said with a half-smile. 'I'm ready for bed by ten thirty these days.'

Alex studied the still on the screen. 'Did she even make it to work?' she pondered. 'Did she meet with someone before she reached there? We need to find out where "work" was.'

Trawling through every pub, club and restaurant in Cardiff was going to take hours the team just didn't have. A check with National Insurance documented that Lola Evans's last paid employment was six months earlier, at a beauty salon in Tongwynlais, a small village on the outskirts of Cardiff. A phone call to the salon revealed that Lola had left after a disagreement about money missing from the till: money the manager of the salon still seemed convinced Lola had taken. She hadn't pursued the matter any further on the grounds that she knew Lola was having personal problems at the time. Alex wondered to what extent those personal problems had really been.

It seemed that whatever other work Lola had undertaken in order to earn money – as a beautician or as a waitress – had been purely on a cash in hand basis. If she was self-employed, she hadn't bothered to register officially. The only other way that they could find out quickly where else Lola might have been working was to go public with her image, but details of her murder hadn't yet gone to the press, and Alex had been hoping to keep it that way for a little longer. The press loved this kind of victim – young, female, attractive – and the publicity the case would no doubt attract in the search for Lola's killer would inevitably lead to time-wasters.

'Any footage of them elsewhere in the shopping centre?' Alex asked Dan. 'Or of Lola, at least?'

Dan moved back towards the desktop computer he'd been working at and clicked another still of Lola and Ethan: this one of them leaving through the doors which led out on to the main shopping street at The Hayes. 'Last sighting of them together. He goes one way, she goes the other. The bar where he works has confirmed he turned up for work that evening at just gone eight o'clock. He was there until gone three.'

'Shit,' Alex mumbled. She sat in the chair beside Dan and studied the image, focusing on Lola Evans. She was a slight girl, her body clearly ravaged by her eating disorder. It wouldn't have been difficult for any man of average strength to have carried her for some distance. But on a Saturday evening in the middle of a city centre? Or perhaps she hadn't stayed in town after leaving Ethan. Where had she gone?

They didn't even know whether or not it was on the Saturday that she had gone missing.

'Any updates your end?' Dan swivelled his chair towards her, his knee nearly meeting hers. She moved away instinctively.

'No.' Alex pressed her fingertips against her forehead. 'Until we find out where she was working, it's going to be difficult to work out her social network. No social media profiles?'

Dan shook his head. 'Seems unusual for someone her age.'

Lola had clearly been a complicated character, a young woman plagued by mental health issues. Checks with her doctor had shown a history of counselling and several prescriptions for varying dosages of antidepressants. By her grandmother's own admission, Lola was rarely fixed to one place, although that didn't necessarily mean she was the party girl that many of the rest of the team had taken this comment to suggest.

'Is everything OK with DC Lane?'

Alex was snapped from her thoughts of Lola Evans. 'Yes, as far as I know. Why do you ask?' The question came a little too hurriedly, she realised.

Dan shrugged. He had a nice face, Alex thought; not conventionally handsome, but kind. Of what she knew of him, DC Mason seemed a hard-working family man. He kept a photograph of his wife and kids on the corner of his desk: an attractive woman aged around forty and two dark-haired girls who both looked under the age of ten. Alex tended to notice family photographs. She had once looked upon them with a hope for her own future, but as time had passed she had come to realise this kind of photograph would never adorn her own desk or the walls of her home. For a while, she couldn't bring herself to look at that kind of photograph at all.

She was getting better. Acceptance came in many forms. This had been one of them.

'She mentioned an email address; she seemed a bit agitated.'

Alex raised an eyebrow. Chloe hadn't said anything about talking to Dan and she wasn't sure how much he knew. 'To do with?'

He shrugged. 'Just said she'd been getting some weird emails.'

'I've not noticed anything unusual.' She gave him a smile and returned her attention to the footage that was paused on the screen in front of them, as though Ethan Thompson might in some way incriminate himself. The smile she had forced evaporated. She was going to have to warn Chloe. If other members of the team were already noticing the fact that her attention seemed diverted elsewhere then it was only a matter of time before the superintendent caught grasp of it.

CHAPTER NINETEEN

Chloe's lasting impression of Patrick Sibley was of a boy no one noticed until he became noticeable for all the wrong reasons. In the weeks leading up to Emily's death, Patrick had made a couple of awkward advances towards her. Nobody knew about the first – no one other than Luke, and later Chloe – but unfortunately for Patrick, most of the town where they'd lived had come to know about the second.

Luke had been at college and there seemed to be a party every other weekend – most at people's houses and the occasional few in the local rugby club – and they each attracted the same faces. Patrick Sibley hadn't been one of them. Not until Amy Patten's eighteenth, when he'd turned up at her house uninvited and drunker than anyone else there. The party was low on numbers. It was the Easter holidays and a lot of the students were away with their families or just couldn't be bothered to venture out into what had been a fortnight of incessant rain. Later, Chloe would ask Amy Patten why she had let Patrick Sibley stay: he didn't belong to their friendship group – he didn't seem to belong to any friendship group – and he'd been so drunk by the time it reached eleven o'clock that he had thrown up in Amy's parents' kitchen sink. Amy had given a surprisingly honest answer. Why not? It was funny watching the class loser make an even bigger tit of himself.

He had left not long after, but not soon enough to spare himself the embarrassment of declaring lifelong and undying love for Emily. Everyone in the room was witness to his humiliation. Everyone laughed when he threw up for a second time, this time across the pale carpet of Amy Patten's parents' living room.

Emily had laughed too.

Chloe knew all this because Luke had told her.

It hadn't taken Chloe long to find out where Patrick Sibley worked. His Facebook profile stated his employment as full-time and his timeline was filled with complaints and ramblings about his job as an administrative assistant at the tax office. The same tax office that was a short distance from the leisure centre where Chloe had met Scott, just a couple of months ago. Was Scott there now, that afternoon, and how would he react if she turned up there today, armed with her apologies and her explanations?

She didn't blame him for losing interest. Everyone else had, sooner or later.

*

The car park of the tax office was blocked by a barrier and no one answered when she pressed the buzzer, so Chloe reversed back out and parked by the shops just a few hundred metres away. She walked over to the tax office and asked at reception for Patrick Sibley, showing her police ID in order to avoid having to use any other reason for requesting to see him. Once the receptionist saw that Chloe was an officer, she didn't ask for further explanation. She put a call through to one of the upper floors, and Chloe took a seat beneath the window as she waited for Patrick to arrive downstairs.

She didn't really know what to expect. She remembered him well enough – and was pretty sure he would remember her regardless of how much she had changed over the years – but time had passed and there was no guarantee that she would recognise him now.

Chloe needn't have worried. She knew him instantly, despite the hair that had been allowed to grow longer and the beard that now partially obscured his face.

'Patrick,' she said, standing from her chair and extending a hand. 'You haven't changed much.'

Patrick Sibley stared at her hand as though it was a weapon she'd just brandished at him. What had she expected, Chloe thought — a friendly hug and a catch-up over coffee? The last time she had seen Patrick she had asked him if he'd murdered Emily. The hostility she'd received was well-deserved. She knew she should apologise.

'Neither have you,' Patrick said coldly. 'Still following people around, I see.' He looked her up and down. 'You're in the police?' The question was laced with scepticism, a tone that suggested he was somewhat disbelieving of the fact.

'How long have you been working here?'

Patrick narrowed his eyes and studied her defensively. Chloe didn't think this was something she should have taken personally; from what she knew of Patrick and was able to remember of him, he was defensive around everyone. The class loner, he had never seemed to have any friends. He had been active on social media — more often than not involved in online slanging matches with trolls who'd insulted him — but in real life he had been far less vocal and had been content (or at the very least had feigned contentment) with merging into the background, lost amidst the colour and noise of his peers.

Until he had too much to drink, apparently.

'What do you want? I'm pretty busy.'

'I want to talk about Emily.'

Patrick rolled his eyes. 'For God's sake,' he mumbled, glancing over to the receptionist. 'I told you everything I knew at the time. I didn't see her after she left that party. I don't know what happened. When will it be good enough for you?'

'I didn't come here to argue with you.'

'No? Just to accuse me of murder then? Again.'

It was Chloe's turn to glance at the receptionist, checking over Patrick's shoulder to make sure nothing had been heard. 'Please, Patrick. If I made a mistake then I'm sorry. But someone killed Emily that night and it wasn't Luke. I just want to talk to you.'

'*If* you made a mistake? We've talked already,' he said, leaning in towards her and firing the words at her face. 'I don't have anything to say to you.'

A wave of doubt and anxiety swept over Chloe, making her momentarily nauseous. What was she doing here? she thought. She had no evidence, no proof, just the deafening knowledge that her brother wasn't a killer.

The words that had been typed into those emails she had received repeated themselves in her head – so few and yet so powerful: *Found him yet?*

No, she hadn't, and that was exactly what had brought her here.

But was this man a killer? Loner or not, Patrick Sibley was no more guilty than anyone else, not without the proof Chloe so desperately needed. Being friendless wasn't evidence of guilt, although Chloe realised that in her own case the same might not necessarily have been so true. She'd been without friends – true friends – for years. There had been no one to share the burden of her own personal guilt.

She felt the colour rise up through her chest and into her face like a swelling surge of sickness. What was she doing here? What was she thinking?

Patrick Sibley's expression changed. He was enjoying her discomfort.

'Those flowers.'

Patrick gave another roll of the eyes. Flowers had been sent to Emily in the weeks leading up to her death. Everyone – including Emily, it had seemed at the time – had assumed they were from Patrick. There had been no card with them, no message or name, but Patrick had been obsessed with Emily for ages and everybody had known it.

'I told you at the time and I'm telling you again – I didn't send any flowers. That girl made me look like an idiot. She knew I liked her and she enjoyed making me feel this big.' He held up a hand and gestured with his thumb and index finger. 'I'm sorry about what happened to her, but it had nothing to do with me.'

Chloe nodded, though she didn't believe him. She didn't believe anyone. Increasingly, the person she was coming to trust the least was herself.

'If you think of anything—' she suggested hopelessly.

'Anything like what?' he asked incredulously. He slowed his voice and punctuated every word with a full stop as though talking to an insolent child who refused to acknowledge what she was being told. 'Listen to what I am telling you. I cannot help you.'

He raised an eyebrow and turned to leave her standing alone in reception; the woman at the desk casting a curious glance in her direction. There had been a time not so long ago when the unwanted attention may have made Chloe's face flare red, but she had grown beyond that. People could think whatever they wanted of her. She didn't care.

How's the search going?

Found him yet?

Someone knew something about the night of Emily's death, and she wasn't going to stop until she found out the truth.

CHAPTER TWENTY

Grace was disappointed. She had spent an hour and a half getting ready and had then sat waiting in the living room with a glass of wine in one hand and her mobile phone in the other. She tried calling Sarah several times, but her phone had kept ringing through to answerphone. Then it had been turned off.

Grace had been impatient at first, but then she grew annoyed. If Sarah hadn't wanted to go out, the least she could have done was call or text to let her know. She would have saved Grace a lot of time spent getting ready, as well as the ten quid she had spent on wine down the Spar, having given up on Sarah coming back with one from the supermarket. Oh well, she'd thought, taking another sip: she would just have to drink it on her own.

But Sarah had been dressed ready to go out, she thought. Why go to all that trouble if she hadn't wanted to? Unless she had actually gone out... with him.

Why did she waste her time with worry, Grace thought as she kicked off her shoes and swung her legs up on to the sofa. Sarah was a grown woman: she could do what she liked.

Grace reached for the television remote control and flicked channels. This was it: a night on her own with only a bottle of red and *Coronation Street* for company. How tragic.

*

Hours later, she woke up on the sofa. The television was still on and she had managed to knock her glass over during her sleep, staining a patch of carpet blood red. She searched for her mobile phone and found it wedged between the cushions at the back of the sofa. She pressed the screen to read the time.

Grace had assumed she'd just nodded off briefly, but it was twenty to eight in the morning. She rubbed a hand across her face and tried to focus her tired eyes. The empty wine bottle on the coffee table was a reminder of why her head was throbbing and her mouth was filled with a sickly sweet aftertaste that was making her nauseous.

She went to the bathroom, peed and brushed her teeth, dragging the toothpaste across her tongue in an attempt to rid herself of some of the wine's aftertaste. She remembered being annoyed at Sarah and resolved not to be a bitch when she saw her. Having a go at Sarah had never got Grace anywhere. If she was going to talk any sense into her, she would have to find another way to go about it.

Back on the landing, Grace noticed the door to Sarah's room was still slightly opened. Sarah could have seen her sleeping on the sofa and not closed it to avoid making a sound and waking her up. Maybe she'd been trying to dodge the lecture she knew she'd inevitably get. Sometimes, Grace felt as though she was playing the role of mother where Sarah was concerned, making constant attempts to keep her on the straight and narrow; failing, despite her repeated efforts.

Grace carefully stuck her head around Sarah's bedroom door, careful not to push it and make a noise. It was dark in the bedroom, the curtains still closed. The light from the landing illuminated enough of the small bedroom for Grace to make out the bed and its crumpled duvet. She narrowed her eyes, searching out the shape of Sarah beneath it. Putting a hand to the wall, Grace flicked the bedroom light switch. The duvet was piled on the bed as Sarah had left it the day before. The bed was empty.

Sarah rarely stayed a night away from the flat. She occasionally slept over when she visited her mother, but those nights were rare. She had never stayed a night away with Connor; of that much Grace was certain. Connor had a family to go home to, and he had made it clear to Sarah that their affair would never involve nights spent away from home. Sarah had made the mistake of mentioning it to Grace on a few occasions, complaining of the fact that she had never got to spend a night with him.

Grace had seen him once, by chance. She had been in the supermarket with Sarah and they had turned into the bakery section and almost collided with a man who was pushing a trolley with one hand and dragging a screaming boy by the other. Sarah and Connor had acknowledged one another silently, each unwilling to speak to the other in front of his son. Instead, Sarah had mumbled an apology at having walked into his trolley, then made some pointless comment to Grace about washing-up liquid. They hadn't needed any: there had been a full one on the kitchen window sill when Grace had cleared away her breakfast things that morning.

'That was him, wasn't it?'

'Who?'

'Connor.'

Once again, Sarah had made an attempt to change the subject.

Grace recalled her frustration with her friend. Here she was once again making the same mistakes, never learning from the things that had caused her so much pain.

Grace had felt frustrated before. Now all she felt was a growing sense of panic.

She went back to the living room and retrieved her phone, trying Sarah's number once more. Again, it went straight to answerphone. She thought about contacting Connor; she knew he had a Facebook account and it should prove easy enough to find him. But what would Sarah say when she found out that Grace had contacted him? She was bound to go nuts. She had assured Grace that the affair was over – why would she lie about that?

A mounting sense of worry crept through her.

If Sarah wasn't with Connor, then where was she?

CHAPTER TWENTY-ONE

Alex stood in the superintendent's office deliberating over the words that were perched on the tip of her tongue. She had gone over it in her head countless times, weighing up the pros and cons of requesting permission to access the files relating to Emily Phillips's case. Although she remained adamant that this wasn't the right time to go over old ground and reinvestigate anything relating to either Emily's or Luke's cases, Alex was convinced that if she could reassure Chloe that they would get permission to do so once Lola Evans's killer had been caught then Chloe would resume normal practice and devote her full attention to the case she was supposed to be working on.

She fully expected the request to receive a less than warm response, but for Chloe's sake it was a reception she was prepared to face.

'Hypothetically speaking, how averse would you be to the idea of having a closed case reopened?'

Superintendent Harry Blake studied Alex cautiously. He still looked so tired, Alex thought. He had been off work for almost a year and, although his treatment had been deemed a success by doctors, the general consensus was that he had returned to work too soon. In his absence, Alex had acted as investigating officer in a couple of key cases, one of which had drawn closer to home than anyone had been comfortable with. The experience had taught Alex a lot, but she hadn't been ready to park herself in the firing line on a permanent basis. She was happiest and, as far as she was concerned, most efficient when she was working amongst the team.

She was glad to have Harry back, but she wasn't happy to see him looking so exhausted so soon upon his return.

'How's the search into Lola Evans's murder going?'

Alex's lip curled slightly. She wondered, briefly, if she had in fact spoken her own question aloud or merely run it through her brain one final time before airing it.

'I... we're following up a couple of leads and trying to establish Lola's final few hours.'

'"Trying",' the superintendent repeated. 'As in, you've not got very far? So why are you asking me, hypothetically or not, about closed cases when we've got an open and very much ongoing one already on our hands?'

Alex made a conscious effort to uncurl her top lip. She knew it was a habit, a reaction that occurred when she found herself annoyed or angered by something, and often she could feel herself slipping into the gesture. Other times, she remained oblivious to it.

'The investigation into Lola Evans's murder is moving forward, and the case I'm referring to won't impact upon it.'

'So there's nothing hypothetical about this "case" then?'

The inverted commas were audible. Alex's brain exhaled an expletive at her careless turn of phrasing.

'It was just a question.'

'And I'm just giving you an answer. Until Lola Evans's murderer is found, everyone's attention remains on him. Or her,' he added. 'What case is this, anyway?'

'It doesn't matter.'

'It matters enough for you to have come to me about it.'

'And I shouldn't have,' Alex told him. Never a truer word spoken, she thought. She realised now why Chloe had been so adamant that the super's attention not be drawn to it in any way. She regretted the decision she'd made, and she hoped it wouldn't find its way back to Chloe.

His stern expression relaxed. 'I'm sorry,' he offered. 'Coming back to all this… it wasn't quite what I'd anticipated. How are you?'

As though he should be asking me that, thought Alex. She shrugged. 'Things can always be worse, can't they?'

He gave her a smile that was tinged with sadness. 'True enough.'

'Things are as they are.' She knew exactly what he was referring to. Harry knew plenty of the details of her marriage breakdown, as well as the events that had led up to it. It now seemed little in comparison to what he'd been through during the past eighteen months.

'Look,' he said, shifting the focus of conversation from Alex's personal life, 'if you want to go back to something, make sure you find me a convincing reason for doing so. But not now, OK? We've all got plenty to be getting on with.'

Alex gave him a nod and left the office. She hoped she hadn't just made a mistake, for both her own and Chloe's sakes.

*

She went back down the corridor and into the main office, having barely a moment to breathe before one of the DCs called her over.

'Boss. We've had a young woman reported missing.'

Alex felt a knot tighten in her stomach. Instinct told her that their caseload was about to get even more complicated.

CHAPTER TWENTY-TWO

She didn't know what time it was, but beyond the boarded windows, through a narrow gap that was uncovered by the drapes that had been hung there, Sarah was sure she could see daylight. Her head felt heavy, like the onset of a migraine. She didn't bother trying to move, knowing her efforts would be futile. She was too tired to do anything other than sit and wait. Whatever he had given her, she felt as though it was still flooding her system.

Her mouth was dry and her tongue was stuck to whatever had been crammed into her mouth. She thought about crying again, but realised her tears had all been wasted. Crying had worsened the headache and they hadn't got her anywhere. She was still in this room, still bound to this chair, still not knowing who had brought her here and done this to her.

Of course, she did know, but she still couldn't quite bring herself to believe it was him.

Sarah narrowed her eyes, waiting for them to adjust to the darkness of the room. She had thought there were only floorboards beneath her – she had heard his footsteps pacing across them hours earlier – but now she was able to see a patch of carpet further away in the room, frayed and dirty. It might have been a deep red colour, but in the darkness she couldn't be sure.

The smell of blood was everywhere, filling her nose. She could taste it in the dryness of her mouth; she could feel it on the coldness of her skin. She didn't know who it belonged to. She felt pain everywhere: it was impossible to pinpoint where she might have been injured. Closing her eyes, she tried to focus on the source of her pain. Concentrating made the screaming in her head louder, more profound, so she quickly stopped and tried to empty her thoughts.

It was impossible.

She looked down at her legs. They were bare, though she had been wearing tights the previous evening when she had left the flat to go to the supermarket. It was so cold that her skin was almost glowing white in the darkness. Not for the first time, she tried to push back thoughts of what had happened to her when she'd been unconscious, between the times she had accepted a lift home from him and woken up hours later. The thoughts brought with them fresh tears, hot and fast against her icy skin.

If he didn't kill her, the cold was going to finish the job for him.

Sarah shifted, pushing the dress she was wearing further up her thighs. Then she felt them, smoother than the dress against her skin. Her underwear was still on. Crying with relief, Sarah allowed her head to loll backwards. She looked up at the ceiling, at the strange artexed patterns that in the darkness took the forms of all kinds of strange and alien images.

It was then she heard him. His footsteps sounded distant at first; she could hear him on a flight of stairs. She wasn't on a ground floor, she thought. Where had he taken her?

Moments later, the door to the room creaked noisily as he pushed it open. She saw his face lit by the light that poured through the windows in the next room, and at the sight of him Sarah began to sob again.

She had thought she had known him. Why was he doing this to her?

He was carrying a large bottle of water and a plastic cup in his hands. With his hip, he shoved the door closed behind him, leaving only a narrow stream of light to enter the room.

She tried to scream at him, but the noise was muted, pathetic. Her eyes sought out his, forcing him to look at her. When he neared her, Sarah's body froze. He put a hand towards her, his fingertips resting on the cloth that filled her mouth.

'You must be thirsty,' he said. 'You can scream if you want to, but there's no one to hear you. You won't get a drink if you do.'

He yanked the cloth from her mouth and Sarah gasped for air, though it tasted thick and dirty. She swallowed it in, desperate to fill her lungs.

'Why are you doing this?'

She barely recognised her own voice. It sounded feeble, weak; all the things she had feared she'd always been, but had never wanted to show.

Ignoring her, he poured a cup of water and held it to her lips. She kept her mouth shut, refusing the offer.

'It's just water.' To prove the point, he took two long gulps of the drink.

When he held the cup to her lips for a second time, Sarah took a mouthful of water. She held it in her mouth before spitting it back at him, soaking the bottom half of his face. As soon as she'd done it, she had no idea why she had. In that briefest of moments it had felt empowering, but she instantly realised she wasn't empowered, she was trapped, and now she had made things worse for herself.

With a single shove, he sent her and the chair crashing to the floor. Sarah felt a surge of pain through her spine as the chair fell back on to the wooden floorboards, and she screamed as he straddled her and placed a hand over her face.

With her nose pressed tightly between his fingers, Sarah had little choice than to open her mouth for air. He was sitting on her chest now, crushing the air from her body. She gasped for breath, but it was cut short when he held the bottle of water above her face and poured it in a steady stream over her opened mouth.

She felt the water fill her mouth and run down into her throat. She couldn't swallow it fast enough; within seconds she was choking on it. She closed her eyes in an effort to block the sight of him. He was still there when she opened them, his impassive face still mocking her.

She heard herself choking.

She could feel herself drowning.

CHAPTER TWENTY-THREE

Alex and Chloe sat in the office of the care home. It was chaotic, Alex noticed: files and paperwork stacked on every available surface; half-finished mugs of tea and coffee abandoned by the desktop computers. There seemed to be few staff members present, and the buzzer in the corridor had been sounding since they'd got there.

'Do you think something's happened to Sarah?' the care home manager asked. She had been unsettled by the appearance of police. She had ushered them quickly through to the office, trying to keep them invisible from the cleaner at the end of the corridor and a resident who was wheeling himself from the day room, his slight frame bent forward and his bony fingers clutching the tops of the wheels of his chair.

The man had caught Chloe's eye, his gaze vacant, and Alex had noticed her colleague staring. It wasn't like Chloe; she was usually so sensitive and discreet. Alex understood how unsettling these places were to someone who'd had no previous experience of them. She imagined Chloe had never been inside a care home before. She knew Chloe had fallen out with her parents and had subsequently changed her surname, but Alex didn't know what their disagreement had been over. Until that week, she hadn't known Chloe had a brother. All she knew of Chloe's life prior to the last six months was that she had trained with the Met in London after graduating with a degree in Psychology. Her teenage years and childhood were something Chloe had never spoken of.

The wailing sound that came from the end of the corridor evidently upset Chloe. She cast Alex a look that said *why aren't they doing something?*

A reminder of her own mortality and the fragility of time were the things Alex realised had confronted Chloe as they'd stepped inside the building, as she too had once experienced.

'We don't know,' Alex said, 'but by all accounts it seems out of character for Sarah to not let anyone know her whereabouts. Has she done this before, just failed to turn up to work?'

The manager shook her head. 'She's always been pretty reliable.'

'"Pretty reliable"?' Chloe repeated.

'Look,' the manager said with a sigh. 'There has been the odd time when she's not come into work, and we know she's had her fair share of problems over the years. But if she wasn't coming in she'd always let us know beforehand, even if it was at the last minute.'

'What problems has she had?' Alex asked. They'd already heard plenty from Sarah's flatmate, Grace, but hearing the details from someone else would corroborate the account.

'Sarah had some problems with an ex-partner,' the manager said, seeming to select her words with caution. She looked anxiously at both women. 'You know this already, I suppose?'

'We know about the violent ex-boyfriend, yes.'

The manager nodded. 'He turned up here once, while she was working. The place is obviously secure so he couldn't gain access, but we had to call the police. He was waiting just around the corner for her, refusing to leave. Sarah was pretty shaken up by it. I wish we'd done more.'

'In what way? What more could you have done?'

'I don't know. Anything. Two weeks after that, Sarah ended up hospitalised.'

The manager's eyes were glassy. She clearly felt a responsibility for what had happened to Sarah on the day of the attack. 'She's in some sort of trouble, isn't she?'

'We don't think her ex-partner is in any way connected, but it's helpful to know as much about Sarah as we possibly can.'

'I wish I could tell you something more, but I really don't know much of Sarah beyond this place. You might like to talk to some of the other girls here – she seems quite friendly with a few of them.'

Alex nodded and noted the names the manager provided. 'If we could speak with whoever's here now, that would be really useful.'

The manager left and came back moments later with a lady wearing a green tabard and a hairnet.

'Marianne has some information for you.'

She gave the woman what may have been intended as an encouraging smile but managed to make her look even more anxious. 'I'll give you some time,' the manager added, closing the door as Marianne stepped into the office.

'Sarah,' the woman began, 'is she OK?'

'She's missing. We want to find her as soon as possible.'

'I saw her arguing with someone. In the car park. It was a man.'

Marianne sat beside Alex and gave her the details: which day, what time, and a description of the man that was as detailed as she was able to recall. Either the woman's powers of observation were finely honed, or she'd had years of experience in being generally nosy.

Alex shot Chloe a look. The woman had just described Connor Price, the man with whom Sarah Taylor's flatmate had claimed her friend was having an affair.

CHAPTER TWENTY-FOUR

Connor Price drummed his fingers on the desk in a way Chloe assumed was intended to be annoying. Since the man had arrived at the station, he'd said little. His body language was stiff, defensive, and every time he was spoken to by one of the officers he would flinch slightly as though bracing himself for an attack.

They knew very little about him, but enough to know he was ex-army, married and had children. Enough to know that his alleged affair with Sarah Taylor was something he was unlikely to have wanted made public knowledge.

'When was the last time you saw Sarah?' Chloe asked.

Alex was sitting by her side, pen poised in her hand. She was taking notes despite the fact that the interview was being recorded. It was a force of habit, something she insisted on doing as though she couldn't trust technology in the way she could trust herself.

'A few days ago. Thursday,' Connor said, translating Chloe's raised eyebrows as a need to be more specific.

'Where did you see her?'

Connor sighed. The police knew where he'd seen her; they'd already been told he'd been to see her at her workplace, thanks to the nosy cow who had spotted them arguing in the car park.

'At her work.'

'Is that something you do often?' Alex asked. 'Go to see her at work?'

'I didn't see her at work,' Connor snapped, unable to hide his frustration. 'I saw her in the car park. I just wanted to talk to her about something.'

He sighed again at the second rise of Chloe's eyebrows. 'Here.' He reached into his pocket and retrieved his mobile phone. He unlocked the screen and searched for the message he'd received. 'There.' He held the mobile phone out across the table and waited as DC Lane and DI King read the brief message.

'But that's not Sarah's mobile number?' Alex clarified. 'So why did you think she'd sent it?'

Connor sat back in his seat and returned his mobile to his pocket. 'No one else is supposed to know… about us.'

'Where did you meet Sarah?' Alex asked.

'At the support group I run. She started coming about nine months ago. She's had problems with depression, anxiety; her ex-boyfriend beat her up pretty badly.'

His eye met Chloe's and she held his stare. 'She knows how to pick them then.'

Connor's jaw tightened. 'Look, we had a fling, all right? It was no big deal.'

'Did Sarah see it that way?'

'Yes. We agreed to finish things and she didn't make a fuss about it. I haven't seen or spoken to her since Thursday. I don't know where she is.'

'That message you received,' Alex said. 'Have you tried calling the number?'

'Of course I have.'

'And?'

'And no reply.'

'Could you give us the number please?'

Connor took his mobile back out from his pocket, found the message and passed the phone to Alex. She copied out the number into her notebook.

'Was Sarah upset by the end of the affair, Mr Price?'

'She didn't seem it, no.'

'You don't think she seemed upset? You said she suffered with depression. You don't think she'd have done anything to hurt herself though?'

Connor's expression changed and his face paled at the implication. 'No. I mean, she wasn't like that. She'd never done anything like that, she just… she liked to talk things through. She wanted to be around people who understood her.'

'And that was you, was it, Mr Price? You understood her?'

Alex shot Chloe a look that didn't go unmissed. She knew what the look meant. She was angry, and her anger was manifesting itself in the wrong way, directing itself at the wrong people. This wasn't like her, and both Alex and Chloe knew it.

'What the hell is all this about?' Connor said, his focus shifting between the two officers. 'Look, I'm not in love with her, OK? I admit it. Is that a crime?'

'It's just sex?'

Connor gave a shrug. 'People do it every day,' he said, holding Chloe's stare longer than was comfortable. 'Look, I assume I'm not under arrest?'

'What would you be under arrest for?' Alex asked. Sarah Taylor was missing, but as yet that was all she was. Under 'normal' circumstances her disappearance wouldn't have yet been considered a priority, but with another young woman recently found murdered they weren't going to take any chances.

'Exactly,' Connor said. 'She's probably just having a couple of days to herself. Clear her head or something.'

'Why would she need to do that?' Chloe asked. 'You just said she wasn't upset by the end of the affair, that she'd accepted it?'

Connor scraped back his chair and stood. 'I don't know. You'll have to ask her when she turns up. Can I go now?'

Chloe watched the man hesitate before he got the nod from Alex that he was free to leave.

He headed for the door.

Alex got up and followed him back down the corridor to reception. She hoped for Sarah Taylor's sake that when she did turn up she'd be capable of explaining where she'd been.

CHAPTER TWENTY-FIVE

Chloe hadn't been to her parents' house in over eight years. Her last visit had ended with her father telling her it was best she never came back, so she'd adhered to his wishes and hadn't returned. A year later she had moved to London, a city where it had been easy to lose herself, and it was there she had joined the police after finishing university. She had spent over six years in London trying to cast off her old self and prove what she was made of, to herself as much as to others. Six years spent trying to forget. Then she had realised she couldn't. She never would. So she returned home, to Cardiff.

She had seen her parents only once since moving back to Wales a little over six months earlier. She had been in Cardiff city centre shopping for a pair of shoes to wear to a party she didn't end up going to. She remembered standing in the shoe section of Debenhams, deliberating between a pair of sensible flats that didn't look that great but were likely to be comfortable and a pair of high heels that looked amazing but she knew were likely to attract unwanted attention.

She ended up with neither. Whilst playing eeny-meeny between them, Chloe had looked up and seen a familiar figure standing near the menswear department. She recognised her mother immediately. The short, solid frame and the hair swept back and piled high on the head: she hadn't changed one bit. Her mother was wearing an outdoor jacket, the windbreaker kind that came in lurid colours that made her even more conspicuous amongst the busy crowds of Saturday afternoon shoppers.

Her mother had turned to speak with someone, and there was Chloe's dad, larger than life, towering over his wife by a good eight inches, as he always had.

Chloe had never been able to look at her father without being reminded of Luke. The thought of her brother never failed to throw her off balance and she put a hand to the shelving unit on which the high heeled shoes she'd been eyeing up were displayed. They were so similar. Both tall, both with the same wiry frame – an athlete's figure – and with dark hair that even in her father's case showed minimal signs of grey. Chloe watched as something was said between them. Her mother gestured to a pair of sunglasses, took them from the stand and handed them to her father who tried them on and turned to his wife, seeking her approval. She gave a shrug and he passed them back.

Chloe had never known her father to wear sunglasses. Why would he have needed any? The sky that ceilinged South Wales spent ninety-five per cent of its time bearing an expression of disappointment, and even on its best days was never that sure about it for too long.

It occurred to Chloe that her parents might be going on holiday, and the thought filled her with a sickening anger. Their son was dead. Years had passed, but not that many, and nothing in that time had changed. Luke was still dead. His killer was still out there somewhere.

His parents were shopping for sunglasses.

'Can I help you?'

A girl who looked no older than nineteen was standing beside Chloe, so close she made her jump.

'Sorry,' the shop assistant said with a smile. 'I just wondered if you needed a hand with anything, or a second opinion maybe?'

Chloe had forgotten the shoes. She had forgotten what she was doing there. She was momentarily distracted by the thick line of orange foundation that framed the girl's face before saying, 'No. Thanks.'

She left the shop, nearly walking into a woman pushing a pram on her way out. Once out in the wide main space of the shopping centre, she took a deep breath and promised herself, once again, that she would never be like them. They might have forgotten Luke, but she never would.

*

Now Chloe stood at the gate of her parents' house, hesitating. She had grown up here, in Fairwater in Cardiff, in a house her parents had always quietly – and sometimes not so quietly – been ashamed of. The semi-detached was a standard three-bedroom on an estate both Malcolm and Susan Griffiths had always regarded as beneath them. From early childhood, Chloe had been encouraged to believe her family was better than those of her peers at school, better than the neighbours; better, in fact, than anyone she came into contact with in her relatively sheltered life. Her parents were big on exam results – anything they could use as a means to confirm themselves more successful than the parents of the other children at Luke and Chloe's school. It had all seemed sadly hypocritical considering how little real interest they had taken in their children.

Chloe had grown up knowing she was different, but only because her parents had made her so. Her clothes were old-fashioned and when the other kids in her class spoke about television programmes they watched and music they listened to, Chloe was rarely able to join in with their conversations. Her father believed television rotted the brain; she and her brother were occasionally allowed to watch a programme, but only if it was educational and had been vetted by both parents first. Pop music – or 'popular' music, as her mother insisted on calling it – was filled with expletives, debauchery and disrespect of women, so that was off limits too.

They had wondered why both their children had insisted on rebellion.

Chloe walked up the short front path that led to the front door and pushed the button for the bell without allowing time when she might talk herself out of it. Everything about the house brought a heavy pain to her chest. The front step on which she and Luke had sat side by side most afternoons after school when it wasn't raining, watching the other children playing on the small patch of grass on the far side of the street and wishing they were allowed to go; the same dark curtains hanging at the front windows where she would stand and lose herself when she and Luke played hide-and-seek and it was her turn to disappear: the sound of the bell, flat and dull, that rang for deliveries and the gas man, but never for the friends Chloe would long so much to see.

As a younger child she had thought their lives were normal. Then Chloe grew a little older, started comprehensive school, and had realised she wasn't living in a home but under a regime.

Chloe had wondered which of her parents would be home – whether either of them would be there – and which one of them would answer the door. She didn't wait long to find out.

'Mum.'

The word almost got stuck to her tongue. It had been so long since she had needed to use it, it sounded foreign as it left her lips.

Her mother said nothing. She looked so familiar, yet now she was this close to her Chloe could see how much older she had become, heavy lines framing her eyes and the skin at her jaw beginning to slacken. Her thick hair was piled high on her head in its usual way, pinned carefully in place with an array of slides and grips. The smell of baking wafted past her as she shifted uncomfortably in the doorway.

There was something behind her eyes, words she couldn't bring herself to say. She kept them there, unspoken.

'Dad home?' Chloe asked when it became clear her mother wasn't going to say anything.

The question was answered for her when Malcolm appeared at the end of the hallway; his face paled as though he'd seen a ghost. Chloe guessed that in many ways that was exactly what she must have become to them.

'What are you doing here?' he asked.

There had been a time when the hostility in his welcome and the curtness of his words might have offended or hurt Chloe, but they were way beyond that now.

'I want to talk about Luke.'

Her father hurried along the hallway and pushed past his wife, his urgency almost violent. He gripped the side of the front door. 'I told you not to come here again,' he said, his voice shaking across the words. 'Not until you'd found something else to talk about.'

Chloe opened her mouth to speak, changed her mind and said nothing. Her focus moved from her father to her mother. Why can't we talk about him, she wanted to scream. He's my brother, your son. Why shouldn't we talk about him today, tomorrow? We should never stop talking about him.

Yet Chloe knew the words would be pointless. They had been there before, so many times; so much anger and bitterness; so many recriminations.

'Mum...' She looked at Susan pleadingly, knowing she was wasting her time. She couldn't appeal to her mother's softer side – as far as Chloe was aware, she didn't have one. It had been there, once, in occasional appearances, but time had hardened it, eroding the soft edges that once might have existed.

This was the woman who had stood and watched on as her husband had beaten their son with a slipper. While Luke later sat locked in his bedroom, Chloe had cried to her mother in the kitchen, begging to know what her brother had done that had merited such punishment.

She would never forget her mother's blank expression as she put Chloe's dinner on the table in front of her and coldly said the words, 'He shouldn't have answered back.'

Chloe looked from her mother to her father and felt a burning flame of hatred race through her. These people had ruined her childhood – had ruined Luke's childhood – yet here she was, standing on their doorstep and pleading with them.

It made her feel pathetic and humiliated all over again.

She might have cried, but in that moment her anger was stronger than her sadness.

'I shouldn't have come.'

'No,' her father said coolly.

Chloe reached into her pocket, her fingertips touching the cold metal of the house key.

She wondered whether her parents had ever thought to change the locks.

CHAPTER TWENTY-SIX

When he'd left the room, he had left Sarah lying on the floor. Her arms had deadened behind her, but at least she was able to breathe again. She had thought he was going to kill her, but she was still alive. He had left her mouth uncovered and, at first, she hadn't made a sound. Then she had screamed and called for help. It hadn't taken long for her throat to become raw with the effort and, even as she'd screamed, Sarah had realised the sound was going nowhere. It was merely bouncing from the walls, returning to her.

She had tried to get herself upright, but with her arms numbed and her legs still tied to the chair, it was impossible. All she had managed to do was end up on her side, but at least this had relieved the pressure from one of her arms.

*

He returned later. It might have been hours; it might have been days. Sarah had lost all concept of time. He pulled the chair upright, lifting her with it as though she was weightless. She saw a glint in the darkness and for a moment she thought he had brought a knife.

'Please don't,' she said softly.

The hours she had spent alone in the darkness had given her time to think. She knew him, or at least she thought she did. There would be things she could say to him, ways she might be able to talk him down. She had seen it on TV: if she kept him talking, she might be able to get him to change his mind about what he was doing.

She didn't want to die here.

She didn't want to die.

When his hand moved, she realised he wasn't carrying a knife. It was a pair of scissors.

'That dress makes you look like a slut.'

She didn't like the dress either. She had chosen it in an act of defiance against Connor, but she hadn't thought it too bad with the tights she'd been wearing. Where were they and when had he removed them?

'Please don't,' she said again when she realised his intended use for the scissors. 'I'm so cold already.'

He reached for the front of her dress and Sarah began to scream. With the back of his other hand, he hit her across the face. She could feel every inch of her body shaking, every nerve tensed as the scissors moved to her chest and he began to cut through her clothing. Sarah squeezed her eyes closed and tried to shut out the sound of the metal slicing through the fabric. She tried to block out the sensations of the scissors' coolness against her already frozen skin; the feel of his gloved hands against her body.

When he was finished, he stepped back to look at her. She was now in just her underwear, cold to the bone and humiliated. She could sense him staring at her, but refused to open her eyes to look at him.

'If you're going to do it, just do it,' she said, the words catching between sobs.

'Do what?'

Sarah opened her eyes and looked at him reluctantly.

'Oh,' he said. 'That. You think that's what I want?'

She was so cold that she didn't know how long her body could survive the temperature inside the room. When she next spoke, she heard the shiver in her words. Despite the darkness, she could see the cool cloud formed with every syllable.

'Let me go. Please. Just leave me somewhere, anywhere; I won't tell anyone, I promise.'

'Leave you somewhere?' he repeated. 'Like that? You'll catch your death.'

Sarah squeezed her eyes shut again. The mocking tone of his voice rang in her ears, taunting her. 'I'll catch my death if you leave me here.'

'I won't be leaving you here.'

She opened her eyes. This time she was determined to look at him; to really look at him, and to make him see her back. 'Why are you doing this to me?' she asked again. 'I've never done anything to you.'

He tutted. 'You all say that.'

When he moved back towards her, Sarah braced herself for what she thought would happen next. She'd been wrong. He reached into his pocket and took something out, something that he pressed over her mouth and nose though she fought to try to get him off her.

Within seconds, there was nothing but darkness.

CHAPTER TWENTY-SEVEN

Alex switched on the TV and turned up the sound. In the kitchen, she began to prepare herself a sandwich and a cup of tea, leaving both half-made when she heard the sound of Superintendent Blake's voice coming from the living room. She went into the hallway and stood at the living room door, watching her colleague face the news crews and reporters as he prepared for the announcement recorded earlier that evening.

Harry still didn't look well. The grey pallor of his skin blended with the grey at his temples and there was something missing from his eyes, some kind of lost spark that seemed to Alex an unspoken admission. Why had he come back to work so soon? Had he even wanted to come back at all?

There had been an air of detachment surrounding him these past weeks; a hopelessness that wouldn't allow itself to go ignored. It shouldn't have been so surprising or unexpected. Harry hadn't returned under the most usual of circumstances. Besides that, he wasn't the only person at the station whose attentions had seemed more than just a little diverted.

Alex's thoughts drifted involuntarily to Chloe. She glanced back through to the kitchen, to the oversized clock hanging on the wall to the side of the sink. It was just gone ten thirty. Whatever Chloe was doing at that moment, Alex hoped it wasn't something reckless.

'We are currently investigating the murder of local woman Lola Evans, as well as the disappearance of another young woman.' Superintendent Blake addressed the camera with a solemn expression fixed upon his face. 'Miss Evans was from Rhydyfelin and her body was recovered from the River Taff at Bute Park on Tuesday morning. She was last seen on Saturday, the ninth of January in Cardiff. Another young woman, Sarah Taylor, is currently missing. We have no reason at this time to believe the two cases are in any way connected, although we are keen to make contact with Miss Taylor as soon as possible. While I'm unable to give any further details about either investigation at this time, I would ask anyone with any information regarding either of these two young women to please come forward and speak with police. As in any other circumstances, we ask everyone to take sensible precautions when in the city, particularly during the evenings and at night.'

There followed the usual barrage of questions from the press, despite the fact that Harry had just made it clear he could give no further details. The camera panned back to the news reporter as an image of Sarah Taylor appeared on the bottom right hand of the screen. It was a photograph of her in a pastel pink bridesmaid's dress, taken at her sister's wedding. She was smiling, her eyes focused on something or someone to the side of the camera and her face caught by a ray of sunshine that made her squint.

Alex turned off the television as the newsreader moved to the next story. Harry was taking precautions by advising people to remain vigilant, but they didn't believe that Lola had been taken at random. If it had been a mugging or a sexually motivated attack, her injuries would have been more frenzied and less methodical.

And Sarah Taylor could be anywhere. She might have visited a friend, stayed out and got so drunk she'd ended up somewhere she hadn't planned; there was no reason to believe she was in any danger.

She went back to the kitchen and to her task of making tea. The file she had left on the kitchen table still lay opened, its front page waiting to be turned. She felt a surge of guilt. She had made a promise to Harry and she had broken it. She had known that if she didn't, it was likely Chloe would get there first.

Alex finished making the sandwich she'd been midway through preparing when she'd heard the superintendent's voice coming from the living room. At the table, she pulled the file closer to her.

POST-MORTEM REPORT: EMILY PHILLIPS
A 16-year-old female was found deceased secondary to what was claimed to be a staged suicide in the family home. The body displayed signs of primary flaccidity. Attempts at resuscitation had been made.

REPORTING PARTY INITIAL STATEMENT
At approximately 00.32 on the morning of the 3rd April 2009 I was requested to attend the scene of an apparent suicide. I arrived at the residence at approximately 01.13 and was met there by Detective Constable Thomas McKenna, Detective Sergeant Alex King, and Chief Inspector Harry Blake. I was briefed by Chief Inspector Blake who provided the following information:

The subject was a teenage girl, Emily Phillips, who lived with her mother, Jane Phillips. Ms Phillips was away for the weekend with her partner. Present at the scene when the responding officers King and McKenna had arrived had been Emily's boyfriend, Luke Griffiths. DS King found Mr Griffiths on the stairs, holding the deceased body of his girlfriend. She checked for a pulse but there was none. There was a ligature attached to the subject's neck, in the form of a belt. DS King described Luke Griffiths as 'distressed and incoherent', but managed to glean that he had found her hanging from the top of the staircase. He claimed to have taken a chair from the kitchen and used it to stand on in order to release her body.

He then called 999. Dispatchers logged the call at 23.41.
Paramedics were at the scene at 00.04 and determined the
subject's death at 00.07.

DEATH SCENE INVESTIGATION
  An assessment of the scene took place at around 01.25.

Alex scanned the next two paragraphs of the report, which
included a long and detailed description of the hallway of the
Phillips's house. She took another bite of her sandwich before
focusing her attention on the description of Emily.

The subject was on the floor at the foot of the staircase. She
was wearing a black dress and no shoes. There was purple
colouring to her lips and her skin had reddened above the
place of strangulation. Clear ligature marks were seen around
the subject's neck. The belt from which the subject was said
to have been found hanging had been placed on the stairs by
Luke Griffiths after removal from the girl's neck.

Alex scanned ahead, knowing what was coming. So much had
flooded back to her upon reading the report. Though she had not
worked directly on the case after that night, it had received so much
press coverage and garnered so much talk at the station that it was
impossible to not have known what had been going on.

During post-mortem, marks found to the front of the sub-
ject's neck are consistent with the belt found at the scene of
death, identical in width and pattern. The placement of the
markings at the back of the neck indicates that the subject
suffered asphyxia caused by the pressure of the belt around
the neck. However—

Alex looked up from the report. It was here that everything came back. This was why no one had believed the death was suicide: it had been impossible. According to the pathologist and to the report, the buckle of the belt used to strangle Emily would have had to have come into contact with her neck, if she had in fact committed suicide in this way. But it didn't. There was a clear ligature line straight around her throat, devoid of any markings that would have been left by the metal of the buckle.

Emily hadn't killed herself. Someone else had held that belt around her throat and had tightened it until the last breath of life had escaped her.

There was another detail that made her suicide increasingly unlikely and, according to the pathologist, impossible:

Fibres found beneath the subject's fingernails match that of the belt, suggesting a struggle to free herself of the noose.

The only fingerprints found at the scene were Emily's, her mother's and Luke's. Luke had been arrested, but the evidence was circumstantial. Of course his fingerprints were to be found at the house: Luke was her boyfriend. He had been to the house countless times, having sometimes stayed there overnight. It hadn't been sufficient evidence with which to charge Luke, but it had been enough for everybody to assume him guilty of Emily's death.

Alex sat back on the sofa and closed her eyes. She wanted to help Chloe, but she had no idea where she was going to start.

CHAPTER TWENTY-EIGHT

During the previous few months, things had got even worse. His mother seemed to loathe him more than ever – so much more now he was the only child still around on which to offload her anger.

He had seen the way she looked at him. There was so much hatred in her face sometimes and yet she managed to look through him as though he wasn't there at all.

When he was younger, it had confused the boy. Later, he came to understand her anger, if only in part. Her bitterness had been explained to him in ways his teenage mind would never have fathomed alone. His sister had tried to comprehend their mother's behaviour, despite all the ways their parents had so unfairly treated her.

There were times he found himself almost feeling sorry for his mother.

And then there were all the other times.

That day, he got home earlier than expected. He hadn't been to college that afternoon, though he would tell his mother that his classes finished early. He had been somewhere she wouldn't approve of, with someone she didn't like. He told his mother anything he thought she might want to hear. He had found that life was safer that way.

He came in through the side door that led into the kitchen. On the table, his mother's laptop was opened. She wasn't there. He glanced at the screen and saw a part-written email. Saw who it was addressed to. Curiosity told him to take a closer look, and he would have managed to overrule the urge if he hadn't seen the name at the start of the message.

He wasn't really sure what to make of what he read.

'What are you doing?'

He hadn't heard his mother come back down the hallway and into the kitchen. She stood at the doorway, hands fixed to her hips; her face frozen in a look that was part indignation, part panic.

The boy felt a shift in control, one so subtle yet so empowering. What he'd read was incriminating. They both knew it.

'I could ask you the same.'

It was only in the past few months his confidence had started to develop. Despite his mother's growing anger, he felt stronger than he ever had. He had been shown a different way of doing things and he wanted to emulate it. He hated this life. He wasn't allowed to question; he wasn't allowed to disagree. There were so many rules, and none of them seemed fair or even logical. He hated his every move being watched; his parents seemed able to do as they pleased; his father, at least. If he stayed there, they would suffocate him. He wanted out.

'I thought you weren't supposed to contact her now?'

'Get away from my things.'

Despite the growing confidence, he obeyed his mother. She hurried to the table and flipped shut the lid of the laptop. 'You say nothing,' she said. 'Understand? Nothing.'

In that moment, all his previous suspicions were confirmed. He saw what she feared most and where her priorities lay. The child still in him wanted to scream at her, to beg her to stop this. Didn't she care what she was doing to her family?

The young man in him knew that doing either would be pointless.

He swallowed the words he wanted to say and went upstairs to his room. Thoughts of revenge continued to plague him, though he fought so hard to push them to one side.

He didn't know then that just weeks later he would find a way to put that email to good use.

CHAPTER TWENTY-NINE

The boy sitting in interview room two had a string of snot sliding from his left nostril. His face was red and his cheeks puffy from an assault of prolonged tears. Beside him, his mother sat with the back of her hand pressed firmly to her mouth. She too looked as though she'd been crying.

DC Mason had filled Alex in on what had been said by the woman when she'd come into the station with her son ten minutes earlier. With a rising sense of disheartenment, Alex closed the interview room door behind her and sat at the table opposite the mother and son.

'It's Jake, isn't it?' Alex said, tilting her head in an attempt to get the boy to make eye contact with her. Jake lowered his head further, trying to conceal the evidence of his tears. He was about eleven years old, Alex guessed – last year of primary school or maybe first of secondary – and the partly shaved scalp might have given him the misleading look of a boy who wouldn't be seen crying anywhere, least of all in front of his mother.

'You're not in any trouble,' Alex told Jake, looking to his mother. 'I just need you to tell me what your mum told the man down at reception.'

The boy turned to his mother, managing to avoid eye contact with Alex. He elbowed her gently in the ribs, prompting her to do the talking for him.

'I really need this to come from you, Jake,' Alex said, stopping the boy's mother before she could begin. Had the boy seen what he had claimed to, or had his child's imagination and the tricks of the dark made him see things that weren't truly there? 'It was the night before last, is that right? Can you tell me exactly what happened, from the beginning?'

The boy looked at Alex for the first time, his dark eyes still glassy with tears. When the words came they came shakily, tripping over one another. 'We shouldn't have been in there,' he stammered.

'It's OK, Jake, you're not in any trouble. It doesn't matter if you were somewhere you weren't supposed to be, OK. I just need to know what you saw. Start from the beginning. Where did you meet your friend?'

'At his house,' Jake said, the stammer easing slightly. 'He lives just round the corner.'

'And you were on your bikes?'

Jake nodded. Alex raised her eyebrows slightly, gently prompting him to continue.

'Come on, Jake,' his mother said impatiently.

Alex kept her focus on the boy, but from the corner of her eye she could see his mother anxiously shifting in the chair beside him. Alex felt a sinking weight drop inside her. The boy's mother had seen the news. They were both thinking the same thing.

'Jake,' Alex said, putting her hands on the table. She felt a sense of urgency now, an inescapable feeling that they were wasting valuable time. 'You are not in trouble, but it is really important that you tell me what happened. Where, when, what, OK? Everything exactly as it happened.'

The boy gave a loud sniff and dragged his sleeve across his running nose. 'We found this place a few days ago,' he said, looking awkwardly at his mother. 'It's all boarded up, but we got in around the back; we found a place we could climb up and get in. We just wanted to explore. We didn't take anything or break anything, I swear. There was a room, upstairs. We went in and there—'

The boy's words broke on his tears. 'He made me promise I wouldn't tell.'

'For God's sake, Jacob,' his mother snapped. 'That doesn't matter. The detective told you you're not in trouble – this isn't about you.'

The boy's sobs grew louder.

'Jake,' Alex said calmly. 'Tell me what you saw in that room.'

Between gulps of air, Jake began his account. 'It was dark. There were things everywhere, like bits of old furniture and stuff. It was really dusty in there. We didn't go in – we only pushed open the door and just poked our heads round to have a look. Riley had a look first. He told me to follow him.'

He stopped. What neither Jake nor his mother knew was that officers were already on their way to the building. Jake and his friend Riley might have been mistaken in what they thought they'd seen, but Alex wasn't going to take any chances.

'Go on, Jake.'

The boy took a deep breath. 'There was someone in there. I think there was anyway. She was sitting in a chair. We ran when we saw her. I don't know if she saw us. I think she might have been sleeping.'

Alex looked away from the boy and to the table, hoping that Jake's naive assumption might have been right but knowing it probably wasn't.

'You didn't tell your mum straight away?'

Jake shook his head. 'Riley said we'd get into shit. Sorry,' he said, his hand moving to his mouth and his young face flaring red. 'Trouble. He said we'd get into loads of trouble and made me promise not to tell.'

'But you did decide to tell?'

Jake's mother caught Alex's eye. 'That woman on TV,' she said. 'The one they showed a picture of last night…' She left the unfinished sentence dangling in the air between them.

'Was the woman you saw the same woman in the picture on TV?' Alex asked Jake, wondering why the boy had been allowed to stay up so late the previous evening. She was thankful that for whatever reason he had been. 'Is that when you told your mum?'

The boy sobbed loudly and turned to his mother, hiding his face in the curve of her arm. His tears answered Alex's question for him.

She was distracted from her thoughts by one of the DCs entering the room.

'Sorry to interrupt you, boss. Have you got a minute?'

Alex followed him into the corridor, about to reprimand him for his abrupt intrusion.

'We've just had a call in,' he told her, before she had the chance. 'Lola Evans. Turns out she was a stripper.'

CHAPTER THIRTY

The pub was in Groeswen, a tiny village that sat between Caerphilly and Pontypridd. It was on a lonely path that although just a few hundred metres from the main road – the main road itself being little more than a narrow country lane – managed to seem as though it was far out in the countryside, isolated from the rest of civilisation by high trees and overgrown wasteland. Alex pulled her car up to the front of the building and parked alongside the couple of other vehicles already there. She could see the appeal of the place for any curious child of an adventurous and risk-taking persuasion. A stretch of land surrounded the building, now thick with bracken but still showing evidence of its former life: a broken picnic table upturned and partially burned, abandoned signage growing moss and left to decompose on the shadow of a path; broken glass still littering the ground like some haunting reminder of a party that was long since over.

Scene of crime officers were already present, having been alerted by the original officers who attended to check the place over. There was no one inside the building when they'd got there, although it quickly became clear that there had been.

Chloe stepped from the passenger side of Alex's car and looked up at the building that stood tall and imposing before her. Its main doors had been boarded, but had been broken through by officers. The windows on both the ground and upper floors were boarded up and the roof was in a state of disrepair with large sections of tiles missing.

'Place gives me the creeps,' she said, pulling her jacket closer around her to stave off the bite of afternoon air.

She followed Alex through the gap of broken boards that allowed them entry into the former pub. Inside, time had been frozen. The bar stood in front of them, thick with grime and dust. The majority of the furniture was gone, but a few old, red-cushioned benches remained lining the walls, pictures still hanging against the flaking paintwork behind them.

Chloe took her phone from her pocket and the officers stood in the glow of its torchlight. Cobwebs hung like curtains from the ceiling and relics of the pub's past – empty glasses, beer mats and beer bottles – lay scattered on the few tables that remained. Beneath them, their shoes clung to the sticky carpet.

'Boss.'

A male constable appeared in a darkened doorway to the right, beckoning Alex and Chloe with a nod of the head. They followed him into a short narrow hallway and up a flight of stairs.

'There's a flat upstairs,' the officer said. 'We've found where the boys got in. Climbed up on to a fire escape at the back.'

'What else has been found?' Alex said, already fearful of the answer. If only Jake had spoken up sooner. If only his friend had said something. If only—

She stopped her trail of thoughts. Where had 'if only' ever got anyone?

Alex followed the officer through another door that led into a small square kitchen. The place was dark and dank, the damp spreading up the walls in a blackened rash and the stale smell of age and abandonment clogging the air. Other than old cupboard units and a cooker that looked as though it had never been cleaned, the room was empty. The remains of a smashed light bulb hung from the fitting at the centre of the ceiling.

'You'd better come through,' the officer said, nodding to the next doorway.

They followed him through an empty space that might once have been a living room. The door that led to the room where scene of crime officers now worked had been at some time padlocked, the lock found on the floor of the kitchen when the first officers had entered the building.

Alex sensed Chloe's body tense as they stepped into the darkened room. The air was fetid and sour with the smell of iron. Patches of blood stained the already dark carpet at the right-hand side of the room. A wooden chair was upturned. Several lengths of rope lay strewn amidst it.

'Jesus.'

Alex surveyed the scene, realising now exactly what Jacob and his friend Riley had seen. A woman in a chair. Her head hanging low and her long hair covering her face. At first, they hadn't thought the woman was real. She looked just like one of those real-life dolls they dress up in shops. A Hallowe'en version.

Then they'd kept telling themselves that's exactly what she had been, to make the memory of her go away.

Alex put a hand to her mouth. Had Sarah Taylor been here, tied to this chair? Was it Sarah the two boys had seen? Had she been alive? If it hadn't been Sarah, who else had been here? And where was Sarah now?

'We've got prints, boss.'

Alex watched a scene of crime officer collect a sample of blood from the floor at the foot of the upturned chair. The other SOCO was still dusting for further prints.

'Could be the boys' prints,' Chloe suggested. 'Did they actually come into the room?'

'Jake said not. What the bloody hell were they doing out here alone at that time of night? Where were their parents?'

Chloe studied Alex, watching frustration play out in the tensing of her jaw. Chloe didn't think it was suitable to point out that if the boys' parents had been keeping a closer eye on them, they wouldn't have found this place.

When she caught her eye, Alex looked away. She ushered Chloe back out to the kitchen.

'If Sarah Taylor, or whoever else, was here then how were they moved – how were they brought here?'

'Road's pretty isolated. Be easy enough for someone to come and go without being noticed, I suppose.'

Alex went back through to the small landing and glanced along the walls at the side of the staircase. 'No blood out here,' she mused. 'If someone had been brought here against their will, there'd be signs of a struggle, wouldn't there? And if he'd had to move an injured person back down these stairs, where's the blood?' She put a hand to her face and pressed her fingers against her eyelids. She knew that injured would likely mean dead. As she began to consider the ways the woman had been removed from the building, dark images permeated Alex's thoughts.

'We need to get Jake and Riley in and get them printed,' she said, thinking aloud. 'If we can rule them out, we might be able to isolate the killer's prints.'

Her phone began to ring. She took it from her pocket and saw DC Mason's number flash up from the screen.

'Daniel.'

'I've watched some of the CCTV footage sent over from the strip club where Lola worked,' he told Alex.

The call the station had received had been from a young woman who hadn't wanted to give her name. She claimed she had worked with Lola in a strip club in Cardiff – one of the subterranean bars that ran the length of St Mary's Street – and said it was doubtful the manager would have contacted police even had he heard of Lola's murder. It seemed he paid a lot of the girls who worked there cash in hand and was notorious for fiddling the club's accounts. He wouldn't have wanted any attention from the police.

'Anything?'

'Didn't need to watch much to find what we needed,' Dan said. 'Lola didn't leave alone.'

CHAPTER THIRTY-ONE

The desk sergeant raised an eyebrow at the man lingering in reception. He appeared to be sweating, despite the fact that it was bitterly cold outside, and even inside the station's barely capable heating system was doing little to stave off the chill. The man had long hair that was pulled back into a messy ponytail. He was wearing leathers and carrying a helmet under his arm.

'Can I help you?'

Stuart generally didn't like helping anyone. His front of house position at the station was something of an ongoing source of ridicule amongst his colleagues who often claimed he would have been better suited to a role in a prison: his mardy expression and surly attitude were enough to put anyone off reoffending. On the plus side, his general apathy was a deterrent against time-wasters and that was something that was always needed.

'I want to put in a complaint.'

If Stuart could have got away with sighing, he would have. As things stood, he had already been spoken to in recent months about his lack of customer service skills and was subsequently feigning best behaviour. He was supposed to make people feel safe and reassured. As far as he was concerned, it was this kind of soft-soaping that was turning the country to shit. Back in his day, the police had demanded authority and respect. They didn't sit behind desks and offer politeness to people who had the gall to make complaints about the way they chose to run things.

His lips spread into a thin, meaningless smile. 'Against?'

'Against Detective Constable Chloe Lane.'

*

Despite the blast of heat from the radiator on the wall behind them, the air in Harry Blake's office felt colder than it was on the street outside. Chloe stood beside Alex, her face pale and her eyes cast to the floor as though she had been summoned to the head teacher's office. Alex knew she didn't have to be there, but she felt a loyalty to Chloe and was aware of the pressure the young woman was under, something no one else at the station knew of. She had asked Harry if he would consider allowing her to return to a closed case – it wouldn't take him long to work out which closed case that happened to be.

Superintendent Blake shoved a pile of papers aside. Alex watched him pointlessly move things around his desk, feigning productivity in an attempt to delay the real reason they were all there. She didn't think it fair that Chloe should bear the brunt of his disgruntlement. She wasn't yet sure of the details of what Chloe was supposed to have done. She had imagined the worst, but had optimistically decided to hope for the best.

No one else knew of Chloe's connection to either the Emily Phillips or the Luke Griffiths case, and as far as Alex was concerned that was how it should stay. There was no getting away from the super finding out now, but Alex was determined to do everything she could to keep Chloe's secret just that. She and Harry Blake had worked together for years. He had been responsible for her relatively quick promotion to detective inspector. She knew that beneath his cool exterior and his off-puttingly stern demeanour, Harry liked her. He respected her. She was confident she could persuade him, if needed, to keep Chloe's secret between the three of them, if only in the short-term. And besides, there was plenty more going on. There was no way he would want any negative attention drawn to anyone on the team.

'You're aware of the complaint that's been made?' Harry asked, not inviting either Chloe or her to take a seat. Alex hoped that was an indication they wouldn't be kept too long.

Chloe nodded.

'Do you want to explain it?'

'Not really,' she mumbled. She looked up, caught his expression and gave a brief and barely audible apology. 'It's not quite as he said, sir. I never accused him of anything.'

'Mr Sibley claims you accused him of murdering your late brother's girlfriend. He says it's not the first time you've done so.'

Though they weren't within touching distance of one another, Alex felt Chloe's body stiffen beside her. She shot the young woman a look.

What the hell had she been thinking?

'Why have you never told anyone about your links to these two cases?' Harry asked. 'Well, except you,' he gestured to Alex. 'You obviously knew all about it.'

'Only recently.'

The superintendent sat back in his seat and pushed his fingertips to his temple as though forcing back a headache. The fingertips of his other hand beat rhythmically on the wooden desk. Chloe braced herself for the verbal onslaught, but it didn't come.

'I didn't want to be judged, sir. It's never affected my work.'

'Until now?' Harry surmised. He sat forward and put his elbows on the desk in front of him. 'I'm familiar with both cases. You weren't with the police then, were you?'

'I was still a teenager.'

Harry nodded. Alex watched him deliberating over his words, carefully sidestepping the things he really wanted to say. She almost felt sorry for him. What was he supposed to say to this young woman whose brother had been accused of murder and subsequently taken his own life? No police training could ever prepare a person for circumstances as unlikely and unpredictable as this. Everyone believed Luke Griffiths guilty. There had been no real reason not to.

'Cases can only be revisited if new evidence has come to light; neither of you needs me to tell you that. Do you have any new evidence?'

Chloe shook her head, her top teeth clamped on to her bottom lip as though blocking all the things she wanted to say. She knew she was fighting a battle she couldn't win. The case was closed. Guilty.

She was starting to wish she had never confided in Alex. She'd managed on her own for this long; why had she thought she needed anyone else now? All she'd done was open up to other people a past she'd kept a lid on for years.

Those bloody emails were to blame. She had responded spontaneously, her heart ruling her head. Someone seemed to be pulling her strings, as though knowing that the mere suggestion another person might know something of Emily's death would be enough to send her plummeting back into the past. Had she reacted as they had hoped?

By her side, Alex cast Harry a pleading glance, but it went either unnoticed or ignored. She assumed the latter. She thought of the post-mortem report she had returned that morning and felt the same surge of guilt she had experienced when sitting at her kitchen table to read it.

'All right then, I don't want to hear any more about this until Lola Evans's murderer has been found. I need you both on task, no distractions.'

Alex nodded in acknowledgment. Beside her, Chloe did the same.

'I will speak to Mr Sibley about this myself. The last thing we need is negative attention. I'll tell him you've been formally reprimanded, although clearly that's an exaggeration. I'm giving you the benefit of the doubt here. Please don't make it something I'll regret.'

'Sir.'

Chloe and Alex left Harry's office in silence, neither willing to be the one to break it.

'I don't want to talk about it again,' Chloe said, once they were in the corridor.

'But—'

'It's not your fault. I should never have involved you.'

Alex didn't know what to say. She didn't want to let Chloe down, but she didn't want to have to be the one to help her chase a mystery that was never going to be solved. The only people who knew what had truly happened that night all those years ago were Luke and Emily. All truths had gone to the grave with them.

'Boss.'

Alex was distracted from her thoughts by DC Mason. Chloe sidestepped him, barely acknowledging her colleague in her desperation to get away.

'OK?'

'Forensics has come back with the results on the two sets of prints found at the pub. One of them is a match with Lola Evans.'

'And Sarah?'

Dan nodded. 'She was there.'

Alex felt her heart miss a beat. A surge of fear for Sarah Taylor overwhelmed her. 'And the blood?'

'Nothing yet. Said they'll try by the end of tomorrow.'

Alex sighed. She hoped for Sarah Taylor's sake that the blood would be identified as Lola's.

CHAPTER THIRTY-TWO

The forensics department was better than its word and the following morning returned a result on the blood samples taken from the pub. Two different blood samples had been collected from the room where they now knew Lola Evans and Sarah Taylor had been held. One was a match with Lola Evans.

Sarah Taylor's sister was called into the station for a blood test, accompanied by the police officer acting as family liaison. His presence alone had previously been enough to send the family into a tearful panic about what might have happened to Sarah. There were things the Taylor family still hadn't been told. They were unaware that Lola Evans had been held in the room where they now knew Sarah had also been held. They didn't want to give them reason to worry any more than they already were doing; at least not until their fears were justified.

The family was aware that fingerprints had been found at the scene and were being analysed against belongings taken from Sarah's bedroom at her flat. The match that had been found was something Alex was about to have to inform her of. Alex sat with Laura in one of the interview rooms.

'I'm so sorry to tell you this, but one of the sets of prints lifted from the pub is a match with Sarah's.'

Laura Taylor had seen the news and knew all about Lola Evans. No one needed to be told that Sarah's disappearance was being investigated alongside the murder case. Alex had barely started speaking before the other woman was reduced to a trembling wreck.

Vulnerable young women, Alex thought. Lola Evans. Sarah Taylor. Now Laura. All victims of the hands life had dealt them. Or maybe not. Life hadn't chosen this for them: a man had. A man possessed by the kind of evil Alex knew she would never begin to understand no matter how long her career.

Alex had sat through the strip club CCTV footage that Dan had flagged up. He was right: Lola hadn't left alone. A camera at the front doors had picked her up leaving the building at just after 2 a.m. She had walked from the main doors of the club alone, but had met with someone as soon as she was outside. A man had been waiting there for her and it seemed Lola had been expecting him. The footage was grainy and the man was wearing a hood pulled up, though there was a partial shot of his face when he turned to greet Lola. Dark features. Much taller than Lola's five foot four.

Was this the man who had taken and killed her?

Did this same man now have Sarah?

Laura Taylor sat sobbing, her long hair hiding her blotchy, tear-stained face. She looked so very much like her sister, and the thought of their physical similarities was unsettling. For a short while, Alex found herself unable to look at Laura without seeing Sarah's face. It made her all the more determined to find her alive.

'We're doing everything we can to find Sarah.'

'But she was definitely there? In that building. You know that for sure?'

Alex nodded.

As Laura Taylor cried – as her tears grew louder and pierced through the silence of the room – the officer assigned as family liaison stood by her side helplessly, seeking Alex's eyeline for some sort of sign as to how he should handle the situation.

Alex put a hand on the young woman's arm. 'We mustn't assume the worst. Although Sarah's prints were there, there's nothing to suggest she has been injured. It's likely whoever has taken Sarah was panicked by the boys getting into the building. He might have just moved her. You need to stay strong for your sister, OK?' She looked up at the family liaison officer. 'Could you get Laura a cup of tea, please?'

The young woman looked at Alex once the FLO had left the room. 'I know what he did to that other girl. What if he's done the same to Sarah?'

Alex took Laura's hand in hers. 'We have to believe he hasn't. For Sarah. OK?'

She let go of Laura's hand and passed her the box of tissues from the desk. Her own words sounded so convincing when she spoke them aloud like that.

CHAPTER THIRTY-THREE

Connor Price had been brought into the station by uniform and was sitting in the holding area looking agitated. He followed Alex through to the interview room, making no attempt to hide his annoyance at having been called there for a second time that week.

DC Chloe Lane was already in the interview room. She sat with her arms folded across her chest and avoided Alex's eye as she entered the room. She was clearly still smarting from that morning's meeting with Superintendent Blake. Alex guessed that much of what the young woman was experiencing was acute embarrassment. She had kept her past – she had kept herself – so expertly hidden, her backstory packed neatly away like a delicate keepsake, that to watch its wrapping torn away by careless fingers must have panicked her into the shame-filled silence which she now seemed so intent on maintaining. If she hadn't known Chloe better, Alex might have thought her attitude petulant. But Chloe was just a young woman who had been forced to endure more than her life's fair share of trauma.

No one could blame her for wanting to cocoon herself.

'I'm not saying anything until a solicitor gets here,' Connor said, taking a seat and folding his arms across his chest. His stance mirrored Chloe's, an unspoken defiance reaching across the table between them.

'That's fine.'

Alex gave Chloe a nod, gesturing her out into the corridor. Chloe stood, barely tearing her gaze from Connor Price.

Alex waited until they were both in the corridor then pulled the door closed behind her, keeping a grip on the handle in case Connor Price decided to try something stupid, like leave.

'You're upset with me,' she said, not wanting to waste what little time they would have until the duty solicitor showed up. 'I'm sorry if you feel I didn't support you this morning.'

'I'm not upset with you,' Chloe said, pushing a length of blonde hair behind her ear. 'I shouldn't have gone to see Patrick Sibley like that. It was stupid.'

Alex didn't think anything would be helped by agreeing with this statement. Going to see Patrick Sibley like that had been reckless and foolish. Hadn't Alex warned her against approaching any of the 'suspects' on her increasingly neurotic list? And hadn't she failed to adhere to her own advice when making the decision to take that post-mortem report? She wasn't really in a position to judge.

'I know you said you wanted me to leave it, but when things settle down here I will help you, I promise.'

She knew she shouldn't be making promises she wouldn't necessarily be able to keep, and Alex realised she had no idea how she would help Chloe. As the superintendent had reminded them, cases couldn't be returned to unless new evidence had come to light. Without any, they had nothing to work from. Chloe knew it and that was what was making her so angry.

'Things won't ever settle down here,' Chloe said, barely masking her irritation.

Alex sighed. 'I know it feels like that some days, but—'

She was interrupted by the appearance of the duty solicitor, a man Alex had sat opposite far more often that she would have liked. He gave both officers a cold smile and a brief acknowledgment before nodding at Alex's hand, which was still clutching the door handle. She pushed the door open, waited for him to walk past her then rolled her eyes at Chloe before following him into the interview room.

*

A few minutes later, the interview was under way.

'You've already admitted to having had an affair with Miss Taylor,' Alex reminded Connor.

He glanced nervously at the duty solicitor, as though gauging a reaction before he opened his mouth. The look was repeated every time he spoke. 'Yes.'

'But it ended recently?'

'Yes.'

'When was the last time you saw Sarah, Mr Price?'

Connor narrowed his eyes. 'You know when. We talked about this when I was here the other day. I saw her at the care home where she works.'

'And you argued?'

'We didn't argue, it wasn't like that.'

'But another member of staff heard raised voices and saw you in what was described as an altercation—'

'That's not true—'

'With Miss Taylor, during which you slammed the car door in an aggressive manner. Correct?'

'Is there a need for the interrogation stance, Ms King? This isn't a courtroom.'

Alex shot the duty solicitor a stare. 'Objection noted. And it's Detective Inspector King.' She reached for the file resting on the table in front of Chloe and took out a photograph, pushing it towards Connor.

His face changed at a single glance of the image.

'Lola?'

'You know her?' Whatever she'd been expecting, Alex hadn't anticipated that. She had been braced for a fleeting acknowledgment in the eyes, or a flicker of guilt so subtle it might easily go undetected.

Connor looked up at Alex sceptically, as though it was a trick question. 'Yeah,' he said tentatively. 'I mean, I haven't seen her in a while, but she used to come to the support group. I read about her on the Internet this morning. I can't believe it.'

'The support group where you met Sarah?'

'Yes.'

'Lola was a member of the same group?'

'Yes,' Connor said impatiently.

Alex looked to Chloe. A link between the two victims would surely help move the investigation forward, but why hadn't they found this out earlier? Had Alex taken her eye off what was important, missing something that should have been obvious? This was why the super had been so insistent that Chloe's past be left exactly where it was, for now at least. They couldn't afford distractions.

'How long had Lola been a member of the group?' She tried to keep her voice level, steady. The last thing she wanted was for Connor to think he had an advantage over them.

They'd had no idea that Lola Evans had been a part of any such group – her grandmother had never mentioned it, and had therefore presumably had no idea that her granddaughter had been going. Either that or she hadn't known anything about the group. Ethan Thompson hadn't mentioned it either, which suggested Lola had kept it to herself. What else had she kept hidden from those who were presumably closest to her?

Being a stripper, Alex thought, silently answering her own query.

As though the realisation of what Alex was implying had hit him square between the eyes, Connor's expression betrayed his panic. 'Quite a while, on and off,' he told them, his anxiety intensifying. 'More off than on. Why are you asking me about Lola?'

'Do you know where Sarah is?'

'My client has already answered that question—'

'No,' Connor snapped, cutting the solicitor short. 'I told you, I don't know where she is, OK? Why are you asking me about Lola? Do you think—' He stopped abruptly. It was obvious what they thought. 'I didn't touch Lola. I swear to God. I haven't even seen her in months.'

'Did somebody help you, Connor?' Alex asked.

He looked imploringly at the duty solicitor.

'Do you have any evidence that Mr Price is in any way connected to either of these cases?'

They didn't, but Alex wasn't prepared to volunteer that information. She was pinning her hopes on the second blood sample currently unaccounted for. She continued to hope it belonged to the man they were looking for, and not to Sarah.

A swab had been taken from Connor – time would tell.

'Did somebody help you?' Alex repeated, ignoring the man.

Connor gritted his teeth. 'I haven't done anything.'

Alex sat back in her chair and sighed audibly. 'Both women were known to you, both were highly vulnerable. They came to your group seeking support. You were in a position of trust. Did they trust you, Connor? Is that why they went willingly with you?'

'This line of enquiry is based on supposition and circumstance, DI King, of which you're well aware.' The duty solicitor was eyeing her with impatience. It was a look she often attracted from him.

'You're right,' she acknowledged. 'We'll need a little longer to prove it, won't we? Connor Price, I'm arresting you for the abduction and murder of—'

'You can't, I haven't done—'

'Lola Evans and the abduction of Sarah Taylor. You don't have to say anything, but—'

'Anything, I don't know where—'

'You haven't been charged,' the duty solicitor said, placing a reassuring hand on Connor's arm as Alex finished reading him his rights. 'They're buying themselves time, that's all. It's a cheap shot.'

'Interview terminated at fourteen fifty-three,' Alex concluded, glancing at the clock on the far wall.

'Rachel Jones,' Connor said quickly. 'She knew about me and Sarah, I'm sure she did. She's jealous. I bet she was the one who sent me that message about telling my wife.'

'Jealous?' said Alex. 'Quite the stud, aren't you, Connor? Must be difficult to focus on much else, with all this female attention you attract.' She looked to Chloe. 'Would you show our guest to his room, please?'

CHAPTER THIRTY-FOUR

It had been easy to find out whether the weekly group meetings were being held in the same place at the same time, and sure enough, there they were: on the same day on which they'd been running for as long as Chloe was able to remember. Her parents' lives – her own childhood – had been shaped by routine and schedule; by commitments and responsibilities. The fact that her parents were still so predictable gave Chloe a two-hour window when she knew neither of her parents would be home, although she allowed herself less than that, not wanting to run the risk of being caught by them if they were to return home early.

It was like being twelve years old all over again.

She always found that the time to get things done was when you weren't thinking about all the possible things that could go wrong. It felt strange to be standing again in the house where she had grown up. Memories clung to the walls, faint and yellowing like old nicotine stains. There was an eerie silence about the place: something other than the stillness brought about by an absence of life.

In the hallway, a framed picture older than Chloe hung on the wall that led upstairs, taking pride of place at the entrance to the house, as it always had done.

> God is the head of this house, the unseen guest at every meal, the silent listener at every conversation.

When she was a child, those promises had filled her with fear. Did God really see everything that happened? Did he hear their conversations... could he hear her thoughts? A part of her now wished that she was able to believe in God. She understood why so many people did. He offered comfort in a world filled with sadness and despair. He offered the promise of stability to lives otherwise shrouded in uncertainty.

It was a bleak thought that this was all there was.

If He really was all-seeing, all-knowing – if He was able to speak to her now – what might He be able to tell her?

She shook herself from her thoughts. They were silly. Futile. Glancing into the living room, Chloe felt a pang of sadness. The room looked the same – the same crimson sofa, the same beige carpet; the same bare walls that bore none of the usual family photographs or memories – and it was exactly this that filled Chloe with a sense of despondence.

What had she been expecting?

She opened the top drawer of the sideboard, aimlessly rifling through pens and paperclips, bills and receipts. She wanted a trace of Luke, of something, but the house was bereft of any reminder of the other people who had once resided there.

Chloe sighed, sat back on her haunches, and closed her eyes. If she thought hard enough, she could still picture Luke sitting on the rug in the middle of the carpet, his chubby little fingers intertwined with hers. As a child, she had loved having a sibling. She had relished the secret language that had existed between the two of them, codes passed through looks and gestures that only the other would understand. She had loved his smile on dark days, knowing that he invented happiness for her sake, even at such a young age. She had needed her brother to share the weight of everything she had been unable to bear by herself.

She missed him with a pain that was physical.

Chloe stood and went back into the hallway and down to the kitchen. As always, the place was spotless. Cleanliness was next to Godliness, and for a while – whilst still a student – Chloe had revelled in chaos, finally able to rebel against the orderliness that had been enforced upon her all those years. She let coffee cups fester on window sills until their abandoned remains grew fur coats. She allowed her clothes to form piles on the floor of the bedroom, wearing them dirty once she'd run out of clean. She let the dust accumulate until it was thick enough to write in.

For a while it had all felt so liberating.

The kitchen smelled of lemon-scented kitchen cleaner. She felt the urge to open the fridge and empty the contents of every carton over the newly mopped tiled floor.

Chloe went back down the hallway towards the front door. She trod the stairs tentatively. This was the part she had been dreading. How would it feel to stand in her childhood bedroom again? And to look upon the shadows left by Luke in his?

At the top of the stairs, she stopped on the landing. She could almost hear the house holding its breath, its heart pumping as loudly as her own. Facing your fears was supposed to be good for you, wasn't it? Do something every day that scares you. She had already stood in front of Superintendent Blake with the knowledge that he was aware of her attachment to two cases he would otherwise have considered forgotten. She found his moodiness intimidating, but he was nothing compared to the dread she felt at the top of her parents' staircase.

The room to her left had been hers. The door was shut, as were all the others. Her brother's room was straight ahead: the small box room at the back of the house, overlooking the garden. She stood at the closed door, a tentative hand waiting to open it.

She knew when she opened the door that what she'd been scared of was exactly what she was confronted with. The room had been stripped completely. There was a single bed pushed against the far wall – not the bed that had been her brother's, but a cheap self-assembly frame made up with crisp sheets, their straight-from-the-packaging creases still evident – and on the wall to her left hung a long mirror. Other than these, there was no furniture. The blue walls had been painted magnolia. The carpet had been changed. The curtains had been changed. Every trace of Luke was gone.

Chloe felt a surge of anger that tasted like sickness in her throat. She closed the door and went to what had once been her bedroom. For plenty of other children, their bedroom represented a place of sanctuary and escape. But Chloe only ever had one dream, and that was to be as far from the place as she was able to get.

Yet there she was, twenty-six years old and back in the place she had longed to escape from; still trapped by the same feelings of inadequacy that had been forced upon her as a child. She didn't have to do this any more. She didn't have to allow herself to feel this way.

And yet she knew she did. For him.

In her bedroom, Chloe found the same awaiting her. She hesitated as memories of what this place had once looked like filled her vision. All of it gone.

As if she and her brother had never existed.

CHAPTER THIRTY-FIVE

Tim Cole had spent quite a bit of time in and out of prison, his longest stretch three and a half years for robbery. It would have been tempting to treat him with caution based on this fact, but also too obvious. Although he had committed plenty of crimes, there was nothing in his record to suggest he had a propensity for violence.

His crimes seemed to have been encouraged by circumstance – a childhood spent in care; an early adult life characterised by homelessness and drug addiction. By all accounts he was a glowing example of how a person really needn't be condemned by the ex-con branding.

Of which Alex was also sceptical. The man sitting opposite her seemed a bit too eager to project himself as perfect.

Tim had removed the beanie hat he'd been wearing when he'd answered the front door and put it on the kitchen table in front of him. Now he sat picking at a loose thread that dangled from its seam, all the while nodding overenthusiastically at everything Alex said. Chloe was standing by the kitchen sink, her attention momentarily diverted to the window and to the sea of nettles that made up Tim Cole's small square of back garden.

'You know both women pretty well then, Mr Cole?'

His head didn't stop, the bald scalp reflecting the kitchen's strip lighting every time his nods dipped forward.

'Yes. I mean, I knew both of them from the group, but I didn't really *know* either of them particularly well, not personally. We don't really. That's the idea of the group, I suppose – or at least the others seem to think so, at least. They like to talk about how they're feeling, but not really give too much away about themselves or their lives. I suppose it feels safer for everyone that way. People feel less judged. If they just talk about their feelings rather than themselves they're not being judged on decisions or mistakes, only on reactions and responses. Does that make sense?'

Alex wondered how anyone else managed a chance to talk about anything when Tim seemed so fond of the sound of his own voice. She glanced at Chloe, who gave her a knowing smile.

'Perfect sense. Did you know that Lola Evans worked as a stripper?'

His eyebrows rose. He turned to glance at Chloe, as though seeking confirmation. 'Really? No. No, I didn't know that.'

'How long have you known Connor Price?'

Tim ran a hand over his bald head. 'A few years back. About three, I reckon. I was volunteering for a youth charity at the time. I met him on a counselling course.'

Alex had already spoken with the man who had run the counselling course where Tim Cole and Connor Price had met. After his return from Afghanistan, Connor had struggled to readjust to life back home and, like so many other veterans, had received little support after leaving the army. According to the course leader, Connor had sought the help of a private therapist after much persuasion from his family. The therapist had advised Connor to seek activity through volunteering, suggesting he become a counsellor in order to channel his own issues into helping others. Alex imagined the therapist's intentions hadn't been for Connor to end up in bed with the women he was supposed to be helping.

'We got chatting one day about the lack of support we'd both had in our respective situations and it went from there. Look, Connor's a good bloke. I know him. Whatever you think he's done, he would never hurt anyone.'

Alex's lips thinned. Was Tim Cole arrogant enough to compare his stretch in prison to Connor's time in Afghanistan? Besides that, his appraisal of Connor was all well and good, but they weren't considering him for employment and she hadn't asked him for a character reference.

'Do you keep a record of everyone who attends the group?'

Tim nodded.

'What do the details include?'

'Only the basics – names, addresses, next of kin.'

'We're going to need those records,' Alex told him. 'Where are they kept?'

'At the hall.'

If they were unable to find anything solid against Connor, they were going to have to let him go. If it turned out to be the case that they had in fact arrested the wrong man, a lead elsewhere would give them other possible avenues to consider. The support group was the first and only current link between the two victims they had. Checking the group's records would allow them to find out who else had come into contact with them.

'How do you keep in contact with group members regarding changes in meeting times and things like that?' Chloe asked.

'I run everything from a Twitter account. We tend to stick to the same days and times, but if there are any changes I tweet it and if anyone wants to contact me they can do so that way. We keep our privacy by not sharing mobile numbers.'

'We'll need the details for that account as well.'

If Connor wasn't the man they were looking for, would the killer be brazen enough to return to the group? Would he sit amongst the other members of the group, his crimes carefully concealed beneath a façade of vulnerability?

'When's the next meeting?' Chloe asked, as though reading Alex's thoughts.

'It's supposed to be this evening, but—'

'Run it,' Alex told him.

There was only one way they were going to find out whether that support group held the answers they desperately needed. They were going to have to go there to see for themselves.

CHAPTER THIRTY-SIX

'Thank you for meeting up with me.'

Scott sat opposite her, his finger idly tracing the circle of water that the base of his iced drink had left on the wooden table. He looked really handsome, Chloe thought. Too nice for someone like her. Too easy-going and laid-back to deserve being dumped on by the weaponry of baggage she carried with her. She couldn't understand why he was there at all. She had messed him about countless times: had cancelled, rearranged; cancelled again. They'd had the odd drink together here and there, always time snatched between other commitments. There had been so many reasons – and sometimes excuses – for not being able to meet up that Chloe was amazed he still wanted to see her at all. She took some hope from the thought that it could only mean he liked her. Somehow, she had managed to inadvertently get something right.

Once again, she'd had to start their meeting with an apology. She didn't have long – the Lola Evans and Sarah Taylor cases were keeping the whole team busy, and that evening she and Alex would be visiting the support group that both of the young women had attended. There were also the apologies for all the previous times she had cancelled on him, often at the last moment. Scott had casually brushed aside every apology, seeming to unquestioningly accept the busy nature of Chloe's job. She didn't think that he was by any lengths a pushover, but he seemed to have a patience that she could only dream of. She wished it was really all that simple, and that the job was the only thing that had kept her from him all those times.

Sitting opposite him now, she realised how much she liked him. Chloe hadn't liked anyone this much in a long time. Liking him was the very thing that had sent her running from every arrangement to meet. Getting closer to him would inevitably mean having to reveal things she had managed to keep hidden for so long. There were things she wouldn't know how to explain, that couldn't possibly ever make sense to him, even with the best of explanations. They still didn't make sense to her.

And then there would be the issue of sex. The thought of getting physically close to Scott was something that kept sending her running, despite how attracted to him she found herself. It was complicated, but how was she supposed to explain that to him?

'I was starting to think I might have upset you in some way, or—'

'God, no,' Chloe interrupted him, a little too keenly. 'It's not you, I—' She winced at her own clichéd words. 'Work has been hectic – that really isn't an excuse.'

'I can imagine. I've seen the news.'

Chloe gave a sad smile.

'You OK?'

She nodded. 'I like being busy. This is just the wrong kind of busy, you know?'

'It must be really tough, seeing what you see. I spend my days hoping something vaguely exciting might happen. You know, a kid loses an armband or something.'

She laughed. 'It can't be all that bad.'

'It is. Anyway, you're looking well.' He flashed a smile.

She knew he was lying to be polite. In truth, she wasn't looking great at all. The stress of her encounters with Patrick Sibley and then with the superintendent felt etched into her skin. And then there'd been the visit to her parents' house. She hadn't had a proper night's sleep in almost a week, although that was becoming something of a regular occurrence.

She sipped her lemonade. 'I've messed you about. I haven't meant to.'

'It's OK. I understand.'

She knew he didn't, not really, but Chloe supposed it was kind of him to pretend to. She considered how uncomplicated Scott Mackenzie's life might be. She knew this of him: he was twenty-seven; he worked at the leisure centre in Llanishen; he shared a rented flat with a friend he had known since school; he was an only child; his parents lived in Whitchurch, where he had grown up. He saw his parents every weekend, usually when he went over to their house for Sunday dinner, which his dad always cooked. It was this image of domestic family bliss that Chloe knew she had been partly captivated by. It was so unlike anything she had ever known.

Scott seemed to think of his life as boring, but it was the very kind of boring Chloe had always craved.

'I would like to see you, if you're still OK with that.'

'You're seeing me now.' He shot her another smile and Chloe looked away. It had been a long time since she had allowed herself to respond this way to a handsome face.

'I don't want to mess you about again,' she said, 'but I'd like to get this case out of the way and then… we'll see what happens.'

She was lying. Chloe didn't want to wait for the current case to be over – what real sense was there in that? There would be others, the next thing to keep her from living what other people might regard as a 'normal' life, but what was normal anyway? What she was really hoping for – trying to ask for without having to say the words – was that Scott would wait for her until she had found her brother's killer.

She just didn't want to tell him that until after the job was done.

'I can wait. Do you think you'll be using the centre before then? Anyone might think you'd been avoiding the place.' He said it with a slight smirk, his lip pulled in a half-smile.

Chloe felt her face flush. Before Christmas she had been going to the leisure centre twice, sometimes three times a week for a swim, but since meeting and then letting down Scott repeatedly she had abandoned the pool in favour of running. She hated running.

'Sorry. I didn't mean to—' God, what was the matter with her today, she thought. She'd been reduced to someone she didn't recognise: uncertain, apologetic, stammering. 'I've just been busy, really. I haven't been avoiding you.'

She knew he would see through the lie.

He smiled in an attempt to reassure her. 'I'm just messing, you're fine. Look, you let me know when you're ready and we'll go out for dinner or something. Be nice to share something a bit more adventurous than a lemonade together.'

There was a glimmer in his eye that made Chloe wonder whether Scott was actually referring to food at all. A nagging voice in the back of her mind questioned whether she was making a mistake. She liked him too much, and that was all wrong. She had Luke to focus on, and a murderer to help catch.

Did she need to prioritise, or could she juggle her responsibilities with some kind of artful balancing act?

Did she always have to sacrifice her own happiness?

Expecting him to wait for her suddenly seemed an unreasonable request. If he minded, it certainly hadn't shown. She watched him circle a finger through the small puddle of water on the table. God, he was lovely, she thought. She imagined what it might feel like to have those hands on her body – that trace of those fingertips on her skin – and had to shake her mind from the thought when he looked back up at her.

Allowing herself to get any closer might prove a huge mistake. It had happened in the past: who was to say it wouldn't happen again?

Her phone rang in her pocket, rousing her from her thoughts. She muttered an apology and retrieved her mobile, shooting Scott an apologetic smile as she answered the call.

This might be a mistake, Chloe thought, but she was no longer sure how many potential mistakes she was prepared to avoid.

What if, whilst avoiding all the potential mistakes, she missed the very thing that might lead to something perfect? In her heart, she knew she deserved to be happy. There were just so many reasons why her brain couldn't yet allow it.

CHAPTER THIRTY-SEVEN

The sky was threatening rain, which once again seemed a fitting tribute to the mood inside the car. As Alex drove she couldn't keep her thoughts from Sarah Taylor. She wondered for the hundredth time where she was now, whether she was still alive and, if she was, what was happening to her. She had to imagine that she was unharmed. While there remained that hope, there was still everything to hold on to.

The image of Lola Evans's body still hadn't left Alex's mind. When she closed her eyes at night, the young woman's water-ravaged face was the last thing she saw before eventually drifting into sleep. They couldn't help her, but they could still help Sarah.

'If it wasn't Rachel who sent that text to Connor then who did?' Chloe said, dragging Alex from her dark thoughts.

Alex shook her head. 'Don't know. The phone's untraceable – pay as you go. Rachel admitted she'd known about Connor's affair with Sarah for a while, but I don't know what she'd have to gain from lying about the text.'

'You spoke to her?'

'Yeah. She seems scared of her own shadow. I don't know. I don't reckon she's the type to lie to the police, although it takes all sorts.' Alex pulled into a side street that housed a row of terraces and a village hall at the far end. 'This is it,' she said, stopping by the kerbside. 'Tim Cole's empire.'

She shot Chloe a roll of the eyes and Chloe smirked.

'She did say something a bit odd though,' Alex said, undoing her seatbelt.

'Rachel?'

'Yeah. She said Connor was supposed to be helping them not luring them into bed. Timid as she is, she sounded pretty angry about it.'

'Luring?' Chloe repeated. 'Bit predatory, isn't it?'

'Exactly.'

They needed something concrete against Connor, and they needed it soon. The more time that passed, the less chance they had of finding Sarah Taylor alive. The majority of the blood found at The Black Lion had belonged to Lola, yet the second sample was still unaccounted for. Someone other than Lola had been injured there; hopefully, the man who had held them captive. Alex had to take her own advice and continue to believe Sarah Taylor was still alive.

*

The reception they received from the majority of group members suggested Alex and Chloe hadn't been expected. Why it should have come as a surprise that the police might show up to the meeting was something Alex was unable to fathom: one of their group was dead and another was missing. It seemed fairly obvious that the police would make an appearance.

There were only three members of the group there that evening: Tim Cole, Sean Pugh and Carl Henderson. The cold village hall was made colder by the sombre atmosphere that greeted DI King and DC Lane as they entered through the creaking main doors. Tim Cole was as overpowering as ever, offering tea and biscuits as though both officers had just popped in for a cuppa and a catch-up.

'I thought of cancelling… you know, under the circumstances, but then thought maybe it was better we try to keep things as normal as they can be. What's happened to Lola, now Sarah, I can't believe it. We wanted to pay our respects in some way, get together to remember them.'

Alex caught Chloe's eye and shot her a look. Christ, the man was laying it on thick. They had told him not to give any indication that he had known the police would be attending that evening. They had told him to act normal. If this was his interpretation of that then it was a miracle anyone ever made a second visit to the group. It was almost as though Tim Cole thought he was now working alongside the police, like some undercover agent. Was he so arrogant that he didn't realise he was under suspicion too?

Alex scanned the room. A young tattooed man met her eye briefly before glancing down at his hands. The second man seated was older, broad-shouldered and with the kind of physique that almost managed to masquerade fat as muscle. His expression bore a mixture of anger and boredom and when his gaze fell upon Alex she could feel the contempt it carried.

Had she looked upon the young women's killer since entering this hall? Had one of these men been responsible for the injuries inflicted on Lola Evans? Was it one of these men who had taken Sarah?

'Are there usually this few of you?'

Tim shook his head. 'Connor's usually here, but…' He trailed off, silently acknowledging the futility of his words. Everyone knew that Connor was currently still in custody. 'No sign of Rachel tonight.'

'Rachel Jones?' Chloe asked. 'We've spoken with her.'

Tim raised a questioning eyebrow, but neither Alex nor Chloe was going to offer him any further details on the conversation that had taken place with Rachel.

Alex scanned the room once more. Just being in that hall was enough to make anyone depressed. It was bloody freezing in there: she'd glimpsed a radiator as they'd entered the room, but it was colder than the air outside, and the electric heater set up to the side of the seating area was doing little other than choke out the smell of burning dust. How this environment was conducive to supporting anyone's anxiety was a mystery.

'Is Rachel OK?' Tim ventured.

'Fine. Under the circumstances, she's decided to stay vigilant.'

The implication of Alex's words wasn't missed by any of the men in the room. If there was a time to spot a suspect – the slightest flicker of guilt – perhaps now, while they were there amongst one another, would be it.

Tim was shaking his head silently, as though attempting to comprehend all that had happened. Was he too responsive? Alex wondered. Too good to be true? Perhaps all this do-gooder persona was little more than an act, though an elaborate and effectively executed one.

Alex took a chair from the side of the room and joined the small circle of men. Chloe followed. Carl Henderson folded his beefy arms across his chest and regarded Alex with contempt. Sean Pugh's eyes flickered from the hands still linked in his lap to Chloe, seemingly distracted by her. Ignoring the looks, Chloe pulled her chair alongside Tim's and sat down.

'Each of you knew Lola Evans, is that right?'

Sean Pugh met Alex's eye as he nodded. Carl Henderson gave a grunt, but his focus remained on the far wall.

'Sarah Taylor?'

The second name received a similar response.

'Did any of you have any involvement with either woman beyond this group?'

The question was met with shakes of heads.

'Connor Price. Any of you know him beyond this group?'

'He was shagging Sarah, we all know that much.' Sean Pugh shrugged when Tim Cole shot him a look. 'What? Don't pretend you didn't know what was going on. It was obvious.'

'Did you ever say anything to either of them about it?' Alex asked.

Sean shook his head.

'Why do you come to these meetings?'

Sean looked taken aback by the question. Clearly this was one subject he thought might remain untouched. They needed to know why each of these men was there. It seemed to Alex that not everyone in attendance was necessarily struggling with anxiety.

Alex sensed an objection from Tim Cole and raised a hand to silence him. 'I'm investigating a murder,' she reminded him. 'Privacy is a privilege, I'm afraid, not a right.' She returned her attention to Sean. 'I want to know why each of you comes to these meetings. And I want to know where you were on Friday night.' Based on the time between the two boys seeing Sarah Taylor at the pub and the search that had taken place there two days later, it seemed likely that whoever had been holding her there had moved her on Friday. 'I'll be checking up on everything later, so let's not waste time by telling lies. Why are you here, Sean?'

The young man ran a hand over his face, his sleeve of tattoos flashing at Alex. 'I'm on probation,' he told her, his hands twisting in his lap. 'I've been to prison before for car theft. It's one of the things I'm supposed to do to keep from going back in.'

That would be easy enough to confirm, Alex thought. She wondered if car theft was this young man's only crime.

'Where were you on Friday?'

'At home. I'm back staying at my mother's; she was there.'

Alex turned to the third person, a bull of a man who had sat glaring at her the whole time she had been speaking, his bottom lip protruding slightly like a child contemplating a full-blown tantrum.

'Carl Henderson?'

The man nodded in acknowledgment of his name.

'Don't take this the wrong way, but you don't exactly seem the type to attend an anxiety and depression support group.'

'You saying I'm a murderer?'

Alex pulled a face. 'I didn't say that.'

The room was awkwardly silent. Sean Pugh distracted himself by picking dry skin from his elbow. Carl Henderson grimaced at Alex, the look enough to curdle the milk in Tim Cole's cup of tea.

'Could you please tell us when you started attending these meetings, Mr Henderson, and why you started coming here?'

Carl folded his large arms across his chest. 'April.' He held her eyes, defiant.

'Why?'

Carl shrugged. 'Something to do.'

Alex's lip curled. She glanced at Chloe, who had been watching Carl Henderson with fascination. 'That's it? Something to do?'

Carl gave another shrug.

'Friday. Where were you?'

'Work. Pulse, the club in Ponty. I work the doors.'

'You must get to meet a lot of women that way?'

Beside Chloe, Tim Cole's face had reddened so deeply he looked as though he might spontaneously combust. He looked imploringly at Chloe, willing her to say something to Alex. She gave him a shrug, mirroring Carl Henderson's nonchalance.

'S'pose so,' Carl finally responded.

Alex pushed her chair back. 'We'll be looking into the things you've told us, so don't be surprised if you hear from us again soon. In the meantime, you're all required to attend the station for DNA testing.'

Tim Cole followed Alex and Chloe from the building.

'I'm not happy with the way you went about things in there.'

'Oh, I'm sorry,' Alex said, her voice laced with sarcasm. 'Next time I'll try to be a bit more sensitive to people's emotions. I'm sure that'll do Sarah Taylor the world of good.'

Tim Cole had the decency to look away.

'The records we asked for earlier,' she said. 'Have you got them for us?'

Tim looked back to her, his expression altered now. 'That's what I needed to tell you. I went to get them earlier, when I arrived at the hall. They're gone.'

CHAPTER THIRTY-EIGHT

'Where the hell are those records?' Alex asked, giving voice to her thoughts. She gripped the steering wheel between tightened hands. She felt so frustrated by the lack of progress. Every minute that passed was another minute lost to Sarah.

'Tim seemed pretty surprised they weren't there,' Chloe said. 'Unless he's a good actor, I reckon he was genuine. If the only other person who had a key to that filing cabinet is Connor, looks as though we've got even more to go on.'

'Not necessarily,' Alex said, her voice betraying her frustrations. 'It still doesn't give us any real proof of anything.'

The Twitter account Tim Cole used as an emergency contact for group members had thrown up no results. Other than tweets with details of meeting times, there was nothing. No one had used it to contact him privately. It seemed an hour a week's contact with Tim Cole was enough for anybody.

They were going to have to release Connor Price from custody. They had held him for as long as they could, and in that time no concrete evidence against him had come to light. They couldn't keep him at the station for being a liar and an adulterer.

'He could get away with this,' she said, once again thinking out loud.

Chloe's head was turned away from her, facing the window. 'He wouldn't be the first,' she muttered.

Alex cast her a sideways glance. 'You've got to stop doing this to yourself, Chloe. You're torturing yourself.'

'I have to find out what happened.' Chloe turned to face her, her expression defiant.

Alex looked at the young woman incredulously. 'Were you not there in Blake's office the other day?'

'You expected me to just turn it off at his say-so?'

'You need to wait until we've found Lola's murderer before you do anything more about Luke, OK? You managed years without pursuing this – why is it so difficult now?'

'I tried to pursue it,' Chloe snapped defensively. 'I tried years ago and no one would listen to me, no one would take me seriously. I was just a kid back then. Things are different now.'

Those emails, Alex thought. Who the hell had sent them? Without them everything would have been different. Those emails seem to have prompted an accusation: she hadn't done enough. It was this guilt that was driving Chloe to behave the way she was now: so erratically; so completely out of character.

Perhaps it would have been better for Chloe if she'd stayed in London and not come back to Cardiff. Old wounds were bound to be reopened eventually, although maybe that's what Chloe had been hoping for.

'Promise me.'

Alex looked sideways at Chloe. The young woman's head was turned to the window, her face obscured by shadow.

'Chloe.'

'OK,' she said, too quickly. 'I know.'

Alex sighed. Chloe was bright, astute, intelligent, but here was her weakness. Given the wrong opportunities, she would throw her career away over a truth that might never see the light of day. Luke was gone: nothing would change that. Alex felt a responsibility to stop Chloe throwing her own life away.

'Your brother wouldn't want you to jeopardise your career.'

Chloe's head snapped towards her, her face stained with an uncharacteristic anger. 'What would you know about it? Luke wanted the truth. He would still want the truth, whatever it takes.'

'Ruining your life?' Alex challenged.

Chloe turned her head back to the window. 'This is my life. Some of us put our families before our careers.'

The words cut through Alex's reserve. They were all the more painful for their unexpectedness. This was a side to her colleague she had never seen before, and one she didn't want to make a habit of seeing.

'What's that supposed to mean?'

'Nothing. Forget it.'

Alex pulled the car to the kerbside, the engine still running. 'Clearly not nothing. What are you suggesting?' She didn't have a family. That ship had long since sailed. Was Chloe referring to her marriage breakdown?

Could she really be that cruel, to use it against her?

Of course she could. When someone hurt enough, the cruellest of things could pass their tongues.

Chloe reached for the handle and opened the car door. A blast of chilly evening air greeted them.

'Chloe, don't—'

'I'm sorry,' Chloe said, cutting her short as she stepped out the car.

'Don't be silly, Chloe, you don't—'

The car door was slammed shut. Alex sighed, unlocked her seatbelt and got out of the driver's side, calling to Chloe's back as the young woman walked the pavement of the main road that led towards the station.

What was happening to her? Just a few months ago, Chloe had been one of the most resilient young women Alex had ever known. She had seemed so grounded, so focused. But perhaps she hadn't really known her at all.

Alex stood by the car and watched as the distance between them grew. She wanted to believe in the young woman she had championed these past few months; the young woman she had requested to have work alongside her. Was her judgement of character so poor that she hadn't seen what had really been there all along?

Try as she might to push the notion loose, Alex was beginning to feel she had made a terrible mistake. DC Lane wasn't who she had thought she was. She was fragile, vulnerable: distracted. She wanted to help her, but she was restricted by professional boundaries. Without looking at the case files, they had nothing more to work from other than Chloe's suspicions.

Chloe knew it.

And now Alex was watching her unravel.

CHAPTER THIRTY-NINE

Chloe was tired and hungry and the thought of her bed was a momentary distraction from the scene she had created in DI King's car. She was wracked with shame at her behaviour and guilt at what she'd said. She hadn't meant it. She was angry with the world, but mostly just angry with herself. There were things she knew she should do now; things that had been put off and delayed because there hadn't been a right time. She knew now there was never going to be a right time, yet she was filled with a sense of urgency that begged that time should be now.

She stripped off in the bedroom and went to the shower, standing beneath a jet of water that was too hot and made her pale skin flare red. Each sting felt like a punishment, as though she deserved to feel this pain. She couldn't prove Luke's innocence. She had let Alex down. All the people she cared about were the very people she was letting down.

Her thoughts roamed to Scott, a momentary, welcome distraction, yet one that brought with it a sense of hopelessness. The thought of him made the sting of the hot water more acute. She wished she could stop herself from holding back. The old Chloe, a Chloe she hadn't seen for years, would have let him know exactly what she was thinking, regardless of the consequences. She couldn't remember the last time she had felt the touch of a man's skin against her own. She carried too much shame to ever let anyone get that close.

She turned off the shower, stepped out on to the cold tiles of the bathroom floor and wrapped herself in a towel. In the bedroom, she put on underwear and an oversized T-shirt before sitting on the edge of the bed to blow-dry her hair. She ran a finger over the mousepad on her laptop, prompting the screen into life. She had several tabs on the Internet open and she clicked on to her emails as her other hand ran a hairbrush across her scalp.

She would usually delete emails from addresses or names she didn't recognise, but this particular one was titled 'FAO DC Lane'. She felt her heart rate slow as her finger hovered over the mousepad. No one contacted her about work via her personal email. The past couple of months had taught her not to be so hasty with her use of the delete button. She had spoken to DC Mason about wanting to get an ID on an email address, telling him she had received anonymous written abuse. He was the station's resident IT geek: if anyone would know how to gain information from the address, he would. Chloe had made him promise not to mention the emails to anyone else at the station. If Dan had been suspicious of this, his face had failed to betray the fact.

Chloe had given him the email address, but Dan had come quickly back to her with the news that the IP address had been masked. There were ways of gaining further information on the sender, he'd told her, but they would involve needing a warrant.

Chloe had thanked him and told him not to worry about it.

She put the hairbrush down and opened the email. There was no message, only a link to a video file. She clicked on the link, knowing she shouldn't, but unable to resist. As the opening image appeared on the screen, Chloe felt nausea spread through her chest. Unable to watch, she closed the link and sat further back on her bed, her heart thumping beneath the towel she still wore wrapped around her.

She couldn't make sense of what she had just seen, yet the sight had chilled her to the bone.

CHAPTER FORTY

Alex got the call at ten to seven that morning, not long after getting out of the shower. She pinned her wet hair back hurriedly and dressed in the clothes she'd already laid out at the end of the bed. She called Chloe, who sounded so awake that Alex wondered whether she had been to sleep at all. Having agreed to pick her up on her way, Alex headed in her black Audi to the village of Taff's Well, from where she would head to the M4 motorway.

Neither woman mentioned what had happened the previous evening, but it had lingered, unsaid, during the call.

Chloe lived alone in the downstairs flat of an end-terraced house in Taff's Well. The street was tucked behind the main road, close to the rugby club. The noise of the A470 could be heard from the street, but other than that the area was peaceful. As Alex approached, she saw Chloe waiting on the pavement. She usually looked immaculate – something that never failed to make Alex feel comparatively frumpy – but that morning she looked nothing like the Chloe Alex was so used to seeing. Her hair was dishevelled, piled into a messy bun on the top of her head. She was without make-up. When she got into the car, Alex could see dark shadows circling her eyes.

'Is it Sarah Taylor?' Chloe asked, pulling the seatbelt around her. 'I hope not.'

Alex pulled back out on to the main road. It was early, but the morning's rush hour traffic was already starting to build. Chloe was uncharacteristically silent, her head turned away from Alex as she watched the houses slowly pass them by.

'Everything OK?'

'Fine.'

Alex knew enough to know that 'fine' invariably meant anything but.

'If it's what happened last night, it's forgotten.'

'I said I'm fine.'

The clipped tone was so unlike Chloe that it put an abrupt end to any further questions Alex might have had. She couldn't even bring herself to make small talk. She had wanted to discuss what had happened – make sure that Chloe knew what had been said had been forgiven (if she was completely honest, Alex didn't forget much) – and it smarted to have the olive branch she had offered snapped back in her face like that. Biting her tongue, Alex turned the radio on low, letting the sound of the morning's national news headlines fill the car's uncomfortable silence.

She didn't want to think about what might face them when they reached Penarth. She knew Cosmeston Lakes well. It was a beauty spot just over a half an hour drive from Alex's home town of Caerphilly that was popular with families who liked to spend lazy summer afternoons enjoying picnics on the grass that sloped down to the main lake, and with walkers who liked to venture further amidst the paths that intertwined amongst the other, smaller lakes.

The area was affluent. House prices were high and the locals prided themselves on being one of the most respectable and successful areas in Wales. Crime rates were low. Sarah Taylor – if she was in fact to be discovered there – had lived in Pontypridd, miles from Cosmeston Lakes. If she was there now, why had she been taken to a different borough?

And why there?

They slowed to a crawl as they neared the city. Chloe hadn't spoken and Alex was too distracted by her thoughts to attempt a conversation about the weather or the state of the economy as bemoaned by the politician whose voice was the only sound to break the quiet purr of Alex's Audi. She did her best to ignore the frostiness in the car, making no further attempt to question Chloe.

*

Cosmeston Lakes was a beautiful spot during the spring and summer months, but like anywhere else it looked considerably bleaker in the grey half-light of a cold January morning. There were few other cars in the car park when they arrived; the only others belonging to the pathologist and officers who had first responded to the call. The man who had made the call was sitting on a far wall at the side of the car park, near the closed-up café. He was dressed in running gear: neon trainers, full-length Lycra leggings, a skintight Lycra top and a thin beanie hat. Alex wondered why anyone would want to go out running at any time of year, but running on a January morning baffled her.

The man was talking with a uniformed officer. As they approached, the two stopped talking and the runner stood from the wall.

'DI King,' she introduced herself. 'This is DC Chloe Lane. You found the body?'

The man nodded. 'I almost missed it. There was something sticking up from the water, just slightly. I stopped to take a closer look.'

The 'something' the man had seen had later transpired to be Sarah Taylor's elbow. She had been in the water for considerably less time than Lola Evans, meaning there had been minimal damage to her body. Helen, the pathologist, estimated around two days, which made Connor Price's involvement impossible. Two days earlier, he had been in custody at the police station. Unless he was capable of being in two places at once, Connor Price hadn't put Sarah Taylor in the water.

Sarah was instantly recognisable. Her clothes had been removed, as Lola's had, leaving Sarah in only her underwear. Grace had told them the last time she'd seen Sarah she'd been wearing a dress, ready to go out for the evening. The dark thoughts that Alex had tried to keep at bay returned.

Like Lola, Sarah's hair had been cut. Yet there were considerable differences between the two victims. Lola had been tortured before she had been killed. Other than the very early effects of water to the body and some slight bruising to the face, Sarah Taylor showed no signs of physical injury.

Alex stood at the side of the wooden bridge and looked sadly at the body of Sarah Taylor. She had been brought to the lake's edge and laid on the damp grass. Her hands were tied behind her back and her legs tethered together at the knees. As with Lola, plastic bags had been attached to the ropes that held her bound.

'Unbroken,' Alex said, gesturing to the bags. 'Not enough time in the water? The river moves, but it's far more peaceful here at the lakes. Well…' she added, acknowledging the irony of her words.

'If those bags had been filled, would the body have resurfaced so soon?' Chloe mused.

'There's something else,' Helen said, crouching beside the body and placing a gloved hand to the girl's arm. 'Here.'

She lifted Sarah Taylor's arms and gently pushed aside one of the coils of rope that held her wrists bound. Angry tears to the young woman's skin showed an obvious attempt to free her arms. She looked up at Alex. 'I can't say anything for certain yet. The post-mortem will tell.'

She didn't need to explain what she meant: it was obvious to both Alex and Chloe what the pathologist was suggesting.

Sarah Taylor was still alive when she'd been put into the water.

CHAPTER FORTY-ONE

The team was gathered in the incident room. On the evidence board were photographs of Lola Evans and Sarah Taylor, both posing with smiles for the camera; both beautifully ignorant of what a near-fate held in store for them. Their faces filled Alex with a desperate sadness that was almost tangible. The older she grew, the deeper her mistrust in life became. Illness, disease, betrayal, death. Murder. It was so often all too easy to forget that there was any good in the world.

Alex had expected the superintendent to be present at the meeting that morning, but she hadn't seen him since she'd arrived at the station. It would be down to her to relay the details to him later, and she was determined to seek him out armed with something more than vague progress. At the current rate the case was moving that possibility seemed something still in too-distant reach.

Connor Price had been released from custody. The two other men from the support group — Sean Pugh and Carl Henderson — were due to attend the station that day for blood testing. The best possible outcome would be that one of them would prove a match for the second, unidentified, blood sample found at The Black Lion, bringing an end to their search for the killer. Should one of the men fail to show up that day, it would surely suggest an indication of his guilt.

'The records of people who attended the support group have conveniently gone AWOL,' Alex told the team. 'According to Tim Cole, the only two people who had access to them were him and Connor Price. The records are only kept for emergency purposes and the last time they were checked was May last year, when Sean Pugh had a panic attack. It seems the rest of the group thought he was having a heart attack, so Tim accessed the files to contact his mother after an ambulance had been called. The files were there then, so I've asked Tim Cole for a list of people who've attended the group between then and now.'

'So we're relying on Tim Cole to give us an honest account?' one of the DCs asked.

'For the moment, yes.'

There had been a few other developments of which many members of the team were still unaware. DC Mason had spent considerable time gathering information on the history of the pub and the people who had lived and worked there. He now shared what he had uncovered with the rest of the team. Alex passed the focus on to him.

'The Black Lion belongs to a man named Clive Beckett. There's been a dispute over land ownership and freehold which has been going on for the last four years. The pub's a listed building, so application for demolition was refused. The nature of the listing means no restoration work can be undertaken either.'

'Makes sense,' one of the team said sarcastically. 'So the building's just left in that state?'

'Yep. Stupid, right? Clive Beckett seems to be something of a businessman, by all accounts. The turnover at the Lion was small fry. Seems he was happy to just let the place go after a while.'

'He been contacted yet?' asked Alex.

'No. He moved to Australia a few years back. I've contacted his company, spoken to one of his employees. Left a message for him to get back to us as soon as possible.'

'Family?'

'One son and an ex-wife who both still live in South Wales. They were divorced years ago.'

'How long has the place been empty?' one of the other DCs asked.

'About five years,' Dan told him.

'Would either Clive Beckett's son or ex-wife still have access to the pub?' Alex queried. 'We need to speak to them, find out when they last went to the place. We need to find out exactly who's had access, particularly during the past few weeks. By all accounts, there's been no legal reason why anyone should have been inside the building. There was no work going on there, no surveys being done.'

Was there a link between this building and the parks? Someone who had reason to be in the grounds of each?

'Did Beckett and his family live in the pub?' It was the first time Chloe had spoken up since the meeting began.

'No,' Dan answered. 'Clive Beckett and his wife lived in Lisvane at the time. He owned a few different pubs around South Wales, all of which were sold during the divorce. He employed managers to run them, but the recession meant they all took a hit by the looks of it.'

'Do we have contact details for his ex?' Alex asked.

Dan nodded.

She was impressed. DC Mason, though with them only a short time, was already proving to be invaluable when it came to research. He worked quickly and he was thorough. There had been a time not so long ago when Chloe had been the same – in fact, Alex had considered that Chloe Lane and Daniel Mason together would be a partnership worth having on board any investigation – but her younger colleague's focus had since slipped and she seemed permanently distracted.

Despite her feelings of loyalty to the young woman, Alex knew Harry had been right about his emphasis on focus. They couldn't afford anyone on the team to be anything but fully committed to these cases, and to finding out who murdered these girls and left their bodies in the water.

'I'll contact Beckett's ex-wife once we're done here,' Alex told Dan. 'Let's focus on what we know about both women. Sarah's body being found has changed everything. The pathologist reckons her body was in the water for no more than two days, meaning Connor Price couldn't have put her there. He was in custody at the time.'

'Doesn't mean he hasn't been involved.'

'True. There's still the possibility we're looking at two people working together. We know that Lola's blood was found at The Black Lion. We also now know that the second sample isn't a match with Connor or Sarah, but as you rightly say, it doesn't necessarily prove Connor's innocence. Some of the men from the support group attended by Connor, Lola and Sarah are due in for testing today. Quite frankly, the longer this goes on, the more I'm beginning to doubt Connor Price's involvement. Yes, he'd been having an affair with Sarah, but there's no evidence of any romantic or sexual link with Lola. There's no doubt that the same man, or men, is responsible for both women's murders. These aren't crimes of passion – they're premeditated, calculated. We're looking for someone thorough, someone clever, someone who knew both women and had access to Bute Park and to Cosmeston Lakes. CCTV footage from cameras at the entrance to Bute Park on Boulevard de Nantes has picked up a white van. It's not the most helpful footage – the plate blurs out on a close-up. 8.45 p.m. on the twelfth of January. It's a Ford Transit – no other identifying features, obviously. That would make our lives far too easy. I'd like you two to chase up any calls that have come in during the past twelve hours,' Alex said, addressing a couple of officers sitting to Chloe's left. 'Let's see if we can glean anything useful amongst the time-wasters. Any questions?'

'Why water?'

Alex looked to Chloe.

'Why is he putting his victims in water?'

It was something Alex had pondered on her return to the station earlier that day. 'I've wondered the same. But without any further clues as to who this man is, it's almost impossible to say. It was clear today that less of an attempt had been made to sink Sarah's body than had been made with Lola.' Alex paused. Talking about these young women as though they were nothing more than corpses made her nauseous. She always tried to attach each victim to a partner, to parents, to friends, tried to imagine herself at such a loss.

'Something from his past perhaps?' Chloe suggested.

Alex nodded. 'Likely. We need to find out more, and as soon as we can.'

'The other women from the support group, should we be keeping an eye out for them?'

Something else that had crossed Alex's mind. She wished they had the resources to ensure that every other woman who had attended the group had security until this man was identified and locked up, but that kind of service was far beyond their means. 'At the moment, the only other woman we know for certain who was attending the group regularly is Rachel Jones. Tim Cole is supposed to be getting back to us today with the other names. We've already spoken with Rachel and she's aware she's to remain vigilant. Let's be careful not to scaremonger though, OK?'

Her words were received with nods.

'Right. Let's get to work then.'

DC Mason handed her a note with the name and contact number of Clive Beckett's ex-wife. As she took it from him and commended him for being so thorough, Alex watched Chloe slink from the room without acknowledging her colleagues.

What was the matter with her? She'd been like it all day, barely speaking to Alex in the car both to and from Cosmeston Lakes that morning. She found it difficult to believe that all this was over the brief clash of words – barely enough to describe as an argument –

that they'd had in the car the previous evening. Alex went out into the corridor, but Chloe was already gone. She was about to head to her own office when Superintendent Blake called her into his.

*

'I've asked for the post-mortem on Sarah Taylor's body to be considered priority, so I'm hoping we might be able to—' Alex stopped talking, aware that Harry was paying her words no attention. His mind was elsewhere, betrayed by the glazed expression his face wore.

'What's the matter?' she asked, closing the door to his office behind her.

He raised an eyebrow. 'Here.' Gesturing to the screen of his desktop computer, he reached for the monitor and turned it towards Alex.

There was a video paused on the screen: a low-lit room, walls adorned with posters and flyers; an unmade bed. On the bed, naked except for a pair of black French knickers, was a young woman, barely in her twenties and possibly still a teenager. Her brunette hair hung long, partially obscuring her face.

Alex looked at the superintendent questioningly. 'What's this?'

He clicked play. The girl rose on to her knees, a thumb hooked into her underwear as the fingers of her other hand pushed back a length of hair from her face. She stared directly into the camera, her eyes widening as she responded to an unheard instruction from her audience on the other side of the screen.

Alex felt the office floor shift beneath her.

'It's her, isn't it? Harry asked, pausing the recording once more.

Alex looked back at the screen. She looked so different, yet so unmistakably her.

'What happens next?'

'Here, or on the recording?'

'The recording.'

'You don't want to watch for yourself?'

Alex shot him a scathing look. 'No.'

Harry shook his head. 'You can use your imagination.'

They both looked back to the monitor, though neither wanted to acknowledge what they were met with there.

On the monitor, DC Chloe Lane remained poised, frozen; her thumb still hooked into her knickers.

CHAPTER FORTY-TWO

It was easier that day for Chloe to gain access to the things she needed. She had slipped from the team meeting without speaking to anyone and gone to a quiet corner of the incident room to access a computer. There was never going to be a right time. Now seemed as good a time as any, and she already felt she had wasted too much.

No one believed her brother wasn't a killer. Chloe knew that despite Alex's loyalties, she too was sceptical. Why shouldn't she be, when all the evidence stacked against Luke was so incriminating? Until she had something to back up her suspicions, even Alex wasn't going to take her seriously.

Chloe retrieved a memory stick from her pocket. She had tried the previous afternoon to access the files she needed, but had been interrupted by Dan Mason. She'd waited until today for another opportunity.

She turned the sound off on the speakers and logged on to the system. The day before, she had managed to access the files, but there hadn't been enough time to download them. She returned to them now, keeping one eye on a couple of colleagues talking at the far side of the room.

She clicked copy and waited.

*

Alex had been caught in a shower soon after leaving the station and her hair – longer than she had allowed it to grow in some time – was a tangled mess, pulled back and knotted into the smallest of buns at the nape of her neck. Her shirt and jacket were creased and she felt sticky beneath her clothing despite the bite of January air that nipped at her skin as she got from the car.

Her mind was already a messy tangle of thoughts: Lola, Sarah, Chloe. What the hell had she witnessed on the screen of that computer?

It occurred to her later that her first thought when she had seen him had been of her appearance, and she had reprimanded herself for having been so vain. Yet, had she known she would see him there, in the supermarket, Alex knew that despite everything else that was going on she would have made more of an effort. It would have done little to soften the blow of what she had seen, but simply being slightly more presentable might have done something – anything – to prevent her from feeling so inadequate.

As it was, when she saw Rob in the supermarket that evening she both looked and felt a mess.

One of the worst parts of it – a part that insulted Alex so keenly, though there were so many other elements of that moment that caused equal offence – was the fact that Rob had tried to pretend at first that he hadn't seen her. He had glanced along the aisle, looked directly at her, and turned away quickly as though she didn't exist. It had stung like a slap, and even hours later she found herself unable to let it go.

But then there was the other thing: the thing that rendered Alex momentarily immobile, frozen by the rows of baked beans as she looked on in disbelief.

There was a child sitting on Rob's shoulders.

A boy of around five years old was sitting on his shoulders, laughing, as a girl – slightly older, maybe seven – danced in the aisle, her wellingtons making sucking noises each time she lifted a foot from the floor. There was a woman crouched just behind the girl, scanning a row of tinned soups. Alex watched, transfixed, as the woman turned, looked up and said something to Rob. She continued to watch as her ex-husband said something in response and the woman stood, taking the young girl by the hand.

She didn't allow time to talk herself out of it.

'Rob,' Alex said, giving the woman a brief smile as she approached them. The woman smiled back. She was attractive, Alex caught herself thinking. Younger than she was. Quite a bit younger.

The look on Rob's face said he hadn't expected her to be quite so confident. 'Alex.' The word wobbled off his tongue. 'Uhh... nice to see you.'

Alex narrowed her eyes slightly. Then the truth of what she was witnessing hit her. The woman was smiling at her, the kind of pained smile that delivered an unwelcome pity. She had clearly heard the name 'Alex' before. This woman knew who she was, in the context of 'ex-wife' at least.

'And you,' Alex said, having to force the words out. 'Anyway, bit of a rush. See you.'

The little girl smiled up at her before continuing to suck up her wellingtons from the supermarket floor. Alex turned and headed back down the aisle, her heart pounding. How stupid she had been, she thought, as she abandoned her basket of shopping near the foyer of the supermarket. How naive to think that for once she had been the one who had been calling the shots.

She hurried back to the car and locked herself inside. Beneath her shirt, her heart was pounding. She felt sticky and hot despite the cold. She pulled off her coat and turned on the engine. From the pocket of her coat, her mobile began to ring. It linked up to the car's Bluetooth system. She looked to the dash.

Chloe.

Alex hesitated. The coward in her wanted to ignore the call. How was she supposed to talk to Chloe as though everything was normal, when everything was so clearly not? She couldn't rid her brain of the image she had seen in Harry's office. She wasn't sure she could bring herself to hold a conversation with Chloe without mentioning the video. Keeping if from her would be as good as lying and Alex didn't want to do that, not to Chloe. She wasn't sure she could.

She didn't have to. The ringing stopped, her phone cutting Chloe to the answerphone.

CHAPTER FORTY-THREE

The following morning, an image of Chloe similar to the one that had been paused on the screen of the superintendent's office computer adorned the front page of one of the local newspapers. Alex stopped at a garage for petrol on the way into work and was stalled by the weatherproof plastic boxes on the forecourt that were home to the daily papers. She felt physically sickened.

Who could despise Chloe so much they'd want to make her suffer in this way?

Harry Blake had held off from speaking to Chloe about the video file he had been sent the day before, clearly uneasy about how to broach the subject. Now these images adorned the newspaper's front page the entire station would be aware of it. The superintendent was bound to be furious this morning, wishing he had spoken with her yesterday. Alex's heart ached for Chloe. She didn't understand the images – she couldn't imagine Chloe, who she had always known to be so sensible, allowing herself to be photographed or filmed in such a way – but until she had the facts, she didn't want to judge. Over the past six months Alex had grown close to Chloe. But how well did she know her really?

How well could anyone know another person?

She grabbed a paper from the plastic display case and went inside to pay for her petrol. After leaving the forecourt, Alex pulled off the main road and into a side street. She cut the engine and drew the newspaper on to her lap.

Cop a Load of This

Those five words alone were enough to fill Alex with an anger so powerful it might have brought her to frustrated tears. It was typical tabloid wordplay, crass and unimaginative. No doubt the 'journalist' who had written it had been impressed with his or her own efforts.

This webcam stunner is twenty-eight-year-old Chloe Lane,

the 'article' began,

a Detective Constable with the South Wales Police.

Even in the first sentence they couldn't get their facts right, Alex thought. Chloe was twenty-six. How reliable was the rest of the piece going to be in its presentation of the 'facts'?

Taken several years ago, this still from a webcam shows the young DC writhing on a bed whilst accepting payment for her 'services'. For more, see page six.

Alex felt anger course through her. Payment? For God's sake, these parasites just made things up as they went along. What evidence did they have to suggest anything of the sort? Plenty of young women made the mistake of allowing boyfriends to photograph or film them in ways they might later regret, but revenge porn was no proof of anything more. Amidst the previous evening's thoughts of Rob and of the children she had seen him with – the family it looked as if he had become a part of – Alex had kept returning to Chloe. She had come to the conclusion that her young colleague was the victim of revenge porn. It was an area where Alex had little experience, although the numbers of complaints filed to the police was increasing at an astonishing rate. She assumed that the number of incidents was likely to be far greater than the complaints. Many women – and, in an increasing number of cases, men – were likely to be too embarrassed or ashamed to admit what had been done.

The paper was breaking the law. It was an offence to make public any intimate or sexual image or video that was otherwise private. They should be held to account for this, Alex thought. Prosecuted. Yet again, the press seemed to consider itself above the law.

She turned to page six. The words that greeted her plunged her from righteous fury into confusion.

Sent to us by an anonymous user of the webcam site 'GirlsOnline', the two and a half minute footage shows DC Lane responding to requests she receives via the site's chatroom. The recording – in which Chloe Lane appears more like a member of the cast of Geordie Shore than one of Her Majesty's serving officers – sees the young woman accepting instruction from a paying member of the site. Some of the images that appear later in the footage are too graphic to be printed here. Using the alias Belle90, Chloe Lane's profile cites her vital statistics as 32-26-34 (bra size C).

It was everything Alex hated about the modern press and about this publication in particular. She'd previously been pestered by journalists from the same paper. This wasn't about professional conduct or public interest – it was merely about scandal and sex. No doubt the newspaper's website article on the 'story' would feature countless different images from the footage in an attempt to exploit as much cheap titillation from the recording as possible; yet another excuse to flaunt naked flesh amidst the real headlines of the day.

Alex sat back and let the rest of the article swim on the page in front of her as she tried to arrange her thoughts. Had Chloe known this was going to happen? Yesterday morning she had been acting strangely, and though Alex realised she was bearing the weight of her brother's death on her shoulders, she had talked about him over a week earlier without her mood being so suddenly affected. The footage had turned up in the superintendent's email account the previous morning.

Did Chloe know he had received it?

She couldn't make sense of anything the article reported. Chloe would never have done that, surely. And yet, it so clearly was her. A younger her, a different her, but undoubtedly her. Revenge porn; sadly, Alex could comprehend that. But this? Webcam sites. Payment. This was all too much for her to get her head around.

She started the engine back up and flung the paper on to the passenger seat, flipping it over so she would no longer have to be subjected to the sight of Chloe in her underwear.

CHAPTER FORTY-FOUR

The tension in the room was tangible; it snagged at the edges of Superintendent Harry Blake's office desk and caught on every inhalation Chloe took, suffocating her. Every time she opened her mouth to speak, she felt herself choking. She had known this was going to happen, but knowing was never going to be enough to help her prepare for it. How could she possibly have prepared? No matter what she said, she knew what was coming.

The superintendent had asked her to take a seat, which did little to calm Chloe's anxieties. It was embarrassing enough to know what he had seen – to know what the entire station had no doubt by now seen – and now his awkwardness was making everything worse. She could see a sheen of sweat on his forehead, glistening on his pale grey skin.

What was he so panicked about, Chloe wondered? None of the papers had published pictures of him in his underwear.

'Do you want to explain it?'

Of course she didn't. She didn't want to explain it any more than she wanted to be sitting in that office right there and then, burning beneath the heat of the office strip lighting. She could explain it, but what would that achieve? The outcome was going to be the same.

'The money was good.'

It wasn't a lie: the money had been great. More than she had ever earned before. More than she could make as a police officer in a month.

Her flippancy wasn't well received. Harry Blake pursed his lips. His cheeks reddened slightly. 'That's it. That's your explanation?'

'It was years ago, sir, before I joined the police. I didn't break any laws. I needed money. I got a job.'

Blake's left eyebrow rose at the word 'job'. 'We are in the middle of a major investigation, one that has gained a lot of public interest over the past couple of days. The last thing we need is…' he gestured at the newspaper on his desk, as if unable to find the right words, 'this.'

'I'm sorry.'

The superintendent looked at her incredulously. 'Sorry? That's it?'

'I don't know what else I can say, sir. I can't undo it, no matter how much I'd like to be able to.'

Blake rubbed his forehead and sighed. 'Tell me what you've copied from the database.'

Chloe felt her stomach double over. Whatever she'd been expecting, it hadn't been that. How did he know?

'Sir, I—'

'DC Lane, please. Don't waste my time.'

Dan Mason, she thought. He hadn't seen her yesterday, but the day before that he had interrupted her as she'd tried to download the files. Clearly he had seen more than she realised. Had she even logged out after being interrupted by him? She'd been panicked; she couldn't remember.

How much had Dan seen?

'Have you accessed files relating to your brother?'

Chloe nodded.

'Bloody hell, Lane. I told you to leave this alone. This,' he said, pushing the newspaper across the desk towards her, as though she needed reminding of its front page, 'is exactly the kind of publicity we could do without. And now this.'

His voice was shaking with anger. She didn't blame him. He was bound by his duties as superintendent just as she had been bound by her own set of responsibilities at the time that video footage had been taken.

She wished she'd waited to access those files, but like so many other things in her life it was now too late to go back and change it.

'I gave you an instruction to wait with regards to your brother's case and you ignored it. You accessed files you had no right to. Have you taken copies?'

She shook her head.

Blake raised an eyebrow, trying to prompt an admission from her.

'I haven't, sir.' The lie came so easily.

He sighed loudly. 'I need everyone on this team to be focused and, at the moment, Lane, you are not. First the complaint made by Patrick Sibley, then the papers, now this. I'm going to have to suspend you from duties—'

'Sir, no—'

'Until our current case is completed. DC Lane, I'm sorry, I am, but you've not left me with much choice. Accessing closed case files like that is a disciplinary offence, you understand that, don't you?'

'Sir, I… yes. I understand that.' She gripped the arms of her seat and forced back tears. No man had ever seen her cry; she wasn't going to change that now.

Why now? She watched the superintendent's focus shift uncomfortably from her before settling itself on the desk in front of him. Who had sent that clip to the station? Who had sent it to the papers – and why had they chosen to do so now? First the emails, then this. This was no coincidence. Someone seemed intent on revisiting her past, and wasn't that what she herself had wanted all these years?

But not like this.

She stood from her chair. 'I'm sorry, sir,' she said again, knowing her words would be met with derision. He looked away from her, down at his desk but somehow managing to avoid the front of the newspaper.

*

In the corridor, Chloe headed straight for the toilets, moving quickly to avoid colleagues. She flung the door to the ladies open and stood at one of the sinks, the palms of her hands pressed against the cold porcelain. Heat coursed through her, her heart racing and her head pounding. She couldn't bring herself to look at her own reflection.

She had done it for Luke. All of it. And now she would be able to do nothing.

Chloe stayed in the toilets longer than was necessary, once again trying to avoid seeing anyone. She left at the wrong time; as she emerged from the ladies, a group of uniformed officers was heading along the corridor in her direction. Chloe hurried for the stairs, but wasn't fast enough to miss the wolf-whistle thrown back in her direction. On any other day she would have turned back to see which one of them it was – would have confronted it head on – but that day she couldn't bring herself to face him. She just wanted to be as far away from the place as possible.

*

Alex had wanted to stay at the station that morning to check through the list of support group member names Tim Cole had emailed across, but an early call from Helen Collier saw her heading to Cardiff to the University Hospital of Wales. She had asked DC Mason to look into the names Tim Cole had provided, and to check for them on the Niche database: a record of every person who had ever made contact with South Wales Police. Under normal circumstances, she would have taken DC Lane to the hospital with her. She sometimes wondered whether anything was going to be 'normal' again, or whether in fact normal had ever existed.

Now she found herself standing in the pathology lab, knowing it probably hadn't.

Sarah Taylor's naked body was laid out on an examination table. The condition of the examination meant that it was now impossible to see her as the smiling young woman whose face still adorned the board of the incident room. She was a drowning victim. A lost girl. Everything that had been a part of her – all the things that had made her the person her family and friends had loved – was gone, leaving a shell so grotesque that Alex's attention was unable to stay fixed for more than seconds at a time.

'She was alive when she went into the water,' Helen confirmed.

Alex nodded. They had suspected so – feared so – and now she couldn't help but linger over thoughts of Sarah's final moments. Drowning wasn't a peaceful death. It was torturous, violent; desperate. The torn skin on her legs and wrists showed a valiant struggle to free herself, presumably both in the water and before.

'There's rupturing to the muscles in the neck and shoulders, suggesting a struggle for air. The water was so cold that given any further time it might have induced cardiac arrest, but she was likely to have been dead within minutes of entering the water.'

Minutes. She made it sound like such a brief space of time; so inconsequential. When you were facing your own death, Alex imagined it was its very own lifetime.

'There was vomit found in her throat,' Helen continued, sparing Alex none of the grim details. 'Vomiting is common in cases of drowning, usually occurring soon before loss of consciousness. It seems in this case that the vomit was trapped. It was likely her mouth had been blocked with something, meaning she drowned through inhalation of water through her nose.'

Alex looked down at the table, her eyes fixing on the cool length of steel that ran beneath the young woman's body. Once again, she couldn't quite bring herself to look at the greying skin of the body that had once been a living being, young and beautiful.

'Her body didn't sink,' she said, thinking out loud.

Helen shook her head. 'She wouldn't have resurfaced that quickly. Given the temperature, that would have taken longer than a week. She was probably visible the duration she was there. Not many people passing this time of year, obviously.'

Lola Evans had sunk to the bottom of the River Taff, resurfacing when the effects of the water had begun to bloat her body. She had been in the water for anything from ten to fourteen days and obvious attempts had been made to keep her body submerged. It didn't seem logical that the killer's efforts to hide his crime would be better first time around than the second. Either he had panicked when he'd put Sarah Taylor in the lake, or—

'The bags.'

Helen looked at her questioningly.

'The bags on her wrist weren't broken, were they?'

Helen gestured to the worktop that lined the left side of the lab. 'They're over there. All intact.'

Lola's body had been weighed down by the plastic carrier bags tethered to the ropes at her wrists. The bags had been ripped and torn: maybe by the force of the water that had swept her downstream; maybe by whatever had been placed into the bag to hold her body under. Perhaps by both. Either way, they had been little more than scraps of plastic by the time her body had resurfaced.

Alex glanced back at Sarah Taylor's corpse. What if those bags hadn't been used to weigh her down, to keep her submerged?

What if they were merely a sign?

It's me again.

I was here.

Alex allowed her focus to linger on the body of Sarah Taylor.

Whatever happened next, she couldn't let yet another woman to fall victim to the killer.

CHAPTER FORTY-FIVE

Clive Beckett's son was a handsome man in his thirties. He was dressed in a suit, having come straight from work. Alex had already found out that he worked in a bank and that he was married, with a newborn baby who he cited as the reason for his permanent sleep-starved state. He sat opposite Alex and drank an Americano in record speed, getting up and leaving her while he went to the café's counter to order a second.

'Sorry,' he apologised, as he returned and sat back down. 'I'm all over the place today.'

'You wanted to speak to me about your father,' she prompted.

At the mention of the man, Martin Beckett's expression altered. 'You've spoken to him?'

'Not yet. We've spoken with one of his colleagues. We're waiting for your father to get back to us.'

'Right. Good luck with that.'

'What do you mean by that?'

Martin Beckett gave a dismissive shrug. 'Doesn't really put himself out for other people. He'll get round to it in his own time, when it suits him.'

The animosity Martin felt towards his father was in no way subtle. Alex wondered whether any information he had would be reliable.

'Why do you want to speak with him?'

'Routine, that's all. I'm afraid I can't say too much. While a case is ongoing, everything is confidential, I'm afraid.'

'Of course. Sorry.' Martin sat forward in his seat and looked across to the counter as though checking that his coffee was on its way. 'Something's happened at the pub though, hasn't it? A few people have mentioned the police cordon. A young woman's body was found there, wasn't it? Was it that missing woman who's been on the news? There are all sorts of rumours flying about.'

Alex's thoughts flitted once more to DC Lane. How many more rumours would be circulating in the aftermath of the paper's actions? One of the duties of the police was to reassure the public. Scandal, in whatever form, was unlikely to help them achieve that. Though none of this was directly Chloe's fault, she knew that blame would inevitably be placed at her door.

She hadn't yet had a chance to speak with Chloe, though she knew that Superintendent Blake had temporarily suspended her from duties. Alex realised he'd had little choice, yet the knowledge hadn't been enough to suppress the anger she felt. There were too many questions that needed to be answered; there were too many things that needed to be explained. Until she knew the facts Alex wasn't prepared to assume the worst. Chloe deserved a chance to tell her side of the story.

Alex's lip curled in response to Martin's comment, and he raised a hand in apology.

'Sorry. I get it. I'm not supposed to ask. The place has been empty for years though, you know that, don't you?'

'Yes. Issues with the freehold?'

'My father's given up on it. Tried to fight the authorities, but stopped trying in the end. He doesn't need the money – it became more a matter of principle, I think. He's a man who doesn't like to lose. It's a listed building, you see, so there's no knocking it down and no converting it. Stupid really. Gets to stand there empty. Not that anyone would want it, I wouldn't have thought.'

'Why do you say that?'

'Well, not the nicest history.'

'What do you mean by that?'

'Well, there was a death there, years ago. Woman who lived in the flat above the pub. You know about this, do you?'

Alex's face made it obvious that she knew little of the pub's history. Over his second coffee, Martin Beckett filled her in on some of the details. He told Alex that his family had never lived in the pub, but had had a house on the outskirts of Cardiff, in Lisvane, as DC Mason had already found out. His father had rented out the flat above the pub. The woman who had lived there had drowned in the bathtub – an accident whilst she was drunk.

Alex wracked her brain for a memory of the case, but she couldn't recall one. She would look into it later.

'That woman split my family apart.'

Alex sat back in her chair, studying Martin curiously. She said nothing, allowing him to continue.

'Mind you, if she hadn't, someone else would have. My father – he probably won't tell you this bit when you speak to him, if you get to speak to him – he had a bit of a problem with keeping it in his pants, shall we say. He was sleeping with the woman who lived in the flat. Seems that's how she kept up with her rent.'

Alex tried to guess at Martin's age, working out how long ago all this had taken place.

'Your mother found out?'

'I think she might have known for a while, but she stayed with him for me.'

Alex wondered if a chat with the former Mrs Beckett might be necessary. For now, she couldn't see how any of this would be relevant to the cases they were currently investigating. Whoever had taken Lola and Sarah had needed somewhere secluded, secure.

Their killer might not have chosen the best of places, but perhaps it had been his only option at the time. But clearly he had known the flat was there.

'I'd like to take your details please, Mr Beckett. Just in case we need anything later on.' She took a small notebook and a pen from her bag, turned to a clean page and passed both to Martin Beckett. He wrote down his name and number and passed them back to her.

CHAPTER FORTY-SIX

Alex had never seen Chloe like this. She was without make-up and dark circles shadowed her usually bright eyes. She looked as though she'd been crying. Chloe was usually so strong, so in control. What was all this doing to her?

Chloe held the door aside for Alex, though she refused at first to meet her eye. Despite her frustration with Chloe's breaking of the rules, Alex knew she was in no position to judge. She should have admitted to her own taking of Emily Phillips's post-mortem report, but she couldn't while their current case was still ongoing. She felt sympathy for Chloe; she felt a loyalty towards her, but she also had a commitment to catching Lola Evans's and Sarah Taylor's killer.

Alex had felt an initial anger towards Daniel Mason for reporting Chloe to the super, but the reaction had been short-lived. The detective constable worked by the rules, as Chloe should have: as she knew they all should. He had done what he thought was right.

Though she had never seen the inside of Chloe's flat before, Alex assumed its current state couldn't possibly be its usual one. Chloe was usually so immaculately presented, so seemingly in control and organised. That day, the place was chaos. The files she had previously taken to Alex's house now lay strewn on the living room's laminate flooring, their contents sprawled at random. Amongst them, the occasional face stared up at Alex, each pair of eyes seeming to follow her as she tiptoed through the debris of Chloe's past.

It seemed to Alex that the flat was sparsely furnished, as though it wasn't inhabited fully but merely used by someone who was just passing through.

Did Chloe have any intention of staying here when she first moved in?

Did she have any intention of staying with the police when she first joined up? With hindsight, Alex speculated whether everything the young woman seemed to have worked so hard for had been with a singular aim: proving her brother's innocence. Though her intentions were in many ways honourable, it all seemed to Alex such a tragic waste.

'Tell me,' Alex said. 'I want to help you, I want you back at work, but I can't do anything until I know the truth. All of it.'

'Coffee?' Chloe offered.

Alex wondered how many she'd already had – she seemed wired. 'Thanks.'

Alex followed Chloe through to the kitchen. The flat was small, with one bedroom, but it was neatly appointed, making maximum use of what was minimal space. She watched silently as Chloe set about preparing coffee for them both.

'It's you in the pictures?'

'Yeah, it's me,' Chloe said, her back turned to Alex.

Alex had studied the face in the newspaper photographs, though it had saddened her to do so. Chloe had looked so different back then – her natural hair much darker than the bottle blonde she now chose; her frame much slighter now than it had been then – but when she looked closely, there she was: the pale skin, the high cheekbones; the bright eyes. She had hoped not to find her in the image, as though not seeing her would make the stark reality of the photographs untrue.

She was beginning to feel an almost maternal loyalty to Chloe, a need to keep her protected from all the nastiness that life seemed intent on throwing at her. It now felt to Alex she had arrived far too late. Chloe's young life had seen plenty before it had barely begun. Alex realised that what she knew was likely to have barely skimmed the surface. She couldn't have been more than nineteen in the images that the papers had so happily spread amongst their pages. What had driven her to it?

'I could tell you I did it because I had to, but it all sounds a bit pathetic,' Chloe said, turning to Alex and handing her a coffee.

She went back into the living room and sank into a corner of the sofa, clutching her mug of coffee to her chest. Her small frame seemed engulfed by the cushions that surrounded her.

To the side of the sofa, on the floor, lay several newspapers. Alex recognised their front page stories: knew that Chloe's own lay not-so-hidden somewhere amongst the pages of each.

She sat at the other end of the sofa.

'What's been said back at work?'

'Don't worry about what's been said,' Alex said too quickly. Her hasty response gave Chloe the answer she'd been looking for: too much had already been said. Stopping gossip was sadly beyond Alex's powers. There were certain male officers at the station who'd been not-so-secretly enjoying the rumours that the previous couple of days had generated. Colleague solidarity was something they were unfamiliar with, and she imagined, with disdain, that there were a couple who had returned to the images splashed across the papers with relish.

It had always been obvious Chloe's looks garnered a fair share of male interest, and why wouldn't they? She was slim, attractive, the kind of pretty that didn't flaunt itself but was nonetheless obvious. Alex had once thought she might have been involved with a former male colleague, but her suspicions had been proven wrong. Rather than enjoying the attention her looks received – as many young women might have – Chloe shunned male interest. Perhaps here was the explanation for that.

'I was brought up as a Jehovah's Witness.'

The comment came from nowhere and took Alex by surprise. Chloe had never mentioned this before, although she had never really spoken of her past before. Something else that was now beginning to make sense.

She didn't know what to say, so said nothing. Thankfully, Chloe filled the silence.

'It wasn't a religion, not where my parents were concerned. It was a cult. For years I thought it was normal, but then I got to about eleven, twelve, and realised it was far from it. My brother and I weren't allowed to do anything. We couldn't mix with the other kids at school, so eventually they stopped bothering to make the effort. We were outsiders. They thought we were weird. The teachers used to be nice to us – overly nice. As I got older, I realised they just pitied us. We were the resident freak show.' Chloe looked down at the coffee in her hands. She had wanted this moment for so long – had wanted to be able to confide in someone with all the things she'd kept hidden for so many years – but not like this. She'd been forced into this. It felt like a confession. She supposed that's exactly what it was.

'Things just got worse at comprehensive school,' she continued. 'It was like all our abnormalities became highlighted. My parents began to realise they were losing their control. The more they fought for it, the more Luke and I rebelled. Especially me. I did everything I could to piss them off.'

Chloe stood from the sofa, turned and lifted her sweater. A tattoo of a black butterfly spread across the base of her spine. 'They both went mental,' she said, sitting back down. 'And I enjoyed every second of it.' She gave Alex a sad smile. 'I bloody hate that tattoo though.'

'I was excommunicated from the watch tower at seventeen,' she explained. 'It was a wonder it hadn't happened earlier really, but I think my parents had done some grovelling with the elders. It hadn't been for my sake. They were worried about their own reputation amongst the group, about being kicked out themselves.

That church meant more to them than anything. Anyway, three months later I left home. I was still studying for my A-levels. I actually liked school – it was the only escape I had.'

'How did you manage to finish school?' asked Alex. 'Where were you living?'

'I rented a room.'

'But how did you—'

Alex cut herself short, realising the naivety of her own question. Of course, she already knew how Chloe had made the money she'd needed to move out of her childhood home. Everyone now knew.

'I worked in a garden centre at the weekends; you know the one over in Morganstown? Sometimes I'd skip school to get extra shifts. It didn't take long to realise it wasn't enough. The girl I was renting a room from, she more or less made her living, you know. It didn't matter to me by then. I'd already lost everything. Well, except Luke.'

'Is he the reason you stayed in Cardiff when you went to university?'

Chloe nodded. 'I'd have gone as far away as possible, but there was no way I was leaving Luke with them. I was saving up for us. Once I had enough, he was coming to live with me. I think that's why he got so close to Emily, to be honest. We'd always had each other to keep us going, but then I left him. I had to. Despite what my parents might have thought, he was with Emily because he'd wanted love, not sex. He wasn't like me.' She reached across and took Alex's empty coffee cup from her hand. Her face had flushed with embarrassment. 'I'm sorry. I don't know why I'm telling you all this.'

It seemed to Alex that someone should have heard all this much sooner. Had she shared her secrets with another person, perhaps things may have been different for her now. Nobody should have been expected to carry the weight of all this alone.

*

I haven't been completely honest with you, Chloe thought, knowing she couldn't bring herself to say the words aloud. *There's something I haven't told you.*

She sat back and closed her eyes, pushing her head back against the sofa as though trying to expel the memories that now flitted beyond her closed lids. She could sense Alex's eyes on her, watching her.

Chloe wondered whether keeping her eyes shut tightly for long enough would eventually make the thoughts go away. Why should it? It had never worked before.

She snapped her eyes open and stood hurriedly from the sofa. She gestured to the empty coffee cup in her hand. 'Do you want another?'

CHAPTER FORTY-SEVEN

Alex returned to the station after visiting Chloe at her flat. She still felt certain the press had broken a law in publishing those images of Chloe and nothing would be more satisfying than being able to prove it. When had people stopped becoming culpable for their actions? When had it become acceptable for everyone's private business to be made public knowledge? Alex was hell-bent on making sure the press was made answerable over their printing of those images.

But it wouldn't change the mess Chloe had managed to get herself into by accessing those files without permission. Whatever happened next, Alex wasn't going to let her face up to that alone.

She got herself a coffee and went to her office. The station was busier than usual that evening, with investigations into the Lola Evans and Sarah Taylor cases ongoing. In her office, Alex was able to shut out the noise of the rest of the building and submerge herself in her thoughts. There was something they were missing; something that had as yet managed to elude them.

She had barely had two minutes to herself when there was a knock at the door. DC Mason entered, carrying a notebook with him.

'Don't you have a home to go to, Dan?' Alex asked.

He sat at the desk beside her. 'I could ask you the same. Anyway, look.' He gestured to the notebook, where a list of nine names was written: four female and five male. 'According to Tim Cole, these are the additional names of everyone else who'd attended the support group between May and December of last year.'

Alex scanned the names: Zoe Morris, Katie Finnegan, Fiona Williams, Rebecca Marsh, Callum Davies, Christian Cooper, Joseph Black, Tom Meredith and Michael Reid.

'Only one of them has a criminal record,' Dan said. 'Tom Meredith. Drink driving charges. I've spoken with him this afternoon – he's got alibis for the night we think Sarah was moved from the pub, as well as the evening Lola was last seen. I've checked both of them out and they're solid. He was in work.'

'And the others?'

'We got Tim Cole in this afternoon and asked him to identify the remaining people from their social media account profiles. We've accounted for seven of them. I've spoken with three of them today – again, they've all got alibis. I'll contact the other four first thing tomorrow morning.'

Alex gave him a tired smile. 'Thanks, Dan. You've done a great job.'

She was aware her focus had been distracted that day. She couldn't allow it to happen again. It was likely their killer would find a next victim. Time was a luxury they didn't have.

'Which two are still unaccounted for?' she asked.

'Christian Cooper and Joseph Black. Neither has a criminal record and neither was identified from any social media accounts. Tim has given a description of both, but they're pretty generic. He doesn't seem to know much else about them.'

Alex nodded. 'I'll get straight on to it,' she said. 'Can I take this?' She gestured to the notebook. 'You should go home now,' she told him. 'Get some rest. Tomorrow's likely to be another busy day.'

Dan stood and went to the door. 'See you tomorrow. And try to take your own advice.'

Alex sighed and sat back in her chair. There were things that were bothering her, some similarities between the two victims they were unable to ignore. Both were of a similar age: Lola, twenty; Sarah, twenty-four. Both were attractive. Yet there was no evidence of any sexual assault on either of the victims. If the killer's motive wasn't sexual, why had he chosen these particular women? Why had he made them suffer in such precise and horrific ways?

There was an obvious link to the water, one that had been playing on her mind since they had learned about the history of the pub. One victim in a river, the other in a lake. A woman had drowned in a bathtub at the place where these young women had been held. There had to be relevance, but Alex was unable to see it.

Why would anyone put their victims in water if not to try to conceal them for a lengthy period?

There was a fifteen-year gap between the woman's death and these murders.

What was the relevance of the pub?

Had the person – or people – who'd been responsible for the deaths of both women known about the drowning of Julia Edwards all those years ago?

Alex turned on the computer. The backlog of work she had intended to tackle nearly two weeks ago still sat waiting for her, beginning to gather dust. She logged on to the computer and opened an Internet search page. Thinking back to what she had found out from Martin Beckett that afternoon, she searched for the woman who had drowned in the bathtub at the pub to which Lola and Sarah had been taken.

There hadn't been much coverage of the woman's death in the media. Alex knew exactly why that was. Forties, working class: a nobody, as far as the press was concerned. No one worth the print space in their publications. Big news made big money. Had she been young and beautiful her photograph would have been splashed all over the local, maybe national front pages. As it was, she was just another woman who had met just another unfortunate end.

The article Alex found was from a local newspaper's website. Presumably, Dan hadn't found the article in his research of The

Black Lion pub because at the time of the woman's death the pub
had been called The Farmers' Arms. Perhaps Beckett had changed
the name of the pub in the aftermath of the event, not wanting
his business to be tainted by the inconvenience of the death that
had occurred there. Either way, the details of the place should have
been found earlier.

It was barely a paragraph – just the woman's name and age along
with a brief summary of the circumstances of her death.

> *A woman has been found dead at the flat above The Farmers'*
> *Arms pub in Groeswen near Caerphilly. Julia Edwards, 42,*
> *was found on Sunday, but is believed to have died days earlier.*
> *Her body was found in the bath by one of the staff working*
> *at the pub. She is believed to have drowned whilst drunk,*
> *and police have described the death as a tragic accident.*

The sum of a life, Alex thought. A short paragraph on a web
page few people had probably visited. She now understood why
Martin Beckett had doubted anyone else would want to live or
work there. The place seemed cursed by darkness.

She glanced at the clock on the far wall of her office. It was
7.40. She couldn't help wondering where Rob was. Who he was
with, what he was doing. She imagined him in a living room, that
woman sitting beside him on the sofa; her two children playing
on the carpet at their feet. She was angry with herself for sparing
him the thought; angry with herself for bothering to care. Was he
with her now? Would he have told her that he'd been going round
to his ex-wife's house regularly for sex?

Of course he wouldn't have.

She sipped her coffee and returned her attention to the computer
screen. She had some footage to sift through: the CCTV taken
from the strip club where Lola had been working. There was a

chance the man Lola had met that morning had been inside the club some time during the evening, and though other officers had looked through the footage Alex realised how easily details could be missed.

The same might have applied to Christian Cooper and Joseph Black.

Until she did it herself, she wouldn't be satisfied there was nothing more to find.

CHAPTER FORTY-EIGHT

Chloe turned off the television and turned her phone to silent. She wanted to be alone and rid of the world. She had seen their faces, the people at work. She had seen the smirks of some of the men and, even worse, on some of the women. After leaving the ladies' toilets, it was as though every officer in the building had waited in the corridors to greet her, waiting to catch a glimpse of her shame while it was still fresh enough to be seen worn across her face. She had worked every day for months alongside these people. She had respected them. They had respected her, or at least she'd believed they had.

Everything had gone so horribly wrong, and she had been powerless to stop it.

She thought of DI King: how easily she had accepted her revelations, though they must have been so unexpected. Or perhaps not. Perhaps Alex had seen so much in her life, both in and outside work, that nothing came as a shock to her any more. Maybe nothing was unexpected.

She thought of the image that had graced the newspaper front page. If she was only able to remember that exact day, that exact request, then perhaps she might have remembered who she'd been speaking with that evening. But there had been so many, over such a length of time. She had never known who was at the other side of the screen, and what good would her being able to remember do her now? Whoever had been on the other side of that screen – whoever had sent that footage to the superintendent and to the newspaper – had been nothing more than a made-up name on a computer monitor; nothing more than a voiceless, faceless person who had paid her to take off her clothes.

. She had thought that changing her name, dyeing her hair, moving away, would be enough to shed her old life as Chloe Griffiths. As Belle90. How naive that had been, she thought. You couldn't escape the past. It stayed with you, there, in your shadow. It lurked at your shoulder, breathing on your neck like a ghost. Running away hadn't worked. Confronting it might, but there were other things she had to do first.

Casting thoughts of her own problems aside, Chloe turned on her laptop. She had wanted to avoid it, but there were things she needed to do: things she owed Detective Inspector King. She had let her down. She had been too wrapped up in herself – in Luke, in Emily, and now this – and she had let her own priorities take precedence over their current case. She may have been suspended, but that needn't mean she had to be completely useless. She didn't matter any more. All that mattered now was Lola Evans. Sarah Taylor.

She finished the last of her barely warm coffee and pulled the laptop on to a cushion on her lap. There was so much she had wanted to say during the last meeting she'd attended, but her thoughts had been interlocked amongst others and she had allowed them to become lost.

She opened the Word document on the desktop and began to write.

> *He hates women. The injuries inflicted on Lola's body suggests some sort of punishment, although there is nothing in his behaviour to suggest that he gains anything sexual from his actions. Why does he hate women? Who has harmed him? He preys on women who are vulnerable: women who put*

their trust in him. They know him. For now, it seems likely they know him from the support group. He lures them, makes them feel safe then traps them.

There were no signs of a struggle in the downstairs of the pub, or on the stairs or in any other room of the upstairs flat other than the room where the victims were held. In order to get them into the pub, he must have incapacitated them somehow. Were the women drunk? Even drunk, it seems likely they would have put up some sort of a struggle against him. There was no evidence of any drugs in the post-mortem of either woman, but it might be worth considering the use of Rohypnol. It is tasteless, odourless, and a person's system is cleared of any evidence of its consumption within twenty-four hours.

The victims would have been incapacitated long enough for him to transport them to the pub and get them into the upstairs flat. Neither victim was heavy — both were easy enough for a man of only average strength to move. The other implication here is that he owns or at least has access to a vehicle, possibly one that might allow him to conceal the women easily. What job does this man have, if any? Is he using his own vehicle, or someone else's?

His taking of items from the victims' bodies, as well as his apparently specific selection of his victims, is conducive with the pattern of a serial killer. He has found, wooed, lured, killed and collected from his victims and is likely to now be in what is known as the Depression Phase. I fear this man may kill again — in fact, it is likely he has already identified his next victim. It may well be another woman from the support group. If he fails in his attempt to trap and kill this woman, it is likely to result in a bitter disappointment that fuels his anger and he may attack at random in response to

*this. He is likely already upset – we have found his base,
disrupted his plans; he will be anxious and angry and will
therefore regard himself as forced to behave in ways that may
not follow the pattern of his two previous crimes.*

Chloe saved the document under the file name 'EVANSTAY-
LOR' before closing it. She logged into her email account and
found Alex's email address. She attached the saved document and
clicked send just as the doorbell sounded.

CHAPTER FORTY-NINE

Alex had been back at the house for less than ten minutes when she was interrupted by the sound of the doorbell. She had been upstairs changing from her work clothes into a pair of pyjamas, too tired to be bothered to take a shower before bed. It had been such a long and eventful day and she felt exhausted by it. The last thing she needed was to see Rob on the doorstep, waiting with the look of someone who wasn't going to leave without much persuasion. She knew it was him through the frosted panes of glass, and she considered how easy it might be to ignore him and leave him standing there. Facing what was bound to come next was something Alex would have preferably avoided, although she knew that not facing it now meant leaving it for another day.

'Can I come in? Please.'

Alex looked at him incredulously. She felt conscious of the pyjamas she had chosen, realising she was dressed like a lazy teenager. Yet again, she reprimanded herself for fickle thoughts of her appearance.

'Who is she?'

'Alex, please—'

'"Alex, please," what? I'm not allowed to ask?'

Rob glanced at the house next door, as though expecting to find the neighbours hanging out of the living room window and listening in on what was guaranteed to be an awkward conversation. 'Can we do this inside?'

'"This"? What is "this"?'

Rob sighed. 'Five minutes, that's all I'm asking.'

Reluctantly, Alex stepped aside and let him into the house. She didn't want him there – it was past ten o'clock and the only place she wanted to be was tucked up in bed – but neither did she want their dirty laundry aired on the doorstep for all to see. If she'd allowed herself the time to consider it, she might have had a chance to think about what she would say to him when she next saw him, but as always she had distracted herself with her work, ignoring the things that, if given a chance, might tip her over the edge.

'How long have you been with her?'

Rob said nothing, his guilty face revealing everything he didn't want to say. At least he had the decency to look ashamed. Alex didn't need him to tell her that he'd been seeing this woman – she still didn't even know her name – for some time. The boy sitting on Rob's shoulders had seemed to know him pretty well: well enough to laugh with him, to keep his small hands clamped to Rob's neck to stop himself slipping; well enough for the four of them to appear as any other family out together to do their weekly shop.

Family.

The word struck Alex, momentarily stalling every other thought.

She had lain naked with Rob, had let his hands undo all the bad things that lurked elsewhere in her life. She had showered with him, returning to his body for second helpings with the kind of thoughtless abandon she hadn't experienced since their early days together; the kind of physical need that had kept her returning to him long after they had both known the emotional element of their relationship to be over. The very thought of it now filled her with shame and anger.

If he and that woman, that woman's children, were in fact a family – if they had welcomed and accepted him as part of theirs – what did that make her?

'It's not what you think.'

'It's everything I think,' she snapped. 'What was your plan – you'd keep a nice little boil-in-the-bag family to go home to after shagging the ex-wife who couldn't give you kids?'

The look on Rob's face said she may as well have slapped him. A part of her wanted to.

'That's not fair, Alex. None of this is to do with—'

Her anger spilled into tears, hot and unexpected. They were rare, and Rob turned away from them as though embarrassed. Alex dragged the sleeve of her pyjama top across her face in a vain attempt to conceal the evidence of her frustrations.

What was she even crying for? She didn't love Rob any more; she hadn't been in love with Rob for years, not in any way more than the kind of love borne of mutual respect for the shared time that keeps couples together far longer than their expiry dates. Her tears were for her own wounded pride. They were for everything she might once have had, but would now never know. They were for everything she had no control over.

They were for Lola Evans and Sarah Taylor. They were for Chloe.

'It's always been you, Alex.'

She was glad he said it: the laugh it prompted helped to get rid of the embarrassing tears. He sounded like some bad male lead in a two-star romantic comedy, doling out clichés with all the sincerity of a double glazing salesman.

'Please. Don't make things worse than they already are.'

'It's true. I know you won't believe me; I know I don't deserve it. But you've pushed and pushed and now everything is on your terms, and is that fair, really?'

'Fair?'

'What have the last couple of months been all about, Alex? I've just been convenient, haven't I? A distraction to take your mind off other things.'

He seemed to know as soon as he'd said it that his words were a mistake.

'Meaning?'

Rob raised his hands in surrender. 'Meaning nothing. I shouldn't have said it. I'm sorry.'

'Sorry' just made Alex angry. She could feel her face growing hot. He'd done enough damage at the supermarket, and now this.

'I'm right though, aren't I?' he continued, not ready to take the warning that he'd already said too much. 'It's you calling all the shots, as usual. You just craving control to make up for all the things that have slipped from your grip, and once again I'm just collateral damage.'

'I thought you were sorry? You can stop now.'

Rob shoved his hands into his pockets and lowered his head. He looked pathetic, she thought.

'How long have you been with her?'

He shrugged. 'A few months.'

Alex's lip curled. It was insulting, being lied to in her own home by the man she had once shared it with. Rob would never have met the kids of someone he'd only been seeing for a matter of months – it just wasn't like him. But then, she thought, there were so many other things she had believed 'weren't like him' which now apparently were.

'That night I called you,' she said, 'months ago, when you came to fix the window. You were with her then?'

That night had been the first of many. She wished now she could go back in time and deal with that broken window herself. Letting him back into her life had been an invitation for trouble and now here it was, welcomed into her home by her own stupidity, her own desire to feel a way she had thought was long behind her. She was too tired to be dealing with this.

He couldn't even bring himself to nod in response. He didn't need to say anything: the answer was in his face, in the way he lowered his head and looked at the hallway carpet like some unruly child receiving a reprimand.

What now? She could kick him out, stand on the doorstep yelling and screaming like some woman scorned, but where would that get her? There was a reason they had separated. She was not meant to be with him.

'Just go, Rob.'

'But…'

'Please.'

He put a hand on the handle of the front door. 'I assume I'm expected to apologise. I can't. You've picked me up and put me down when it's suited you. We're really not that different.'

He waited for a reply and pushed down the handle of the door when he didn't get one. There were a hundred things Alex wanted to say to him – spiteful, vicious things that would relieve her momentarily of the bitter taste they were creating in her mouth – but she managed to hold them back. Voicing her anger wasn't going to make it go away.

Rob closed the door behind him, leaving Alex standing in the hallway. She wasn't sure which hurt the most: the humiliation of having been the other woman, or the fact that too many of the things he'd said had been disconcertingly accurate. She had never before considered seeking control a negative thing, but perhaps that's what it was.

She looked around the empty house, breathing in its silence.

Perhaps in her case it was destructive.

She heard her phone ping with a message and went to the living room to retrieve it from her bag. The message was from Chloe.

Check your emails. I'm so sorry for everything. Please catch this bastard.

CHAPTER FIFTY

The following day, Alex took DC Mason to visit Cardiff Council's office buildings to gain details of both ex and current employees within their grounds maintenance departments. Alex realised it was a long shot. The maintenance of the stretch of river running through the grounds at Bute Park involved external services, meaning plenty of people beyond the council's staff would have been able to gain access to the area of land where the pathologist seemed sure Lola Evans's body would have been placed in the river.

'Would someone working in the grounds of either park be brazen enough to abandon the body of a woman he had killed there?' Alex wondered as they walked back to the car.

'Seems crazy to us,' Dan agreed, 'but it takes all sorts. Whoever's done this wasn't right in the head to start with.'

Alex unlocked the car and they got in.

Dan's summary was a simple one, but there was perhaps more to it than he'd intended. To what extent could a criminal mind ever be understood? In cases like this the mind was damaged, perverse, and it seemed to Alex that although no rational human being ever wanted to fully comprehend the workings of a mind that had planned, executed and then lived with the memories of killings such as Lola Evans's and Sarah Taylor's, it was her job to think like a criminal.

'Nice little job for someone,' Alex said, gesturing the pile of paperwork that rested on Dan's lap. It was details of staff members obtained from the council. A lack of physical evidence was making things complicated. Short of arresting every member of staff in turn, DNA testing each and hoping for a match with the second blood sample found at The Black Lion, all Alex could see were dead ends.

'Can you have a quick check through those names, check for a Christian Cooper or a Joseph Black?'

Dan flipped through the paperwork and scanned the list of staff names.

'Connor Price's wife was in again this morning,' he told her. 'She's claiming police harassment. Apparently, his post-traumatic stress disorder is making him an easy target for victimisation.'

Alex rolled her eyes and started the engine. 'I'll give her a detailed description of Lola Evans's corpse, if she likes. Then she can talk victimisation.'

Connor's wife now knew – had seemingly known for a while – of her husband's infidelities, but if she was happy to turn a blind eye to it then Alex figured that was her problem. She had bigger things to worry about than other people's marriages.

'Anything?' she asked.

Dan looked up from the paperwork. 'No.'

It was hard for Alex to ignore the pessimism consuming her. She realised that events of the previous evening hadn't helped her mood, and thoughts of Chloe ate into her. She wished it was Chloe rather than Dan who sat beside her now. Dan was nice enough and proving good at his work, but things just weren't the same. Alex needed some of Chloe's enthusiasm, even if it was now apparent that her enthusiasm was likely to have all been a brilliantly performed charade. But her focus and energy hadn't been.

How had she been able to maintain such pretence amidst everything she had carried with her all that time?

'I got an email from Chloe. Don't mention it to the super. Not that there's anything wrong with it, but it might get his back up.'

Alex talked through some of the ideas Chloe had considered in the email she had sent the previous evening. The psychological stages of a serial killer dictated the man would plan, hunt; kill. There would be a period of euphoria following the initial execution of his crime. Then a stage of depression. He would crave the feelings he had experienced in those moments that had followed the death of his victim. He would long to feel it once again.

'You think he'll kill again?'

Alex nodded. It seemed a given now. 'We don't even know whether Lola was the first.'

It occurred to Alex that the most notorious perpetrators of history's most horrific crimes were people who blended into their communities, whose desires and compulsions went unnoticed by even those closest to them. It was thought that Jack the Ripper had been a timid man on the surface, a man who would easily have been overlooked as a suspect. Yet the brutal and macabre nature of his crimes demonstrated a violent nature that was anything but timid. Similarly, Ted Bundy was said to have been handsome, charismatic: someone his victims had initially trusted and didn't feel threatened by. It was frighteningly easily for a psychopath to blend into his surroundings. Was this the kind of man they were hunting?

A pressing sense of time crept upon Alex's shoulders, weighing them down. Killers such as this – if this man was, in fact, or would become, a serial killer – often had cooling periods between victims, but that didn't mean they could afford to become complacent. Time could mean the difference between life and death for yet another victim. A lack of physical evidence was making their job complicated. He was managing to outsmart them.

If they couldn't trace him, they were going to have to try to understand him.

'Penny for them.' Dan raised both eyebrows and Alex realised how deep in thought she had been. It was worrying that she was able to drive these roads without focusing on the route she was taking; that she knew these streets so well her mind was able to switch off to the routine of it all. 'Should probably be a bit more now, what with inflation. Fiver for them, at least.'

'Sorry?'

'Penny for them. Your thoughts. I was just going to say that—'

He stopped. Alex clearly wasn't listening. Her mind was somewhere else; judging by the look on her face, it seemed to be somewhere she might have preferred it wasn't.

She suddenly pulled off the main road and parked up outside one of a row of terraced houses. 'Shit.'

'What?'

'What do we know about Julia Edwards?'

'What we discussed in the briefing. Forties, alcoholic, unemployed. There's everything Martin Beckett told you about her and his father, but whether it's true or not's another thing.'

Alex opened the door and allowed a rush of cold air to flood the car. Traffic rushed past, its sounds forming a wall around her. Why hadn't she seen it before? Why hadn't any of them seen it?

She thought back through some of the things that had been said at the meeting earlier in the week. Chloe had questioned why the killer put his victims in water. Something from his past, she suggested.

The river. The lake. The water.

The bath.

'Did Julia Edwards have any other partners we know of?' Alex asked. 'Ex-husband lurking about anywhere?'

Dan shrugged. 'Don't know. Why?'

'Perhaps her death wasn't an accident. What if someone killed her there, years ago, and is returning there now with his next victims?'

The scepticism in Dan's reaction was unmissable. 'Fifteen years later? But why? And was there any evidence to suggest Julia Edwards's death wasn't an accident? Surely that would have been investigated at the time.'

He was right, Alex thought: there was no evidence. Prescription drugs and alcohol had been found at the scene: Julia Edwards had been so intoxicated she apparently hadn't felt herself drowning.

Or had she?

'Was someone else with her when she died?' Alex wondered aloud. They needed to make finding out a priority.

CHAPTER FIFTY-ONE

She shoved a foot in the doorway in an attempt to block his entry, but he pushed past Chloe regardless. He eyed the sparse flat with obvious contempt before turning the look upon her. She knew she looked a mess. She hadn't bothered taking a shower that morning and her hair was pulled into a knotted bun on the top of her head. Yesterday's make-up still circled her eyes. She was wearing leggings that were ripped across the knee – the results of a previous accident involving an attempt at home DIY – and a shirt that had a coffee stain down the front. She looked like someone whose grip on their life was starting to slacken, and the look her father gave her was sufficient to confirm it.

'Get out.'

'What are you going to do?' he asked. 'Call one of your colleagues? Oh, sorry, you can't do that, can you?'

Chloe hated her father. She had feared him when she was a child, resented him when she was a teenager, and now those years had escalated into one wall of hatred: one she couldn't see a way over or around.

He glanced at the opened laptop on the sofa. 'Applying for jobs?'

Christ, he was cruel. But then he always had been, she thought. Every time he had locked her inside her bedroom, deaf to her cries. Every time he had taken his belt to her brother, each time reminding him that he had brought it on himself. Of course he was cruel. She had always known it.

'Why are you here?'

'You've been to the house.'

Chloe felt her face flush. She had always been a terrible liar, despite her frequent attempts at the contrary. As a teenager she had lied about where she had been, who she'd been with, and her parents had always known she was lying. As though they had followed her. As though God had been following her and had reported back.

'One of the neighbours saw you.'

'And what did they see exactly?' she replied sarcastically. 'A daughter visiting her childhood home?'

'It stopped being your home a long time ago. The day you decided to reject us. The day you decided to reject everything we stand for. You'd no more right to be in my house than—'

'Than you've got to be in mine?' Chloe challenged, interrupting her father mid-sentence. Suddenly she was seventeen again. She was standing in her parents' hallway, the front door opened for the street to bear witness to just what an awful child that poor Griffiths couple had been cursed with, shouting and swearing, pledging vows to never set foot within that house again. And she never had. Until that week.

'Why were you there?'

Chloe shrugged. 'Just fancied a trip down memory lane.'

The irony of her choice of phrasing didn't pass her by. She had changed her surname to Lane in an attempt to escape her former life, now here she was, immersed back in it, and all her own doing.

'I told you before not to come back, and I meant it. You can't keep your meddling little nose out, can you? You were always the black sheep of our family. Always the one to question everything. Thinking you knew it all. Leading your brother astray.'

At the mention of Luke, Chloe felt her pulse quicken. She knew that 'astray' referred to his relationship with Emily. She hadn't been the one to lead Luke astray. Luke had been pushed that way by a childhood ruined by rules and routine and punishment. He had sought affection, love, in an attempt to replace all that had been missing whilst growing up. If they hadn't liked what Luke had become, it had been all their own doing.

'And now you've truly shown yourself up for what you really are. Tabloid whore.'

Her father's face had turned a deep crimson, as though even the words embarrassed him. He was trembling slightly, as though blaming her for having been reduced to such use of language.

At her sides, Chloe's hands clenched into fists. What would it feel like? How satisfying might it be if she were to hit him, to launch her fury at him, let him pay for every time he had raised a hand to her or Luke? She had lost her brother, her best friend. She had lost her career.

What did any of it matter now? What was there left to lose?

'What did I ever do to you?'

An unexpected sadness swept out with her words. This anger she felt wasn't borne out of hatred. Somewhere, in another life, it had been borne out of love. She had loved her father as any daughter might. He had berated her: she had loved him. He had punished her: she had loved him. He had shunned her and she had continued to love him, still desperately seeking his approval. She had only ever wanted him to stop. She had only ever wanted him to be the man she had once thought he was, back when she had been young enough to be easily deceived.

His face softened, for a moment, and in that moment Chloe saw her other father: the father who had made himself known on rare occasions. He had made sandcastles one summer: a summer over twenty years ago that Chloe was still able to remember despite the fact that she had been so young. He had helped Luke bury his pet gerbil, making a wooden cross to mark the grave at the bottom of the garden. He had read Chloe stories. There had been good times, once upon a time. She might have tried to fool herself into believing it had all been bad, but she realised that was a lie.

Nobody was ever all bad, not completely. Wife beaters ran bubble baths and made candlelit dinners. Child abusers played games and told stories, made their victims feel as though there was nobody in the world more special.

Then his expression changed, the soft edges gone, never truly there. And there it was, Chloe thought. There was the lie. You couldn't be both: both bad and good. You could be good and do a bad thing – you could be bad and do a good thing – but one or the other had to be the true you, the real you, the one that was inherently in you, impossible to ever really remove or disguise.

Any good was a lie, Chloe thought. This was his true version: the one who sneered and gloated and belittled. And she had stopped seeking his approval a long time ago.

'Why Marcross?'

'What?' Her father's face creased, heavy lines forming across his forehead.

'Luke,' she reminded him, as though he had somehow managed to forget the location of his son's supposed suicide. 'Marcross. Why there? Had he ever even been there before? Why would he choose there?'

'You can't let it go, can you?' he said, his voice wobbling on the words.

She hadn't imagined it: he had flinched. It had been so brief that it might easily have gone unnoticed, but she had been looking for it and it had been there. At the mention of Marcross. At the mention of that night.

Something.

'How can you let it go? He's your son. Don't you want to know what really happened that night?'

'I know what happened,' her father snapped. He crossed the room towards her, making Chloe start. His hands gripped her shoulders. 'Your brother killed that girl. Why can't you accept it? He might not have meant to, but he did. He killed her. He bloody well strangled the life out of her. He knew he wasn't going to get away with it and he didn't want to face up to the consequences.'

He was shaking Chloe, his fingertips pressed into the shallow dips above her collarbones. In that moment, she hated what she knew he could see. Fear. Her twelve-year-old self back again, scared of this man. This man she had just wanted to love her.

She did what she had never been able to back then. She fought back. Her knee rose instinctively and slammed between her father's legs. As he groaned and leaned forward, she shoved him with such force that he staggered into the coffee table and fell back, dazed, on to the sofa. He exhaled loudly through his mouth, breathing away the momentary pain she had inflicted.

There was an awkward moment when father and daughter stared one another out, like some ridiculous cowboy film, each waiting for the other to make a move for a pistol from a back pocket. She had braced herself, expecting her father to react, to make a lunge for her, but he did neither. He sat on the sofa, puffing like an old man as he tried to catch his breath.

'The porn,' he managed to stammer beneath breaths.

'The what?'

'The porn your mother found.'

Chloe looked down at her father, contempt consuming her. Luke had told her about the magazine his mother had found. He'd been fourteen at the time. He told Chloe how their mother had held his head under water to wash out his eyes. She treated him so cruelly: even more so, it seemed, when neither Chloe nor her father was there to see it.

Was that her father's explanation for events? Was that his justification for believing his own son had been capable of his girlfriend's murder?

Just after Emily's death, Luke had turned up at the flat where Chloe had been living. He had sat on the edge of Chloe's bed, red-faced and tear-stained, a sixteen-year-old boy suspected of murder. Luke had been inconsolable. He had sobbed through his words, retching on them as he explained how their mother and father had accused him of being depraved. They had wanted him to admit it. They wanted him to confess to what had happened: that he and 'that girl' had engaged in some warped, sick sex game and he had accidentally strangled her. He had panicked, left her for dead; gone back. They wanted him to admit to them, and then to the police, exactly what he had done.

'I swear to you, I never touched her. It wasn't me, Chloe. I would never have hurt her.'

And Chloe had held her brother's hand in hers and believed every word he told her.

She still believed him now. She had never stopped. He was an innocent. Nothing like her, regardless of anything their father might say.

'He was fourteen and he looked at some porn,' Chloe said, looking down at her father. 'Jesus, what teenage boy doesn't?'

'Jesus? How typical of you, Chloe, to use his name in vain. Your religion means nothing to you, does it? And that's where we're different, you see. Your mother and I. You and Luke. You think that behaviour is acceptable. We don't. You think looking at pornographic imagery is acceptable. We don't. You think accepting payment for sexual favours is acceptable. We don't.'

He stood from the sofa and Chloe held her breath, expecting his worst.

'Get out of my flat.'

'Gladly,' her father said. 'Come to the house again and I'll call the police. Be nice for you, I suppose. Think of it as a reunion.'

'Come to this house again,' Chloe said, yanking open the front door, 'and I'll make sure everyone knows you killed your son. Luke didn't kill himself, did he?'

There was a moment before he headed back out onto the street and Chloe was able to slam the front door behind him. But not before she saw it again. There it was, so faint she might have missed it. That flicker beneath the arrogant, horrible exterior that acknowledged that his secret wasn't entirely his own.

Guilt.

Now all she had to do was prove her father was a murderer.

CHAPTER FIFTY-TWO

The first call Alex made when she got back to the station that morning was to Martin Beckett, the son of the man who had owned The Black Lion. She had gone straight to the coffee machine for a caffeine fix before shutting herself away in her office, wanting to be alone with her thoughts. Dan had returned to the main investigation room to continue his research into Julia Edwards. Finding out as much as they could about the woman now seemed their best chance of finding a link with the two girls whose bodies had been retrieved from the water.

Alex searched through the contacts on her phone for his mobile number. As it continued to ring without answer, she cursed.

'Hello?'

She kept her fingers crossed that he might hold the information she needed. She had made the link between the bath and the water when they'd found out about Julia Edwards's death at the pub, but she wished the missing pieces had fallen into place earlier. They needed names. A solid link to Julia Edwards would finally give them something concrete from which to work.

'Martin? It's Detective Inspector King. Have you got a minute?'

She heard noise in the background, the sound of voices and movement.

Martin spoke to someone at his end before redirecting his attention back to Alex. 'I do now.'

'Julia Edwards, the woman who died in the bathtub at your father's pub: how much do you know about her?'

'Not much. Like I told you though, I knew too much. More than I was comfortable with.'

'Look, I know this can't be easy to talk about, but I need to know as much as possible about what was going on in that flat. You suggested your father had been having an affair with the woman who lived there?'

Martin gave a bitter laugh. 'Not how I'd describe it.'

Alex paused. 'How would you describe it?'

There was a loud exhalation at Martin's end of the conversation. 'More of a business transaction, shall we say. An exchange of services.'

This much Alex knew already. Clive Beckett appeared not to have been too pushy about the rent on the flat above his pub, providing missed payments were accounted for through alternative means.

'How did you find out about your father's...' She had been going to use the word 'relationship', but Alex realised it would most likely lead to insult.

'I heard my parents arguing,' Martin told her, saving Alex the awkwardness of having to rephrase the question. 'Not just the once, either. I think she had a bit of a reputation at the pub – the staff used to gossip about what was going on in the flat.'

Alex doodled distractedly across the notepad on her desk. 'So you're suggesting she saw other men there? Men she might have been accepting payment from?'

'I don't know. I don't want to speculate. Like I said, there was a lot of gossip.'

No smoke without fire, thought Alex.

'Do you remember her moving into the flat?'

'Yeah. Couple of years before she died.'

'Did she move into the flat alone? No husband or boyfriend?'

Martin sighed. As responsive to her questions as he had been, Alex realised revisiting this old ground was something Martin had no desire to experience.

'Look,' he said, 'I was only a teenager back then. I don't know. I think she lived there alone, but I can't be sure. I'm sorry I can't be more help, I really am. I've seen those girls on the news. I know what all this is about. You don't think it's got something to do with that woman though, do you? I mean, all this was years ago.'

'I can't give any details of the case, I'm sorry. You've been really helpful. I'm sorry to have dragged it all back up for you. One last thing: do the names Christian Cooper or Joseph Black mean anything to you?'

'No,' Martin said. 'I'm sorry, I really am. I wish I was able to help you in some way.'

'You have. Thank you.'

Alex ended the call and sat back in her chair, pressing her eyes shut tightly. Despite the links with the water and the pub, nothing was making sense. Why would anyone who had known Julia Edwards all those years ago be now targeting women who, back then, were just kids?

Why couldn't they find out who these two missing men were? It was rare these days for people to leave no trail behind them, particularly with the popularity of social media. People made themselves easily traceable, even if they failed to realise they were doing so.

Had one of these men removed the records from the support group's filing cabinet in a bid to make himself more difficult to find? Tim Cole so far seemed entirely plausible, and they had no evidence with which to arrest Connor Price for a second time. If the man they were looking for was either Christian Cooper or Joseph Black, one of them was being careful to do everything he could to conceal his tracks.

He had gone to that group with the intention to kill, Alex thought, and the notion made her sick to her stomach. The guilt she carried about the death of Sarah Taylor was overwhelming. They should have got to her in time, but they hadn't. They had failed her.

She had failed her.

CHAPTER FIFTY-THREE

Chloe flicked on the kettle before going into the living room and taking her laptop from the sideboard. She turned it on and waited for the darkened screen to light. She inserted the memory stick and waited for the list of files to appear.

There was so much to work through she barely knew where she would begin. All Chloe knew was that there was no more time to be wasted. She had already wasted far too much. It didn't matter any more that these files had come at such a high price. Now she had them, she could finally do something constructive.

She opened the file that contained the police interview with her brother. Just seeing his name at the top of the screen brought a lurching sickness to her stomach, a sense of sadness so intense that Chloe had never been able to describe it in just one word.

She turned the volume up on the laptop and sat hunched forward as though to cover it, as though to prevent any detail it held from escaping her. She knew that hearing Luke's voice for the first time in so long was going to throw everything off balance.

DS Barrett: For the purposes of the recording, could you please confirm your full name.

Luke Griffiths: Luke Griffiths.

DS Barrett: You understand that you've been arrested on suspicion of the murder of Emily Phillips? You've been read your rights and understand that this interview is being recorded and anything you say may be used against you later in court?

Silence.

DS Barrett: Please respond verbally for the recording.

Luke Griffiths: Sorry. Yes, I understand.

DSB: You've told officers that you went to a party with Emily Phillips last Saturday night, is that correct?

LG: Yes.

DSB: Could you tell us where that party was?

LG: Michael Parry's house. He's in our year at college. He was having a party while his parents were away. He lives on the other side of Emily's estate.

DSB: Did you meet Emily there or somewhere beforehand?

LG: I met her there.

DSB: Can you tell us what happened when you and Emily left the party, Luke? What time did you leave Michael's house?

LG: About 10, I think.

DSB: We have eyewitnesses who say it was 9.15.

LG: OK. 9.15. I can't remember exactly.

DSB: Please tell us, in as much detail as you can, what happened after you left the party.

LG: We walked back to Emily's house. We stopped at the shop for a bottle of Coke. She had a headache. I thought maybe a bit of sugar would help. She'd had too much to drink. When we got back to the house I made her a cup of tea and some toast. She went into the living room to sit down and take off her shoes. She came through to the kitchen then, when I was making the tea. She was crying. I thought it was just because she'd had too much to drink. Silence.

Then the faint sound of crying. Luke.

Chloe closed her eyes, gripping the sides of the laptop. She pictured her brother sitting there in that interview room, eyes red and nose running, alone with the realisation that the people who might prove his innocence were the very people who were convinced of his guilt.

She remembered sitting in the waiting room at the station in Cardiff that day. Her parents had been there; her mother's visit so brief that she might as well not have bothered at all. Chloe and her father had sat opposite one another, both with their heads bent forward, each avoiding eye contact with the other. So many hurtful, hateful things had been said between them in those previous few months. This should have brought them together.

DSB: Do we need to stop the interview for a while?

LG: No. I don't need time, I just... I didn't kill her. I swear; I didn't touch her – you've got to believe me.

DSB: Let's stick with the facts for now, please, Mr Griffiths. You say Emily took her shoes off in the living room and then came through to the kitchen where you were making tea. She was crying. What happened then?

LG: I asked her what was wrong. She said she was sorry, that she—

The recording became inaudible; Luke's words lost amidst his sobs. The interview was terminated.

Chloe went to the kitchen and made herself a coffee. She longed for something stronger, but she needed to keep a clear and sober head. Against her wishes, tears escaped her. She gripped the edges of the kitchen worktops, trying to cling to some remnant of normality. She hadn't allowed herself to cry enough, fearing where those tears might lead her. Once she started, how would she stop?

Trying to push back a flow of tears, Chloe returned with her coffee to the living room and to the recording of her brother's police interview. What she'd heard was painful, yet she knew what was still to come would be so much worse.

> *DSB:* Interview resumed at 11.42. You said Emily came into the kitchen. She was crying. You said she apologised. What was she apologising for?
>
> *LG:* She said she couldn't do it any more. She said she was sorry, but she didn't want to be with me any more.

The cup in Chloe's hand wobbled slightly, sending coffee trickling down its side. She didn't want to hear about this, not again. This was why everyone had assumed Luke was responsible for Emily's murder. She had wanted to end the relationship with him. He couldn't accept it. So simple, when it was put like that.

The sound of her brother's tears, muffled by the interviewing officer's words, filled the room. She wasn't sure they would ever leave. She would continue to hear them long after she stopped pausing the recording.

> *DSB:* She wanted to end the relationship?
>
> Silence.
>
> *DSB:* For the recording, please, Luke.

LG: Yes.

DSB: And how did you feel about that?

LG: I was shocked. I thought everything was fine.

DSB: Emily hadn't given any previous indication that she didn't want to be in the relationship any more.

LG: No.

Even in his single word responses, the change in Luke's voice was obvious. His increasing hesitation, his heightened tone: he knew the implications of the interviewing officer's questions.

DSB: What did you say to her when she told you that?

LG: I said I didn't understand. Everything had been fine, I didn't know why she was saying that.

DSB: Did you argue?

There was a lengthy pause. Chloe had abandoned her cup on the coffee table, the smell of it alone making her nausea worse.

LG: Yes.

DSB: Did the argument become physical?

LG: No! I asked her why she was doing it and she wouldn't give me a proper answer. I told her she was drunk, that she didn't know what she was saying. I left. I slammed the front door behind me; I was upset.

DSB: Where did you go when you left Emily's house?

LG: I just walked around the estate for a bit. I was going to go home, but… I don't know, I didn't want to. I just wanted to be by myself.

DSB: But you went back to see Emily?

LG: Yeah. I wanted to sort things out with her.

DSB: Even though she was drunk? By your own admission, it sounds as though you thought she didn't really know what she was doing or saying. Why go back then? Why not wait until the following day, until she'd sobered up, to go back to speak with her?

LG: I didn't want to leave her on her own. Her mother was away and—

Luke stopped mid-sentence. It was almost as though he'd sensed the trap he was about to walk into and had decided not to venture any further. Honesty didn't always pay. Sometimes saying nothing was far less incriminating than speaking the truth, even when that truth fell from the mouth of an innocent.

DSB: And that gave you an opportunity to go back and kill her.

There was an objection from the duty solicitor. Luke had refused the presence of his father, and Chloe didn't blame him. He'd been better there alone than with either of their parents.

DSB: You were angry with Emily, weren't you, Luke? Angry that she was ending the relationship. Angry that she wouldn't give you a reason for it.

LG: No, it wasn't like that. I wasn't angry. I was upset.

DSB: So upset that you went back to the house and you argued with her. She said something and you snapped. What happened, Luke? Was it an accident?

LG: I didn't touch her. I didn't do it. For God's sake, please, I didn't kill Emily; I loved her.

Chloe leaned forward and paused the recording. She closed the file hurriedly. She couldn't listen any more. Her brother's voice filling the room, panicked and desperate, was like having his ghost there beside her, and though she had always been haunted by what had happened to him, the words spoken on the recording were more painful than she could ever have imagined.

She didn't want to question him. She didn't want to doubt.

She couldn't listen any more, not while she still wanted to believe.

CHAPTER FIFTY-FOUR

After speaking with Martin Beckett, Alex contacted the register office at Caerphilly Council, telling them she would be there within the hour. Her main focus now was finding out what ex-boyfriends or husbands might have been lurking in Julia Edwards's past. The rest of the team had been given the priority of trying to find Christian Cooper and Joseph Black. The plan was for officers to speak again with the remaining support group members to see what they could remember about either man. Lola Evans and Sarah Taylor had known their killer well enough to have trusted lifts from him. Presumably, others from the support group would also have got close to him; close enough that they may have known relevant details about the man's life.

Before Alex left the station, Dan tracked her down in the corridor.

'Christian Cooper,' he said. 'We've found him. He works in the cinema at Nantgarw – he keeps off social media because of his anxiety. Bullied at school, history of self-harm.'

'How did you find him?'

'Sean Pugh remembered seeing him at the cinema once, a few months back.'

'Alibi?'

'He was at his aunt's fiftieth birthday party on the Saturday Lola went missing. There were seventy-odd other people there. He's not short of witnesses.'

Alex nodded. 'It's narrowed it down. What have we found out about Joseph Black?'

Dan exhaled loudly. 'Not a lot, I'm afraid. No record of him on Niche. Physical description is pretty general – could describe forty per cent of the male population. Rachel Jones seems pretty sure of one thing though: he drives a van.'

Alex's eyes widened. 'Right. OK. Get on to the DVLA, see if we can trace a vehicle registered to Joseph Black. I'm going to the council offices in Caerphilly – I shouldn't be too long. Call me if there's any news.'

*

When Alex arrived at the council offices early that afternoon they were obviously expecting her. She had given them Julia Edwards's details over the phone and was hoping for a result that might reveal an ex-husband on the scene.

The words of Chloe's email echoed in her head.

Who has harmed him?

Martin Beckett's views on whether or not Julia Edwards might have been selling sexual favours to men other than his father had been vague, but there was no denying the insinuation that had been present. Had Julia angered a former husband or lover? Had one of her clients held a grudge against her for some reason?

Had someone else contributed to her death?

Alex pulled into a parking space at the council office car park and turned off the engine. The direction her thoughts were taking her didn't make sense. Why would someone connected with Julia Edwards all those years ago be victimising young women now? Julia had died years ago; if someone had meant her harm but hadn't killed her, surely her death had spared them from taking matters into their own hands?

Yet it was clear that whoever had tortured and killed Lola Evans and Sarah Taylor was connected with the pub in some way. It was too much of a coincidence that the place would have been chosen at random. Though it was remote and derelict, South Wales had its fair share of such places. There had to be a reason for its relevance, and Alex was determined to find out what it was.

She entered the council building and went to the reception. The woman there pointed her in the direction of the register office, which was tucked in the far corner of the ground floor of the building.

'DI King? I'm Diane. We spoke on the phone earlier.'

A woman about Alex's age stood from the department's front desk and reached out a hand to greet her before leading her through to the office. There was a young man there; Diane asked him to go and get them tea, presumably as an excuse to give them some privacy.

'I've found the lady you're looking for,' Diane told her, gesturing to a seat. Alex sat beside her and looked at the computer screen as the woman pulled up her search results. 'Julia Edwards. Death registered as the fourth of April 2002. Accidental drowning while under the influence.'

'That's her. Any record of any marriages?'

Diane shook her head. Alex felt her heart sink. She had been so hopeful that today might be the day they found their concrete lead, something substantial that would lead them to their killer before he had an opportunity to identify a next victim. 'There's a son though,' Diane said, switching between the opened windows on the database.

Alex's reaction made it obvious she'd known nothing of a son. There had been no mention of a child living at the pub when Julia had died. There had been no mention of him at any time during the investigation.

'Adam Edwards. Born thirteenth of November 1987.'

Alex stared at the details on the screen, trying to keep her expression impassive. 'Could you print this off for me, please?'

Diane nodded and set about the task. When she got up from her seat and went to the printer at the far side of the room, Alex moved closer to the computer screen, her mind racing as she absorbed the details. Adam Edwards was fourteen when his mother died. Where had he been at the time? He couldn't have been living at the pub with her: Martin Beckett would surely have made mention of him and none of the reports relating to Julia's death made any reference to any children.

Where had he been? Why hadn't he been with his mother?

CHAPTER FIFTY-FIVE

It took the rest of the afternoon to build just a brief profile of Adam Edwards, the son of the woman who had died in the flat where both victims had been held. Did the unidentified blood sample taken from The Black Lion pub belong to him, Alex wondered. The list of employees obtained from Cardiff Council gave no match with the name Adam Edwards, so the team was left to search for other links he may have had to both victims and the areas where their bodies had been found. Adam was twenty-nine years old and had a criminal record: a caution received for a shoplifting offence thirteen years earlier. A check with the Inland Revenue revealed a long history of employment, with Adam having frequently changed jobs. However, the records showed no known employment for the previous eight months, his last job having been with a building firm based in Bridgend.

The image on the criminal records database showed a teenager with unruly dark hair and pale grey eyes. He had an angular face and soft features. Alex wondered how much Adam had changed during the past thirteen years, and whether anyone who knew him now would recognise this boy as the same person.

His police record had thrown up another interesting detail of his past: since the age of eleven – and at the time of his arrest when he was aged sixteen – Adam had been living in care. That explained his absence from the reports on his mother's death.

Had this shoplifting teenager become a criminal slick enough to kill two women without leaving behind a trace of himself? There had been no unidentified fingerprints lifted at the pub, but perhaps one of the young women had helped police by causing her killer an injury and leaving a blood sample at the scene. Perhaps he hadn't been as clever as he'd thought.

Alex brought Adam's details up on the Police National Computer. After his arrest, fingerprints and a swab sample from his cheek would have been taken. Both would have been recorded on the database. All she needed was a DNA match.

She clicked back and re-entered the database page. Something was wrong.

Adam Edwards's fingerprints had been taken and stored, but the results of his swab test were nowhere to be found on his file.

'For God's sake.' She shoved back her chair and left the office.

*

She eventually found Harry in the staff canteen, staring through the window whilst a plate of what might have been lasagne, but was really anybody's guess, lay congealing on the plate in front of him. So much for keeping everyone on task, she thought.

'Boss.'

He looked up and stood hurriedly, leaving his food as though ashamed to be associated with it.

'We've got a potential suspect. He's got previous, but his swab test results haven't been recorded on the system. If we had them, I could try a match with the unidentified sample from the pub. Why the hell isn't it there?'

Harry sighed. 'Human error,' he said, the scathing tone unmissable. 'Isn't that the popular get-out clause? Someone fucked up. Who is he?'

'His name's Adam Edwards. His mother lived in the flat above The Black Lion.'

'The woman who drowned in the bath?'

Alex nodded. 'Victims in water. Can't be a coincidence, can it?'

Harry looked sceptical. 'Is that all you've got?'

'If we can get him in and his swab's a match, I think that's enough, don't you?'

He raised a hand as though in surrender. He was rarely in the mood for a confrontation with Alex and today was no exception. 'Do we know where he is?'

'Not yet. A few of the DCs are on to it.'

'Let's get him in as soon as possible. You can get a swab test sent off then.' He paused. 'How's DC Lane?'

Alex gave a shrug. 'As you'd expect. She's a good officer. I don't want to lose her.'

The superintendent gave a look that acknowledged the challenge in her tone. 'There's a procedure that has to be followed. It's out of my hands.'

'There's a lot you don't know. That girl's been through so much. She got here with so much stacked against her.'

'I'm sure that's true. But rules are rules.' Harry gave an apologetic shrug and made his way back to his office.

Alex felt a sting of injustice on Chloe's behalf. When this case was closed she was going to do everything she could to get Chloe back to work, whatever it took, even if it meant risking her own position.

*

She made her way back up to the central office, a streak of determination pushing a spring into her step.

Through employment records, Adam Edwards was traced to an address in Ystrad Mynach. Alex headed there with DC Mason, but en route she took a detour. She explained to Dan that she wanted to pop in on Rachel Jones, to make sure the young woman remained vigilant. Though this was true, there was also another reason for her

visit. Something had been nagging at her: a suspicion she hoped
Rachel Jones might be able to confirm or deny.

She parked the car outside the terraced house and asked Dan
to wait.

*

The young woman was small and timid, something birdlike about
her sharp features. She answered the door cautiously, having checked
past the living room curtains before going to the door.

'Everything OK?'

Rachel nodded, but everything about her expression and
demeanour spoke the opposite. She was scared, Alex thought. Given
the same circumstances, what person wouldn't be?

'I've been thinking: is there anyone you could go and stay with
for a few days?'

Rachel's features stiffened. The young woman seemed a bag of
nerves.

'For peace of mind,' Alex attempted to reassure her. She held
back from saying she didn't think Rachel was in any danger: how
could she possibly know that? They didn't know the reasons he
had selected Lola and Sarah as his victims. She would be trying
to second-guess a mystery, and Alex wasn't prepared to take those
chances.

'My brother lives in Bristol.'

'Go there for a few days, if you can. I promise you we're doing
everything to find this man. For now, there's something I need to
ask you.'

The young woman shifted her weight from one foot to the other,
looking down at the hallway carpet.

Alex reached into her pocket. 'Do you recognise him?'

She held the picture out to Rachel. It was Adam Edwards's police
photograph, taken years earlier. The support group was the only

link between the two women. It made sick sense. Where better to target vulnerable young women? Until now, their main suspects had been first Connor Price and then the elusive Joseph Black. Yet Joseph Black seemed untraceable. Perhaps because he didn't exist.

Rachel took the image from Alex's hand, holding the face closer to her own. 'When was that taken? That's Joseph.'

'Joseph?'

The girl looked back to her. The look of anxiety she wore as a second skin had been replaced by something else. Fear.

'You don't think—'

'I don't think anything,' Alex interjected. 'Not yet. Rachel, this is definitely the man you know as Joseph Black? He attended the support group?'

Rachel nodded, her eyes clouding with tears. 'What do you mean "the man I know as"?' She looked again at the face in the photograph. It might have been a different version, a younger version of the person she had known, but there was no doubting she knew the face that stared back at her.

'What else can you tell me about him?' Alex asked.

'He used to come to the support group, a while back. Haven't seen him since before Christmas. He looks different to this now, though. Much shorter hair. Older. Do you think he—' She cut her own words short this time, hanging on to the unspoken implication of Alex's interest in this man.

'Is there anything else, Rachel? No matter how small it might seem, anything is helpful.'

Rachel was shaking her head, her tears now beginning to fall. 'No one ever asks too much. But we trust each other – that's why we go there. It's supposed to be a safe place. Joseph was quiet. Nice. He was a good listener.'

Alex exhaled audibly. Quiet. Nice. Presumably the very things that had made him seem trustworthy to the young women whose lives he had gone on to end so brutally. 'Go to Bristol,' she said, putting a hand on Rachel's arm. 'Go today and I will keep in touch, I promise. This will all be over soon.'

She hoped to a God she was dubious about that this might be true. Her head was ringing.

They needed to make contact again with the other four women who'd been named on Tim Cole's list of members. Each of them needed to know that if they saw Adam Edwards – Joseph Black – they were to contact police immediately.

*

Alex went back to the car where DC Mason was waiting.

'She knows him, Dan.'

He gave her a questioning look.

'Rachel knows Adam Edwards. He was part of the support group, only he called himself Joseph Black.'

'Jesus Christ.'

Alex pulled her seatbelt across her shoulder. 'We need to find him.'

She gripped the steering wheel as her mind raced three steps ahead of her. There was something about that police photograph of Adam Edwards that was bothering her, some familiarity she couldn't allow to go overlooked. Lola. Sarah. The support group. Just how close to his victims had Adam been?

Close enough to have been to the strip club on what would turn out to be Lola's last night there, Alex now realised. Close enough to have waited for her to finish work – for her to have been expecting him. Tall. Dark features. Quiet. Nice.

So close he'd been there all this time, hiding right in front of them.

CHAPTER FIFTY-SIX

The man who answered the door at the address the team had traced as Adam Edwards's was in his early forties. He was wearing oil-stained trousers and a T-shirt that looked as though it had never been washed. The dog at his feet shared the same look.

'Been working on the bike out the back,' he said by way of explanation. He wiped the palm of his hands on his T-shirt and peered down at Alex's ID.

'We're looking for Adam Edwards. Your name is?'

'Simon Watts. What do you want Adam for?'

'Is he home?'

The dog yapped at Alex's feet, jumping up and leaving smeared paw prints on her trousers.

Simon shook his head. 'Why do you want him?'

'We'll speak to Mr Edwards about that. Any idea where he is?'

The man's eyes narrowed with curiosity. 'Not seen him in about two weeks. He's away on a job.'

'Job? What sort of job?'

Simon shrugged. 'Building work, I assume. He didn't say much.'

Alex glanced past Simon and into the cluttered living room. The dog had decided to leave her side, instead turning its attention to what appeared to be a pile of dirty washing abandoned at the end of the sofa. 'Can we come in?'

After a moment's hesitation, Simon stepped aside and let them into the house. The front door led straight into the living room, which looked as though it was housing preparations for a car boot sale. There was mess everywhere: dirty clothes lying in a heap at the end of the sofa; piles of magazines stacked precariously against the fireplace; engine parts and tools beneath the window at the far end of the room. Another dog sprawled on the laminate flooring next to the sofa, its heavy breathing chesty and laboured like an old man's.

'Do you own the house, Mr Watts?'

Simon nodded.

'And how long has Mr Edwards been living here?'

'Year or so. I split up with my ex; she moved out; I needed the money so rented the spare room. Look, what do you want him about?'

'How did you meet Mr Edwards?'

Simon Watts looked from one officer to the other, his mouth twisting into a cynical grimace. 'Why all the questions?'

'We're looking for Mr Edwards as a matter of urgency, Mr Watts, so if you could please just answer our questions.'

'He did some work here for me, on the electrics. A mate recommended him. Mentioned he was looking for somewhere to rent and not long after I had the room going. Has he done something?'

'We'll need the name and contact details of this mate,' Alex told Simon.

'Can we take a look in his room?' Dan asked.

'You got a warrant?'

'No,' Alex told him, 'but it shouldn't take us too long to get one.' She gave the man an insincere smile.

He sighed. 'Go on then. It's the second door on the right.'

He followed them upstairs. On the landing, further clutter welcomed them. Alex expected much the same when she opened the door to Adam Edwards's room, so the orderliness that greeted her was a surprise. The bed was made and obviously hadn't been slept in the previous night. There was a TV mounted on the side wall and beneath it a chest of drawers. Alex pulled the top drawer open. Piles of T-shirts lay inside, all ironed and neatly folded. In the two drawers beneath it there were more clothes. Wherever Adam had gone, it looked as though he was planning to return.

'He didn't tell you where he was going?' Alex asked, turning to Simon who was standing in the doorway watching them.

'No.'

'Where do you work, Mr Watts?'

The man's expression had becoming increasingly hostile. It hardened once again now, as if he was about to be accused of something.

'Cardiff Council. I do grounds maintenance round the parks.'

Alex straightened up and cast Dan a glance. 'Do you have access to a council vehicle, Mr Watts?'

He nodded.

'Has Adam ever borrowed a vehicle from you?'

Simon Watts shook his head. 'They're kept down in the unit. I drive down there start of the shift to pick one up, drop it back off at the end of the day.' He studied Alex with curiosity. 'What's all this about?'

'Does Mr Edwards own a vehicle?'

'He's got a van. Uses it for work.'

Alex shot Dan a second look. 'Do you have a work ID? Something you need in order to gain access to the grounds?'

Simon Watts was looking increasingly concerned. 'This is about that girl, isn't it? The one they found in the river.'

'Mr Watts... the ID?'

'I've got one somewhere,' he said, throwing his hands up as a gesture to the mess, 'but don't ask me where it is. I don't use it very often – we don't tend to get asked.'

Alex reached into her pocket, took out a notebook and pen and handed both to Simon. 'The friend who recommended Adam... his details, please.'

She waited as Simon retrieved his mobile phone from his pocket and searched for his friend's contact number. 'Please have a look for that ID,' she told him. 'If you see Adam or hear from him, phone call, anything, I want you to get straight in touch.'

'Jesus,' Simon said, handing back the notebook and pen. 'What's he supposed to have done?'

'Mr Watts…'

'Yes, yes, OK. I'll let you know.'

*

On the way back to the station, Alex wondered what they were dealing with. If Adam Edwards was, in fact, their killer, exactly what sort of man were they up against? It had seemed they knew so little of him, yet as Alex drove in silence – Dan beside her, scouring the Internet on the iPad – she thought they perhaps knew far more than they realised.

But why was he doing this now, after all this time?

According to Martin Beckett, Julia Edwards had been living in the flat in exchange for sexual favours with his father. Had Adam known this? He had been taken into care years earlier, but had the same thing been happening during the eleven years he had lived with his mother? Had he grown up knowing what she did, and had his perception of his mother clouded his attitude towards women? He had tortured Lola Evans. He had removed her fingernails and cut her hair, essentially stripping her of some of the elements that made her feminine.

'Found anything?'

In the passenger seat, Dan's attention was still focused on the iPad.

'Seems our man's recently reactivated his Facebook account.'

They'd already searched for a profile matching their suspect, but none had been found. His absence from social media and his use of the alias Joseph suggested he had been intent on keeping a low profile.

So why reactivate the account now, Alex wondered.

'You sure it's been reactivated and isn't a new profile?'

'Yep. Posts dating back to last year. They come to a stop in July. Then they started again yesterday. He's shared a post about looking forward to the weekend.'

Reactivating a social media account didn't make any sense to Alex. If Adam Edwards was the man they were looking for, he had so far managed to stay beneath their radar. Reactivating old accounts on social media sites was surely making the work of the police easier for them, unless the man was so arrogant he continued to believe he was getting away with it.

Looking forward to the weekend, thought Alex. She felt her stomach churn. He was going to kill again. He had more than likely already chosen his next victim.

CHAPTER FIFTY-SEVEN

It had taken Chloe a while before she had returned to the work that still lay set out on the coffee table in her living room. On any other day she might have gone out for a walk and allowed the fresh air to clear her head of unhelpful thoughts before returning to the task at hand, but there was no stepping outside the flat that day, and probably not for many to come. Facing the world seemed a daunting prospect, something she could easily do without. Thank goodness for online shopping and home delivery, she thought. Not that she could think of food. She could think of little other than the sound of her dead brother's voice, so frantic and so scared.

It had become so easy for people to disappear from the outside world. People could both earn and spend their money online, having everything they needed in order to maintain survival brought to their doorstep by a person they would have to face for no longer than the time it took to sign a delivery slip. Entire lives could be lived from behind the keys of a laptop. Chloe had always sought company from her own screen and what a sad existence that now seemed to her. Loneliness clutched at her. It was becoming an all-too familiar sensation.

Then something even more painful gripped her: anxiety, clawing her insides. A 'what if' that she had never wanted to consider.

She was interrupted by the ringing of her mobile. Scott's name flashed up from the screen. It was the third time he had tried calling her in the past twenty-four hours. He had left an answerphone message earlier, but she hadn't been brave enough to listen to it.

She wanted to answer his call. She wanted to speak to him, to hear the reassuring tone of his voice at the other end of the line. But how could she? What the hell was she supposed to say to him? I'm sorry you saw me half-naked in the papers. I'm sorry I never told you I used to perform sex acts for money.

She couldn't speak to him. It was cowardly and she realised she might never get another chance to explain herself to him, but she just couldn't do it, not that day. She needed time to think. There were so many other things hanging over her.

She listened to the end of the recording of her brother's police interview. It had ended as she had known it would: with Luke being released without charge. He had been released on pre-charge bail, with the police seemingly confident – or, at the very least, hopeful – that given extra time they would secure the evidence that would justify a charge against Luke and lead to a successful conviction.

Two days later, Luke was dead.

She pored through the file relating to his death. His 'suicide' as the police and the coroner had preferred to label it. Her father's car had been found at the bottom of the cliffs at Marcross in the Vale of Glamorgan. Luke had passed his driving test, but he hadn't had his own car and hadn't been insured on his father's. Luke had made sure he passed his test, Chloe knew, in order to prove himself. In order to prove that, very soon, he would be able to do whatever he wanted and there would be nothing either of his parents could do about it. He had followed Chloe's example in that. He had wanted them to know that they wouldn't be able to control his life for ever.

It was sadly ironic that his act of defiance had finalised the nature of his death. Had he never passed that test – had he never learned to drive – Luke would never have been able to take himself to that clifftop. The police would have looked into the possible involvement of another person, but as it had stood, they had done nothing.

The post-mortem report that Chloe had copied on to her memory stick from the police database confirmed her brother's death as suicide. A blow to the head, sustained on impact. Lacerations to the face and arms where his body had collided with the windscreen. The details were difficult to read, but as always for Chloe the not knowing seemed far harder.

She closed the post-mortem report.

A Facebook message notification pinged at the top of the screen, its narrow banner highlighting the first line of a newly received message. She would have ignored it had it not been for the name that greeted her. At the sight of it, a surge of memories flooded the room, filling it like long forgotten friends. She clicked on the banner and the messenger page popped up to fill the screen.

> *Hi Chloe. I'm not going to ask how you are – I've seen the papers, so realise things must be pretty tough for you at the moment (understatement, I'm sure). Anyway, I hadn't realised you were back in Wales. It's been a long time, hasn't it? I thought you might need a friend, and there's no friend like an old friend (next stop 30, so definitely qualifying on the "old" bit). Let me know if you fancy meeting up for a drink or a chat (or both). You still have my left shoulder x*

A sad smile passed Chloe's lips. His last line resurrected a memory that was so distant she might have come to eventually forget it. She had once told him that she appreciated his shoulder to cry on, and he had asked which one. For a long time, he had been the only person she'd had to talk to. Months after leaving Cardiff, she'd continued to miss him.

As with everyone else, she'd had to let him go. But unlike many others, she had been sorry for it. Somehow, it seemed almost as though he had known when she might need him.

She began to type a response.

CHAPTER FIFTY-EIGHT

There was no sign of Adam Edwards. His vehicle licence number had been obtained from the DVLA, and his van was a match with the same make and model as the one that had been picked up on CCTV near the entrance to Bute Park. Although the plate couldn't be seen clearly on the footage it seemed increasingly likely they had identified their main suspect. Wherever Adam had been keeping the van since Sarah's murder, it appeared he was doing all he could to make sure it stayed out of sight and therefore away from suspicion.

A request to the Department of Work and Pensions for his current and former employment details was being processed; a phrase Alex had come to loathe. It seemed a get-out clause for people who were simply unprepared to complete their jobs quickly and efficiently. She had given one of the team's DCs her own request: to make sure the department's administrative staff didn't keep them waiting, even if that meant standing over a desk and utilising the threat of a search warrant.

Alex wasn't confident about where the information might take them, but she wanted every member of the team kept busy. Any information was to be considered useful, only to be discarded once it had been proven not so. Alex had made the mistake in the past of overlooking the finer details, and at times missing the all too obvious. It was the reason she had insisted on sitting through hours of strip club CCTV footage, though it had turned out to be fruitless. She couldn't afford to make any mistakes.

Adam Edwards's mobile number had already been sought and his phone company contacted. They had been hoping to be able to use the GPS to track him, but as yet there had been no result. His phone seemed to have been disconnected from the network. The only way that this could have happened was for the battery to have been removed. Once again, he was two steps ahead of them.

A search warrant of the house where Adam Edwards had been living recently was obtained.

*

Alex and Dan returned to Simon Watts's house and searched Adam's bedroom, finding nothing there out of the ordinary. The man seemed as meticulous in his day-to-day life as he had been in his crimes.

'This is ridiculous,' Simon Watts said, standing in the corner of the living room and watching with a disgruntled expression as Alex searched through the contents of the drawers beneath the TV unit. 'Adam's hardly ever here.'

Ignoring him, Alex's thoughts continued to focus on the hair that had been cut from both Lola's and Sarah's heads. If Chloe's assumption had been right and the killer had taken the hair as a souvenir, it seemed likely he would keep it somewhere close; somewhere he would be able to return to it. There was no sign of either woman in the house.

Had he taken the hair with him?

Where the hell was he?

'Your work ID shown up yet?' Alex asked.

Simon Watts shook his head. 'Security at the parks is useless anyway.' As soon as he'd spoken the words, he seemed to regret them.

'What are you suggesting, Mr Watts?'

'Nothing,' he said quickly.

'So anyone could gain access with a vehicle if they chose the right moment, is that it?'

Simon's refusal to offer a response answered Alex's question for her. It was frustrating, but why would anyone have expected tight security at a city park or a popular picnic location? People didn't generally expect to have murder victims abandoned there.

'Does Adam have any identifying features?'

It had occurred to Alex that, although Rachel Jones had been able to identify him from his photo as a teenager, she hadn't seen him since well before Christmas. During that time, he'd had plenty of opportunity to change his appearance.

'Got quite a big tattoo up his arm,' Simon told her.

'Of?'

The man shrugged. 'Snake or something.'

'What colour's his hair?'

Simon narrowed his eyes, as though it was a trick question. 'Dark.'

It had been dark in his police photograph, Alex thought, but that didn't mean he hadn't recently changed it. She continued her search of the house, finding a bank statement dated six months earlier that she took with her.

*

Once they left, she and Dan made their way to the nearest branch. If they could gain access to Adam Edwards's account activity, it might give them an indication of where he now was. Any further activity would help lead them to him.

'Did you hear Simon Watts complaining about the mess?' Dan asked as he put on his seatbelt. 'I thought we left it in a better state than it was in when we arrived.'

Alex smiled, though she had barely registered his words. She was thinking of Adam's mobile and how the GPS had thrown up no results. It was the same for Lola's and for Sarah's. Adam Edwards was a clever bastard. He had been careful in concealing his tracks, and Alex was worried that his bank account activity might also prove fruitless in their search.

*

Her suspicions were proved correct. Standing orders had left his account: his phone bill; his monthly payment for van insurance. Other than that, Edwards's account had little activity. He had been paying his rent at Simon Watts's house in cash, presumably from the odd jobs through which he seemed to be earning his living. He must have been making the rest of his purchases that way.

To all intents and purposes, Adam Edwards had disappeared.

CHAPTER FIFTY-NINE

Chloe had barely slept, and what little rest she had managed to cling on to had been permeated with dreams that had left her shaken. Her brother's voice on the recording and the memory of his visit to her shared flat not long after Emily had died all played back to her, the words distorted, incriminating. Why was she now starting to doubt him? She hated herself for even contemplating the notion that Luke might not have been telling the truth. She had come this far. She wouldn't stop believing in him now.

It was twenty past seven. It was early to be calling Alex, although she knew the DI was always up early. She wanted to catch her before she got to the station, or wherever it was that the investigation into the deaths of Lola Evans and Sarah Taylor would take her that morning. She wished she could be of greater help. She felt useless there, confined to the flat and unable to go to the job that she realised had for so long now been the very thing that had been keeping her afloat. Without it, what was she?

'Alex?'

'Everything all right?'

No, Chloe thought, but of course they both already knew that. Nothing was all right. It was starting to feel as though nothing would ever be all right again.

'Any updates on the case?'

Alex exhaled loudly down the phone. Chloe realised what a difficult position she was putting her colleague in, and she had already asked too much of her. Relaying details of a current case to an officer on suspension would be yet another round of ammunition the superintendent could use against Alex, were Harry to decide that her involvement in Chloe's closed case investigations was sufficient to take action against them both. Alex had already made herself vulnerable for the sake of helping her.

'Chloe, you know I can't give you any information.'

'I know. I'm sorry. I just feel so bloody useless sitting here, not doing anything.'

There was a pause.

'Something's happened, hasn't it?' Chloe pressed, reading the unspoken suggestion in Alex's silence.

'You're not useless, OK. We have a suspect, and that's all I can say, but something you wrote in your email… we wouldn't have got there without you. You're not useless.'

The DI was trying to offer her reassurance, but Chloe couldn't bring herself to accept it. She should be there with her now, she thought, helping her catch the bastard responsible for the deaths of two innocent young women. She had allowed herself to become distracted. She had failed those girls. Words had their place, but it was actions that solved crimes and ensured convictions.

'Who is he?' Chloe asked, knowing she was pushing her luck.

'I'm going to put the phone down if you ask me anything else. How are you?'

'Like I said, useless.' Chloe played distractedly with a loose thread of cotton at the seam of her duvet cover. 'Look, I know we can't do anything more about Luke now. I realise I might not be coming back. I just want you to know something.'

There was silence again as Alex waited for Chloe to resume her speech. Chloe had wanted to tell Alex of her suspicions about her father so many times before, but there had never seemed to be a right time. Whenever she had thought to tell her, she had visualised Alex's likely response. She knew how erratic her suspicions already appeared, what trouble they had already led her into. Accusing her father was likely to help her lose what little credibility she'd had left.

There was never going to be a right time. Somehow, the urgency to tell her now seemed pressing. If someone else knew what she thought had happened at least she would no longer be alone with her suspicions. Even if they chose not to listen, she had told someone.

'I think my father killed Luke.'

Chloe could hear the scepticism in Alex's silence. To anyone else, her words were those of someone barely clinging on to common sense. First Patrick Sibley then all those other names she had reeled off that morning in Alex's office, crowding the room with events and accusations that seemed to hold little coherence even to her. Now her father.

'Do you have any evidence?'

There was a tiredness to Alex's question – a 'here we go again' sigh mingled between the words that Alex couldn't have hidden even had she attempted to.

Chloe looked at the screen of her laptop. She knew what she wanted to say. She wanted to tell Alex, louder this time, what a controlling bully her father had been throughout her and her brother's childhoods. She wanted to tell her again – had she not heard it the first time? – that she had watched her father beat Luke for little more than what he had referred to as insolence.

Luke had been accused of murder. What had her father been capable of under those circumstances?

She looked again at the screen in front of her. She couldn't tell Alex – not without admitting to having copied the files. Not without forcing Alex to an even greater scepticism of her integrity. 'No.'

'You need to stop this now. For your own sake, please.'

She thinks I'm losing the plot, Chloe thought. 'I wish I was there to catch him with you.'

Was she talking about Lola and Sarah's killer, or was she talking about the man she believed responsible for her brother's death? Was it now more important to find that man than it was to find the one responsible for the death of Emily? The boundaries between everything seemed blurred. Chloe wasn't sure of anything any more.

Except maybe one thing.

She looked at her opened laptop and at the CCTV footage that was paused on the screen. A main road, not far from Marcross where her brother had been found. Her father's car stopped at a set of traffic lights. A driver who wore a hooded jacket – a jacket that was one of Luke's.

A driver she was certain was not her brother.

CHAPTER SIXTY

He stood on her front doorstep still looking so much like the younger man Chloe remembered with such fondness. Time had altered him, tracing the finest of lines at the corners of his eyes, but that smile – that front tooth that crossed ever so slightly over the other – was still instantly recognisable as his. It brought a comforting sensation that she felt enclosed by, as though nostalgia had wrapped itself around her like an old blanket, cosy in its familiarity.

'Chloe? God, it's been so long. You haven't aged though. What you taking? I'll have some.' He smiled that familiar smile again, though it was quick to fall from his face. 'Sorry. How are you? Stupid question, I suppose.'

Seeing him brought back a host of memories. He had always been so nice to her; so supportive, even though she had so often taken advantage of the fact. Chloe supposed there were a lot of things she had taken for granted back then. She'd had to grow up quickly – far too quickly – but despite her circumstances, her teenage naivety had been strong enough to blind her to the hardships that were yet to come. When it had seemed she had lost everything, she'd still had the person closest to her. The person who had made it possible to survive anything.

But once Luke was gone, Chloe had really known what losing everything truly meant.

Perhaps that was why she had lost touch with him. She couldn't cling to the remnants of a past, not when the solid structure of it was no longer in existence. It was a shame, she thought, but life and everything it had thrown at her had forced her away from everyone.

There was also the issue of that awkward night she didn't really want to remember.

She stepped aside and let him into the flat. He handed her a carrier bag. She peered inside. There was a bag of mixed salad, a packet of tomatoes, some spinach and ricotta ravioli and a bottle of non-alcoholic fruit cocktail.

'Thought you might need some dinner. If you're anything like me, you don't bother cooking for one. You still a veggie?'

Chloe nodded. 'Thanks.' She stepped aside to allow him into the flat, but he hesitated.

'I don't want to be presumptuous. We can go out if you prefer, though? Might be good for you. The longer you stay in, the harder it's going to get to go back out.'

Chloe realised this was probably right, but she couldn't face the outside world just yet. She considered it for the briefest of moments, but it was far too soon. 'I invited you over, didn't I? Look, I know you're right, but... not yet.'

What would other people say if they were to see her out with a man, just days after those photographs had been splashed all over the front of the newspapers? She would be adding fuel to a fire that, as far as Chloe was concerned, couldn't die out quickly enough. Keeping a low profile would mean keeping herself protected to what little extent she was now able to. Surely it didn't mean, though, that she needed to keep herself entirely isolated?

'How long have you been living here?' he asked, taking a look around the sparsely furnished living room.

It did look as though she had only just moved in and hadn't yet had time to unpack any items beyond the basic furniture needed to make the space liveable, but this was exactly as Chloe had always liked it. She had never wanted to become fixed to any one place, presumably because being fixed had once meant being trapped. Since working with Alex – and now since meeting Scott – her ideas had altered. She felt a sense of belonging in her job, something that had previously been an alien sensation to her. Scott had been the first person in a long time with whom she could imagine something fixed, something permanent, and it was those very thoughts that had sent her running.

What must he think of her now?

Chloe followed her old friend's eyes as they scanned the room, embarrassed suddenly by the sum of her life. 'About six months.' She took the bag from him and ushered him through to the kitchen. 'Thanks for these.'

In the kitchen, she flicked on the kettle and took two mugs from the cupboard next to the fridge. For someone who had craved her own space, Chloe had found herself attacked by loneliness at a worryingly rapid rate. Isolation had been acceptable when she had chosen it. Once it had been forced upon her, it had quickly lost its appeal.

'It's good to see you.'

She turned from her task of making tea and shot him a smile. 'You too.'

In a way, having him there made it feel as though the previous eight years of her life had never happened, as though she had been transported back to a whole other lifetime: one that despite being so relentlessly battered by sadness had been punctuated with the occasional moment of hope. Before Luke's death, she had been happy, occasionally. Those times they had laughed together over something stupid – the times he had walked her home, deliberately extending the route taken in an unspoken effort to keep her a little longer from a flat he had always seemed to know she would never be able to call her home.

Would she want to be eighteen again? she thought.

Not the version of it she'd been given, certainly not. But in another past – in another life that had led down a path much different to the one she had been given – most certainly.

She turned to him. 'Still take sugar?' she asked.

He gave her a smile. 'Good memory, Chloe.'

CHAPTER SIXTY-ONE

The local press had been informed of the search for Adam Edwards and one of the team was updating social media websites with his image and a request for any member of the public who might see him to contact them immediately. If he was to gain knowledge of the fact that the police had identified him, there was always a chance he might give himself up. He had nowhere to go, and nobody could run for ever.

Alex had to acknowledge that the likelihood was slim. If the conditions Sarah Taylor had been put into the lake at Cosmeston offered anything by which they were able to judge this man, Alex predicted that he had come to view his criminal activity as some sort of game. It was likely he had known her body would be found, and sooner rather than later. He may have already known that the police were aware of him, probably enjoying this game of cat and mouse where he had, until now, exercised control.

Wading through Adam Edwards's copious employment history for any clues as to his current whereabouts seemed a daunting task, one that Alex realised they had little time for. With Rachel Jones safely at her brother's house in Bristol, she had no longer to fear for the young woman's safety. But that wasn't to say Adam Edwards hadn't set his sights elsewhere.

While the rest of the team worked on contacting those who might have known or worked with Edwards, Alex paid a visit to the mutual friend who had referred Simon Watts to Adam when he'd needed electrical work on his house.

*

She found the man working in a pub in Hopkinstown. The man had once worked in another pub, years earlier, and it was there he had met Adam. It made sense that Adam Edwards might have worked in pubs: he had grown up in one, would be familiar with their running. According to his former workmate, Edwards had trained as an electrician but had never fully qualified, although he still took on cash-in-hand jobs to make an extra bit of money on the side. The man claimed not to have seen Edwards in months, not since he had moved into Simon Watts's house as a lodger.

As far as Alex could fathom, the part-time sideline in electrical work seemed the main way that he was earning money. There was no formal record of employment for the past nine months. He had been able to live under the radar for months, the nature of his income allowing his bank account activity to remain quiet. Tracing him through a transaction seemed unlikely.

The pub where both men had worked was called The Bar on the Bridge and was situated on a roundabout just off the A470 between Caerphilly and Pontypridd. It had recently been turned into a gastro pub – she remembered the days when they had simply been known as pubs that served food. She had her fingers crossed that someone working there would remember Adam Edwards and might still know him. She spoke with a young woman working behind the bar who looked no older than twenty-one and asked if it would be possible to speak with the manager. When the manager arrived, Alex felt her hopes sink. He also looked too young to have worked there at the same time Adam Edwards might have. She had a brief chat with him, knowing her efforts here were futile.

In the car park, Alex sat in the driver's seat with the engine running. Where next? Adam Edwards had as good as disappeared. His landlord hadn't seen him in weeks and he had no colleagues to have missed him or wondered why he hadn't shown up for work. He had no family that he might have been staying with.

Where the hell had he gone?

She looked again at Edwards's long list of former employments. Was it possible he was now staying with someone he had met through work? Was someone helping him conceal his whereabouts?

Two young women were dead. With every wasted moment that passed, they might be risking the life of a third. Alex felt herself afflicted by a pressing sense of urgency.

She scanned the employment history. She wasn't that far from another of the places where Adam had once worked: a garden centre in Morganstown, just outside Cardiff.

*

It took her less than ten minutes to get there. Thankfully, there were members of staff beyond their twenties, and one of them remembered Adam Edwards.

'Worked here about seven, eight years ago,' the woman told her. 'Nice boy. Helpful. Don't know where he ended up working after he left here though – I think he might have been one of those types to do a bit of travelling before he settled down. We used to have a lot of students working here around that time, I remember; a lot of them from the school down in Radyr. I think he was a bit older, mind you, probably…'

Alex had stopped listening. A wedge of anxiety lodged in her chest. The conversation she'd had with Chloe at the young woman's flat just days earlier played back through her mind, the lost details that had seemed so insignificant at the time now sounding through her brain like alarm bells. She had worked at a garden centre as a teenager trying to save enough money so that her brother could go and live with her once he was old enough to leave his parents' home without their consent. There weren't that many garden centres in the area any more, not since the big chain DIY stores had taken over. Chloe had mentioned Morganstown, Alex was sure of it. She had gone to school in Radyr.

Seven, eight years ago, the woman had told her. About the same time Chloe might have worked there.

'Chloe Lane,' she said, interrupting the woman. 'Griffiths,' she corrected herself. 'Do you know her?'

The woman gave an apologetic shrug. Alex reached into her pocket for her mobile phone and scanned through her photos. There weren't that many on there, but she hadn't deleted the selfie Chloe had insisted they take to document the night out they'd had at Christmas. She held out her mobile to the woman.

'She used to have dark hair. Do you recognise her?'

The woman studied the photograph. 'I remember her now. Lost a bit of weight since I last saw her, mind.'

Alex felt sick. She left the garden centre hurriedly and tried Chloe's mobile. It went straight to voicemail. She called Dan. 'Where are you? Can you get yourself over to Taff's Well? I'll explain when I see you.'

Chloe's image had been splashed over the front of the local papers and it was now public knowledge she had been suspended. An old friend might have contacted her during this time, when she needed a friend the most.

Alex pulled out of the car park and took the roundabout back onto the A470. She needed to reach Chloe before anyone else did.

CHAPTER SIXTY-TWO

'You OK?'

Chloe had lost track of time. After eating the food he had brought over, she and Adam had talked about where their lives had taken them since they had last seen one another. They tried to omit certain details – Chloe's family, what had happened that week with her job and with the newspapers, Luke – but avoiding these subjects entirely left Chloe with little to talk about. These were the things that had come to characterise her entire existence. She still couldn't bring herself to consider what she would be without her job and where her life might take her if her suspension was to lead to a permanent dismissal.

They had talked about Adam and what he had been up to in the eight years that had passed. He had travelled for a while, admitting he'd had his own ghosts he'd needed to escape. When he didn't elaborate, Chloe didn't push him on the subject. She didn't want to talk about the things that haunted her; she had no right to force him to do something that she wouldn't.

'You OK?' he repeated. He was sitting in the chair opposite her, the coffee table separating them. He tilted his head, his eyes glazed with concern as he looked at her.

She pressed her fingertips to the side of her head. She felt light-headed. 'I just feel a bit funny.' She could hear the slur in her words, although they sounded as though they were being spoken in another room, somewhere distant and remote, from another person's mouth.

Adam stood. 'Shall I get you some paracetamol? Are there some in the kitchen?'

She shook her head, though it hurt now to do so. It felt as though something was pulling at the sides of her brain; the same kind of feeling she'd experienced plenty of times, years earlier, when she'd had too much to drink. It had been that very feeling, along with the anxiety and guilt that had all too often inevitably followed, that had prompted Chloe to cut alcohol from her life several years earlier, around the same time she had signed up to join the police.

But she hadn't been drinking. They had shared the bottle of non-alcoholic fruit cocktail that Adam had brought over to the flat with him. Other than that, she'd had nothing but tea.

'I'll be OK in a minute,' she said, not entirely convinced this was true. The room shifted slightly; she leaned forward and gripped the edges of the coffee table as though keeping herself from falling off the sofa. Her hair fell in front of her face. She left it there.

Adam sat beside her. 'Glass of water?'

Chloe shook her head. What was wrong with her? One minute she'd been chatting – she had almost laughed a couple of times, which was something that just hours earlier she had thought she would never again be capable of – yet now her head felt soaked with sickness. Her eyelids felt heavy. Her body longed for sleep, yet her mind was trying to fight off the desire. Her limbs felt detached somehow. It was a horrible sensation, one that made her study her own skin as though she no longer recognised it.

Adam reached for her hand and took it in his. He gently stroked the back of her knuckles with his thumb. She could barely feel his touch. She was watching it, but it looked as though it was someone else's skin he was touching, someone else's hand that rested beneath his. She didn't feel really there. Why was her vision so blurry? Why did her jaw feel as though it was no longer capable of forming words?

'Lola had such pretty hands. Small, pale, like yours. But everything that's pretty on the outside is ugly when you scratch beneath the surface, isn't it?'

His words were pooled in a muffled cloudiness. Chloe watched his mouth moving, but the words seemed to be lost, slowed down. She tried to speak the other woman's name, but her mouth refused to form the word and any sound she might have made was caught in her throat and suffocated.

His hand closed around her wrist, tightening. Then the room went black.

CHAPTER SIXTY-THREE

Alex was fraught with worry, and when she again tried Chloe's mobile phone it went straight to answerphone. You're worrying unnecessarily, Alex told herself. Chloe had wanted to shut herself from the world for a little while. That's what she had done. She was fine.

She wished she could believe it, but a nagging anxiety kept whispering in her ear, reminding her she couldn't be so sure.

Her thoughts had collided into a knot of facts and assumptions. If Chloe was there beside her now, sitting alongside her in the passenger seat, as was so frequently the case these days, she would have taken that knotted mess and unravelled it all as though dealing with a ball of Christmas lights of which Alex could no longer see either end. Or would she? The Chloe she had known just a few months earlier would have. She would have dragged the once messy bundle behind her, presenting it back in a neat line that would make perfect sense, stress free and rationalised. But recently... things hadn't been quite the same recently. Under similar circumstances, Alex doubted anyone would have worked to their usual standards.

Those emails had started it all off. Chloe hadn't been quite herself after Christmas. It had been so easy to miss and Alex might have put it down to any number of things. Christmas wasn't a time of fairy lights and anticipation for many people. For many it was a time of loneliness, regret and nostalgia, and Alex had been caught up sufficiently in her own problems to have easily missed the struggle of others. Had she noticed Chloe's shift in mood at the time, she might easily have put it down to something ordinary brought about by the supposedly festive season.

Those emails. Alex's foot pushed further to the floor. Chloe had told her those emails came from an address she didn't recognise: an address with the username 'theserpent'. She had dismissed them so easily as somebody messing about – a prank undertaken by someone who had too few brain cells and too much free time – and now she wished she had done more to help her when she'd had the chance.

Adam Edwards had a tattoo of a snake on his arm. When Simon Watts had been asked for any identifying features, this had been the first thing he had mentioned.

She stopped the car to find Simon's number in the notepad she had stashed in the glovebox. Connecting the call with the car's Bluetooth system, she resumed her drive to the village where Chloe lived.

'DI King,' she told him, hearing the immediate sigh that escaped him at the sound of her name. 'That tattoo you mentioned—'

'The tattoo? Yeah. What about it?'

'You said it was a snake?'

'A snake, yeah.'

'Do you know what Adam's email address is?'

'His email address?'

Alex wondered whether Simon Watts was going to continue the conversation by simply repeating back everything she said to him. It would have been frustrating anyway, but with so little time in front of her Alex didn't have the patience for it now.

She ran a red light at a crossroads and swerved to avoid a taxi. The driver came to a screeching stop and slammed on the horn. 'Yes,' she snapped, 'his email address. What is it?'

'I live with him,' Simon Watts said impatiently. 'Why would I need to email him?'

'Just check,' Alex told him.

Simon Watts sighed before moving from the phone, presumably checking the mail on his email account via his mobile: 'adamedwards25@yahoo.com,' he said eventually.

'Thank you,' Alex said through gritted teeth. 'Not too difficult, was it?' She cut the call and put through another call to DC Mason. Her mind was racing. Of course he hadn't used his normal email account; that would have been far too risky. It was likely 'theserpent' had been set up just recently, in the past month or so: just before Chloe had received that first email.

'I'm on my way to Chloe's,' Alex told Dan. 'I've tried calling her. It's going straight to answerphone.'

'She could be anywhere.'

Alex's face tautened at the suggestion.

As though somehow sensing her reaction, Dan was quick to correct himself. 'I mean she could be shopping, or with a friend, or—' He didn't bother finishing his sentence. He had unwittingly spoken Alex's worst fears.

A silence fell. It allowed Alex time and space to think again, but her thoughts were leading to the darkest corners, each separate piece stretching itself and linking with the next in an attempt to create a whole.

Lola Evans had been a young woman with an eating disorder, without parents and separated from the grandmother she had lived with on what seemed to have been very much a part-time basis. Sarah Taylor had been recovering from an abusive relationship that had left her hospitalised. Both victims had been taken at a time when they had been vulnerable, which went a long way to explaining Edwards's choice of the support group as a place to meet the women upon whom he would come to prey.

And then there was Chloe, a young woman whose twenty-six years on this earth had been blighted by more tragedy than most people would have to endure in a lifetime. Her vulnerabilities had lain with her brother. All Edwards had needed to do was resurrect Luke – bring his memory back so he dominated Chloe's consciousness.

Those images he must have stored – that footage he had kept in his possession all this time – had secured his hold over Chloe, making sure she was at her lowest ebb when he made his move. It must surely have been Edwards who had sent it.

'I'm nearing Taff's Well now,' Alex told Dan. 'Please be as quick as you can.'

Her grip tightened around the steering wheel. She hated this bastard with an intensity she had never felt towards anyone. She needed to get to him before he got to Chloe first.

CHAPTER SIXTY-FOUR

When she woke, Chloe found herself still in her own flat. Her head felt woozy, as though nursing a particularly violent hangover, and though it was her flat everything around her looked different. Her hands had been pulled together in front of her, crossed and tied with gardening wire. The thin wire cut into her wrists painfully, pinching her skin and cutting off her circulation. Her ankles were shackled in the same way.

Opposite her, Adam sat in the chair, his body tilted at an angle from Chloe's prone position on the sofa.

'Wakey wakey.'

Her eyes stung. Their corners were gritty with sleep and her chin felt damp, as though she'd dribbled during her unconsciousness. The room seemed to move as she twisted her head against the seat of the sofa.

Lola.

The woman's name rang in her mind like an alarm bell. He had mentioned Lola. Right before she'd blacked out, Adam had spoken Lola's name.

God, she felt sick. Whatever he had given her seemed to have soaked through to her core. Was it Rohypnol?

She had predicted this. She had written it down, told DI King it would happen.

She hadn't once imagined it would be happening to her.

Nothing made any sense.

DI King. Alex had told her they had a suspect, but hadn't been able to tell her his name. Was it Adam? Would they be looking for him, or would the investigation have led them to another false path, one that would direct them further and further from him, from her?

'Why are you doing this?'

Adam smiled. That smile that had seemed so reassuring in its familiarity just hours earlier now made Chloe feel physically sick.

'Because I can.'

He sat forward in the chair and rested his forearms on his knees. He'd taken off the long-sleeved sweater he'd been wearing earlier and was now in a T-shirt, his arms bare. His exposed skin revealed a tattoo of a snake that looped up and around his elbow.

Chloe moved her head, though the motion sent a painful ringing through her ears. There was something wrong. Something missing. She glanced over to the floor and saw it. Her hair… thick blonde chunks of it lying on the laminate.

'It was you, wasn't it? You killed Lola. You killed Sarah.'

Just hours earlier, she had welcomed this man who had appeared on her doorstep. She had invited him there, to this place she called home but knew had never truly been and now would never be. She had welcomed that smile back into her life, believing him to be the man she had known all those years ago: the young man who had been so silently supportive and so predictably dependable when she had most needed it.

Was that why this was happening to her? Had she taken him for granted? Did he feel used by her, betrayed in some way?

Memories were surging back, mingled with the foggy cloud that the drug had left floating in her brain.

That night, the night he had gone back to the flat with her. Luke had died a couple of weeks earlier, and Chloe had spent those weeks existing in a kind of half-slept haze that later made it difficult to recall the details of anything. She had drunk too much, argued with her parents, argued with the police. It was only months later that snapshots of those days would come back to her, seeping into her consciousness like unwanted visitors.

She had gone out to get obliterated, by whatever means possible. Adam had seen her in town, arguing outside a pub with a bouncer who had refused her entry because she was already too drunk. Adam had coaxed her away from the man, put her in a taxi and taken her back to the flat. Then he stayed with her as she threw up, making her tea and toast afterwards.

When the memories of that night began to resurrect themselves, the thing she would remember most about Adam was the fact that he had listened. She couldn't really remember him doing much talking, or if he had she'd forgotten the things he had said. She had spoken to him about everything: about her parents, her childhood, Luke, Emily. It was as though everything she had carried with her was offloaded in one outpouring of grief and drunken confession, and Adam had listened without comment or judgement, allowing her to relieve herself of all the demons that were haunting her.

She wondered if he'd done the same for Lola. For Sarah.

She had tried to kiss him that night. The memory of that moment made itself much clearer than the others, returning to mock her. He had gently pushed her away. He had said something, but she couldn't remember what it was.

Had Lola made advances on him? Had Sarah? Did Adam reject them too?

'Whores,' Adam said, as though he had somehow been capable of reading her thoughts. 'All of you.'

He reached to the opened laptop on the coffee table and ran a finger across the mousepad, sparking the screen into life. There was a still on the screen: the image that had seared itself into Chloe's mind all that week.

Sickness lodged in her throat. She tried to speak, but she choked on the words, on the realisation that sprang from the laptop screen to assault her. When he pressed play, a strangled sob escaped her.

'Please turn it off.'

He sat back, ignoring the request. The tattoo on his arm flashed black and green at her.

The serpent.

Another sob burst from her. Those emails, she thought. It was him. The video clip had been sent to the papers and the superintendent by him. He had set out to ruin her, and he had succeeded. He had been there all those years ago, on the other side of that computer screen, typing his instructions, filming her. Could he possibly have imagined all those years ago that he would be able to use that footage to such devastating effect?

'Please.' The word was now barely audible.

'Lola begged, as well. And Sarah. Do you know what they offered? They said they'd do anything I wanted, both of them. Do you want to make me an offer, Chloe? What do you want to give me? Remember I've already seen everything, so it'll have to be something pretty special.'

Where was the boy who had held her hair back whilst she'd been sick: the one who had rubbed her shoulders and told her everything was going to be OK? How could he be this same man, a man who had tortured and killed?

Alex had been convinced early on in the investigation that Lola and Sarah had known their killer. Had they been fooled by him in the same way she had, lured by the kindness of his smile and by the reassuring comfort of his false words?

Her thoughts strayed to her father's visit. Good men could do bad things.

Bad men were capable of doing good things.

She was going to die here.

The sound of her voice, lowered in mock seduction, ridiculous, played out in the background. 'I'm not going to offer you anything,' she managed, her voice regaining some of its strength. 'You repulse me.'

Adam leaned back to the laptop and paused the footage. He got up from the chair and went to Chloe, crouching beside her.

His presence, so close, made her body stiffen.

'You repulse me, Chloe Griffiths. I liked you, you know that? But you're just the same as all the others. Just a whore.' He wound a finger in a short length of her hair. 'Look at you,' he said, gesturing to the image paused on the screen of the laptop. 'Like Lola. Like Sarah. Like every other woman I've been unlucky enough to know.'

She could have told him that she'd done the webcam work because she'd had to – that there was nothing else she could have done that would have paid the kind of money she had thought at the time she desperately needed – but what would be the sense? She didn't have to justify herself to him. She had to justify herself to Scott, but not to him. Thoughts of Scott filled her with a momentary despair. He had called her. He had been there, at the other end of a phone call, but she had been too cowardly to speak to him. If she had just answered that call it might have been him here with her now, not Adam. Her thoughts were filled with things she wished she'd done and hadn't. Scott. DI King. She had to justify herself to Alex; to her more than anyone. She had let her down repeatedly, though DI King had persisted in standing by her, supporting her when most others would have walked away. She had been so focused on Luke, so distracted by the secrets of the dead, she had forgotten the living.

The thought of never seeing either Scott or Alex again filled Chloe with a renewed energy. She dug her wrists into the sofa, trying to force enough pressure to push herself up into a sitting position.

Adam watched, his eyes unmoving and his expression dispassionate.

'You going somewhere? I was just thinking the same, actually.'

His hand reached for her neck and closed around her throat. She tried to scream, but he was too quick for her. He punched her in the face. She heard the crack as her nose broke and felt the pain flood through her just moments later. Blood trickled on to her top lip. Adam was on top of her, his hand pressed down, covering her mouth.

There was something in his hand: something damp pressed over her mouth and nose. She writhed beneath him, but the room began to blur again, its corners melting one by one.

When the world went black for a second time, all the thoughts that had rushed through Chloe's mind just moments earlier dispersed, leaving her head empty. All the courage she had felt just fleetingly, all the promises she had managed to make to herself in just those few brief moments, were swept into the darkness that awaited her.

When the world went black for that second time, Chloe could have sworn she heard her brother's voice calling to her.

CHAPTER SIXTY-FIVE

They stood outside Chloe's flat and waited for her to answer the ring of the doorbell. When she didn't – and when Alex called her mobile to be greeted by the answerphone for a fourth time – her worries began to morph into a fear that gripped in her chest. As far as she knew, Chloe hadn't left the flat since being suspended over the pictures that had appeared in the newspapers. To her knowledge, Chloe had been intent on hiding away from the world for a while. That might have explained why her mobile phone was turned off, but where was she?

The curtains in the downstairs window were shut. She lifted the flap of the letter box and spoke into the gap.

'Chloe. Chloe, it's Alex. Please answer the door.'

Nothing. Even if Chloe was hell-bent on shutting herself away from the world, Alex felt sure she would answer the door. She imagined that Chloe would keep herself in touch with the case somehow – whether by watching TV, listening to the radio news, or looking for updates on the Internet – and sheer curiosity alone should be enough to send her to the front door once she realised Alex was there on the other side. She had told her they had a suspect.

She would want to know what was going on.

Something was very wrong.

'Radio for backup,' she told Dan. 'We need to get this door down.'

He looked at her in surprise. 'Really?'

'Yes, really. I'm not taking any chances.'

'What if she's in the bath?'

'I'll pass her a towel.' Alex pressed a hand to the outer wall of the building and closed her eyes. Adam Edwards had a distinctive tattoo on his arm. A snake. Chloe had received emails from a Hotmail account with the username 'theserpent'. They had known one another years earlier.

She felt a surge of sickness race up through her stomach and into her chest. Chloe should have been at work, not here at home. Alex had also accessed files without permission. She was as guilty as Chloe, yet she hadn't admitted so to the superintendent. A change of heart and a panic for her own position had snapped Alex into a temporary silence. She had refused to give Chloe the name of their suspect. She had refused to offer any clue as to the person under suspicion.

She had left her unprotected. Chloe had no idea how dangerous this man was.

'Can you break the door through?'

'Sorry?'

Dan had finished putting a call through for backup. He struck Alex as an officer more likely to be able to hack into an email account than break down a front door, but she wasn't prepared to wait for the others to turn up. The unsettling uncertainty she had felt for Chloe's safety had quickly morphed into a full-blown fear.

'I think she's in danger.'

He hesitated. 'You sure?'

Alex's top lip curled.

'OK.' Dan raised his hands. He tested the door handle again, as though the threat to force entry might have somehow willed it unlocked. Then he stepped back before slamming his shoulder into the door. His face contorted into a fixed expression of determination and he tried for a second time, achieving little more than a rattle of the uPVC.

'Christ,' Alex muttered. She went around to the back of the building, along the narrow pathway shared with the house next door. There was a gate in a wall at the back. The downstairs window at the back of Chloe's ground floor flat was obscured by a roller blind. 'I need something to smash the window with,' she said to Dan, who had followed her around to the back of the building.

He might have argued with her, but DC Mason appeared to have resigned himself to Alex's headstrong will. He disappeared, briefly, and returned with a brick salvaged from a crumbling front wall a few houses down. Alex took it from him and threw it through the glass pane of Chloe's back door. Against Dan's protestations, she thrust a hand through the space of shattered glass and grappled with the key that was hanging from the lock of the back door. When she next saw her, Alex was going to have a little chat with Chloe about leaving keys in doors. For someone so smart, the young woman was guilty of some serious lapses in common sense.

Alex stepped into the kitchen. In front of her, pulled shut, was the door that led through to the bathroom. Water. The bathroom. The bath.

She crossed the room to the door, holding on to her plans for a security talk. Time surrounded her, casting her in shadow, goading her as it so often did. Alex placed a hand on the door handle and shoved it open, not allowing time for hesitation and further unwanted thoughts.

There was no one there. There was no bathtub. A glass shower cubicle stood in the corner of the room, a towel flung over its partially opened front screen. Alex exhaled loudly. Behind her, Dan attempted reassurance.

'I'm sure wherever she is, she's fine.'

'I hope you're right.' She turned to her colleague. 'But where the hell is she? Why isn't she answering her phone?'

Alex left the bathroom, sidestepping Dan to get back into the kitchen so she could go down to the living room. There were two glasses on the coffee table; two plates that held the remnants of what had been dinner. Dinner for two.

'Shit.'

Chloe's laptop lay opened beside the plates. Alex passed a finger across the keypad, sparking the screen to life. It asked for a password. She cursed again. Her focus fell to the floor. Chloe's hair. She crouched and gathered the chunks in her hands, her body almost teetering beneath the weight of her fear.

'Boss.'

Alex stood and turned to Dan, who was standing in the living room doorway. He was holding Chloe's mobile phone. 'In the kitchen.'

'1707,' she told him.

'Her passcode? How do you know it?'

'I've sat beside her on plenty of car journeys.'

1707. The date and month of Luke's birthday. She had seen it whilst reading one of the files relating to Emily's case.

She watched as Dan tapped the passcode into the phone. Then she dragged her attention back to the used plates and glasses on Chloe's coffee table. She didn't want to touch anything else for fear of disturbing what might become evidence. There was no doubt in Alex's mind as to who had been here with Chloe. Sick bastard, she thought. He had sent those emails, sent that video clip, made Chloe vulnerable and then preyed on her when he had known she would be at her weakest.

Alex was snapped from her thoughts by a noise at the front of the building. She pushed aside the curtains. Backup was here.

Where the bloody hell was she supposed to send them now?

She turned back to the room, planning to leave the flat via the back door. It was then she saw it. The small smear of blood on the sofa cushion. Her fear morphed into panic.

'Boss.'

Alex looked away from the sofa and up at Dan.

'Chloe's Facebook messenger app. You might want to read this.'

CHAPTER SIXTY-SIX

She awoke to a square of mottled ceiling, yellowing and riddled with patches of damp. The ceiling shifted, swaying from side to side until coming to rest above her. She was cold. Her head felt heavy, tumbled, as though it had been through a washing machine and was still resting at the bottom of the drum, waterlogged and ready to be wrung out.

She was so cold. Her clothes were cold, her skin was cold; the bones that held her body as one were frozen stiff.

It took a few moments of blurry consciousness to realise that her hands were still tied in front of her, the wire cutting into her skin. The same at her ankles. She couldn't feel her feet. They were so cold that it was as though they were no longer attached to the rest of her. She felt drugged by her own heaviness, yet somehow weightless. The leggings and shirt she was wearing clung to her body like a second skin.

Tilting her head, Chloe looked at the shallow water surrounding her. She was lying in water. She was lying in a bath.

She pushed her head up from the cold porcelain. It took all her effort. The dizziness she had experienced moments earlier returned with the sudden movement, giving the false sensation of falling. She was in a roll top bath, in a room painted a pale, watercolour pink. The lines of the old stonework could be traced up to the ceiling; the cracks in each stone creeping upwards, as fine and delicate as spiders' webs. She might, in another life, have thought this room beautiful.

With that thought, a tsunami of others crashed over her. It was him, she thought. She had written it down for Alex – she had described the man they had been looking for – but the pieces of the puzzle had never quite slotted into place to make one complete picture. Not until now.

Amidst her despair there was a flicker of hope. DI King had told her they had a suspect. She had said that something Chloe had written had led them to him.

Had she meant Adam? Were they looking for the right man?

As though sensing his name in her thoughts, the door was pushed open. Adam entered the room. He was wearing a jacket now, the serpent tattoo concealed.

'You won't get away with this,' Chloe managed.

Adam studied her. He sat on the closed lid of the toilet and rested his elbows on his knees, his chin in his hands. 'But I already am. Come on. You know how easy it is to live a double life, don't you, Chloe? Change your name. Pretend it makes you someone else. Only it doesn't, does it? You can change the outside, but you can never really change what lies underneath. You're just keeping it hidden from everyone else for a while.'

'Those women… they'd never done anything to you.'

Adam's mouth tilted into a wry smile. He leaned forward and turned on the nearest tap. 'I know you don't really see things that simply, Chloe. Life's not that straightforward. You're better than that.' He sat back, his eyes still fixed on her.

'Please don't do this,' Chloe begged, watching the water hit toes she could no longer feel. 'We were friends, weren't we? Please.'

'You are my friend. That's why I need your help. I didn't want to kill them. I wanted them to suffer, but once I'd started, I couldn't stop. I want to make it stop. I don't want to do it, any of it. It isn't me. It's like this voice in my head, it won't go away; I try to hide it somewhere, try to drown it out, but it keeps coming back. It's louder than me. It's stronger than I am. You believe me, don't you?'

Chloe's eyes widened as the freezing water continued to fill the bath around her. She felt her spine numb as though submerged in ice. Pain throbbed through her face. Her nose, she thought. She only now remembered that her nose had been broken. The ties at her wrists cut off her circulation as she struggled and writhed, too tired and too desperate to do anything but flop at the bottom of the bathtub like a fish put too late back into water.

'Tell me you believe me.'

She nodded, the words half-choked in her painfully dry throat. 'I believe you.'

Adam moved towards her. He reached for the tap and slowly turned it off. Then he smiled. 'You bitches really will say anything just to get your own way.'

Chloe looked helplessly around the room. She had no idea where she was. She didn't want to die there, in a stranger's home.

She didn't want to die.

There had been so many moments during those past eight years when the thought of death had come to rest beside her, settling at her side with a silent persistence. It hadn't seemed to look as frightening as it once had. Its silence seemed almost comforting, in contrast with the noise and the chaos of everything else that had surrounded her.

Now she understood how wrong she had been. She didn't want to die.

Her thoughts returned to Scott and to that bloody phone call she hadn't answered. She wished she'd just picked up. If she had, she wouldn't be here now.

Adam sat on the closed lid of the toilet. 'Lola Evans made some very tempting offers. Bit like you once. Remember?'

She remembered, but she didn't want to. Two weeks after Luke died, Chloe had confided in Adam. He had gone to her flat, sat with her in her room as she'd cried over her brother, and after finishing the second bottle of wine she'd seen off by herself, she had tried to kiss him. The night had come back later in snapshots, blurry and unordered, and she knew Adam had refused her, pushed back, said something about not taking advantage.

Now she realised that wasn't why he had turned her down.

He hated her.

'You leave your laptop lying around far too readily. Makes it too easy for people to find out what you're up to. What do you reckon, Belle90?'

It was amazing how the mind could restore itself when it needed to, even when her brain felt as addled as it did now. That night came back to her, a daydream so vivid that it seemed to play out in front of her, blurred by time and everything that had taken place since. At some point after trying to kiss him and having her advances refused, Chloe had slept. During that time, what had he been doing?

Her laptop had been in her room. He must have accessed her Internet history, the not-so-secret life she lived online.

Chloe screamed. She had no idea where they were or how long it had been since he had taken her from her flat, but surely there would be someone close enough to hear her cries for help.

Apparently not.

Adam flinched slightly at the noise, but he didn't move from where he was seated. His hand moved to the sink. Something flashed from his hand.

A knife.

The sight shocked Chloe into silence. She stared wide-eyed at the blade, her thoughts consumed with images taken at Lola Evans's post-mortem.

'It's not really how I want to go about it this time.'

Her head lolled back against the side of the bath, too heavy to hold upright any longer. *Keep him talking*, she thought. *Keep him distracted for as long as possible.*

Yet in her heart, Chloe wasn't sure there was any point in prolonging what seemed to be inevitable.

CHAPTER SIXTY-SEVEN

Alex had taken Adam Edwards's phone number from his landlord that morning and had tried several times to get through, each attempt leading her nowhere. The number Dan had found on Chloe's phone at her flat – a number that had called her twice earlier that day – was now being traced. It looked as though Edwards had used a second phone: the one through which he had made contact with Chloe. He had presumably assumed that the police wouldn't be able to trace him through it, had assumed they would have no idea of its existence. His mistake had been leaving Chloe's phone behind in the flat when he had taken her.

It was now clear why his Facebook account had been reactivated. He had used it to make contact with Chloe.

Dan was in one of the police vans with another officer who specialised in the use of phone tracking equipment. The technology was able to masquerade as a mobile phone network, allowing them to access communications and track a location. Once a trace was detected via GPS, he would be able to feed information through to Alex and the rest of the team out on the ground. In the meantime, Alex had to think quickly about where Adam might have taken Chloe.

Waiting outside the flat whilst scene of crime officers secured the evidence left there by Adam and Chloe, it seemed to Alex sadly ironic that she had previously considered the similarities between her young colleague and the two women who had been killed by this man. The similarities were making themselves all the more obvious at an increasingly rapid rate. Lola Evans had been working as a stripper, something few people had known about. Sarah Taylor had been having an affair with a married man. Chloe had worked as a webcam girl. All three were 'guilty' – if that was how Adam regarded them – of living secret lives, double lives, and all in some way connected to sex.

According to the information Alex had received from Martin Beckett, Julia Edwards had also had her secrets.

This man's crimes weren't motivated by sex: they were committed because of it.

What else did Adam Edwards know of Chloe's life? Alex had no idea how close they had once been. She had read the Facebook messenger conversation between the two of them which suggested they had once been fairly close friends. The emails he had sent anonymously demonstrated an awareness of Chloe's desire to find whoever had been responsible for the death of either Emily or her brother. Presumably, he knew of at least elements of Chloe's past.

Alex watched a scene of crime officer head back into the flat. She felt so bloody useless standing here, waiting for Dan to come back to her with something concrete. Chloe had been in the same place, feeling the same way only that morning, and now… where was she? Alex felt a piece of her heart crack at the thought that something might have happened to her. She had already been through so much.

Alex needed to clear her head, to think straight, and to do it quickly.

She paced the narrow length of path that ran between Chloe's building and the house next door. Behind her, out on the street, she could hear a uniformed officer losing his patience with a woman who refused to move along and stop lingering by the police cordons erected by the roadside. Alex shut them both out, focusing her mind on the things she knew: things she knew might hold the answer to where Adam had taken Chloe.

She was distracted from her thoughts by a familiar voice.
'Alex.'

She turned. Superintendent Blake was heading down the pathway towards her, his grey face etched with concern. 'DC Mason's got me up to date. Any idea where this bastard might have taken her? Are you OK?'

He put a hand on her arm, and for once Alex was grateful for the physical contact. His was a reassuring face in a world that had become bleaker than she had ever seen it. Was that how Chloe had perceived Adam? Had he offered her comfort, familiarity, at a time when it seemed the rest of the world had chosen to turn its back on her? Was that why she had let him into her home without a second thought?

Memories of the corpses of Lola Evans and Sarah Taylor flashed into her thoughts. Alex had spent much of her adult life aware of the fragility of time, but she had never feared it as she did now.

She shook her head. There was little point pretending she was OK when she so clearly wasn't. 'I'm trying to think. This is all so complicated. She was sent emails, a while ago now – one a couple of weeks ago and the other back before Christmas. I dismissed them. I told her not to worry about them, that it was just someone messing around.' Alex paused to take a gulp of cold air. It burned the back of her throat.

'This is not your fault.'

'No? I spoke to her this morning. I told her we had a suspect, but I didn't tell her who, and you know why? I was covering my own backside. Looking after number one. And it's led her to this. So please don't tell me it's not my fault.'

Harry's hand twitched at his side, as though he wanted to reach out to her once more but was afraid she might lash out at him if he made the attempt. 'If it's any consolation, DC Mason's also blaming himself. If he hadn't told me about those bloody files, DC Lane would have been at work. You know more about her past than I do. Is there any link to this?'

A scene of crime officer appeared at the garden gate. She nodded an acknowledgment to Alex and Harry as she passed, and Alex waited until she'd gone before she answered Harry's question.

'I just don't know. All this business with wanting to prove her brother's innocence – that was all prompted by those emails. Either he does know something, or he's used it to get at her.'

She knew there was something she should be seeing amidst the murky fog clouding her vision, but it was refusing to draw itself to the surface and make itself known.

The women. Their 'sins'. The water.

Was he trying to cleanse them in some way?

Chloe. Her brother. The water.

Then it came to her, as clearly as though she had always known the answer. She knew where Adam had taken her.

CHAPTER SIXTY-EIGHT

Adam had left the bathroom for a while, leaving Chloe to the stillness and the cold of the water. She lifted her head again, using all the effort she could muster to take a better look around the room. If she could find something, anything, even slightly sharp, she might be able to use it to cut through the wires that bound her. Pushing her elbows to the porcelain, Chloe tried to push herself back. The bath was too slippery and she fell awkwardly, hitting her shoulder against the inside of the bathtub and sending water splashing into her face. It didn't hurt – her body was still numbed by the drugs.

The bathroom was sparse. There was a toilet roll hooked on to a holder screwed to the wall; a bar of soap in an old-fashioned plastic soap dish in between the taps at the sink. Chloe tried again to get herself upright, gaining better leverage with her elbows on this attempt. Now, for the first time, she noticed a corner of window reflected in the mirror to the side of the room. It was dark outside, the window offering nothing but a rectangle of blackness between the opened curtains. She had a sudden longing to know what the time was.

She called again into the deafening silence, but there was no sound from the other side of the closed door. Was it locked? If she could get herself out of this bath, would she be able to get out of this room? Perhaps he had left the building. If he had, she might have enough time to get herself from this room before he returned.

Chloe scanned the bathroom again. Then she remembered the knife.

There had been times, years earlier, when she had thought the things she had lost were enough to send her to her death. Now the things she had yet to gain joined her, gathering to fill the empty spaces in the room. They looked lovelier in that moment than they ever had. Her career. Scott. All the things she had still to do, the places she had yet to see. She had been foolish – blind to what had been in front of her – but she was able to see things so differently now.

She had wasted so much time dwelling on what she'd lost. It was only now that she realised how much more she had still to lose – and to live for.

With all the effort she could summon, Chloe heaved her body upright. The sudden movement made her nauseous, and the room seemed to sway once more as she tried to gain balance, using the side of the bath to right herself. She glanced to the sink. She couldn't quite see over its rim, couldn't tell whether or not the knife had been left lying there. She tried to slide along the bottom of the bath, bring her knees up so she could gain some momentum, but the surface was too slippery and the drugs he had given her had rendered her body near useless.

She felt tears of frustration catch at the corners of her eyes. Chloe lay back and studied the goose bumps that had spread across her skin like a nettlerash. Her limbs had turned a pale purple colour, her veins prominent. She breathed in slowly, taking a long lungful of air.

Then she tried again. Sheer determination forced her upright. She brought her knees up to her chest, gritting her teeth against the pull of weight that fought to keep them fixed beneath the water. With her feet flat to the bathtub, she propelled herself upwards and forwards, not considering the physics of her movement or the angle at which she might land. Whilst she was still in that water, he had her at her most vulnerable.

Chloe felt exhausted by the effort, but she was out of the water. She sat perched precariously on the edge of the bathtub, her bound feet still in the water, her tied hands resting between her knees. She leaned forward slightly, just enough to shift the swirl of clouded vision behind her eyes without allowing her to fall back into the bath. Her head hurt so much. Every muscle in her body screamed in pain.

She caught a glimpse of her reflection in the mirror. Her hair had been haphazardly cut short. Like Lola Evans's. Like Sarah Taylor's. There was dried blood staining her top lip and smeared across her left cheek. Her nose was knocked off its path at the bridge.

It would have once mattered, but now these things meant nothing. She needed to get out of there. She wouldn't let him win.

She stretched forward and peered into the sink where the knife still lay.

CHAPTER SIXTY-NINE

Alex headed to Marcross in one of the squad cars. She sat in the back beside Harry, checking her mobile every thirty seconds in the hope of getting a call from Dan. They had ordered an immediate appeal for any sightings of Chloe or of Adam, but it was late and most people would be tucked safely in their beds, sleep rendering them oblivious to the horrors that lay beyond their locked doors.

Every officer available had been employed in the search for Chloe. Alex prayed their efforts wouldn't prove in vain.

'You sure he'll have taken her to Marcross?' Harry asked.

'No,' she admitted, 'not exactly. I think he's taken her to the area, but I don't think they'll be outdoors. He knew Chloe wanted answers about her brother and about Emily. He takes his victims to water.' She closed her eyes and tried to block out the tightness she felt in her chest. They were travelling so fast it was making her feel sick, yet it still wasn't fast enough. 'I don't think he'll take her to where Luke died, but I think he'll take her somewhere close. He wants things on his terms. His mother died in the bath. That's the one thing he's not attempted yet with either of his previous victims. Maybe he sees it as apt in some way. I don't know. I can't think like a fucking psychopath.'

Alex's right hand gripped at the door handle, her nails embedding grooves in the plastic.

Harry watched his colleague's anguish and felt a wave of helplessness that had become, unfortunately, familiar to him. He couldn't remember ever having heard Alex swear before. The look that had fixed itself upon her face was fraught with worry. She cared about every victim, but this was far too close to home for them all.

'We'll find her,' he said.

As soon as the words had left his mouth, he knew he shouldn't have spoken them. It sounded like a promise and promises were so easily broken.

It wasn't finding her that was Alex's concern. It was finding her in time. The thought turned Alex's fear to bile she could taste in the back of her throat.

'I let her down.'

'How?' Harry reached out and tentatively touched the back of her hand.

His skin felt cold against hers, as though the blood that warmed them had been drained from him.

Lola Evans's torture. Sarah Taylor's drowning.

What horror was Chloe being subjected to in these moments?

'I should have kept her protected somehow. I knew she was vulnerable; I knew better than anybody. She came to me for help, she trusted me, and I did nothing to help her. Then I turned my back on her; I covered my own back.'

Harry slid his hand from hers, unsettled by the intimacy. The officer driving had cast his eyes to the rear-view mirror, distracted from the road by the sound of Alex's anguish.

'Chloe is an adult. She made some choices that neither you nor I nor anyone else could have controlled. Come on, please. This is not your fault.'

Alex turned from him and looked out of the window at a black night that was rushing past them. The trees lining the side of the road formed a continuous train, racing beside them as though in competition.

'Those files she accessed: her brother's case. I'm as guilty as Chloe is. I took Emily Phillips's post-mortem report. When she goes to disciplinary, so do I.'

She heard the future tense hang in the air, hopeful but fragile.

On her lap, Alex's mobile rang. She swiped a finger across the screen and hurriedly moved the phone to her ear.

'They're not at Marcross,' Dan told her.

She prayed that wherever Chloe was, they wouldn't be too late. Alex's fingers tightened around the phone.

'He's at Colwinston. The phone's been traced to a rental holiday cottage there.'

Alex lowered the phone from her ear and spoke to the officer driving. 'Get on the radio. They're in Colwinston. It's not far. Do we have an address?'

Dan read out the postcode, Alex repeating it to the driver.

'We're trying to make contact with the owner now,' Dan told her. 'I'll get back to you as soon as we hear anything.'

Alex ended the call and glanced at the satnav on the dashboard. They were another ten minutes away. She hoped to God a squad car was nearer. Anything could happen in ten minutes, she thought.

Anything.

CHAPTER SEVENTY

Chloe lifted her legs and swung them out of the bathtub. Her ankles were bleeding; the wire that bound them had torn into her skin as she had fought to gain momentum and get herself out of the water. She felt breathless and exhausted, and the earlier sensation of coldness that had chilled through to her bones had been replaced with a hot panic that flared the colour in her cheeks and made her skin damp with fear. She didn't have much time. If Adam was still in the house, he would have heard the squeaks and thuds that had accompanied her efforts to free herself. If he wasn't there, she doubted he would leave her long before returning.

She grabbed the knife in both hands and reached down to saw through the wire that bound her feet. It was going to be more difficult to cut through the wire at her wrists, the angles all wrong; if her feet were freed then at the very least she would be able to run from him. The wire didn't give easily. It was pulled tightly, making it tricky for her to get the knife beneath, to work upwards and avoid cutting into her skin. Panic made things even more difficult. The handle of the knife was slippery with the sweat from her palms, and she took a moment, took a deep breath and told herself to calm down.

It was difficult to calm down when she had no idea where he was or what he was doing.

The wire began to give way. At the final snap of thread that held it bound, Chloe felt the blood rush back to her feet. She stood, but fell back, hitting her heels against the foot of the bath. She moved her wrists to the sink, using them to balance herself. She still felt so sick, so dizzy. She looked up again, barely recognising the woman who stared back at her from the reflection in the mirror. Her eyes were small, shadowed with grey, but her pupils seemed unfeasibly large. Her skin looked washed out, as though the water had drained it of life.

But she was alive, she thought. She was here and she was alive.

There was a noise outside the room. Chloe tightened her grip on the knife she still held in her hands, trying to stop them from shaking. She stood upright on wobbling legs, willing them to work as they should.

The bathroom door was pushed open. He stood in the doorway, blocking Chloe's only exit. His face spoke his surprise at seeing her out of the bath. He'd clearly thought the drugs more powerful, or he had underestimated her.

'Clever girl,' he said. He glanced down at her legs, at her freed ankles.

She wanted to lunge at him, to attack him, yet at the same time she knew that doing so might mark the end of everything. He was stronger than her, faster than her; her judgement and balance had been so altered by the drugs that it would be easy for him to overpower her. She would get it wrong, and getting it wrong would cost her everything.

'Stay away from me,' she warned, jabbing the knife in his direction. She stepped sideways, moving back from him. 'I swear to God, I will cut your throat. For Lola. For Sarah. An eye for an eye, what do you think?'

Her words sounded brave, but inside Chloe could hear herself crying. Having the knife in her hands hadn't put her ahead of him. She was still as isolated, still as vulnerable.

'I don't think you have it in you.'

Chloe held his eye, knowing he saw straight through her attempts at heroics. This man had seen her at her weakest, at her most exposed. He knew her. He knew he still had her exactly where he wanted her.

'Let me go,' Chloe said, knowing the words would be pointless. 'Let me go now and I can make sure you're given mitigating circumstances. You'll go to prison for what you've done, but I can make sure you get a lesser sentence.' She caught her breath as the words tripped over one another. It still seemed so impossible that this man who she had known for so long and had trusted so unquestioningly was a murderer. He stepped further into the room, and she lashed across the air between them with the knife.

'Get the fuck away from me,' she screamed, tears now betraying her fear.

He studied her with dark eyes; eyes where she had once found comfort. How could she have got him so wrong? She had believed she could trust him with the things she had entrusted with no one else since Luke had died.

'Or you'll what?' Adam said, raising his hands in mock surrender and taking a step backwards, away from her. 'You'll kill me?' He took another step back and sat down on the closed lid of the toilet seat. 'Go ahead. Only, then you'll never find out the truth about what happened to Emily.'

CHAPTER SEVENTY-ONE

Alex ran an Internet search for the property to which Adam's mobile had been traced. It was a small, one-bedroom cottage in the village of Colwinston, seven miles north of Marcross. It was advertised on just one website; not one of the more popular holiday home search sites but a page on a tourism site dedicated to the local area. The description of the property boasted beautiful rural scenery and an idyllic location free from any neighbours.

She stopped reading and looked up from the iPad. The bastard had planned this, had probably been planning it for a while. He had chosen somewhere they wouldn't be seen. Somewhere they wouldn't be heard.

They were just a few miles away now, but the distance seemed impossible and time felt as though it was dragging its feet, once again not on their side.

She tried to make a map in her mind of the moves Adam might have taken to get Chloe into the van. It would have been so easy to do: the lane at the back of the building was accessible to vehicles and Chloe's flat was on the ground floor of the last house on the row of terraces. The lane at the side was wide enough for a vehicle to access, and Chloe's back gate was at the side of the house, giving it total privacy from the neighbours. All Adam had needed to do was carry her from the door to the van: a distance of only four metres. There wouldn't have been time or opportunity for anyone to have seen him, especially not at that time of the evening.

A voice on the radio alerted her attention. One of the other cars had already arrived there. Alex leaned forward, putting a hand on the side of the driver's seat.

'Do not approach the property,' she said. 'Wait for armed backup.'

She turned and looked at Harry, who gave her a nod. She knew that, were she there alone, she would likely do the stupid thing and barge straight in, heedless of the possible consequences for both herself and Chloe. But she wasn't there yet. One officer in danger was one too many. She wasn't going to jeopardise anyone else's safety, not unless it was her own.

'There's a vehicle outside the property,' one of the voices on the end of the radio told them. 'A white van. No plates.'

Alex glanced again at Harry. She imagined his thoughts were in that moment a mirror of hers.

Chloe was smart, Alex tried to reassure herself. She would keep him talking, try to stall him.

Sitting back and pushing her head against the seat, Alex closed her eyes for a moment. She was fooling herself. Chloe was facing the worst kind of horror imaginable. She knew what that man had done to two other women. She knew everything he was capable of. Given what she knew – having had the images of Lola's and Sarah's bodies imprinted on her brain – any sense of rational thought, any former courage, was certain to escape her.

Alex opened her eyes and focused on the darkened world outside the window. Don't give up, she muttered to the glass, as though somewhere, wherever she was and whatever was happening to her, Chloe might hear her.

CHAPTER SEVENTY-TWO

The knife was shaking in her hands. His words echoed in the small room, bouncing off the stone walls and deafening her. She didn't want to hear them. She didn't want to believe them. Chloe had thought he had used her past to weaken her, to push her life off balance. She hadn't once considered he actually knew something.

He didn't, she thought, holding his stare as he looked up at her. He didn't know a thing. He was trying to put her off, trying to weaken her once more. The more she tried to believe that, the more she was able to stifle the sounds his words still made.

'Don't look so surprised,' he said. 'You always knew your brother didn't kill her.'

A sob escaped Chloe's throat, half-strangled. She felt tears coursing streaks down her cheeks, but she no longer cared if he was witness to them. Why was he doing this to her? What had she done to deserve any of this? What had Emily done?

She moved her focus to the knife, willing it to steady. She would use it. If he moved now, she would use it. She wouldn't think twice about what she was doing.

'You're lying.'

He gave her a sad smile. 'Easier to believe that, isn't it? A bit like poor Luke, really. He didn't want to believe the truth either.'

Chloe felt her jaw tighten, the drugs that had earlier rendered her face immobile now beginning to wear off. She clenched her teeth.

'Emily didn't want to be with him, did she? She told him, but poor little Luke didn't want to believe it.'

'You don't know what you're talking about.'

He was bluffing, she thought. It would have been so easy for him to gain the details surrounding the night of her death: they had been splashed across the papers and all over the Internet. Everyone had known that Emily had apparently tried to end her relationship with Luke that evening. It was the reason the police had decided him responsible for her murder.

'She was so excited. She couldn't wait to tell me that she'd dumped him. Couldn't wait to tell me that we could be together.'

Chloe felt the floor of the bathroom give way beneath her feet. Her body tilted to the side, as if drunk. The words seemed to circle her, tangling, making no sense.

'No,' she said, with a quick shake of the head.

Adam nodded. 'We only see what we choose to, don't we, Chloe? She thought I actually wanted her. That little slag. Now why would I have wanted to go anywhere near that?'

Chloe felt emptied. She wasn't prepared for this – she could never have been prepared for this – and none of it made any sense.

They had once met through her, she remembered. Chloe had moved from one shared house to another: Adam had helped her move her things. Luke and Emily had popped over to see the new place. Adam had been there. As far as she knew, he and Emily hadn't seen one another again after that.

They would never have met if it hadn't been for her. All of this was her fault.

'You're lying,' she said again. The words sounded pathetic. Feeble. Their lack of conviction gave all the evidence that proved she knew them to be incorrect.

'She used to turn up at the garden centre quite a lot,' he told her. 'Always when you weren't working. Wouldn't have looked too good to be seen flirting with me in front of her boyfriend's sister, I suppose.'

'Shut up,' she snapped.

Adam raised an eyebrow. 'Really? You don't want to know what happened? All these years and now you don't want to hear the truth?'

He was right. She had wanted to know the truth about what had happened to Emily. She had always believed that knowing what had happened to Emily would lead her to the truth of her brother's death. But not like this. Now the words were being spoken – now the truth was being aired in front of her – she no longer wanted to hear. Like a child, she wanted to put her fingers in her ears. She wanted to close her eyes in the hope that if she couldn't see the monster, it couldn't see her.

'She tried it on with me so many times,' he told her. 'She was gagging for it. She was so easy to lure. A few cheap flowers. A few cheap words. I did the honourable thing, told her I wanted it to be more than sex, that she was special. Told her I wouldn't do anything while she was seeing someone else. She stalled a bit. She said she felt guilty, said Luke was nice, she didn't want to hurt him. But she still did. Women are all the same really, aren't they?'

She was sixteen, Chloe thought. Not a woman. Just a girl. In that moment, she couldn't bring herself to hate Emily for the way she had behaved. It didn't matter what she'd done, what any of them had done. She didn't deserve what happened to her. None of them did.

They had all paid for someone else's choices.

'Who are you, Adam?'

His family had rarely come up in conversation, but she remembered him telling her once that his mother lived in North Wales with her second husband. He said he visited her a few times a year and that he'd never met his father and didn't know anything about him. Now she didn't know what to believe.

All lies, she thought. She didn't know the first thing about him. Everything had been a lie.

'She threw herself at me,' he said, ignoring her question. 'Tried to kiss me. Everything happened so quickly. I hadn't planned it. Not that time.'

'You let Luke take the blame.'

Adam shrugged. 'Sorry. Collateral damage.'

All thoughts left her. Her mind went blank, a white sheet dropping behind her eyes, filling with a screaming tinnitus that threatened to deafen her. Her balance was lost again. She moved her feet, shifting back against the wall, steadying herself.

He watched her, his expression fixed. No sign of remorse. No traces of anything she could recognise as human.

He stood from the toilet seat. Chloe raised the knife, holding it poised. His hand moved to his pocket. She felt herself trembling. The cold had come back to her, her still-wet clothes clinging to her body like a second skin. There was a piece of cloth in his hand.

'What use is that now?' she asked, her words shaking as she studied the dampened cloth.

'I came here to do a job. I never leave until the job's done.'

Chloe thrust the knife at him, but he was quicker than she was. He grabbed her bound wrists with one hand, twisting them so that the knife pointed away from him. She kicked out at him, her foot meeting with his shin, smashing into the bone. It knocked him off balance, momentarily, and she flailed as he faltered, redirecting the knife and yanking her wrists from his hands. She swung quickly. The knife met his side, embedding itself inside him.

His eyes widened at the shock of the pain. 'You fucking bitch.'

She tried to pull the knife back out, but he hit her away. He grabbed her by the throat and pressed her against the wall, closing his hand over her mouth and nose. There was a sweet smell, sickly. She flailed helplessly, a fish out of water, but within moments there was nothing but darkness once more.

CHAPTER SEVENTY-THREE

'That's it.'

Alex saw the building at the end of the narrow lane they had turned on to. Backup vehicles were now on the road behind them. They pulled up alongside the car already there, parked behind Adam's white van. Alex barely waited for the driver to come to a stop before getting out.

The cottage was small, secluded from the neighbouring houses by an expanse of fields and a cluster of wide trees that formed the boundaries of the garden. There were no signs of any lights on, but if Adam and Chloe were where she feared they might be, then that particular room may not be visible from the front of the house.

Armed officers got out of the van that had pulled into the lane behind them.

'The bathroom,' she told them. 'Unless you see him or Chloe anywhere else, head straight upstairs.'

She followed behind four armed officers. A lever was used to break open the wooden front door and the officers rushed inside, heading straight for the stairs. Alex ran after them. There was a man's jacket hanging from the end of the stairs. She followed the officers up to the first floor. One of them called Edwards's name. There was movement upstairs.

The bathroom.

The door was shoved open. Adam Edwards was on his knees on the carpet of the bathroom floor, his body straddling a limp and lifeless Chloe. His hands were closed around her throat. The first officer in the room hit Edwards with the butt end of his gun and sent him toppling sideways. Another two officers helped pin him to the ground as he struggled violently against the first. Alex rushed to Chloe. She was soaking wet, her sodden clothes clinging to her slight frame. There was dried blood on her face. She wasn't moving. It seemed they were already too late.

She pushed Chloe's severed hair from her face and touched her fingertips to her throat, trying to find a pulse. Alex could feel and hear nothing but the pounding of blood in her own ears.

Then the sound of Edwards's voice ripped through it.

'If you'd got here a bit earlier, you could have watched.'

Alex turned to the officers restraining him. She refused to look at Edwards. She would face him in the interview room, on her grounds, her terms. Not here. 'Get him in the van.' She saw the blood for the first time then; saw the knife still embedded in his side. She wanted to grab the handle and push it deeper, give it a good twist. Finish what Chloe had started.

She turned her attention back to Chloe as Adam Edwards was taken from the room. 'Chloe. It's me. It's Alex. Come on, I know you're with me.'

Where was the bloody ambulance?

Her fingers retraced the skin at Chloe's throat, finding the place where a pulse would make itself known.

'Get me something to cut this with,' she said, speaking to the officers who remained in the room with her. She gestured to the wire still binding Chloe's hands. 'Chloe. Come on, sweetheart.'

She glanced to the corner of the room. There was a rag lying on the carpet. She reached for it with her free hand. She brought it carefully to her nose before quickly throwing it back to the ground.

Then she felt it. The pulse was slow, distant, but it was there.

He hadn't killed her. He had drugged her.

Alex exhaled loudly. Her fingers slid from Chloe's throat and moved to her still-bound hands. She took the young woman's hand in hers, clutching on to her fingers as though scared she might lose her for a second time. She heard the scream of an approaching ambulance. An officer returned with scissors. Carefully, Alex cut Chloe's wrists free. Her hands slumped to her sides.

The paramedics arrived, filling the bathroom with their urgency. Their noise burst the awful silence that had fallen upon the room.

Alex stepped aside as one of the paramedics crouched beside Chloe, checking her vital signs. She left the bathroom, passing the waiting SOCOs who would retrieve the evidence that would be needed later. She walked back downstairs, past the super who was talking to one of the armed officers, and out of the building into the cold night air.

It was only then, with the start of rain falling fresh on to her face, that Alex felt relief slump over her. She sat on the front step of the cottage and allowed herself to cry tears for what might so easily have been.

CHAPTER SEVENTY-FOUR

She had never seen this woman. She had heard plenty about her during that difficult conversation at Chloe's flat, but she had yet to meet her. As with so many other people, Susan Griffiths was nothing like Alex had expected. The woman's face remained a blank until Alex explained who she was. Then Susan ushered her into the house, looking up and down the street as though checking that none of the neighbours had been witness to the police presence on her doorstep.

It seemed typical, given what Chloe had told Alex about her parents.

Alex hadn't told Chloe she was going to visit her parents. Nor had she told her she intended to visit their church and sit in on one of the meetings. By ten that morning, events of the previous evening would be well broadcast on television and on social media, although it had been requested that, for the time being, the name of the officer involved remain withheld from the press. Alex wanted to get to Chloe's parents before the media managed it first.

'Is everything OK?' Susan asked. 'What's happened?'

She seemed for ever concerned with her appearance, Alex noticed; forever touching her hair and searching out her reflection in the many mirrors that seemed to decorate the house. But Chloe had already told her this. For the Griffithses, appearances were everything.

Exactly what were those appearances concealing?

'Is there somewhere we could sit down, Mrs Griffiths?'

Her husband appeared at the top of the stairs then, a tall man, slim, with a presence Alex could easily imagine a young child might find intimidating. He came down the stairs with his eyes fixed upon her, a definite defiance in his expression. Everything Alex knew of this couple was clouded with Chloe's experience of them and the suspicions that had only developed over time. She knew she must try to ignore them, but it was difficult not to view the couple in the same way as Chloe.

It was also difficult not to suspect them now she had spoken with one of the elders from their church.

'Mr Griffiths,' she greeted him. 'I'm Detective Inspector Alex King.'

He didn't offer her a hand, or even a response.

'Through here,' Susan said, gesturing to the living room doorway. Alex followed her into the room and sat in a chair opposite the sofa on which the couple sat. They were nowhere near each other, she noticed; each taking a separate end of the sofa. She wondered if it was habit.

'I'm afraid there's been an incident involving Chloe.'

She watched the couple carefully for their reactions. Malcolm's face didn't change, his defiant expression remaining fixed and emotionless. There was a flicker in Susan's face; a tensing of the jaw.

'Is she OK?'

'She will be,' Alex told Susan. She had to hold back her anger. They hadn't even asked her what had happened. 'Incident' could have meant anything.

'You're aware of the images of Chloe that were sent to the press last week?'

She spoke to Malcolm this time. She already knew he was aware of the photographs: Chloe had told her how he had gone to the flat and taunted her about them. The man's eyes left her for the first time, casting down to the living room carpet at his feet.

Susan gave a slight nod.

'The man who sent those images is responsible for the murder of three women. He's also guilty of the attempted murder of your daughter.'

For the first time there was a reaction that Alex might have described as normal.

Susan's hand moved to the arm of the sofa, gripping it as though stopping herself from falling off. Her face paled. 'You said she's OK though? She's going to be OK?'

Alex nodded. 'She's pretty tough, your daughter. But then, I'm sure you already know that.' She looked again to Malcolm. His gaze had risen from the floor, back to her.

Had this man really done what Chloe suspected him of?

'The three women I mentioned,' Alex continued. 'One of them was Emily Phillips.'

Susan's head turned sharply to her husband. His eye met hers, but still his expression barely changed. He refused to look at his wife. When Susan looked back at Alex her face looked frozen. 'But, Luke?'

'Luke was wrongly accused. He will be formally cleared. As a result, the case into his death is going to be reopened.'

'Why?' It was the first time Malcolm had spoken. It was the first time a reaction had been evident on his face. He didn't seem to have any idea that she was lying, that she was testing the waters. There had as yet been no talk of reopening an investigation into Luke's death.

Alex had let Chloe down. There was only one way that she was still able to help her. She hadn't yet found out what had happened to Luke. Adam Edwards claimed to know nothing about Luke's death; like everyone else, he thought it had been a suicide. It was better than he could have hoped for: Luke's suicide had meant the police were no longer looking for Emily's killer.

Alex hoped she might be able to find the truth for Chloe. She felt she owed it to her. Finally, Chloe would be able to move on with her life.

'Emily was murdered, Mr Griffiths, we knew that. Your son was falsely accused of her murder and was awaiting charges. At the very least, this new information about Emily's death makes someone responsible for Luke's suicide. The police are culpable in many ways.'

She watched him carefully as she spoke, gauging his reactions. There was a lot she had learned from Chloe in those past six months. Faces could reveal so much more than words were capable of. She hadn't missed it: at the mention of the word 'suicide' the tension in Malcolm Griffiths's jaw had relaxed slightly. He knew something. He was hiding something, and had been doing so for all these years.

Susan was crying now, silent tears that ran streaks down her face.

'Chloe's in the University hospital, if you want to go to see her,' Alex said, standing from the chair. She wondered if Chloe would want to see them. It didn't seem to matter: Alex doubted that either of Chloe's parents would go to visit their daughter. They didn't seem the type of people to admit when they'd been wrong.

'In the meantime, if you need anything, please take my number.'

Susan hurriedly rose from the sofa, running her sleeve across her face. She went to the sideboard and took a pen and paper from one of its drawers, handing it to Alex. Alex wrote down her name and number and handed the pen and paper back to Susan. It was Susan who saw her to the door, though Malcolm lingered in the hallway behind them, watching every move.

'If I could have a moment alone with your wife, please, Mr Griffiths.'

'Why?' He stepped nearer and put a hand around Susan's wrist. 'This is my house. Anything you want to say to my wife can be said in front of me.'

Alex raised an eyebrow. 'Fine. We'll talk outside then.'

She opened the front door and waited for Susan to leave ahead of her. The woman did so reluctantly. So this was what life had been like, Alex thought. Malcolm Griffiths dominated his wife. He had been the same with his children. Once again, Alex felt in awe of the way Chloe had managed to succeed despite the terrible start her young life had been given.

*

She unlocked the car and gestured for Susan to get in. Malcolm Griffiths stood on the path to the house, watching, with arms folded.

'Chloe tells me you're a Jehovah's Witness.'

Susan eyed Alex suspiciously, as though wary of falling into a trap. She glanced past her and through the window to her waiting husband.

'Yes.'

Alex nodded. 'It must be a relief to you, knowing your son was not a killer. Perhaps your church will have you back now.'

Susan's face dropped. 'How do you…?' She pushed a hand through her hair.

'I spoke with one of the elders earlier this morning. Do you want to tell me why you were excommunicated?'

'I'd have thought that was obvious. Our son killed a girl.'

'Only he didn't. You know that now.' Alex glanced at Malcolm. Would his wife now be brave enough to tell the truth? 'You have my number. When you're ready to talk, call me.'

Alex started the engine, her eyes returning to the house where Chloe had grown up. She waited to watch Susan walk back up the path and return to the house with her husband, wondering what would be waiting for the woman once the door was closed behind them. She wondered what secrets lay beyond that door, and what words were being spoken now that the rest of the world had been shut out.

CHAPTER SEVENTY-FIVE

There were two detectives sitting opposite Adam: a man he didn't recognise and the bitch that had turned up in that bathroom. Neither of them had taken their eyes off him, as though staring long enough was going to make him cave in and reveal everything.

It wasn't.

The woman pushed a couple of photographs across the table towards him, prompting him to take a look. 'You recognise this place, don't you?'

They were photographs of the pub: the room where he'd held Sarah and Lola, and the bathroom where his mother had drowned – the bathroom where he had found her dead one Friday evening fifteen years earlier.

He could still remember that night so clearly. He had been living in care for a few years by then – a supposed home where he kept himself to himself and didn't bother with any of the other kids. He had gone to the pub to see her. He had already been a couple of times, on the afternoons he'd bunked off from school and lied to the home about hanging around town. Even after all that time, he still wasn't sure why he had felt the need to return to her. He didn't like her. She had never liked him. He hated going to the pub. He hated the noise from downstairs, the smoke-filled air of his mother's living room and the raucous voices of the girls who worked behind the bar. He hated it because it reminded him of every other pub they had lived in. It reminded him of the fat, sweaty men he would see coming out of his mother's bedroom, of the grunts he would hear through the flimsy wall that divided her bedroom from his.

'Adam,' the detective said, dragging him from his thoughts. 'Or would you prefer me to call you Joseph?'

He'd given them the name Joseph Black; made up an address and a false contact number. Nobody had ever bothered to check them out.

'We found the support group member records in the glovebox in your van. Want to tell us how you got them?'

He had taken them when Connor had been 'otherwise engaged' with that tart, Sarah. They thought everyone else had left.

He met the detective's gaze. If he could, he would close his hands around her throat and squeeze until those eyes bulged from her head. He hated her. He hated all of them.

His mother had claimed to hate those men, although that never stopped her from letting them back into their home time and time again. She would be all painted smiles and low-cut tops when they arrived, then scowls and slurred expletives when they left. When he was small, he hadn't understood what had been happening on the other side of the wall. Then he'd got older and he had grown to realise what his mother was. As soon as he did, she had hated him for it, as though it was somehow his fault.

'Why did you take them to the pub?' that bitch King asked him. 'What did she do to you there, Adam? Or was it the men? Did one of the men do something to you? Do you blame her for letting it happen?'

He sat back and closed his eyes. If he focused hard enough, he could drown her out, just like he drowned out the others. He had come to think it was the coldness that cleansed not the water itself. Warm water soothed the skin, but the cold could drive right through it, hitting the heart of all that was truly dirty.

It could seep through to the rotten core of any person.

The bathroom door had been ajar. He could see a hand, so pale it looked almost transparent, with thick turquoise veins, rested on the edge of the bathtub. He pushed the door aside slowly using his foot. His mother was in the water, her face submerged. She was naked, although he couldn't bring himself to look at her. He kept his focus fixed to her face, lifeless and blurred beneath the water.

There was a bottle of vodka at the end of the bath, nestled between the taps. To the left of the hot tap, two bottles of prescription medication.

Her hair clung to the sides of her face, partly covering it. Later, it would be her hair he would remember the most. He hated it. He hated the way she wore it long: pretence at a youth that had long since passed her by. He hated the way it concealed the ugliness of the person who hid beneath it.

Like the make-up she wore caked in thick layers on her skin, her hair hid the truth of what she really was.

He put out a hand and touched the top of her head, pushing down slightly. Her body nudged further below the water, weighted to the bottom of the bath.

The detective produced another photograph from the file on her lap. She put it alongside the others and waited for him to react. He took a glance, knowing straight away who the girl in the image was.

Emily Phillips.

'You confessed to her murder. Why did you kill her?'

Everything was his fault, his mother had told him. She did it for him. To keep a roof over his head. To keep food on the table. She could have had a nice life without him. No man wanted to keep her. That was because of him.

Eventually she'd given up on him. She had told social services she couldn't handle him. She told them he'd be better off with someone else, as though she was getting rid of him for his benefit rather than her own.

Detective King was still staring at him, still waiting for a response. He supposed he should give her one.

'She was a little whore, just like the rest of them.'

There was a flicker of a reaction in the woman's face. He had touched a nerve, it seemed.

'And Chloe?' she said. 'You knew about the webcam work. You sent that video clip to the paper, didn't you? And here, to the station? Did that make her a whore, as well?'

He had never felt such bitterness towards his mother as he did in that moment he realised she was gone. He had wanted that moment as his own – had dreamed of hurting her in so many ways, childhood nightmares that had turned into obsessive fantasies as he had reached his teenage years – and now she had taken it away from him, robbing him one last time. She couldn't even leave him with that.

The water had been a final bad joke. She was filthy. Disgusting. And now she was drowned. Cleansed. It was funny, really.

The detective placed both hands flat on the desk in front of her. She looked down at the photographs before focusing her gaze upon him once more. 'Seeing as you're not prepared to talk to us,' she said, 'let me tell you what I think. I think you're a coward. I think you believe you hated your mother, but more than anything you were desperate for her love – so desperate, you would have killed her rather than gone ignored by her any longer. But she took that opportunity away from you, didn't she? And to compensate for it, you've been making other women pay. Innocent women. Women whose vulnerabilities you sought out and then preyed upon. Women who made no other mistake than to trust you.'

She sat back, still staring at him, waiting for a reaction.

'There's no rush for a response,' she told him. 'You're going to have plenty of time to think it over in custody.'

CHAPTER SEVENTY-SIX

Glancing in through the window of Chloe's hospital room, Alex saw the young woman sitting on the side of the bed. She had a bag opened on the sheet beside her and was moving things from the bedside table, packing them away.

'Not leaving already? I've heard the food's so good here.'

Chloe turned and gave her a tired smile. She looked so much better than when Alex had last seen her, lying in this same bed unconscious, the drugs and the exertions of her fight in the bathroom at the cottage having exhausted her. She had come around long enough to tell Alex what Adam had told her – that it was he who had murdered Emily. She had rambled incoherent words about Luke, a car, something about CCTV footage, and then she had left them again for a while.

Her nose had been reset. There was bruising to her neck and her eyes bore dark circles from the effects of her broken nose. It seemed to both Chloe and Alex that she had paid a small price in comparison to that which they had both feared.

'Has he told you, about Emily?'

Alex nodded. Adam had known Chloe was alive and conscious and that she had told them what he had confessed. What had chilled Alex most was the man's lack of remorse. Adam Edwards seemed to think himself on some sort of one-man crusade, ridding the world of impure woman. The cutting of their hair seemed a stand against dishonesty, ridding his victims of part of the mask he felt they hid behind. His moral crusade had stretched to Connor Price – to the text that had been sent threatening to tell his wife of the affair with Sarah Taylor. And yet throughout his interviews, Adam Edwards failed to acknowledge any sin in his own actions. His only regret seemed to be that he hadn't achieved a greater number of kills.

What exactly had he seen and heard as a child growing up in the flat above that pub? What had his mother done – what had she allowed to happen to him – that had led Adam to become so consumed with hatred and fixated on revenge? They would never know all the things that had driven a young boy to become the man Alex had just two days earlier charged with three counts of murder and one attempt.

Not for the first time that week, Alex considered how criminals could so easily blend themselves into the rest of society. No one had considered Adam – Joseph – anything but a kind man, someone reliable, someone to be trusted with their secrets. Vulnerable women had befriended him, regarding him as non-threatening. They had seen him as safe, and it was this that had empowered him.

'This is all my fault,' Chloe said.

'How?'

'If I'd seen him years ago for what he was—'

'Chloe,' Alex said, sitting on the bed beside her. 'No one saw him for what he was. Not Emily, not Lola, not Sarah. Is it their fault too?'

Chloe looked down at her hands, not meeting Alex's eye. 'I've done some stupid things. Really stupid.'

'So have I. I've been sleeping with my ex-husband.'

Chloe looked up quickly. Alex wasn't sure whether she looked embarrassed or was trying to suppress a smirk. She wouldn't mind if it was the latter. It would be worth her own momentary embarrassment just to see a smile on Chloe's face again.

'Sorry?'

'It's been going on a while. Every time I felt a bit stressed out, a bit lonely, I called him. And I didn't once realise that he'd been with someone else for months, not until I saw them out shopping with her kids.'

Chloe's eyes widened. 'Christ. What a prick.' Her face coloured slightly, as though she thought herself guilty at having spoken out of turn.

'Exactly. And I'm almost twice your age. What's my excuse?' Alex put a hand on Chloe's arm. 'You trusted someone you'd known for years. That doesn't make you stupid.'

Chloe smiled. She looked her beautiful self, despite the tiredness and the broken nose. Alex wouldn't tell her yet, but short hair suited her.

'Thank you. For everything.'

Alex felt a wedge of guilt at the sound of Chloe's gratitude. It wasn't deserved. If she had acted earlier – if she had trusted Chloe with the name of their suspect – they wouldn't have been in that hospital room.

'I haven't forgotten Luke, by the way.' She moved her hand from Chloe's arm. She wasn't sure whether or not telling her she had been to her parents' house was a good idea. Chloe was still in recovery. Her physical injuries would heal quickly enough, but the things that lay beneath the surface were going to take far longer. She didn't need any additional stresses. But she had always wanted to know the truth about her brother's death. Alex wanted her to know she hadn't forgotten that.

'I need a bit of time now,' Chloe told her. In truth, she was beginning to wonder if what Alex had said the previous week had been right. Perhaps she would never know the truth. Perhaps not knowing wouldn't be such a terrible thing after all.

Alex nodded. 'Of course you do.' She stood from the bed. 'By the way, there's someone waiting in the corridor to see you.'

'Who?'

'I don't know, but he's very good-looking, he's got lovely manners, and unless he belongs to one of the nurses I'd suggest you snap him up.'

Chloe smiled. Scott.

'If you need anything, you know where I am. Is he giving you a lift home?'

Chloe nodded.

'You're going back to the flat?'

She shrugged. 'Can't let him beat me, can I? Scott offered his place, but I don't think it's really appropriate that I stay there. We're not even together. He's been so nice. I don't deserve it.'

Alex pulled a face. 'Don't deserve to be happy? Well if you don't, no one else is entitled either.' She paused. She didn't really believe Chloe wanted to go back to that flat, not after everything that had happened there.

She thought about the deafening silence that filled her house. 'Why don't you come and stay at mine?'

Chloe looked up at her, surprised by the offer. 'Really?' she said, the single word soaked with scepticism.

'Really. I have a four-bedroom house I can't really afford alone. You can help me pay the mortgage.'

Chloe rolled her eyes. 'Thank you. I'll think about it.'

Neither of them suspected she would need too long to make a decision.

CHAPTER SEVENTY-SEVEN

She found Harry Blake in his office. He was at the window, staring out at a rainy February morning. A mug of tea had gone untouched on the desk beside a pile of paperwork that looked as though it hadn't been disturbed in quite a while.

'Sir.'

He turned to greet her, his daydream broken. 'How are you, Alex?'

She exhaled loudly. It seemed a sufficient answer.

'I second that.' He took his seat and gestured for her to sit opposite him at the desk. 'Seen Chloe?'

'I went this morning. She's going home today.'

He nodded. 'You want to talk to me about her, don't you?'

It was disconcerting how transparent her thoughts were. But she had made no secret of the fact she championed Chloe as an officer. Even from a distance, DC Lane had proven her merit once more. They may have eventually reached the link to Julia Edwards's son, but Chloe's email had got Alex there quicker than if she'd been left to her own devices. Chloe was sharp, perceptive. She had been knocked off focus by the resurrection of her brother's memory and an unsolved mystery which she no longer wanted to remain in the dark, but once the truth of Luke's death was uncovered Alex was confident Chloe would be able, some time, to return to her true form.

And she was now determined that the truth would be uncovered, somehow.

'I know this is out of your hands to a certain extent,' Alex told Harry, 'but help me persuade professional standards she has to come back.'

Harry moved his hands to the desk, interlocking his fingers. 'What's happened in the past few days will go in her favour, strange though that sounds.' He shook his head. 'I don't know, it's a lot to ask them to overlook.'

'I know. But they can't afford to lose both of us.'

'You don't have to do this. I doubt Chloe's going to mention your involvement, and I certainly won't.'

Officers had been allowed to stay in the job following worse offences than Chloe's, but Alex also knew of those who'd been dismissed from duty for far less. There were mitigating circumstances. She had to believe that Chloe would be allowed a second chance. Admitting her own involvement was the right thing to do.

'A while back you were talked out of handing in your resignation.'

Alex sighed and sat back in her chair. 'There was a lot going on. I had some difficult choices to make.'

'I know how that feels,' Harry muttered. He looked away from her, his eyes drifting to the photograph on his desk.

It was turned away from Alex, but she knew what the image depicted. Harry's children: two boys standing on a sandy beach, clutching surfboards, wide smiles stretched across their young, sun-kissed faces.

'I'm glad you changed your mind. You're a great detective, Alex. And you've been a good friend over the years.'

She didn't like where this was going, but supposed it had been inevitable. Harry had never really returned to the station, not fully. Now his absence of spirit made sense. She had suspected weeks earlier that he no longer wanted to be there.

'Why the past tense?'

'I'm standing down. The past eighteen months have changed my priorities. This job has given me a lot over the years, but it's taken a hell of a lot more. I want to see my kids grow up.'

He looked away once more, uncomfortable by his own words. 'I'm sorry.'

She waved away the apology. She didn't expect other people not to talk about their own children because of her situation. It wasn't something she wanted either. She'd had years of pitying looks and awkward platitudes. She was beyond all that now. Harry had supported her in the past. She knew she should now offer him the same.

'You've got to do whatever you think is right for you and your family.'

They were interrupted by a knock at the door. A uniformed officer entered the room. 'DI King, there's a woman asking for you in reception.'

Alex gave him a nod and turned back to Harry. 'No rest for the wicked.'

*

She headed downstairs to reception.

Sitting on one of the plastic seats of the waiting area, her hands clasped together in her lap, was Chloe's mother.

'Mrs Griffiths.'

Susan Griffiths stood hurriedly and reached for her bag from the chair beside her. She clutched it to her chest as though using it as a barrier between her and Alex. There was a shadow to the side of her face, a blur of muted purple that looked like the beginnings of a bruise.

'I need to talk to you about Luke.'

CHAPTER SEVENTY-EIGHT

Alex took a seat opposite Susan Griffiths in one of the interview rooms. Chloe's mother glanced at the tape recorder on the desk to the side of them, but she looked calm and composed, as though she had accepted what was to come. 'I wasn't entirely honest with you when you asked why we'd been excommunicated. I suppose you already know that.'

Alex nodded. The elder she had spoken to – an obnoxious, arrogant man who held the Griffiths couple in contempt even after all these years – had filled her in on the details that Susan would later choose to omit.

'You maintained contact with Chloe after she'd been disfellowshipped; that's what it's known as, isn't it?'

'They had no choice but to let Chloe go – she'd already been given so many chances. We begged for them to give her another chance, but she refused to acknowledge any of our teachings. She was so headstrong, so defiant.'

'She had a mind of her own, you mean?'

Susan's jaw tensed. 'She was still my daughter, despite everything. I wanted to know she was OK.'

Alex sat back in her chair and eyed Susan with an anger she was struggling to keep hidden. Susan might have thought that keeping contact demonstrated loyalty to her daughter, but when it had come to a choice between her family and her religion, her commitments to her children had been pushed to one side.

'You weren't supposed to maintain any contact with Chloe?'

Susan shook her head. 'It's for the best, I know. Isolation is meant to teach people where they've gone wrong. I thought that given time to think about the choices she'd made, she would realise her sins and come back to us.'

'"Her sins"?' Alex repeated, incredulous. Susan Griffiths was indoctrinated. She knew she was supposed to be without bias, but this concerned Chloe and that made everything different. 'What were "her sins"?'

'She disobeyed us; she told lies; she drank; she got tattoos – she did everything she could possibly do to defy us.'

'She was a teenager, you mean.' Alex couldn't bite her tongue. Somewhere amidst the indoctrination her religion had been responsible for, Alex was certain Susan realised it wasn't Chloe who was the real sinner. She wouldn't have been there otherwise. 'How did the elders come to find out about the emails you'd sent Chloe?'

'Luke.'

Alex's eyes widened, surprised by the answer. It hadn't been what she was expecting. The elder she had spoken with told her Chloe had sent copies of emails that had shown Susan Griffiths was continuing communication with her wayward and excommunicated daughter.

'The emails were forwarded from Chloe's address, but it was Luke who sent them. He took great delight in telling me what he'd done.'

She cast her eyes to the hands she held clasped on the desktop. 'I lied to the police on the day Luke's body was found. I told them the last time I'd seen Luke was the previous afternoon. I told them he'd been upset and had confessed to me that he had killed Emily.'

Susan stopped and glanced up at Alex. The bruising on her face seemed to have deepened in colour since they had left reception and gone to the interview room. Her husband's doing, Alex assumed. Chloe had told her what a bully her father had been. Luke and Chloe hadn't been spared his violence. Why would it be any different for his wife?

'I did see him that afternoon,' she continued. 'We argued at the house, about the emails. He told me he'd sent them. He said now I'd know how it felt to have everybody turn against me. He was still refusing to admit to us that he'd killed Emily.'

'Us?'

'Malcolm and me.'

Alex nodded. She thought she knew what was coming next. 'You thought Luke had killed Emily? Why?'

'The same reason the police thought he had. She'd tried to end the relationship and Luke hadn't been able to accept it. He'd been obsessed with her, wanting to see her all the time and spend all his time with her. It wasn't healthy. She wasn't a good influence on him. We tried to keep them away from one another, but he was pretty deceitful.'

One interpretation of his character, Alex thought. Either he had been deceitful, or desperate to escape the suffocating clutches of his controlling parents. Desperate to be loved. Alex decided to opt with Chloe's version of events.

'So you argued about it?'

Susan nodded. 'I told him to tell the truth. I told him that if it was an accident, if he hadn't meant to do it, he should tell the police.' She stopped. Her face was fixed, emotionless. It was as though she was reciting a rehearsed script. She'd had plenty of time to learn the words, Alex thought. *Tell the truth*. Surely the woman could hear the irony in her own words?

'Tell me about the argument.'

'Luke lost his temper. He said he couldn't believe his own mother didn't believe him. Then he told me he'd found a way to make me pay for what we'd done.'

'The emails?'

Susan nodded. She looked angry – resentful at her son's betrayal – yet Alex believed that something else must have once existed where that anger lay. At some point, there must have been love. Maintaining contact with her daughter had once, if even for the briefest moment, been more important to Susan than their church. If only she had acknowledged this moment and clung to that notion a little longer, all their lives might have been so different.

'Where in the house were you?'

'In the kitchen. I'd been making dinner. He told me what he'd done and I just saw red. I wasn't myself for a moment. Everything we'd already been put through – Chloe's behaviour, Emily's death, and now this. We were shunned by everyone important, everyone that mattered to us. The church had already given us so many chances. They didn't want to be associated with our family, not in the state it was. Chloe's behaviour had already condemned us all. Sending those emails was the worst thing Luke could have done. I was branded a traitor. I had a tart for a daughter and a murderer for a son, and the emails made them decide I couldn't be trusted either.'

Alex's hands had tightened into fists in her lap. She knew what was coming next, though she wished she was able to somehow change it.

There was silence.

'And then what happened?'

Susan's gaze remained on Alex, her expression still devoid of all emotion. 'I hit him.'

'Was your husband there when this happened?'

Susan shook her head.

Alex felt a shiver pass through her. Luke had died because his parents had always expected the worst of him. He had died because the police had assumed him guilty and had failed to look elsewhere. His mother had chosen her church over her children and her decision had proven fatal.

'Tell me what happened.'

Susan's hands slid from the table and rested in her lap. 'I hit him just once, with a glass vase. It was standing upside down on the draining board, drying. I just lashed out. Everything happened so quickly.'

Alex closed her eyes. She was going to have to tell Chloe all of this, and then what? The poor girl had already been through so much. She had wanted the truth, but surely not this.

'He fell to the floor. I thought he was trying to scare me at first, trying to punish me again for not believing him, but when I said his name he didn't move. There wasn't even much blood, just a trickle on the tiles. It was so quiet. I called my husband on the phone. He said not to touch anything until he came home, so I waited in the kitchen with Luke.

'Malcolm was very calm when he got there. He made me see sense. I told him I wanted to tell the police, but he said we couldn't. We'd lose everything.'

Alex's jaw tensed.

'Did your husband move Luke's body, Mrs Griffiths?'

Susan nodded. 'He told me that when the police asked, we should tell them that we thought Luke had killed Emily. We agreed to say he'd been acting strangely all week, that he hadn't seemed himself, and that he'd taken my husband's car and we hadn't seen him after that.

'Malcolm moved Luke's body to the car in the garage. I stayed at home and cleaned the kitchen. We arranged where and when I would go in my own car to collect him. I didn't intend to kill my son, but I did believe he had killed that girl. It seemed justice had been served in a way, through God's hands. Malcolm helped convince me of that.'

Alex eyed the woman with disbelief. It seemed impossible that she was so indoctrinated by her religion – by her husband – she could allow herself to believe this. She wondered how long it had taken for Susan Griffiths to become convinced by the lie. Eventually, the guilt must have subsided and acceptance taken its place. An eye for an eye: so simple when she thought of it like that.

Yet now it wasn't. She now knew her son hadn't killed Emily, and that changed everything. Enough for her to be there now, finally confessing to her crime. Enough for her to have confronted her husband, prepared for the repercussions she would face.

Driven by her loyalty to her colleague, Alex felt contempt for the couple. How Chloe had managed to become the woman she was now showed that miracles existed in some form.

God's hands, she thought. The only hands that had been responsible for Luke's death had been Susan's own. Was this really how she'd managed to convince herself for all these years that she had done no wrong?

'"That girl",' Alex repeated slowly. '"That girl" was someone's daughter. Someone's child. In the same way Luke was your child. Innocent. But of course you know that now, don't you? Your son wasn't a murderer. He was a victim. Why have you waited until now to tell the truth?'

'You won't understand. You have independence; our lives are very different. I made a promise to my husband and I had to stand by it, even though he's hated me since the day Luke died. He misses the church. He hates the stigma that comes with having been disfellowshipped, and he's been punishing me for my disloyalty for the past eight years. I've lived in fear of my husband, Inspector King, but I feared prison even more. Now I don't. Now I think prison will be an escape.'

Alex paused the interview and left the room, leaving Susan Griffiths alone with whatever thoughts filled her head. She couldn't escape the thought that Luke's revenge had cost him his life. But was it really that simple? Chloe had spoken in such detail about her brother. None of what she'd said reflected a malicious boy who'd have sent those emails purely based on spite.

Alex turned back to the door and looked through the glass at Susan Griffiths. Only a certain type of person could carry a secret of that enormity for all those years; one Alex knew she would never understand. She would never want to.

Even now, the woman wasn't sorry for what she'd done to her son and to her family. She was sorry she'd been banished from the church. She was sorry she was being punished for it and she was confessing to free herself.

In the corridor, Alex leaned against the wall and took a deep breath.

Just as Chloe was beginning to mend, this was going to break her.

CHAPTER SEVENTY-NINE

Scott carried the last of Chloe's things upstairs to the bedroom Alex had made ready for her. She had given her the back room, the one with the view of the garden, and had made up the bed with new sheets she had bought the previous evening. She put fresh flowers in a ceramic jug on the window sill. Alex knew enough to realise the flat Chloe was leaving behind had never been a home. In so many ways, a home was something Chloe had never known.

She might have tried to convince herself she was doing this purely for Chloe's sake, but Alex realised that was only partly true. Chloe wasn't the only one who had lost a sense of home. Roaming around that house listening to the conversations that took place amongst the ghosts she allowed to remain there had become a habit Alex needed to break free from. It had kept her in limbo, stuck between a past to which she could never return and a future that wasn't hers to claim.

Chloe would give her something other than herself to focus on.

Chloe hadn't said too much about what was going on between her and Scott. Alex imagined she didn't want to think too far into the future. There had already been too much thinking about the past. For now, Chloe seemed happy to exist in the moment. Alex was pleased to see glimpses of Chloe's former self, though she was sorry she and Scott hadn't been able to get to know one another under different circumstances, ones that hadn't involved Chloe's shame and secrets laid out bare between them.

Scott had visited Chloe several times in the hospital. He had given her lifts. He had helped her pack her limited possessions into boxes and then transported them from the flat to Alex's house. He hadn't judged her, despite everything he now knew.

Small things. Kind things. The things Chloe's life had been missing for so long.

Scott came back down the stairs and thanked Alex for the tea she had made him, handing her the empty mug. She took it from him and headed into the kitchen, closing the door behind her to give Scott and Chloe some privacy.

*

'Thanks for all your help.'

He smiled. 'You're welcome.' He gestured to the kitchen. 'This is good of her.'

Chloe nodded. She didn't know how she was ever going to repay Alex. By being better, perhaps. By making sure she learned from her mistakes.

'There's something I want to ask you.'

'Sounds ominous.'

Scott took her hand in his. 'I was wondering if you would do me the honour of going for dinner with me one evening. I think you've made me wait long enough now.'

Chloe laughed. She squeezed his hand. His skin felt good against hers. Safe.

'I'll have to check my diary.'

He leaned in and kissed her. It was brief but perfect. 'I checked it for you. You're free on Thursday.'

Chloe raised her hands in mock surrender. 'Thursday it is then.'

She saw him from the house and went into the kitchen.

*

Alex was sitting at the table, her laptop opened in front of her and her chin resting in her hands. 'He seems lovely,' she said, without turning. 'Really lovely.'

Chloe stood behind Alex, reluctant to sit down. Since Alex had arrived back from the station she had been quiet, withdrawn. Just as Chloe had thought the worst to be over, there always seemed to be something else, something just waiting to disturb any chance of peace and normality.

'Has something happened?'

Alex turned to face her. She gestured to the seat beside her. Chloe sat, her focus fixed on Alex. She had always thought herself so good at reading people, but the past week had proven her skills in that particular area less than impressive. She had no idea what the other woman was thinking, no idea of what could now be bothering her.

She took a seat. 'Oh, God.'

How naive she had been, she thought. There was only one thing left: one vast and gaping question to which she had for so long sought an answer.

'Chloe—'

'It's about Luke, isn't it?'

She saw the answer in the other woman's eyes, her hesitation over the words she had to speak. Chloe had the urge to run from the room. The child still in her was there once more, yanking at her side, begging her to run away with her. She wanted to put her fingers in her ears, to sing as loudly as she could and not have to hear what Alex was about to tell her.

Chloe's hands moved to the edge of the table, her fingers clinging to it. She looked at Alex. Her jaw was taut, tensed around the words she was seemingly as reluctant to speak as Chloe was to hear.

'Was it him?' she asked, her words barely audible.

Alex shook her head. She reached for Chloe's nearest hand, prising her fingers from the edge of the table. 'Listen to me, Chloe. You're going to get through this, OK? I'll help you, I promise. You've got this far. You're going to be OK.'

'Just tell me,' Chloe said, her eyes filling and her fingers tightening around Alex's.

Alex told her everything: the argument between Luke and her mother; the emails from their mother to Chloe that Luke had forwarded to the elders of their church; the excommunication of her parents that, until now, Chloe had been ignorant of. She told her about her father's involvement in Luke's death; of the ways he had persuaded his wife justice had been served. Alex held Chloe as she cried and wished she could somehow make things different.

'Do you ever delete the sent items in your email account?' she asked, when Chloe's tears had begun to subside.

'No.'

'Can you log in for me?'

Chloe reached for the laptop and logged into her email account with shaking hands. Alex took over from there, typing the email address Chloe's mother had given her into the search bar. A short list of results was thrown up.

'It was the night Luke came to my flat,' Chloe said. 'It must have been. The night he'd argued with my parents and they'd accused him of Emily's murder. He asked if he could use my laptop. He must have gone into my emails then. He always said he'd make her pay, but I thought it was just anger talking.'

Alex stared at the screen. Chloe hadn't yet seen what she was looking at. Seeing it would change everything.

'Did you ever reply to any of your mother's emails?'

Chloe shook her head. 'There was too much damage done. She didn't mean anything she wrote – she just wanted to get back some sort of control.'

Alex looked again at the laptop. Whether or not that was true, they would never know. She thought it might be better now – less painful for Chloe – if that had been Susan Griffiths's only motive. Chloe hadn't replied to her mother, yet a message sent to Susan was in her email outbox. It had the same date as the email that was forwarded to the elders. When Alex looked at the times each had been sent, this one had been sent just minutes later. She watched as Chloe read the email and as tears coursed down her face again.

> *Mum, I know you hate me and I understand why, but we're not all the same. I am not like the men at church and I am not like dad – I wish you would stop punishing me for all the ways these men have treated you. You'll be mad at me for sending that email to the elders, but I hope one day you'll understand. It's not too late, Mum. If you leave, you, me and Chloe can be a family again. I know Chloe still loves you, no matter what she says. Please don't hate me. Luke.*

Alex put a hand on Chloe's arm, knowing nothing she could say now would relieve the agony of what Chloe was reading. Luke hadn't sent those emails in an act of revenge against his mother's cruelty; instead, it had been a desperate attempt to hold together a family that had been falling apart around him.

Just like Chloe, he had longed for the affection of a parent who had continually mistreated him, ever-hopeful that one day things would be different. Alex still believed there had existed a time when they might have been.

'Did she mention this email?' Chloe asked through her tears.

Alex shook her head.

'He just wanted her to love him. He just wanted her to be a normal mother. What sort of God allows a woman like her to be a mother when someone like you can't?' She ran the end of her sleeve across her eyes, smearing her mascara. 'Sorry, I shouldn't have said that.'

'It's fine.'

'How do you do it?' Chloe asked, turning to face Alex. 'How do you keep going despite everything being thrown at you?'

Alex gave Chloe a smile and squeezed her arm gently. 'What are you asking me for? You already know.'

TO THE READERS:

Thank you so much for taking the time to read *The Girls in the Water*; it really does mean the world to me.

Alex and Chloe have been in my life for over five years now; a pair of invisible friends that refused to go away. *The Girls in the Water* was not their first story that I tried, but it was the place where they both fully came alive. I hope you've enjoyed their company as much as I have.

If you have, I would be so grateful if you could spare an extra couple of minutes to write a review. I would love to hear from you with your thoughts on the series, and am always happy to chat via my Twitter account and Facebook author page. Any writer knows that writing can sometimes be a lonely business, so thank you to the people who've offered words of support and encouragement online: I already feel that I have made a wonderful new group of friends.

Alex and Chloe's next story is under way, and I hope you join them there. If you'd like to be the first to hear about my new releases, you can sign up using the link below.

www.bookouture.com/victoria-jenkins

Thanks again for reading.
Victoria Jenkins

ACKNOWLEDGEMENTS

First, a huge thanks to my brilliant agent, Anne Williams, for all her guidance, support and continued faith in my writing. We got there in the end. Thank you to my editor, the lovely Jenny Geras, who has made my dream of becoming published a reality.

Thanks to 'Uncle' Chris Richards and Michael Owens for their advice on police procedure – if I've got anything wrong, I'm sorry!

I wouldn't have finished anything without the support and encouragement of my family – I love you all. A special thank you to my dad, who never stopped believing in me, even when my confidence wavered: this book is for you. To Kate, my lifelong sidekick and original partner in crime – thanks for the reminders that I need to get off social media and get down to work.

Lastly (but never last), thank you to Steve, for everything – you are the main character in all my life's favourite stories.